Nikko and the No-Life King

'made in h5 vs. made in h3' project

by T.B.O.A. Sad

Nikko and the No-Life King ©
Copyright 2012 Richard A. Schroeder Jr

All rights reserved.
No part of this book may be reproduced in
any form, with the exception of graffiti
and / or positive review, without written
permission from the Author.

This is a work of fiction. All characters,
situations, and contents are creations of
Richard's brain and a boring life. Any resemblance
to actual events or humans, living or dead,
is purely coincidental.

ISBN 978-0-615-61549-3

Printed in the United States by:
Morris Publishing®
3212 East Highway 30
Kearney, NE 68847
1-800-650-7888

Visit tboasad.com

~ Let go of my hand, and now here goes nothing, literally, letting every memory die inside of my Heart tonight ~

CHAPTER 1

Empty Sky Stargazing

    It was the summertime from so long ago ~ Or was it just late spring? The air was warm, not hot, and the sound of everything was coming back now... The birds and voices, the old cars driving by and sounding new, the sound of Mom's voice humming a made up song.. The old beautiful music of yesterday, matched only in this memory by the smell of the clean laundry hanging to dry, perfect white sheets swaying like slow waves on the ocean, clothes pinned up 1 by 1.
    And there was Nikko - Herself, only younger. Her entire life ahead of her, no troubles or worries, no boy problems.. Just and only the unimaginable effortless things that captured her early mind, taking for granted the happiness all around her as it surrounded her now again in thought.
    And Mom - Was she always this beautiful? All before the sick life. She could be seen here as a woman, a young woman and not just a Mother. Someone who would turn heads and still had the presence of her youth about her.
    These times, something as mundane as the drying of laundry outside in the warm weather, these were the things so important to the true happiness of her Heart.
    Nikko looked back at it now in peace, watching herself and her Mother, watching the day go by and the beams of the sun shining down. A blue sky and sunny dream held in memory as if happening again, growing clearer as she lost herself in the yesterday. This was the treasure, the gift that no bad friend, no hospital or medicine could take from you..
    But Nikko was different. For every happy memory that she would remember, she struggled to put it aside. To stop thinking about the thinking. To pretend that she hated it and pull herself back into an empty reality. That was always the plan, but her memory and active imagination were so vivid, so lifelike, that revisiting an old thought was the same as to live it all again. And before she knew it, she was trying to soak in every inescapable detail. The things she saw back then but of course didn't really see, the details surrounding her forever lost in time now once again staring her in the face..

Nikko and the NLK

~ The red cardinal in the tree ~

~ Mom looking back toward the driveway, waiting for Dad to get home from work ~

~ The dogs in the neighbor's yard, a shelty and old english sheep dog, watching intently at everything from the way across ~

All of the little things, trying to pull them all in, 1 desperate attempt to keep them close. The grass, the leaves, the trees, the blue-blue sky. A piece of Nikko remained lost in it's comfort, while another piece stayed desperate to collect everything into her Heart. To try and save every small trace of this feeling before what was about to happen began to happen - To salvage or to even escape before the inevitable could take place..
1 happy memory in the the broken clock of her Heart and brain - Just 1 small piece that helped make it as complete as it could be, a tiny gear doing it's part to keep the entire system intact.

But now, try hard to dislike it. Take the memory and say it wasn't good.. Close the eyes inside of her brain, try to turn away and be distracted from the change to the past..

+ And then, like always now, he came +

The uninvited Black Knight, the ruiner of her inside things and part of her memory that didn't belong. Just as Nikko could vividly re-enter her happiness through memories, so it always seemed so could this monster.
The newest past invasion, and the sky wasn't so blue anymore. The sheets swayed in the breeze... Upgraded to a wind now? It was too violent - Small drops of rain fell in the wind, darkened skies and flashes of lightning too. This was it. The watching Nikko desperately cried out to her memories, to her younger Mom and to her young self, but nothing. To them they went about the day as it had originally happened. Smiling, laughing, oblivious to what was changing in it's now post-existence.
A new end was happening to something already over..

Nikko and the NLK

Nikko cried out with her silent voice. These black skies and this rain, the lightning and drum-like pounding of thunder, and then the arrival of the shadow that had been tormenting her for what seemed to be so long now. From the driveway and right out of nowhere, the nameless Black Knight took solid steps through Nikko's mindscape and personal place.

+ An invasion of her secret world from yesterday +

He was a being of complete death black - An armor covered man from head to toe, the 7 foot build of a devil's barbarian. His armor was decorated with dark fur, a black helmet with bat wings on both sides atop his hidden face, and a massive axe attached across his back. Stomping slow, but even so, too fast through this moment.

+ Ready for destruction, and Nikko braced herself to never see it again +

Cry out loud, scream, nothing..

The tornado tempest of the storm was now in full swing, the sky like a black hole twirling high above, and the remembering Nikko ran towards the man, the thing, in a desperate attempt to hold him back. To the driveway fence, near his approach, and already this part was in ruin. The smell of storm and rain - This wasn't part of the memory! This was something killing her, piece by piece of the Heart.
He approached the fenced-in yard, the giant axe removed from his back and swinging to demolish all in his step.

This was a parasite of her soul...

Nikko stepped into the path like always, and as always, he stepped through her like a ghost, able to affect her past where she could not.
Run in pursuit, a black furred cloak flowing behind him, the grass blowing in waves and the rain rolling off of the trees like bleeding veins. The sheets flew up and Nikko's Mom was oblivious to it all, even as a white sheet blew out of the laundry basket, lifting off into the vortex of the black sky and gone.
And the younger Nikko stood there, standing so innocent, waiting to

hand the clothespins to her Mother - What was the point of this? Why was this thing killing all of these small moments?
Reach, grab, pull at nothing.. Such a perfect day, and now..
Nikko fought hard with it, throwing unlanding punches that swung through him so violently, pushing air and scratching space, trying it all, but nothing.

And like so many now-forgotten times before, it came to this -

Smiling her years-ago sunshine smile, Nikko's memory of her Mother from this moment was cut down in death, the black axe of the uninvited man cutting clean through her body, his motion-blurred weapon against her skin. Cut skin to muscle, muscle to organ, organ to spine, and then out through the other side. A body split in half... Face unphased, still smiling in no pain at all -

No..... Nikko screamed and suffered, knowing that while it wasn't real, the death of this happy moment somehow was real, killing what was in her memory - Again..
The blood and black sprayed across the hanging sheets in the wind, and the younger memory of Nikko looked on, unseeing what had happened in the present version of this past.

The evil thing turned away from the killed memory of the Mother, looking now to the child version of Nikko.

No.. Not again.. Not another time like the other times that were now already lost...

The young memory of Nikko set the clothespins down and turned to walk away - Just as the watching Nikko remembered - Running to the fence to talk to the neighbor's dogs, just as the memory was supposed to play out.
Present-time Nikko fell to her knees in the changing time, helpless to the power of this black thing, no voice left in her, sitting in another ending day of her life.
The young girl ran, and the Black Knight faced her direction, putting his axe into a firmer 2 handed grip.. Nikko tried to look away, but now even closing her eyes only left her eyes open in the altered memory. Everything began to speed up quickly - The running to the fence, the

movements of the dogs, the sheets in the wind and the rainfall..
Without effort, as lightning crashed into trees and power lines, sparks and flashes all around, the memory-invading black being swung his weapon, ruthlessly cutting down the innocent child -

- Pouring out a river of blood -

+ Another day, another memory so close to her, that piece of life now missing and another black hole in her Heart +

And then the return to reality...

Nikko stood staring blankly at a wall in her parent's house, in her room, in the early hours of the night.. What had just been happening? The thoughts escaped her already, but the emotions did not. 1 more time in her head - But what memory was it this time? She tried to think but couldn't remember, an overwhelming depression setting in and the feeling of something else now missing too.

The curse, or whatever it could be called, was the only thing she could remember when she blacked out in such unusual ways. It was a standing sleep.. An unwanted dream, a nightmare always ending with the Black Knight and the shadows, the dark sky and his killing axe..

"Nikko?" a voice called up the stairs. "Nikko!"

"Yeah -" Nikko called back down from her bedroom. "Yeah, what, Mom?"

"Are you still going out tonight?" her Mother answered back and then a moment of silence.

Nikko thought, her mind feeling completely blank and wading through these bad emotions. Looking around her room, she saw all of her things, reality seeping back. A meow from her bed, her cat standing on top of the clothes that she had laid out to wear for the evening -

"Kimby!" Nikko greeted her little friend as if she had been gone, picking up the black and white kitten into her arms. It purred as she caressed it, rubbing the fur beneath it's black choker-like collar, the light reflecting off of it's connected nametag.

"Nikko?" her Mother asked as she opened the door, stepping in with an ever-worried look drawn across her face. "Nikko..."

"Mom!" she said back in surprise, just now realizing that she was dressed in only her black bath towel and black bra. "Mom, can't you knock??"

"Oh relax, you -" her Mother comforted her, taking Kimby from her daughter's hands and into her own. "I used to dress you everyday - But back then this was the time for clothes to go to bed, not clothes to go out.."

Nikko looked to her Mom - The years had been going by so fast, her sickness had aged her so rapidly now. She stood there in her off-pink nightgown, ready for bed, her grey-black hair pulled back behind her ears. They had been close friends, probably closer than even Nikko's Father and herself, but it was difficult in this depression. Growing up at last, and seeing her Mother falling away before her eyes - This was something she was never prepared to handle.

"I'm old now," Nikko told her with a turn to her desk and vanity, sitting down to face the mirror and put on her make-up. "We always go through this every time that I go out."

"You've been crying," her Mother noticed as she set Kimby back by Nikko's clothes on the bed, walking over and placing her hands on her Daughter's shoulders.

Nikko saw her own green-amber eyes in the mirror.

"It's nothing," she said, wiping the back of her hand at them. "You know how I get sometimes."

Kimby hopped down from the bed and began wandering the room, looking for things to play with out of boredom.

"Your Father and I worry about you, Honey. We've all been through a lot lately - Maybe you can think about staying home tonight?"

"I'm not staying home," Nikko said as she went to applying make-up to her face. "This place is like a prison to me.. You and Dad never let me go anywhere anymore."

Nikko looked away. Her parents had been through this for too long now. Depression watch, suicide watch, dementia watch.. Whatever it was called, it didn't matter anymore - Mixed with her Mother's health, it had all taken such a toll on the family.

"Honey, the hospital -"

"I don't want to talk about the hospital!" Nikko interrupted as fast as she heard the word, not caring if it would be about her own visits or her Mother's. "I just want to go out and be like a normal girl on a normal night - Just do what I want to do, you know?"

"I know, Sweetie," her Mom comforted, her grip a little tenser on Nikko's shoulderline. "But what was it tonight? This time?"

"What? What are you talking about?"

Kimby hopped up onto Nikko's lap, only to be set back down on the floor again.

"Was it the thing we talked about? Did you see the same thing again? Do I need to call the doctor??"

"No-no-no," Nikko quickly shut down her Mother's guessing. "Don't freak out, it wasn't anything.."

But her Mother's eyes were already tearing up. "Sweetheart, you need to tell us," she said, her hands and fingers shaking just a small bit and felt on the shoulders. "Your Father and I just want to help you. We can call the Doctor, you can talk to him about these things.."

But Nikko knew better. The last time she had opened up, she was put into the hospital to be opened up, only for what was said to be her own well being. Now out and under her Parent's watch, she did everything that she could to hide the reality she was facing.

"No, no, I'm fine now, really," she said, her Mother's doubtful eyes meeting hers in the mirror. "That's behind me. A totally normal girl now."

"Totally normal girl?" her Mother joked, letting go of her shoulders and going over to her clothes laid out on the bed. "And what totally normal girl has the fashion sense of you?"

"Hey, come on!" Nikko laughed, getting up from the chair and then pushing her Mom back with 1 hand, her other holding the black towel together. "Would you just go to sleep? I have to get ready!"

"Fine, fine," she agreed as she slowly stepped across the room to the door, stopping to give her daughter 1 last hug. "Nikko, you know that we love you - I love you - And we just want to take care of our girl."

"I know, Mom, I love you guys too. But you have to let go of my hand sometimes, ok? Like now? Like maybe a few hours for the night?"

"Maybe *just* for a few hours," her Mother said back with a smile, letting go and letting Nikko push her back out through the door. "Who's even picking you up tonight? It better not be -"

"Yeah, yeah - It's him, Mom," Nikko interrupted as she knew what was coming. "Just let it go? He's the only guy I wanna hang out with, so please be ok with it?? Be a good parent!"

"Be a *good parent*? Ha! Isn't there anyone else??" she asked back, this time from the other side of the closed door - Kimby pawing at it from the inside. "What about Maria? Or Richard Allan??"

"Mom! Don't be mean to me! Go to sleep! I haven't talked to them in forever!"

"...Well, ok," she said, her voice going into a whisper then, "just don't let your Father know who you're running around town with.. He would kill both of us if he knew that you still talked to that guy."

"Goodnight, Mom."

"And not too late tonight -"

"Goodnight, Mom!"

"Sorry!" her Mother said, at last the sound of her footsteps returning down the stairs, heading off to bed at long last.

Another close call, and now Nikko rushed to get ready -

What a struggle..

It wasn't that she didn't appreciate what her Parents did for her, it was just being held nothing short of a prisoner here, everyday the same, looking at the walls and staring at the ceilings, back and forth forever.. There was only so much she could take! And of course she couldn't go out alone. Going out with her friend was trouble enough with the family. But going out by herself? Forget about it..

With Kimby laying on the vanity desk before her now, Nikko set to quickly finish her make-up and hair. Her eyes stared at the mirror, staring at herself and hating what she saw. A beautiful 24 year old girl. Japanese eyes and fair German skin, small freckles just under her left eye. With black eyeliner and shadow, black red lipstick applied, she finished brushing her long, mid-back length black hair, black bangs to the left only a little over her eye.

The thought of him again.. The black-out and disorientation...

Don't let it into your head...

With her make-up and hair close enough to how she wanted, she hurried now to get dressed.

"Watch out, Kimby," she warned with a friendly smile and again set the small black and white cat to the floor. "I have to go get ready really quick!"

First were the white knee-high socks, 2 black stripes at the top. She quickly slid on a short black skirt, key chain charms at the right belt loop - A silver cross, a black cross, and a generic furry monster. The skirt tight-buttoned at the waist, and now she put her arms through a short sleeve white button-up shirt, leaving it unbuttoned for the time being, and started to lace up her black combat boots - Time to rush!

"Kimby!" Nikko called to the kitten as it attacked the lace every time it was pulled through a hole. "Come on, Kimby - I can play with you later, ok? I promise!"

1 boot and then the next, Kimby now swatting at the 3 keychains of her belt loop, and then -

Hoooonnnkkkkk!!! Honk Honk!!!

"Jesus, Jigoro!" Nikko said to herself and jumped up, rushing to the bedroom window.

There he was already, the pitch black car sitting idle in the street, rumbling like a stockyard train - Her friend Jigoro leaning across the passenger seat with a giant smile across his face.

"Just - 1 - more - minute!" she widely mouthed the words down to him, holding 1 finger up, his smile unrelenting -

Oh, crap! Her shirt! Nikko quickly pulled her shirt together and then drew the curtains together, now frantically jumping back to her bed.

What a creep!

Button the shirt up, a stomach-length black tie tied correctly around her collar, and she was good to go.. But wait, a coat - It was still only the beginning of February.. She threw on a small black leather jacket, making sure that she had her ID and lip gloss, and gathered them up into her rubber black Heart backpack - The zipper closing up in a zigzag broken Heart style. Silver backpack chain straps over her shoulders, a kiss to Kimby, and it was time to go!

"Ok, you have food and water, so you be good tonight and don't wait up!" she told the little cat. "I will see in the morning, and then we can nap all day together, ok? And play - We'll play too, I won't forget!"

Kimby let out a big-cat purr that made her entire small body vibrate, and Nikko shut the light off before slipping out through the door.

Down the stairs without the light switch, quiet walk past the Parent's room, through the living room, and out the door. Keys, lock, and now a brisk walk to the waiting car... It actually wasn't so bad out tonight!

Nikko and the NLK

A little warm and the melting snow, the crisp air of night energizing her with each free breath - Like a day out of prison -
"Hey, you -" Nikko's friend greeted as she opened the heavy black door, stepping in and sitting down and closing the door in 1 rapid motion. "Hey! Why so fast? I didn't even get to see those legs -"
Nikko interrupted him with a quick and fast forced kiss on his scratchy cheek - "There, that's all you get tonight," she told him, his lips puckered out for an ungiven lippy kiss. "And stop looking at me, Jigoro -"
"What?" he asked in pretend surprise, his voice 1950's and whiny at the same time. "Why are we talking about me like this?"
"Come on, let's just go already," Nikko told him, putting her seatbelt on. "My Dad's gonna freak out if he gets up and sees your car out here."
Jigoro gave her the look and then turned to face the road, the engine roaring as he raced off down the street.
"It's always kinda cool how you're like a trapped princess up there, waiting for me to rescue you," he told her, taking a quick look at Nikko's legs in the dark. "You want some rock and roll tonight?"
"Sure, whatever -" Nikko answered, noticing that he didn't even wait to hear her before he turned the volume up.
Jigoro Himoff, a.k.a. the 'Monster Party..' What a jerk.
It was difficult to see him in the nighttime car, but she could tell he looked the same as always - That ridiculous black greaser haircut, an exaggerated and fake pompadour wig, his head being silhouetted with a square nose and jaw. His features, even in just the blue glow of the dashboard, were as always almost a skull shade. Nikko never knew if it was make-up, tattoo, facepaint or just old skin, but he always had this weird ghost-bone face about him.. And those ripped up jeans again? Every time.. It was hard to tell, but it looked like under his white-bone black leather jacket was that faded "Monster Party!!" t-shirt that he always had to wear - Too tight for his muscular frame, and with a stupid cartoon skull screaming the words out like an explosion. Jigoro always said that he had designed it after he nicknamed himself, but Nikko of course had no reason to believe anything that he said.
And that in itself was the thing about people like him - Or 'Monsters' like him, as he would prefer her to say. She didn't have to trust him. She had absolutely no faith in someone like this, so what was the risk? If he did something bad - So what? He wasn't a good person,

and she already knew that. He was in his own little world. But what was so wrong about bad people? Jigoro made no bones about who he was, and Nikko could at least respect someone like that. It was the people, the humans, that only pretended to be good that hurt her the most..

Her mind almost drifted..

God, this was really bad rock and roll! The 'Monster Party' was bobbing his head along, looking back over at Nikko with a raised eyebrow and sneaking-glance.

"So what trouble are we getting into tonight?" she asked, turning the volume knob down just enough to not have to yell across to him.

Jigoro automatically turned the volume back up, a slow twist as if Nikko wouldn't notice or see, and leaned over closely to talk and to be too close. "We're going to go show you off at the club tonight!"

"No!!" Nikko's Heart jumped as she told him, her eyebrows going up into a fast sad angle. "Please don't take me back to that place?? The people there - I hate it!"

"Listen," Jigoro told her, his car pulling onto the highway from the ramp now, full speed racing, "you were a pretty popular girl, Nikko. You know that. You made a big name for yourself around here. So humans know you, so what?"

"But still -" she complained. "Can't we just, I don't know, maybe go somewhere without people?"

"Haha!" he laughed, head moving with his wig haircut staying still like a rock. "That's a good idea! But it's a Saturday night, isn't it? Humans are all over the place.. The lonely insects, all swarmed out to simulate their reproduction, right?"

Jigoro looked up from her legs, back at the road for 1 second, and then at Nikko's face before noticing that she truly didn't want to go to the club -

"Ok, listen," he told her again, "you're already all dressed up, and we're already heading to the city anyway.."

"I just really don't want to..."

"Well, me neither," he tried to agree, his foot pressing heavy on the gas pedal, "but why are we going to 'not go' somewhere because of a bunch of scuzzy humans? Who cares what they say? They pay 5 dollars to go in there, and then they wanna talk about you or me? Then they paid 5 dollars just to look at us - That club should pay us for providing the entertainment!"

Nikko laughed at the same old stupid ways Jigoro would always try to convince her that things were ok. At least he tried, so that was something. "Well, ok, but now *you* listen," she said back to him. "If I let you take me there, you have to promise to take me to a place with no people - no 'humans' - afterwards. Deal?"

"Oh, ho ho!" he laughed back and sat up straight, sitting all of the way back on his side and talking loud enough for her to hear him. "Oh yeah, Nikko! That is definitely a deal!!"

"And I do not mean a motel, Jigoro!" she told him, loud over his rock and roll, Jigoro snapping his finger in defeat. "I know how that brain works, Mr. Himoff. Don't even think about it."

Jigoro went back to driving and Nikko tried to settle in. Even with such a guy, it was always great to get out of the house, regardless of where to go. The old black car rumbling through the night, silver skull locks, a silver skull suicide ball on the steering wheel, the as-always XXX magazines scattered about the floor and back seat - It wasn't exactly the friendship that she had always wanted, but it was the closest thing to it that she had.

Racing down the city highway, the city limits and the skyscrapers loomed overhead ahead. As much as Nikko hated the city, hated the place Jigoro was about to take her, she underneath it all loved this feeling of flying like bullet, rocketing into the giant mess of towers clustered out of the land. The rock and roll music played loud and Nikko turned it down just a little more again, enough to still be loud enough and still be able to comfortably talk.

"Did you find any new articles on Shiva?" she asked, interrupting his lip-syncing of the horrible lyrics.

"Shiva! Yeah!" he quickly turned his body, leaning back into the back seat. "I actually found a.. Somewhere back here.. I've got a new..."

"Jigoro!!" Nikko yelled, the car veering out of it's lane. "Watch what you're doing!!!"

The vehicle swerved in and out of the cars around it, horns blaring and tires screeching -

"Relax, Nikko!" he unsuccessfully calmed her as he turned back into his seat, pulling back over into his original lane. "I've got it all under control! Here's the book, check it out -"

Jigoro handed over his binder of clipped newspaper and magazine articles of the woman known as 'Shiva.' Nikko had seen it before, being forced to look at it and hear about it every time that they saw each other. She took it and opened it, quickly flipping past the old stuff she had already seen so many times over.

"I got a new magazine on Wednesday with her in it!" he bragged, truly obsessed and at the same time positively hoping for some form of ungiven jealousy.

Nikko fast-flipped through the pages of clipped articles, personal thoughts and printed pictures off of a computer - "Adult Film 'Actress,' Cold Blooded Killer?" 1 headline read. "Triple X Queen 'Shiva' Murder / Suicide : What Went Wrong?" another read. Pictures, pictures and pictures.. Articles, articles and articles.. And near the back, there it was.. Yet another grizzly photo of the blood drenched apartment..

~ Shiva ~

Another of girl-crazy Jigoro's obsessions, Shiva stood alone at the top of his list. She was the 'plastic-surgically' beautiful adult movie queen, a hometown girl, despised the entire country over. Now hated double time by the mass of humanity, first for making movies that men like Jigoro rented, and now again for the bizarre murder / suicide that she had been involved with. Her life made no sense whatsoever to the people - An impossibly beautiful woman making those movies, and then going off on the killing rally. It was a double strike of hatred from the country's human majority.

"She was such a Sweetheart, wasn't she?" Jigoro asked as Nikko read the photo-accompanied article.

She nodded and read on. Sweetheart was maybe a little strong of a description, but Nikko didn't share the same hatred that the rest of the population seemed to hold for this lady. For some reason, she often found herself sympathizing with the villains of the news rather than the victims.. Of course no person would understand that, maybe not even Jigoro - Who for all of his claims of understanding Shiva's deep mental suffrage, still found himself upset that she wouldn't be starring in any new video releases more than anything.

Such a bizarre case, and it had caught the public's eye well enough that even now, a few years later, they were still publishing guess-work articles on what the people involved must have been thinking..

~ A beautiful adult film actress locks herself up in her apartment with her live-in boyfriend, not coming out for days. The reports and stories varied, but the general agreement was that they came to an agreement, possibly out of boredom and misery for life, to fight and to hurt each other until death ~ Laugh and joke, still be friends, punch and kick, use things around the apartment, silverware, fingernails and teeth.. As soon as 1 of them killed the other, the survivor would turn themselves in to the authorities and spend the remainder of their life behind bars. Nothing left to do in the doldrums of life, except try to push each other off of the edge and past the physical limitations of existence..

Shiva got as far as the killing her boyfriend part, but then instead of turning herself in, she chose to drive off of the downtown city bridge to her watery death..

At least these things sounded a little more interesting than just an ordinary lover's double suicide... ~

"It seems like forever ago," Nikko said as she handed the binder back to the Monster Party. "How long has it been now?"

"2 years and 4 months," Jigoro replied without even needing to think, setting the binder back into the back seat. "Coming up on the 2 and a half year mark. We should celebrate that with an all-night Shiva-only movie marathon!"

"Count me out!" Nikko uninvited herself as fast as possible.

"Heh.. Really though, you know, things could have been so much different if she had just turned herself in," he went on, the highway entering completely into the towering city now. "I could've went straight into the penitentiary, and we could've broken her right out.."

"What?" Nikko laughed, looking out through the window at the city lights and illumination. "Not that again - Look, I don't care how many video games you say you've played -"

"Exactly! At some point we need to accept that things like this are my destiny! Think about it - *All* of my *entire* life, rescuing *all* of those Princesses - What have I rescued, like 1 million Princesses by now? And Shiva was like a Princess, they called her the Queen, right? It would've been like she was held captive in, like a dungeon, sort of.."

"Jigoro..." Nikko slowly shook her head, this coming up pretty much every time that they hung out it seemed. "Don't even think about it anymore. She's long gone now.."

"Well, I'm just saying.." he went on in defeat. "Someone needs to step up in those situations and be a hero to the ladies sometimes, that's all."

Such a guy.. Eyes on the road, and the reckless hero was now off of the highway, driving down through the city's bustling streets. The windows were cracked open just enough for the warming cool air, the snow melting even faster here in this downtown area.

"Well, you can think I'm crazy," Jigoro defended himself, "but I won't ever think you're crazy, even with all of those stories you talk about. That's what happened to Shiva, you know. People didn't believe any of the things she was saying - Talking about seeing things and talking about the 'Death Wish' and all of that."

"Talking about seeing what sort of things?" Nikko curiously asked for her obvious reasons.

"Relax," he calmed her. "Trust me - Nothing like the stuff that you come up with. Not even close."

"Well... I suppose I can take that as a compliment then," Nikko said back, sticking a tongue out that thankfully Jigoro didn't see.

Jigoro's rumbling black car turned and pulled onto *the* street. The familiar place Nikko had seen so many nights in the past days of her life. Rats, they were already here so soon.. She felt the butterflies in her stomach, a crossbreed of the old excitement with a bit of 'no, thank-you,' and without even having to look, the Monster Party immediately found a parking spot nearly straight across from the entrance...

~ Might as well try to make the best of this.. ~

Parked car, out the door and now a short walk across the street, and Jigoro hooked his arm through Nikko's as they did their best impersonation of an awkward couple. Through the 2 lanes of taxi traffic and drunk drivers, and Nikko got a brighter look at her friend under the city lights, just then noticing something she had prayed not to see.

"Oh, come on.." she moaned and stopped in her tracks for a brief moment, her eyes looking down at his side belt loop.

"What? You like what you see or something?"

"You're *so* not wearing that thing again, are you?"

And sure enough, as Jigoro smiled his sharpened tooth smile, she could see that it was in fact what she thought it was. Worn at his belt as said and hanging like a gun holster, it was the 'Monster Party Microphone' that Jigoro had been wearing from way back when he met her. A simple black and silver cordless microphone with a cheap built-in speaker hidden inside - He could pull it out at a moment's notice and sing through it, talk loud through it, make noises or just about do anything annoying that he could think of - And he was still finding new ways to use it in the worst possible ways.

"Come on, Nikko!" he said as he grabbed her hand and continued their walking path. "We can't be all super lame like the rest of these humans, you know? Sometimes we have to *Stand Out Loud!*"

And now with the catchphrases.. Stand Out Loud... What did that even mean??

With the now added possibility of even more embarrassment, Nikko let her friend lead her by the hand and down the alleyway that led to the club's hidden door. The walls on both sides were covered in messy graffiti along with club and concert posters. 1 seemed to be put up more than others, and caught the passing eyes of Nikko - "Black Queen, Black Stacy" it said, Black Queen on top, Black Stacy on the bottom, and a mugshot photo of a blonde girl sticking her tongue out.. No mind to the walls, and this was so nerve wracking.. She could already hear the muffled-in music from the stone walls beside them.

To divert her bad anticipation, she pulled her backpack off and went looking for her ID busily, letting go of Jigoro's hand and trying to hide her uneasiness.

To the hidden door, open, and the club smell and smoke machine sfx rolled out into the alley - The music and club bass louder and clearer now - Look up and - Oh, no..

"MONSTER PARTY! JIGORO HIMOFF, BABY!!" Jigoro was sing-saying into his unholstered microphone, his ID already in the hands of the black-clothed gorilla looking bouncer.

Embarrassing!

The man just shook his head slightly back and forth, then handing the ID back to her obnoxious friend, and then looked at Nikko to take hers.

- And here it would come.. -

"Nikko Heinlad, huh?" the man said to her, looking her over with a look of surprise and probable disgust. "It's been a while.."

Another slight shake of his head, and he handed the ID back to her with it held between 2 fingers, his eyes looking away as if she didn't even exist.

Awkward moment '1' down, and still many more to go..

Into the club they went, dark colors and neon lights flashing, ugly people dressed like horror monsters and a few beautiful girls here and there mixed in. Smoke air and a long bar, low ceilings and a dropped down dance floor - Centered and surrounded by stripper poles, topless girls crawling all over them and spike-wearing men as close as they could get.
This wasn't a bad place. Foreign music, unexpected sights, enough of a crowd to hopefully come and go unnoticed, and a happy clash of scary versus disgusting.
Maybe it wouldn't be such a bad night after all?
"Now we're gonna party, Nikko!" Jigoro yelled to her, his stupid microphone out but thankfully not being used.
He guided her through the crowd near the bar, parting men that stopped their conversations to give him their universally ticked off look. Nikko noticed the effect that Jigoro had of killing almost every conversation that he passed. Guys and girls, even the 'guygirls' too - Everyone stopped and stared, glaring and snickering with a look up and down. Jigoro took her through to an open spot at the bar, and all nearby club people stepped a few steps away, making room for someone they feverishly did not like.
All of the better for Nikko.
"2 *CAAAAANS* OF POP, PLEASE!" Jigoro sang loudly into the uncool microphone device, Nikko putting her hand over head to shield her eyes in humiliation. "You want a soda, right Nikko?"
"Sure..." she answered so quietly she doubted that he had even heard her.
The bartender served it up fast as if to move Jigoro along, and in a moment, the Monster Party was guiding her back away from the bar and down toward the poles and the dropped sunken dance floor.
"OUT OF THE WAY, HUMAN SCUMBAGS!" he announced as they passed attractive people, the looks of disdain even more widespread over here. "MONSTER PARTY, GIRLS!"
Nikko sometimes couldn't believe this friend of hers.. She followed uncomfortably as they walked through the crowds and found a bat-shaped couch to sit at - A little too tight for her and the muscular build of Jigoro, but he would've sat super close anyway, so it didn't

even matter. Both settled in, taking in the scenery of the unreal characters dancing and the gorgeous girls stripping all at once. Creepy looking guys and a handful of girls so flawless, it was of course no wonder that someone like Jigoro would come to a place like this.

A place that some time ago had been a fit for her as well.

"So what are you, like the Devil here now or something?" Nikko asked, noticing that even the people on the dance floor were unhappy by his arrival.

"Aw, the Devil?" he asked, looking around as if he hadn't even noticed the reactions. "That's cool, but nah.. These guys think I want to kiss their girlfriends or something. You know what? I probably already did! All these girls just get crazy with the Monster Party around them - What can I say? Last time I was here, I had to wipe some throw-up off of a girl's lips before I let her kiss me!"

"What??"

"Well I wasn't going to put my mouth on the throw-up!"

"Seriously, Jigoro..."

There actually were a small number girls eyeballing him now that Nikko looked for it, though she seriously couldn't imagine any of them continuing on if they had a chance to know him like she knew him..

Some staring, looking, glares.. There were so many people out there on the dance floor...

~ And then in the crowd, the sight of her old friend Maria, dancing along with Nikko's ex-boyfriend, Richard Allan...

Exactly the last thing she needed to see now.. ~

"So..." she said to Jigoro with an uncomfortable sip of her soft drink, trying hard to look every other way but there. "What do we do now?"

"What do we do now?" he asked back, unaware of the friends from her past. "We monkey around! Come on! It's a Monster Party, let's go! Let's dance!"

Nikko dodged his reaching hand and instead sat back, watching him go tough guy dance off and into the crowd, all along hoping that her ex-friends wouldn't notice her here now..

She focused on Jigoro -

The way that he danced, it was always way too much..

He was like a really bad rock concert.. Everyone had their own style at the places like this, but Jigoro.. He was on stage in his brain. Although as she watched him, forcing herself to avoid her old friends, she had to admit there was something unexplainably cool about him. Not 'fitting in' in the outside world, and then here, not 'fitting in' in the outsider hang out - That was kind of cool. Well, maybe only a little bit cool..

But her attention wandered.. All of these people around, her ex-friend and ex-boyfriend out there... Together... It was a lot to handle. Even the little things, like the way the doorman had treated her as soon as he saw her. People didn't like who she was around here anymore, and though she hid herself a bit better than the flamboyant Jigoro, she could even now see some of the people whispering to each other, their eyes then quickly looking away when they met her catching glance -

Nikko crossing her fingers that those 2 certain people would never notice her sitting there...

And stupid things like this were the reasons why she couldn't go to places like this anymore. This drama, this neverending storyline where even if some of the faces eventually changed, the storylines would always repeat. Raise in popularity, fall in popularity, loved, hated, courtesy hugged and cheek kissed, whatever. Friends, dating, breakups, cheating.. Nikko had been a popular girl at this place at 1 point in time, and it was actually the same place where she had originally met Jigoro.. But that was such a long time ago now that some of the old faces had gone on and vanished. New employees, new dancers, new troublemakers - All mixed in with these few left originals that hadn't yet moved on with their lives and / or died.

It was the same thing as ghosts.

Jigoro was back and forth on the dance floor as the night went on, a lot of time seeming to pass, though in actuality only very little. Nikko's discomfort multiplied as it seemed that more people grew aware of her presence. For all she knew, they were talking about 'that girl' who was with Jigoro, but her brain was going crazy in panic, believing they had figured out that she was 'that girl,' the stupid suicidal girl that everyone had heard about.

"Hey, you!" Jigoro interrupted, waving his microphone in front of her comatose eyes. "HEY, YOOoooouuuUUU!!"

"Stop it, Jigoro, please," she asked him, quickly snapping out of her thoughts and hoping to not draw attention to herself. "Please, can we go now? I want to get out of here.."

"But already? We just got here! They don't close for like 3 more hours!"

Nikko looked around fast - It was all beginning to freak her out, as if she was cornered in the dark. "Yeah, can we go now? Please?"

Jigoro took a deep breath in and took a fast look around himself, mostly a look to the stripping girls at the poles of course..

"Yeah, yeah - Ok, let's get out of here," he told her, Nikko getting up in a stretch of relief, the tension freed from her face. "This place is like a coffin anyway. Most of these humans should be black-listed from this place.."

Microphone surprisingly back into his holster, and Jigoro parted the sea of drunken fools, Nikko led along by the hand. Past the disgusted looks 1 final time, the evil eyes and the whispers, Nikko doing all that she could to not look back at the people from her past. A few Jigoro tough guy brushes past the unmoving and to the entrance, a small huff of a sarcastic laugh from the idiot doorman, and -

~ Freedom ~

~ Out into the cool night air again ~

Nikko felt the phobia of the cave-like club evaporate now. The night sky and melting snow, only a small chill in the air and the fresh breath taste of the breeze against her lips..

"Did you at least try to have a little fun?" Jigoro asked, taking her by the hand, walking down the alleyway toward the street and car.

"It was..." she stopped and thought, trying to be appreciative of him even taking her down to the city. "Yeah, it was fun.. Sorry we were just in and out.. There were a couple of people in there I wasn't ready to see yet -"

"Really? And you didn't even dance!" he told her, backdown and to the street now. "I guess it's better that way.. We don't need those creepy guys checking out your legs when your skirt spins around.."

And then Jigoro leaned away from her and looked down, trying to lift the edge of her skirt with the tip of his finger -

"Jigoro!!" Nikko yelled and laughed, jumping away from him and staring him down face to face.

"Heh, sorry!" he apologized and reached for his microphone.
"No!! Don't!"
"LOOK AT THIS LADY!! LOOK AT THESE KNEE HIGH SOCKS!!"

Nikko and the NLK

Nikko hurried across the street in yet another embarrassment, her hand once again shielding her eyes as she stepped around the black car to the passenger side.

"Aww, come on - Are you kidding me?? I think my microphone battery just died..." Jigoro complained as he unlocked the doors for both of them to get in. "What the heck..."

"Good," Nikko sighed in her relief, a match of getting out of the crowded club and the temporary death of the microphone. "I don't know why you love talking so much anyway."

"I have alot of things to say!" he defended himself, climbing into the driver side and ready to head off.

With a loud rumble of the engine, the car came to life, the rock and roll back on and a pull out onto the street.

Drive and leave the club behind...

"So, do you remember your promise?" Nikko asked as she put her seatbelt on.

"... Maybe we should just stop somewhere fast and pick up some batteries..." he said, tapping the unresponsive microphone against the steering wheel to no avail.

"Come on! You promised to take me somewhere without a million people!"

"I know, I remember," he told her. "We'll go somewhere good this time, I still promise!"

Nikko pretended to believe him, his car taking all sorts of strange routes and turns in the span of just a few city blocks. Jigoro was up to his usual tricks of sneaking looks over at her legs from time to time, driving in so many different directions she hadn't the slightest idea where they were heading now.

"So where's this place going to be?" Nikko asked, the music at a decent level where they could almost comfortably talk.

"Actually, it's going to be right up and around the corner here.." he looked toward her with a flash of his eyebrows. "Nikko, did you know that this city is where Shiva ended up killing herself? In our river?"

"Yes, Jigoro," she told him with a roll of her eyes. "You ask me that every time that I see you."

-"Well, nerdy smart girl -"

Nikko and the NLK

"Hey!"

"I bet you didn't know this!" Jigoro continued. "When they went to look for her, her body was never even found! Even her car is still in there! Like a sunken ship!"

"Is that really true?" Nikko asked, not knowing if anything he ever said was fact or not. "I don't think they would just leave the car sitting down there, but that's kinda cool.."

"Up here's going to be the exact spot," he said, pointing down the road, pulling his car over to park streetside again. "Come on.. We're gonna go check it out.."

Before she could say yes or no or anything, Jigoro had the keys in his hand and was out the driver side door already. Nikko exited the car as well, following his lead down the last patch of street before it crossed over the bridge.

"Well I'm glad you aren't going to be crashing your own car off of it, at least," she said as she caught up with his anxious steps. "You seem just a little bit obsessive.."

"You know what? I've actually thought about doing that!" he said to her with no surprise shown on her face. "That's usually on my mind when I come here!"

Cars raced by, the bridge-street separated from the pedestrian walkway by a waist-high barrier.

"You don't think that she survived the crash, do you? If her body was never found?" Nikko asked him, walking along the divider from the road, on the walkway and at the edge.

"Are you kidding me? Shiva?? The things that she could do would shock you! If she wanted to die, you bet she died! When she set her mind to something, everybody stood back!"

They continued, and the bridge rounded up a little, an arching walk up a half-lit, under-construction facelift to the bridge over water. Nikko walked along the edge, looking down at the river far below. The water was up higher than usual, the warmer day and now night melting all of the snow into a runoff.

"So we're just gonna.. Hang out here?" Nikko wondered out loud, Jigoro stopping his walk and jumping up to sit on the railing, feet and boots hanging over the side.

"Yeah, come on!" he said. "You're not cold are you? It's beautiful out!"

It wasn't quite the 'place with no people' that she had in mind, but come to think of it, there weren't many city places this separated

Nikko and the NLK

from the crowds. The people raced by behind them in their cars, but nobody could be seen out walking around over here.

"It is pretty nice out tonight," she climbed up and sat down next to him. "And you're saying this is *the* spot where she drove and crashed her car off?"

"Well, actually I'm not 100 % sure on the exact spot," he explained, "but from what I've been able to figure out - Yeah! I'm pretty sure of it.. Awesome, right??"

"Heh, yeah. I guess this is pretty neat.."

They looked on, able to see the city in such a beautiful view. As much as Nikko hated it, it was difficult to resist it's allure from afar - Up close and inside, not so much - But out here, sitting on the under-construction suicide bridge, it temporarily didn't feel like such a bad place..

"She picked a good spot to die," Nikko said, looking around at the lights bounding off of the flowing water below.

"You've got that right," he agreed with her, his head up and looking into the city's eternally starless sky. "So - What's been going on with your head now? Same old things?"

He actually asked..

As bad of a friend and all around person that he was, Jigoro from time to time could find ways to catch Nikko totally off guard, times like this, actually sounding like he maybe cared about something other than himself.

Nikko looked up from the river, staring off at the buildings ahead. "Yeah, same old stuff. I go about my day, my night, so bored and nothing I want to do anymore, and all of a sudden I find myself just standing there - Like my brain shut off for a minute.."

"You and your standing sleep.. You still see that guy in your head? Still feel like you can't remember stuff?"

"Heh, yeah... Yeah to both."

"And still telling your parents it's not happening anymore so you don't have to go back to that hospital?"

"Well, I'm glad to know that you were actually listening all of those times," she smiled, slightly at ease about the entire situation for the moment.

"At least your only problem is not knowing what your problem even is, that's a good thing, right? Who knows. Maybe you're just a crazy girl after all -"

"What the.. Hey, are you seeing this??" Nikko asked Jigoro fast, looking down at the water's reflection again, then quickly back up and looking back over her shoulder.

"Huh? Seeing what?"

"You wanna talk about crazy girls, look at this!"

Nikko looked back down at the water, seeing the reflection of a girl rollerskating across the bridge -

Jigoro looked down, then back up behind him and all around -

"What am I supposed to be seeing?"

Just below and difficult to see in the distortion of the water, there was the reflection of a tan girl rollerskating across the bridge - Long straight blue hair, giant bulky headphones, big oversized white socks, and the most unusual of all - A rainbow colored bikini? In the winter??

"You said it was a girl??"

"In a bikini!" Nikko laughed, trying to find her on the bridge but not locating her at all.

"Did you just say a bikini?!?" Jigoro nearly spun completely around looking back and forth, freaking out to try and see something like a spring preview, maybe even a summer preview, right here during the melty snow of winter.

"I can't believe you didn't see her," Nikko said, not being able to find the actual person and looking back straight down for the reflection.

And with Jigoro still on search, the unexpected image skated away and beyond -

"I wonder how the heck..." he said and scratched his head, careful to not touch the rock-hard pompadour. "You better not be making things up, Nikko! That sounded too good to be true! A bikini in the winter? Come on..."

A confused look around, and Nikko gave up. Even with the rush of cars going by, there was no way the girl could have skated directly behind them without Jigoro being able to man-radar the presence of a female... It was almost as if her reflection was swallowed up by the river..

So random..

"What were we talking about again?" Jigoro asked, trying to relax but obviously still wondering about the bikini skater.

"Just the same old stuff, nothing important."

"Hmm.. Anyway.. You know how I was saying earlier that Shiva was talking about a 'Death Wish' before she closed herself up in that apartment?" he went on, quickly falling back into his obsession. "Even on her movie sets, they say it was all she could talk about. But what do you think it means?"

"What, a Death Wish? That's just when you want to die, you know?"

"Yeah, but I always wonder - What was it to her, really?" Jigoro asked. "Was it like a wish on a shooting star?"

Nikko swung her legs inward and outward from the bridge. 'Death Wish?' It struck her inside with a weird feeling just wondering about it.

"I think about 'Death Wish' all of the time," Jigoro confessed to her. "Ever since I read that Shiva talked about it, I haven't been able to get it out of my head."

"So then have you made a 'Death Wish' yet?" Nikko asked Jigoro and gave him an elbow nudge into his ribs.

"Me? No way! That's serious stuff, man..."

Nikko laughed and a few moments of no talking passed, only the sounds of the passing car horns and the far-off voices of the city.

"Hey, um..." Jigoro started saying, sounding just a bit unsure. "You want to do it?"

Nikko looked over at him with both of her eyebrows up. "Do... Do what exactly?"

"The Death Wish! We can make it now!"

"Ha!" Nikko laughed in relief. "Yeah, sure why not? It sounds like fun.."

"Oh yeah? But are you really, *really* sure, Nikko?"

"I'm sure, Mr. Himoff..."

"... Oh, man, how cool is this?" Jigoro asked himself in excitement, following Nikko's eyes up to the no-star sky of the city. "Let's find like a 'Devil Star' or something.."

Nikko brought her head back down and away. "I don't think we can make a wish on a star if there aren't any."

"That's the problem... Do you think maybe it's something different, something even crazier or more exciting?"

"Possibly. Something like Death Wish sounds like a really big deal."

"That's what I'm thinking.." Jigoro said back with a strong pondering glance. "I think about it a lot, but I can't figure out how a guy could even make it.. It can't be just like a prayer, can it?"

Nikko went on explaining what it possibly could be, at least to her, and as she did so she soon noticed Jigoro was paying no mind to her at all.

"Nikko Heinlad, I'm about to ask you such a serious question," he proclaimed, sounding dramatic like he was holding his dead-battery microphone out -

"Jigoro Himoff," she proclaimed back to him, trying to sound serious while so silly, "I am prepared to make a statement."

He turned his head to face her, face to face. "Do you, Ms. Heinlad, officially announce your Death Wish before this Living World?"

Nikko tried not to smile. "I 100% do. This is the real deal to me.. But do you, Mr. Himoff, officially announce *your* Death Wish before the Living World here tonight as well?"

Surprisingly, Jigoro took a moment to answer, taking a deep breath and then a gulping sound from his throat before talking. "I do. More than just my friend's 'real deal,' this is the 'actual factual' to me."

"Is that so?" Nikko asked, amused that he always had to try and be cool no matter what.

"It is 'very' so," he confirmed. "And with that, I officially announce 'Monster Party' Jigoro Himoff and Nikko Heinlad as true-blue Death Wish... *Wishers...*"

"This isn't the part where you say 'you may now kiss the bride,' is it?" Nikko laughed to him.

And just as she started to smile and almost caught herself enjoying his company - He pushed off, propelling his body forward and off of the under-construction bridge, pulling Nikko by her hand as he did -

"Jigoro!!! What are -" Nikko cried in shock but it didn't matter now -
The weight of her muscular friend dropped her along with him all of the way down, her Heart racing up into her throat as they plummeted the short but so far distance into the river's water below. All of the emotions and shock and confusion going on at once, and then the impact -

The dark water splashed as their bodies hit, his first followed by hers not a moment later.. The cold water blasted through Nikko's body, her bare legs freezing and boots so heavy, the momentum of the drop pushing them underwater and both fighting back to the surface.

"Jigoro!!!" she gasped as the water rushed into her mouth - "Are you crazy???"

He tried to tread water, struggling more than Nikko was, and then opened his mouth to talk.. But out of it came nothing, just gasps for air and the chattering of his brittle old teeth - his wig somehow still in place.

"Take your coat off!!" Nikko ordered him as she saw the trouble he was having staying above submersion.

And as he did so, the black leather skeleton print coat now floating alongside them, her eyes raced around to the riversides, looking for an easy place to swim to.

"Oh, my God.." Nikko freezingly turned in a circle, seeing the same thing on both sides.

The melting snow had brought the water level higher than normal, but even with that, the sides of this part of the river were concrete man made. Pointless little ladders were higher up, but out of reach even with the levels so high..

"The bridge!" Nikko cried and shivered, her legs going numb and gradually her entire lower body. "There's gotta be someone up there to help us! Jigoro - you really - Why??"

But as she swung around, he was nowhere to be seen.

"Jigoro??" she screamed out. "JIGORO?!?"

But all over was just the freezing dark water and no trace of her friend.

"No!! Jigoro! What were you thinking, you stupid idiot??"

Tears mixed with the water in her eyes, and the shock of her Heart combined with the freezing compression of her lungs - It was too much - She desperately struggled to stay afloat in the cold, her numb legs barely moving. She slid from her backpack, her jacket coming off too, and then tried to move her arms more freely, but it didn't help. There were only small feelings remaining at this point.. And what was the point to helplessly struggle?

Her head bobbed under the water and she raised it back out, a failed kick of her legs, but no use as she could hardly even sense them anymore. So many people, all over the city - Unable to escape them, but now not even a single person to help her out, or to even give her a ray of hope..

~ And now it seemed that maybe things really weren't so bad before ~

Nikko and the NLK

Parents who cared? A cat that wanted to play? A friend that wanted to take her out dancing? These were the things that she thought about as her head was slipping beneath the surface. Imagining all of the people out having fun, or at home comfortably sleeping, and here she was at the edge of her life..

~ 'Kill Yourself?' ~

She had always wanted to die, but now she found herself fighting to stay alive.

~ Flailing, fighting, trying to float ~

The sound of the city, the unseasonably-warm though still cold day, the cars passing by overhead, the reflection of the city's lights on the river, and Nikko missed her last chance at a deep breath of air.

A sink into the deep river body, all sounds muted and lights blurring into the black.. Garbage beneath the surface and this river would be her death bed - Jigoro too - All unexpected and with the worst war of pains imaginable as her brain received no oxygen. Her eyes opened and closed in the icy temperatures of the water - 1 hand at her throat in pain and the other reaching pathetically for something, for anything at all, to grab onto.

But nothing.

Thoughts in mind now not of the things she loved, not of the things that haunted her, but just of the all-overriding pains that engulfed her head this far beneath the surface.

~ At the edge of life now ~

And at the river's bed, there slept the actual wreckage of Shiva's car, now a forgotten afterthought - The last thing her freezing eyes would ever see in this Living World..

~ Sinking boy + sinking girl, goodbye to this stupid world ~

Nikko and the NLK

Her zipper Heart backpack floated atop the February river, the water and world moving on now without her..

Nikko and the NLK

"This is crazy.. Are we really going through with it?"

"Of course we are! It'll be fun..."

"I don't know. I just.."

"You're not backing out on me now, are you?"

"... No... I'm ok. I can do it."

"That's what I wanted to hear! So, did you lock the door?"

"Yeah... We're locked away from everything now."

"Good! I'll let you hit me first! This is going to be so crazy!!"

Nikko and the NLK

CHAPTER 2

It Doesn't Die

    Black riverbed to deathbed, all turned to black and a stillness came soon after.. No more flailing, no more panic, just the motionless shutdown of the Heart. The brain clicked off as if a bullet had been shot directly through it..

    ~ And then? This should be heaven then.. ~

    But something else happened.. Particles of a consciousness were coming together, back and forth, an alive-meets-dead system synchronization.. All senses began slowly feeling back online for the body, and Nikko felt an awareness in the way of a tiny spark. She was a match lit in the dark, a small sense of what was what -
    Voices - Sounds - Nerves..
    Blankets?
    Her eyes opened in a rush, her lungs ready to burst at the flowing in of air all at once.
    And where was she? Not dead? Her body was completely dry - Was this an afterlife dream? She found herself draped in blankets, the uncomforting paper thin sheets and coverings of a hospital room bed..
    No... Not again!
    All of this looked so familiar, but it couldn't be.. Nearly a replica of the hospital she had been to so many times and back again. And Jigoro - There was no way...
    Beside her was another bed of the same generic design, holding Jigoro amid a gathering of unusual women..
    "This is bad.." Nikko said in a drowned voice to her friend. "Jigoro? What happened to us??"
    Nothing was said back as Nikko looked closer - She could roughly make out 5 of them, all women and dressed like a boy's dream of how nurses should dress. They wore white and short-skirted 1-piece buttoned outfits, each woman identical to the other, with unnaturally long, nearly exaggerated-long long legs. There were sprits of blood

Nikko and the NLK

over their bodies and gloves, and worst of all, though somehow the last detail noticed, each nurse had no head - Or at least no human head.. In place of each of their faces were slightly oversized skull heads or masks, or possibly something horrible in between.

The skull nurses stood around Jigoro with 2 even crawling atop him, long needles and medical instruments poking and prodding, drawing blood and injecting colored serums into his motionless body..

Something was going horribly wrong here.

"Jigoro!" Nikko called back over to her silent friend. "Wake up! I think we're dreaming or something! Wake up! Please!"

He remained still, his body and wig dry as if nothing had happened.

"This can't be good..." Nikko said silently to herself, so much of a disorientation between the reality of what had happened on the bridge and the now unbelievable reality before her..

She closed her eyes and leaned the back of her head deep into the stiff pillow. Try to focus.. Try to wake up if she was asleep, or try to just die if she was in some weird mental state..

And within a moment, she felt the tip of a needle touch her upper arm and she jolted up - Sitting up and opening her eyes again -

"What are you trying to do??" she yelled out and reactively brushed her arm before her, pushing off 1 of the skull headed nurses. "Get away from me!"

The nurse stepped back slowly, the other skull nurses in the room looking up from Jigoro and toward her.

"Why are you doing that to him?" she cried. "What's happening? Where are we??"

But without speaking, the remaining number with his motionless body went back to their actions. Non-stop medical attention, crawling all over her friend's body like insects across a dead animal.

And before Nikko, the nurse that had attempted to inject her was now just standing there. Speckles of dried blood over her long-leg body, the faded-white skull face just staring eyelessly toward her.

"You can get out of bed when I say that you are better," a cute voice said, static-filled and coming from overhead. "But try it even a moment sooner, and we will have to sedate you, Sweetie!"

Nikko looked upwards at the hospital's ceiling - And now that she looked, was there even any? As bright as the hospital's white lighting was, where were the lights? The walls went so high that they faded off into black, almost the same black as the river's depths she had only just seen before death.

Nikko and the NLK

"Barbie Turates," the new voice went on, "please keep an eye on the pretty girl. Don't just focus all of your medicine on that good looking boy!"

Nikko, who would have normally laughed at the good looking boy comment, continued her look into the black reaches of the impossible ceiling. Confused about everything, and then she saw the outlandish shadow of the speaking woman coming into view.

"I see that you are awake finally, patient #81," she said. "My nurses and I would like to welcome you to the Medikiss Hospital! I am the Head Nurse, you can call me Miavia ~"

The girl calling herself 'Miavia' came down slowly from the ceiling. She was sitting atop a giant cartoon shaped Heart, floating down and closer near the beds. She had a physical appearance similar to Nikko, with pale asian skin and long brown hair. She sat with her legs overhanging the Heart, comically big white platform boots, and from the floating organ, straight up and to her hands, was an old-fashioned 1950's microphone stand that she used to talk. Her body was dressed in something like a honeymoon nurse's outfit, white and red, with a Heart eyepatch over her left eye, white lace all around it. Bandages were across her thighs and arms, and as the Heart ride dropped in closer, she was in the middle of wrapping yet another white dressing over a dry-blood spotted gauze patch.

"We don't like seeing attractive people in pain," she said, her cute voice a close static to an old time radio voice. "So we are going to take care of all of your little needs for now."

".. I have no idea what's going on here," Nikko said with a shaky voice, moving around a little in her bed. "I'm not supposed to be here - We aren't supposed to be here -"

She looked over at the bed of Jigoro and saw the skull head nurses still attending him, climbing over his body to get at different angles, their needles pricking like bloody mosquito heads.

"And what the heck are they even doing to him??"

"They're taking care of patient #82 for me," Miavia unsuccessfully tried comforting Nikko. "He was admitted just a few minutes before you, as you would've been #83, had our original #81 not died during the brief moment between your arrivals.. So once they have him stable, they'll get to you ~ Please be patient, patient!"

She laughed a little bit at her own words, and then finished the self-dressing she had been busy applying. With both hands, she lifted 1 of her legs slightly and set it nearer to the other - They looked so

Nikko and the NLK

lifeless even compared to the sickly rest of her. Were they broken?

   Nikko didn't pretend to care, and instead tried to get up from her white-blanketed bed, the nearby standing nurse pushing her back down quickly.

   "What the?" Nikko tried to sit back up, being pushed back down again.

   "No-no..." Miavia warned her, the Heart gliding nearer the side of her bed and hovering. "You've been through some serious trauma! Please be calm and wait for your turn, #81!"

   The Head Nurse reached into a Heart-shaped carryall box and pulled out a neon green prescription bottle, taking 2 or 3 pink-yellow pills before putting it away. A small cough and she covered her little mouth, then uncovering it with a few drops of blood at her lips.

   "I'm ok," she said with a glance at the red on her fingertips. "Just a cold ~"

   Nikko went to get up again, the needle-holding nurse standing over her with 1 knee on the bedside, ready to pounce on top of her if need be.

   "Jigoro!" Nikko yelled over again to her uncomfortably quiet friend. "Jigoro, will you wake up already??"

   "*Nikko*!" Jigoro's voice at last called out from the mass of nurses. "Would you please just 'shhhhhhh,' and let me enjoy this??"

   "What?!? You're ok??"

   "I've never been better!" he said back. "I think we ended up in Heaven! Let me just lay here and let these young ladies take care of me!"

   "You have to be kidding me!"

   "You know," Miavia said down to Nikko, "you really should just let #82 rest, a hospital is no place for all of your yelling and shouting.. We really don't want to have to put you to sleep.."

   "I don't need you to do anything to me, I just want to get up and get out of here - Jigoro, can we go? Now?"

   The Heart loomed nearer - A nearly solid red, it must've been at least 7 feet tall. This close, Nikko could make out the slight image of.. What was it? It looked like colored organs bunched up inside of it, a subtle pulse-like vibration every few seconds or so.

   Another cough, and a little blood coughed up, the Heart pulsing just a small touch harder.

   "Jigoro, we're not staying in this place for another minute," Nikko sat up straight, pushing the watching nurse off of her and swinging her legs out of bed - Taking her 'afterlife' fate into her own hands. "Come on, let's just go already!"

Getting out of the bed, and Nikko was still dressed exactly how she had been on her night out with Jigoro - Minus the coat and backpack left in the river, and somehow dry again - And as she stood up, an instant unsteadiness filled her brain. The nurses all in shock, Miavia letting out a gasp, and Nikko stepped over to Jigoro's bed, pushing at the skull headed long-leg nurses between her and her friend.

"Get off of him!" she yelled, pushing at the 2 that had been draped atop him. "This isn't what nurses do!"

"Sedate that girl!" Miavia yelled orders into the microphone, Nikko staying alert with her arms and ready to swing.

"Don't even touch me!" she screamed.

"Nikko!!" Jigoro shouted and opened his eyes. "What do you do this for?? These ladies - Whoa - Who's that on the Heart??"

Jigoro's eyes were trained on Miavia, his head staying still and not even the slightest of movement from his body. Nikko looked back at the Head Nurse for a fast moment too, Miavia waving a girly wave to the bedridden Jigoro.

"Look at *you*!" he said, half to her and half thinking out loud. "Look at that outfit! And look at those bandages! A microphone too?? Oh... And your legs.. Is there.. Something wrong with them??"

"Jigoro!!" Nikko pulled at his arm. "Would you get real??"

"Actually," Miavia said back to him, "they're both broken, #82.. I haven't figured out how to fix them yet.."

"Oh, this is so hot... Nikko, we don't have to go just yet - Hey! What are you, what?? Hey!!"

And as Nikko gave up on listening to his conversations with Miavia, she yanked on his arm as hard as she could, the surrounding nurses standing back and making room in an expectant manner.

"Nikko!!" Jigoro yelled to her in a rare panic voice. "Something doesn't feel right!!"

And just as he was pulled almost into the sitting up position, his lifeless body went even limper, the skin across his face breaking up into small disintegrations -

With a fleshy rip, his skull fell out from his face and hit the bed, dry and no blood, bouncing to the ground and the eyeballs rolling away -

"Oh, my God!!" Nikko screamed and jumped back.

"Oh God!!" Jigoro's skull screamed back. "What just happened now?? Why am I on the floor??"

Nikko stood with her mouth hanging open, staring and then looking back at the expressionless nurses, and then back again at the self-medicating Miavia.

"Nikko! What happened?" Jigoro asked, the voice coming from the jaw and teeth mouth of his disconnected skull -

Talking with no vocal cords??

"I, um, I.." she said and trailed off. "I don't know.. Are you... Ok?"

"I'm fine! Just help me off of the floor! I can't feel my arms!"

"This is so messed up.." Nikko carefully went to lift him.

"Wait! Wait, give me a second!" he interrupted her. Taking a moment to just sit there in silence -

Nikko paused and then realized, even as a skull, she could see his mouth smiling, presumably trying to see up the skirts of herself and the long-legged nurses.

Seeing without eyeballs!!

"Are you serious, Jigoro??" Nikko scolded him. "Even at a time like this??"

"It's so weird! I can't even move my head!!"

"You need to get back into bed," Miavia ordered Nikko, the nurses clenching their syringes. "You don't want to end up like #82, do you?"

Nikko bent to pick Jigoro's skull up and stared over to the Heart-riding Head Nurse.

"Hold on," Jigoro interjected. "How come I can see my body still laying there in the bed??"

"We aren't sticking around here anymore," Nikko told Miavia and her associates. "I don't know what this place is, or what the heck you did to Jigoro.."

"What the..." the talking remains of Jigoro went on, still in his panic mode. "Am I just a head?? Nikko, please tell me I'm not just a head!!"

She took Jigoro with both hands and held him face to skully-face with herself. "You're a skull, Jigoro, a slightly oversized, talking skull. Don't ask me why, I have no idea what's going on in this place.."

Jigoro's skeletal jaw hung open, an expression of '?!?' across his bone face, not saying even a word for just a moment.

"Look," Nikko called to Miavia, 1 hand cradling Jigoro up against her arm. "I don't know what any of this is all about, but we're getting out of here - We're not staying in a hospital, and we're definitely not staying in a horrible place like this!!"

Nikko and the NLK

"Wait!" Jigoro called up to Nikko from her holding hand. "We're not just gonna leave my body here, are we?? You can't do that to me! I need it!"

"Consider it a favor!" Nikko told him as she dashed right through the gathered nurses, pushing off a few of them as they reached for her with their long unnatural fingers. "We'll leave your body with all of these creepy ladies you seem to like so much!"

"Oh, this isn't right.." Jigoro moaned to himself. "Nikko, I don't think I like this anymore..."

"Don't think for a minute that this sort of behavior will be tolerated here!" Miavia called ahead to the fleeing patients. "Nurses, don't let them get away! We have to take care of them still! Sedate them!"

And as Nikko fled through a garage-sized door and into the hallway now, the group of nurses abandoned Jigoro's leftover body and followed in a voiceless pursuit. Nikko looked back, catching sight of the floating Heart exiting the room as well, just barely fitting through the oversized door and scraping against the walls and floor, Miavia holding tightly on.

"Nikko, do you even know where you're going??" Jigoro frantically asked her, still uncomfortable coming to terms with being only just a skull. "I think we need a plan right about now!"

"Plan what?" she asked him back in a rushed laugh. "And this is coming from the jerk that pulled me off the bridge?? You've got some nerve to talk!! Just let me try to get us out of here!"

Running in a near sprint down the hallway, Nikko rounded a corner and then another, hoping to find some sense of an exit. Out here there was an actual ceiling, the decor of the hospital seemingly static and plain, and not any much more different than what she had seen at her 'real life' hospital back home. But that in itself was bad enough for her, and she anxiously fled the pursuing nurses just as much as the hospital itself to escape that unrelenting memory.

"This wouldn't be so difficult if I didn't have to lug you around!" she told Jigoro's skull, the awkward size of it requiring her to use both hands every so often.

"Well you can't just put me down! Why don't you carry me in your backpack?"

"I took it off when I was drowning!!"

"Then I don't know, put me on your head or something - Like how the nurses look -"

"You think those are just skulls on their heads?" Nikko asked and wondered herself. "They looked like they were really attached!"

And now that Nikko looked closer, Jigoro's skull wasn't just shaped like an actual skull either - It was cartoon exaggerated, to an extent, and actually seemed to be hollow inside? No brain??

"Just try it! Do whatever you gotta do!" he begged her. "I know you're really mad at me, just do whatever you have to do!!"

As Nikko gained more distance from what seemed to be the only people in the entire hospital, she stopped for just a moment and lifted Jigoro over her head -

"It's not gonna fit, it's too small," she said and then stopped off -

It actually did fit? Somehow, Jigoro's skull fit like a helmet over her head, her black hair hanging out through the bottom and against her neck.

"How in the world..." she wondered out loud, her eyes looking out through the empty sockets of his skull.

"Who cares??" Jigoro answered, his voice ringing in her ears as his jaw moved atop her mouth. "Does any of this make any sense to you so far?? Just move, woman!!"

"Don't be so bossy!" Nikko started jogging again, seeing the nurse brigade and Miavia just behind and down the hall now. "And I'm still mad at you - Hey, you can't, like, read my brain or anything right now, can you?"

"Who cares?? Just move!"

Nikko passed by empty rooms, glancing in as she passed in hopes of seeing someone or anything normal. No doctors, no nurses, no other life of any kind in the entire building it seemed -

"I thought you said you liked it here?" she said with her breath a little heavier, the running wearing her down. "Didn't you think you were in heaven?"

"Heaven until my head fell off!"

"Ha! Serves you right!"

Just on the right side of the hallway, near it's end and a dead end, there at last came an opened-door elevator, and Nikko with her skull head stepped in as fast as she could. It was completely wallpapered with mirrors, and she hurried to the button board, 81st floor.. 81st floor?? How tall of a hospital was this?? Scan down the panel, and there - Ground level..

"Push it! Push it!"

"Relax, Jigoro! I'm doing it!"

With a push of the button, the doors of the mirrored elevator closed, cutting them off at last from the approaching look-alike nurses and their Heart-mounted leader.

Finally, a few moments to catch their breath as the elevator very slowly began to descend.

"...This is without a doubt the best you've ever looked," Jigoro laughed, the reflection of Nikko with his skull head helmeting hers.

"Oh you like it?" she laughed back, confused beyond belief by the absurdity of this all. "I could say the same thing about you, punk!"

And as Nikko and Jigoro admired their singular appearance, her body and school girl clothes with his skull headed face, something moved around in the inside of the air. It was unnoticed by them at first, so many things now running through their heads, but as it moved about, it caught the eye of the invisible eyes of Jigoro -

"Nikko, move your head back to your right.."

"What? Why, what do you want?"

"There - What is that thing?"

"What are you looking at?" she asked him, but then saw the same distorted space he was seeing.

Like a lump in the air, a see-through mass of warped nothingness was twitching and moving about, almost as if something was trying to break through.. And then something actually did break through - A book flew out, hitting the floor and then another just atop it, as if materializing from mid-air. 'The Scarecrow Dream?'

"Whoa!" Jigoro shouted out. "Look at that! Books!"

Another book fell from the invisible mass, and then 2 more - A book titled 'CoolToDie World??' What was this? And then the book drop stopped off, the see-through bulge of air still moving in the slightest invisible way, something much different then a book squeezing it's way out now..

"What the heck??" Jigoro shouted loud enough to rattle Nikko's own skull. "How cool is that?!"

Out of the space of disrupting air, the dog-sized head and body of a miniature donkey leapt out, landing on the elevator floor and prancing about as if nothing unusual. It had a mangy look about it, dirty and matted short hair, mixed in an assortment of grey and dirty black.

"Now this??" Nikko asked, becoming less and less surprised about anything that happened in this place after death. "Jigoro, it looks like there is now a *donkey* in the elevator with us.."

"Eee-Haw! Not a donkey!" it shouted up at Nikko, shocking them both with it's words. "I am the Dorchester Burrow!"

"It talks and it has a fancy name too!" Jigoro applauded by voice, Nikko a little hesitant to be so excited.

"Look, we aren't here to.. talk to donkeys..." she told the Burrow. "So if you don't mind.."

She turned and faced the closed elevator door, patiently waiting for it's turtle speed descent to reach the ground level.

"Nikko..." Jigoro said under his breath, even that sending an odd vibration against her head. "If we aren't here to talk to donkeys, eh, a Burrow, then why *are* we here exactly? We need to make the best of this, starting right now! Talk to it!"

"Jigoro," Nikko said in her own under-the-breath whisper, "we don't know why we are here, or even 'where' here is exactly... All I know is that we need to get out of this hospital as soon as we possibly can!"

"Well, I'm talking to it!" Jigoro defied her. "Dorchester, is that what you said your name was? I'm the Party Monster, Jigoro Himoff -"

"Jigoro!" Nikko pointlessly complained.

"2 voices from a single body?" the Burrow asked. "That's pretty impressive!"

"It's just a trick!" Jigoro explained. "Normally, I'm a really strong, good looking guy. But for now, my friend Nikko is wearing my skull on her head, at least until we can go back and get my body -"

"We aren't going back to get your body..."

"Oh my, that's a tight spot... But speaking of bodies..." the animal went on, a short awkward silence followed by a boy-looking-at-a-girl whistle.

Nikko rolled her eyes behind the skull, and then saw the reflection of the Dorchester Burrow in the mirrors of the elevator - Catching the small donkey standing near her and glancing up her skirt!

"Are you kidding me?!" Nikko complained as she twirled around and held her loose-fitting short black skirt against her legs. "What is wrong with you? You're worse than Jigoro!"

"Eee-Haw!" it sounded and ran around the elevator, Nikko turning in step with it and holding down her skirt. "Just a guy! Can't resist a real beauty!"

"This guy's alright!" Jigoro announced, Nikko rapping her knuckles against the side of her head and his skull. "Oww! What was that for??"

"Don't encourage it!"

"But in all seriousness," the Burrow said with a calmer tone, then suddenly coming to stand on it's hind legs like a small donkey-shape

Nikko and the NLK

of a man -

"Oh, this is excellent!" Jigoro cheered on.

"If I may," it continued, seemingly unphased by the talking skull's comment until it gave a knowing wink, "though normally I only offer this to those characters with a certain.. *animal*.. I would like to make an invitation.."

"Out of thin air?" Nikko asked. "How did you even get in here? And what's with the books?"

"I was getting to the details! And nevermind the books! Who reads them anyways? Now this is very important, so please hear me out.."

~ PING ~

The elevator sounded as it at last reached it's floor, and Nikko quickly turned again to face the opening doors.

"Sorry!" she apologized over her shoulder. "We're gonna have to take a pass on that offer! Nice meeting you!"

"Nikko, no!" Jigoro cried. "Let's hear him out!"

"Don't go! Hear me out!" The Dorchester shouted, Nikko dashing out through the doors the moment that they opened wide enough.

"You could've at least.." Jigoro complained and then stopped off as Nikko stopped off herself.

"Wait a minute - I don't think this is the ground floor.."

She turned back quick, feeling that the elevator had stopped short of it's pressed button, and standing beside the now-closed door was 1 of the skull head nurses -

"Shoot! She must have pressed the button!"

Nikko turned back around to face the direction she had been facing first, and now a small gathering of the nurses had rounded the corner. Nikko gritted her teeth and forced her way into the group, pushing and punching her way through.

- A stab of a syringe into her arm -

"Hey!!" she cried out in pain, shoving her way through and then a run again down a similar hall. "That really hurt!!"

"See??" Jigoro told her. "We should have listened to Dorchester! He was trying to help us!"

"He was a donkey!"

"That could talk and stand on 2 legs!"

"Yeah, and come out of thin air like some sort of a demon! I had a bad vibe about that thing!"

Rushing down the nondescript hallway of hospital whites and utter chaos, Nikko found and ran through the open door of an emergency staircase, jogging down as fast as she could without tripping over herself.

Down a flight of stairs, a floor of stairs and then another - 1 more, and then -

"You are in no condition to be doing this, patient #81!" came the familiar broadcast voice of Miavia, her floating Heart entering the stairwell from the next floor down's entrance.

"Rats!" Nikko quietly complained.. "I knew that elevator was moving too slow.."

"If you will just allow my nurses to escort you both back to your room," she put another pill on her tongue before swallowing it with a cringing gulp. "And please remove patient #82 from your head, #81? That looks a little unhygienic.."

Nikko continued down the stairs, 1 hand on the wall's guardrail, cautiously approaching the meeting point - Looking for her opening to race down and past them.

"Nikko," Jigoro advised his friend, "maybe we should just go back up - Just until we're better?"

"Listen to you," Nikko said without moving her lips, quiet so only he could hear her, "you probably just want to go back for your body, don't you?"

"Well, maybe it wouldn't hurt to at least try?"

"You can never make up your mind.."

And just as Nikko made her downward sprint to pass Miavia, 2 nurses raced in from the floor's hallway entrance, pushing a hospital stretcher and running directly into Nikko, knocking her to the floor -

She yelled out in instant agony, the pain in her leg feeling as if they had nearly fractured it with their stretcher bed.

"Quickly, nurses!" the Head Nurse Miavia instructed. "Restrain them right away!"

And as Nikko tried in desperation to roll her body down the next few steps, the nurses came at her - The first stabbing her in the same arm with another sedative syringe, and then the next weakly picking Nikko's body up and slumping it onto the hard white mattress of the stretcher.

Nikko fought back, a failing attempt of swinging arms and kicking legs, but the more she struggled the more her body was poked by the needles and sedation.

"Nurses.. Um, nurses?" The radio-style cutesy voice of Miavia interrupted the struggle. "Um, the Head Nurse needs your assistance for just a moment.."

The 2 skull head nurses and Nikko looked from their wrestling and to Miavia at once..

"Um.. Yeah... Help?"

The Heart-riding Head Nurse had snagged her floating Heart on the banister of the stairwell, the thing trying to move while it's semi-transparent red skin stretched and pulled from it.

Nikko leaned up from the mattress, and just as the nurses ran to their leader, a ripping sound came from the hot-air balloon-like Heart, the sound of skin ripping from skin. And in a moment, the entire shape emptied out - A sea of bloody juice and malcolored organs, pouring out swiftly like red raging white-water.

"Oh, Jesus!" Jigoro screamed. "Too gross! We're gonna throw up!!"

Nikko braced her body on the wheeled stretcher in fast reaction - The complete stairway filled with the flood, Miavia falling to the floor helplessly with her broken legs, her nurses beside her, and the swift momentum of the blood current pushing Nikko's stretcher down the stairs like a speedboat.

"Hold on tight!" Jigoro yelled into the rush.

Down and around the bends, following the stairs down so fast, Nikko held on with a desperate grip and Jigoro screaming the entire ride down. Blood waves splashed all around, pieces of the Heart's organs slapping into the walls with wet thuds, and Nikko with Jigoro's skull rode it all of the way down to the hospital's ground floor.

The end of the staircase, and the crimson river carried them through an empty lobby, through a courteously opening automatic door and out, at last, into the outside world. The bleeding flood spread itself out and thin, the momentum of the stretcher rolling now just on it's own.

"We did it, Jigoro! Haha, we did it!" Nikko shouted to him and sat up on the slowing down red-splattered stretcher. She pulled his skull from her head and held it in front of her face - "I told you I would get us out of there!"

"I think that the was the most exciting thing that has ever happened to me.." his skull seemed to smile against the odds. "Now can we go back and... Get my body? Maybe?"

Nikko and the NLK

"Ha.. I wonder where in the world we ended up, Jigoro," Nikko said to him, completely ignoring his request. "We should keep moving - But check it out.. This isn't like anything we've ever seen before... Oh! Sorry!"

She laughed and turned the skull around, forgetting for a moment that he had no way to function now without her. Stepping off of the stretcher and onto the street, they looked and saw this world, now from the outside of the hospital, for the first time -

It was something like a city, empty streets and a midnight sky. There were buildings like the buildings they had been by earlier in the night, pre-death of the night, but these were something different.

"Everywhere I look," Jigoro surveyed the land that Nikko held him to see, "it's like 1 giant reminder! What's the deal with this place??"

Bothering the now skull-only Jigoro, most structures seemed to have a skull shape and design to them. Cartoon style, with extra large eyeholes and chubby teeth at the ground. Were those the doors? And towering even higher than the skull buildings were cross-shaped skyscrapers, filling the starless-sky like an oversized cemetery city.

Nikko walked fast through the street, her leg still aching and the sedatives kicking in stronger now, an all encompassing empty feeling lingering over the skull and cross city. Did anyone even live here? And where could such a place exist?

"You didn't have to kill me too, you know," Nikko said to the skull carried in her hands. "What were you possibly thinking back there?"

"You said that you were making a Death Wish with me," Jigoro defended himself, still an odd feeling for Nikko to have her friend in such a state. "That's a serious thing! I even told you it was serious!"

"Well, we say things like that to each other all of the time. You could at least tell someone before you try drowning them."

"Well fine, now I know for next time."

"Now you know for *next* time?? Only you would say something like that! And just look at you now.. It serves you right, Mr. Himoff.."

Suddenly, from a block or 2 behind, the sounds of an ambulance siren filled the silent air and installed a fear within Nikko's Heart.

"What now?? This is getting ridiculous!" she worried and looked back, hurrying from the center of the street to the shadows of a skull building's side.

"What? All of this, and something like a siren bothers you?"

"Shhh..." Nikko tried to quiet him, creeping through the shadows as the howl of the ambulance grew louder. "Even when you're dead you talk too much!"

"Who said I'm dead?!" he asked back as if shocked at the idea.

"You'll know when I'm dead! You'll have no doubts about it, and you'll miss me, and you -"

Nikko quickly turned and held the skull again to her face, giving Jigoro such a look that he bit his non-existing tongue and kept quiet for the moment. The approaching siren was so near that Nikko stopped and held her ground against the unlit wall of a skull-shaped building, trying not to move as her head began feeling so dizzy that she felt like falling over..

"Nikko?" Jigoro interrupted his own brief silence. "I can't see behind us, but I'm guessing that standing up against these white-skull things isn't going to help us hide - If that's even what you're trying to do."

Shoot.. Nikko's brain was so groggy now from the injections that she couldn't think straight. Where to run to? With the siren practically before them now, though no vehicle yet in sight, she made a fast stumbling attempt to cross the street - Looking for anything dark to hide behind or in.

Things started feeling fuzzy, and the medicine was really.. kicking... in...

"Nikko??" Jigoro called up to her in panic as he felt her grip on his remains loosening. "Nikko? What are you doing? Get out of the street!"

Nearly midway across, and Nikko felt so overdosed on the injected sedatives that she stumbled left and right -

Eyes half closing, Jigoro saying something that she couldn't even come close to making out, and she dropped down in the center of the asphalt roadway. The sight of an ambulance slowly pulling up, and it's flashing lights blended into the drowsiness of her brain...

Eyes closed, lights now just flashing in her mind...

~ Asleep, in death, and drifting off into another wonderful memory ~

In the place of a dream, Nikko's mind took her away into a happy place. Years ago, her first love then - She could see it clearly now,

Nikko and the NLK

with no recollection of what was just happening in the new place where she and Jigoro had ended up..

Just this, a dream of the past in her sedative-induced sleep. This place, it looked familiar, and then Nikko remembered it crystal clear. It was the oasis reststop over the old 294 tollway. She could see herself sitting at 1 of those counter-tables that lined the glass window walls, the middle-of-the-night view of the cars driving beneath. Headlights in the dark, people rushing off to who knows where, truck drivers on the long road, and families heading home from summertime vacations..

It was an escape, 1 that she and her at-the-time friend Richard Allan had enjoyed together. A secret meeting place, a checkpoint for traveling strangers, and a peacefully empty hangout spot for these late forgotten hours.

Nikko could see him now, in this memory, sitting beside her, writing in his notebook as she typed at her laptop computer. Telling pointless jokes, playing with worthless 25 cent toys from the vending machines, and forgetting about the busy world around them. This was a time prior to her suicide attempts, prior to her hospital stays, and..

It came to her at that moment.

It was always the realization for her after feeling the warmth of any memory. The reality of Nikko's problem and the repeating nightmare. It was at these brief times that she could remember not only what the thing was, but what it did to her - Killing these happy days until she would open her eyes and forget they ever existed.

Nikko's returning presence in the memory walked over to her only years-younger self and the boy named Richard Allan, both oblivious to her as expected. She wanted to feel the moment before it would be taken away forever. That boy, so confusing to her but so important, sitting there with his uncomfortable looking fake foam hair braided in, pulled back into a fake foam-strip high ponytail, real hair shaved off around the sides and half bottom back.

He smiled, and her few-years-ago self smiled back, none of the mental health problems plaguing her back then.

Nikko took it in - All of it - From the passing cars, to the worker mopping the floors, to the tiny reflections of the reststop store lights filling the wide glass window walls.

+ And then, as prepared for but in no way ready for, the unnatural

Nikko and the NLK

creature was spotted +

Already?

Richard Allan and the memory's Nikko lost in their individual works and shared conversations, the looking-back Nikko saw the man in her dreams arrive so soon again.
Her eyes gazed out through the giant windows that lined the oasis, and she could see him there, walking straight down the center of the oncoming tollway. Red sky in the night coming to life behind him, clouds like fire, and the memory was now polluted and changed according to him. The black armor barbarian, walking unphased, the memories of the passing cars crashing into his unbreakable body and spinning off into each other. Vehicles out of control, fires bursting from the wreckages, semi trucks hitting him and bounding off of his body as if a concrete wall was walking. Faster and faster he was slowly approaching the oasis.
Nikko looked at her time-ago friend and the joy that he had brought her, now re-remembered as she saw it again across her younger face. Trying now to absorb it all in..
But there was never enough time. These 'memory visits' were like having a final visit with someone on their deathbed. Trying to feel all of the emotions at once, to relive the past and appreciate it with a hindsight view...
Though all along knowing it was already too late.

Nikko stood with a defeated posture, not fighting the arriving defeat this time. Nothing could change it anyway..

The window wall of glass instantly shattered as the Black Knight came bounding through - An inhuman leap from the below tollway and through the window, Nikko's memory of herself and friend of course unseeing.

And with the fires of the automotive wreckage below, the armored Devil swung his axe 1 time around, cutting memory-Nikko's head from her body - And with a spray of his friend's blood across his face, Richard Allan was then split clean down his middle, 2 pieces of 1 body cut perfectly in half.

Nikko and the NLK

Nikko looked at the rearranged scene with her hands over her face. The broken window walls of what had been her long-ago escape were now destroyed, nighttime air blowing through unblocked. The body of 1 of her last real friends, when he was still a friend, now divided into bloody bone and muscle halves. And her own body's head from years ago yesterday, now severed at the floor, smiling, and looking right in the direction of Nikko's own remembering eyes..

And the Black Knight stood over them, Nikko's memory now fading away so fast.. Lights to black... Sounds, rumbling, a voice...

That voice...

~ "Nikko!!!" ~

Nikko's eyes flashed open fast, tears at her cheeks and she sat up immediately -
"Nikko!" Jigoro's voice was yelling. "Wake up already!"
Taking it all in at once, Nikko came back out of her now forgotten memory and found herself, along with Jigoro, strapped down onto a bed.
"They put us in the ambulance!!" Jigoro screamed at her. "I want to go back and get my body, but this is freaking me out!!"
The back of an ambulance?? Nikko looked around, but it wasn't like the back of the ambulance that she had rode in long before. This was sealed off and they were separated from the medics, locked back by themselves and left alone on barely-secure strapped down stretcher beds.
"What happened to you back there??" Jigoro kept talking during her cloudy return to possible reality.
"I don't know... I think I..."
"Was it that nightmare guy again??"
"The black armor guy.." Nikko said to herself. "Yeah... I think it was.. I can't remember.."
"Well, you sure picked a fine time to fall asleep on me! The nurses picked you up and almost left me laying on the street alone!"

Nikko and the NLK

"I'm sorry," Nikko said as she finally gathered her head, shaking off the violent forgotten memory and small amounts of the sedative already. "Hey, do you think we can get out of here?"

"Well, first you can get me out of this!" Jigoro demanded, Nikko then looking over at the 2 belt-like bed straps pulled tightly over his skull to the thin mattress.

"Yeah, of course.. I'm sorry.."

Nikko easily undid her own mattress straps from her stretcher and stepped over in the moving ambulance to Jigoro.

"How long was I out?" she asked, unbuckling his skull and taking it up into her hands.

But before she could hear his answer, out through the tiny circular windows of the speeding ambulance, Nikko thought that she saw something hauntingly familiar traveling alongside it -

~ The moving rainbow ~

The rainbow girl, outside and rollerskating in the same direction as the ambulance.. It was a closer look this time than the reflection on the river, and even stranger yet, the tan girl seemed to be creating rainbows in the wake of her long skating strides.. It was all in the flash of 1 brief moment, but Nikko saw her in detail now. She was tall and fit ~ Tan skin as said and straight mid-back length blue thin hair, oversized baggy white socks and 1980 California-style rollerskates. Her rainbow bikini was knit-together soft colors, and her eyes were hidden behind movie star sunglasses with oversized headphones covering her ears.

"Jigoro! Look!" Nikko told him as she quickly held the skull up to the window, just in time for him to catch a glance of what he had missed on the bridge.

"Oh.. my... God..." his skull said in a panting breath.

"That's the girl I thought I saw back on the bridge, remember??"

"She's like a dolphin -" Jigoro continued, oblivious to Nikko as he was held up to the window, "like a dolphin transformed into a beautiful rainbow cartoon girl...."

"Uh, yeah.. Whatever, but that's her for sure!" Nikko said as she pushed her head next to Jigoro's, squeezing in tight to both see through the tiny window.

"Don't take the time to put me over your head," Jigoro said as they

Nikko and the NLK

were both pressed so close, "I don't want to miss a second.. She even looks kinda like you.."

"What? Get out of here, no she doesn't! And what's up with the rainbows?" Nikko wondered out loud. "It look's like they're coming out of her or something.."

"Rare beauty should not be explained.." he philosophized to her. "Just take it all in Nikko - Just take it all in.. "

And in that quiet moment, as Jigoro was in deep admiration, the ambulance slammed into a complete brick-wall type stop, slamming Nikko and skull into the divider between the ambulance drivers and the back portion - The momentum throwing them hard sideways then from the wall and to the floor, the ambulance dropping from 80 miles per hour to zero in less than a second, a high-impact collision with something unseen. And all in the same moment, the entire inside shape of the vehicle had changed, compacted and condensed -

A wreckage that left Nikko and her skull head friend laying coughing and in pain on the floor of the now in ruin ambulance..

"Does it really hurt that bad?? Maybe we should stop.."

"Of course it hurts.. I didn't think you could hit me so hard.."

"Yeah, well I tried to hold back a little.."

"Do I get to hit you now? Or do we just start fighting?"

"I'll let you hit me since I already hit you."

"Ok.. Maybe you should sit."

"Just try not to break my teeth?"

Nikko and the NLK

CHAPTER 3

Machine To Me

From the wreckage, Nikko pushed and twisted her way out toward safety, squeezing the skull of Jigoro along with her through the frame.

"Are you ok, Nikko?" his muffled voice asked from her hands.

"Heh, yeah," she said, a little trouble talking as she made her way through the bent and now banged-ajar rear doors, "consider it a blessing in disguise.."

And it turned out to be just that - As Nikko crawled outside, then picking herself up off of the ground with the talking skull in hand, she could see the devastation of the ambulance. It was completely demolished and contorted into a scrap heap, a skull head nurse hanging through the crushed windshield and another motionless on the road ahead.

And then the object that had caused such an accident -

"*Good grief, if it isn't 1 thing it's another,*" came a mechanical voice from an 8 foot tall golem-type robot, calmly untwisting pieces of the ambulance frame from it's massive leg. It must have weighed more than a few thousand pounds, it's shapes of gears and rounds, it's colors of faded gunmetal and chipped-away coppers. As it freed itself from the fatal collision, Nikko could see it's oval head with a jawline of grate-like furnace bars, it's eyes glowing with the pumpkin colors of an orange fire.

"Um," Nikko called out to it without even thinking, her head wound up slightly still from the sedatives and car crash, "are you ok?..."

"Nikko!" Jigoro answered before the robot had a chance. "We can't talk to donkeys or broken-leg nurses, but we can talk to this thing??"

"Shh!" Nikko shushed her friend, holding him in 1 arm and holding her other hand over his mouth. "Those crazy nurses just ran right into him!"

"*Actually,*" the giant robot talked again, it's voice deep and echoed through what sounded like a near-hollow body, "*yes, thank you, I'm not programmed to register physical stimulation - But if I could? You wouldn't believe how bad it hurts!*"

With the ambulance separated from it's leg and body, it turned it's oversized frame to face Nikko and her skull. She could see it now completely, steam bursting out every so often in small shots from all over it's design. It had large, out of proportion 4-finger hands, and a clear circular section on it's stomach area, a white liquid sloshing around it like a mobile washing machine.

"I'm Nikko," Nikko felt obliged to introduce, "and this," she said, removing her hand from the skull's jaw, "is my friend Jigoro... Or at least part of him..."

The copper round robot stepped a step closer to them, the ground quaking just a little.

"*I don't have a real name,*" it said, "*but my machine type is called MilkTank -*"

Jigoro burst out laughing and Nikko quickly covered his mouth again, to the muffled sounds of him trying still to talk.

"*That's an unusual friend that you have with you,*" the robot told Nikko. "*Is that like these things?*"

Nikko looked down at it's line of view and saw the still-bleeding dead nurse in the street, her skull head cracked at the pavement and nothing seen within.

"Um, actually, we're not like those nurses at all.. We were kind of trying to get away from them and got caught..."

"*Processing a statement,*" MilkTank pointlessly announced before it continued. "*Humans would call this a 'mixed blessing,' wouldn't they?*"

"Yes!" Nikko excitedly agreed, something finally seeming unhostile or creepy to her in this new place. "That's exactly what I said a minute ago!"

"*Either I am programmed like you, or you possibly have a brain much like a robot..*" MilkTank half-rotated around, beginning to take it's solid steps away from the wreckage of the ambulance and bodies. "*No difference, I would confirm happiness if I were able to feel it.*"

"Wait!" Nikko called as it began mechanically walking away, the ground taking a pounding. "Can I walk with you? I want to ask a few questions about this place."

"*You are free to make your own choices, human girl.*"

"Well, walking with you is much better than just staying here!"

"~Walking with you is much better than just staying here, la-la-la ~" Jigoro mocked her voice with his mouth free again. "I swear you make no sense! A real-life talking donkey and you pick to talk to this thing. Give me a break!"

"Please disregard Jigoro, MilkTank," Nikko told it as she walked alongside the slow but large-step taking robot. "He's a little out of his element here, as am I.. Where are we exactly?"

"*We are currently in the city-limits of Medikiss City, the hospital city capital of Daiyomi.*"

"Medical what??" Jigoro asked, not waiting for Nikko's response.

"Medikiss City..." Nikko thought out loud. "That doesn't even sound like a real place.. And you said Daiyomi?"

"*Daiyomi is the world's name,*" MilkTank walked strongly down the skull-building city street. "*I'm concluding that you are not originally from here.*"

"Definitely not," Nikko's eyes looked away and all about at the skull and cross cityscape, feeling a small bit safer in the presence of the friendly giant. "We think that we died.."

"*That wouldn't be unheard of,*" MilkTank informed them. "*Many others have come to this place by unusual means. Some -*"

"No need to continue!" Jigoro then rudely interrupted the talking machine. "I can't speak for this lovely lady, but I'm pretty sure I *know* I died, and then I think I even died again! My freaking skull fell out of my skin!"

"Jigoro, relax?" Nikko tried to settle him.

"Well, why should we waste our time listening to this thing? What does it even know?"

"*I know what a loudmouth is,*" it told him back. "*I also have some jerk-recognition programs in here.*"

"What the?!" Jigoro said to himself as Nikko started laughing. "You're going to let him talk to me like that, Nikko? Hit him! Punch him for me! We'll see who a jerk is!"

"*You just stated that '*You are pretty sure you know you died.*' Is that supposed to make sense? Or are my bits malfunctioning?*"

"Nikko??" Jigoro pleaded. "Say something smart back to him!"

"*Hmm..*" MilkTank checked back in. "*It's confirmed. Does not make sense. Please keep your remaining ideas to yourself.*"

"Um, getting back to 'Daiyomi,' then," Nikko interrupted the skull and robot to change the subject back to where it started, "it sounds Japanese.. Have you maybe heard of Japan?"

"*Not registering..*"

"...Idiot..." Jigoro mumbled to himself.

"What about Earth?"

"*Earth... No files.*"

"Great.." Nikko said in defeat, following the path of the traveling robot, it's steam making small whistles each time it vented. "Well, wherever we ended up, all thanks to you, Jigoro, we might as well keep moving. Where exactly are you heading, MilkTank?"

"And why do they call you 'MilkTank' anyway?" Jigoro added on to Nikko's question. "Don't you even know what that sounds like??"

"*Addressing the kind-Hearted girl,*" MilkTank began, getting an 'oh, my!' face of Nikko looking to Jigoro, "*I am returning from an errand of picking up medicine for Ms. Fiona Shelly Rose. I was crossing the street when I was run into, but fortunately it only slowed me down for a moment.*"

"Is she like your owner or something?" Nikko asked, the sedative mostly worn off by now.

"*That could be an acceptable explanation,*" MilkTank replied. "*Miss Fiona Shelly Rose is the daughter of my creator.*"

"Ooh," Jigoro whispered. "A young daughter?"

"*Her age isn't your concern. And to answer your mock question a moment ago,*" MilkTank addressed Jigoro, "*I am very simply an actual tank of Milk. Your name is 'Jigoro?' Do you know what the name Jigoro sounds like?*"

The talking-too much skull had no answer to that.

"*Milk is a very delicious thing -*"

"I love Milk.." Nikko added in.

"*Then you can appreciate this story,*" MilkTank told her as it began to outline it's purpose. "*When Miss Fiona's Father found out that he was going to have a child, he set out to bring this child the most famous Milk in the world -*"

"Oh, come on!! This is stupid!"

"Jigoro! Shh!!!"

"*Now, there are many flavors of Milk,*" the heavy-stepping robot continued, "*but none as sought after as the 'Angel Milk' of Daiyomi's paradise at the End of the World ~The Summerland ~ He decided that traveling there was far too time consuming, and in doing so he would miss the birth of his first and possibly only child. So in the span of 18 restless days, he created me from microchips, gears and heavy kitchen appliances.*"

"Wow!" Nikko admired. "That's really impressive.."

"*Thank you.. Microchipically speaking, I was designed to -*"

"What??" Jigoro cut in. "Hold on, MilkTank. I'm pretty sure that 'microchipically' isn't a real word -"

"*It's programmed into my database.*"

Nikko and the NLK

"So what?? That's a made up word!"

"Jigoro?" Nikko asked him. "Please? Just let it talk?"

"*My database tells me that at some point, all words are made up. Therefore, even if it wasn't a word, 'microchipically' would now be an official word.*"

"You can't do that!"

"How cool!" Nikko made her best attempt at calming the situation. "We got to hear a new word be created today! Jigoro - Let the robot finish?"

"*As I was saying, *microchipically* speaking, I was designed to understand my surroundings and travel to the Summerland, the land beyond the 'World's Teeth,' undistracted, and bring Milk back to the newest member of the Rose family.*"

"So did you make it there? Beyond whatever the 'World's Teeth' are?" Nikko questioned, their walking path heading a little bit away from the looming cross skyscrapers now.

"*I traveled across the world, seeing amazing things, and succeeded in bringing back the Angel Milk shortly after the birth of Miss Fiona. They were happy to see me, and the next year, I was sent back out on the same path to Summerland once again.*"

"So you walked out there twice?" Nikko asked. "All of the way to the End of the World?? How far was that?"

"*I wasn't made to measure the distance, but it was a very long journey. I made the trip not just 2 times, but many times since -*"

"What a waste of time," Jigoro unneedingly added.

"*It would have been rewarding if I was capable to enjoy the things. Over the years, all of the locations I passed became used to seeing the sight of me. I remember when humans were scared to watch me walk through their streets. They would keep their children inside, only looking out through the windows. Heh, I remember -*"

"Did you just laugh?" Jigoro asked.

"*I'm not programmed to laugh. Anyway, I remember the first few years,*" MilkTank went on with the story, Jigoro and Nikko's like and dislike for the robot going in vastly opposite directions, "*they were so uneasy. But each year thereafter, I became a familiar and then welcome sight. I would see the families grow, 1 year older with each passing. The children would eventually run out to the road, their parents coming too - Decorating me with flowers and chalk colors, welcoming my annual pass like a yearly holiday in their village. I've seen the children grow, their parents pass on, and the children's

Nikko and the NLK

children run out to me with the same excitement that their parents once did so long ago..*"

"Geez.." Jigoro softly said to the carrying Nikko. "How old is this Fiona girl?? 200 years old?... You know," Jigoro then said louder, directing his voice towards the traveling robot, "back in our world, if I want some Milk? I just go down to the grocery store, and nobody decorates me with flowers or anything.."

"*Angel Milk is superior to your Milk.*"

"It's the same thing, I bet!" Jigoro argued. "What do you even do when you get to the Summerland? Milk a cow?"

"Jigoro, please," Nikko pleaded again with him. "God, you're so embarrassing some times."

"*Angel Milk is better than anything you've ever tasted,*" MilkTank tried to convince the annoying skull. "*I'd open my body and pour you a glass, but you don't look like you even have a tongue.*"

"And like a robot can taste it?"

"*Programmed to enjoy the taste. Delicious.*"

"How do you even know if what you're programmed for is what -"

"Guys, please!" Nikko shouted. "I'm sure it's very wonderful Milk, but can we just stop getting upset?"

"*I'm not programmed to be upset,*" MilkTank stated.

"Well, that may be so, but what we really need to focus on is where we are right now, and then how we get out of here.. Ok?"

MilkTank stopped it's walk and rotated a degreed angle, turning to walk up the sidewalk path of 1 of the skull-shaped houses.

"Um, MilkTank?" Nikko asked. "Is this your house?"

"*Miss Fiona Shelly Rose's house,*" he corrected. "*So then yes, indirectly, yes it is. Care to come inside and meet her?*"

"Sure," Nikko said without even thinking about it. "I'm sure she is a wonderful person!"

"Nikko," Jigoro asked her. "Do we really have to? You're sure it's a good idea? She sounds pretty old.."

A hand over the skull's non-stop talking jaw, and Nikko followed through the now-opened tooth shaped door, carrying the skull into the skull-shaped home of the Milk-carrying robot.

"*I'm back with your medicine,*" it called out with an almost 'honey, I'm home' type voice.

Walking in, and the complete inside of the skull house was seen in a single glance - Was this normal? 1 large room, with no bathroom or kitchen? The theme seemed to be bone-like whites, but added in over that were the colors of red roses and floral themes, a quick count of 6 bird cages with red cardinals perched 1 inside of each. There were actual butterflies inside the house as well, monarchs that fluttered just a little unsteady, crawling ladybugs and green stem vines extending all about the dome-shaped interior.

And there, against the skull-colored wall across from the tooth shaped door, was an elegant and red-themed king sized bed. It was decorated in red roses and sheets, small green vines and red pillows, and over it was a canopy with sheer see-through red curtains.

"*Miss Fiona,*" MilkTank greeted as it walked toward the bed, "*I have someone stopping by to meet you today.*"

Nikko followed the robot over to the curtained bed, carrying Jigoro and catching a small glimpse through the sheer and parting of the curtains. Wasn't this lady supposed to be really old?

"*Nikko,*" MilkTank introduced, "*this is Miss Fiona Shelly Rose. Miss Fiona, this is Nikko.*"

Nikko stood near now and peered through the curtains between them. The lady was nothing like she was expecting, anticipating along with Jigoro a withered and frail woman - But this instead? She was youthful and full of life, her face pale with meticulous make-up, her hair what looked like a cream-colored powdered wig, a red rose on it's near-upper left side. Though half covered by the sheets on the bed, what could be seen of her looked to be overdressed - Wearing a red dress evening gown, her shoulders and neck bare save for a vintage portrait locket.

~ Her face, beneath the make-up, something hauntingly similar to Nikko's own Mother ~

"It's very nice to meet you," Nikko said to her, caught far off guard by the similarity and beautiful look.

"I'll say!" Jigoro added in. "Not at all what I was expecting!"

Fiona smiled, then moving her red lipstick-covered lips, making the moves for words, though nothing other than the sound of breath being heard.

"*Miss Fiona, please don't strain yourself for our guest. She will of course understand.*"

Nikko looked at her and then about the single room skull house again. Something was off.. The little birds and insects, the blooming roses and vines.. Even though this wasn't a house like she had ever been in before, was it natural to grow roses straight out of the ground indoors? Or these vines - Why were they so overgrown inside while nothing grew on the exterior? And now that she saw the cardinals closer, they were a bit unnatural too, moving their necks in an almost generic type pattern, repeated over and over.

A look back at the bed and Miss Fiona, and Nikko was once again captivated by her beautiful appearance.

"This really is a unique house that you have," she complimented her, trying to say anything while her brain was wondering about it all.

Again the lady's lips moved, though this time Nikko thinking that she may have heard a faint voice -

"Excuse me? I couldn't hear you - Did you..."

And as she leaned in and went to part open the canopy's red curtain between them, her hand hit what felt like an invisible plastic wall, stopping her from moving any closer.

"*Please don't disturb Miss Fiona too much?*" MilkTank asked of her, setting the small bag of carried medicine down on a bedside tabletop. "*I understand it must be difficult for you to understand the amount of pain that she suffers.*"

"I'm sorry.." Nikko said, her hand still pressed in mid-air against the invisible barrier. "But why can't I -"

"Nikko! Quick, look!" Jigoro shouted up to her. "Under the table! It's a raccoon!"

"What?" Nikko asked, leaning back from the bed and then stooping to look - Jigoro's line of vision heading straight beneath the bedside table.

"*Oh! I see that you've noticed Tanuki,*" MilkTank stated, stepping away from the table so that the 2 could get a better look.

"Oh, my God!" Nikko beamed in excitement. "That's a tanuki! That's not a raccoon, Jigoro! That's a real-life tanuki, right here in front of us! I can't believe it!"

"What's a tanuki??" Jigoro questioned, not nearly as impressed as Nikko was sounding.

"*Tanuki,*" MilkTank explained to Jigoro, allowing Nikko time to marvel, "*is a raccoon-dog. Not a raccoon, or a dog, but an animal onto itself.*"

"Well, what is it supposed to be doing right now?" Jigoro asked the robot. "It looks like it's trying to pray or something."

"Oh I don't believe this..." Nikko sang out loud as she nearly laid on the floor to get a better look, "it has a leaf on it's head too?? Now we

Nikko and the NLK

have to be dreaming!!"

"*Tanuki is a magic user,*" MilkTank continued it's explanation, all eyes on the medium-sized animal sitting cross-legged under the table - It's eyes closed and 2 front paws held together in a prayer-like pose. "*With the aid of the mystic leaf he puts on his forehead, he can create illusions on the area around him, or even shapeshift into any sort of thing he can imagine.*"

"But that's just what they say," Nikko told Jigoro. "It's old Japanese folklore - Like they say about foxes and badgers too. My Dad used to tell me about these animals when I was little -"

"*Japanese folklore?*" MilkTank asked. "*I'm sorry, but that doesn't register in my databank. There is only 1 *Tanuki*, and you are looking at him right now.*"

"But that's not true.." Nikko said, her eyes still on the meditating animal. "I know for a fact that there are more tanuki than you could even count in Japan."

"*Japan does not register.*"

"Ha, now you see how I feel talking to this scrap heap!" Jigoro laughed as Nikko at last disagreed with the robot.

"But I know I'm right..." Nikko insisted, a little frustrated with the stubborn machine. "And they aren't supposed to 'really' be able to do magic, but then again, I don't think that they are really supposed to be able to sit like that either.."

"*Sometimes he uses the leaf, sometimes he does not. It's much less strenuous for him to rely on the leaf though. I will allow this illusion to end,*" MilkTank stated and paused, it's orange fire eyes looking toward Nikko, "*if only for the sake of enlightening the pair of you.*"

The robot rotated and walked away from Miss Fiona's bed and the under-table animal, walking across to the door-side of the 1-room skull house.

"What's his name?" Jigoro asked as MilkTank then rotated to face the bed and table again, now from the far side.

"*Tanuki.*"

"That's it?" Jigoro moaned in disappointment, unbelieving. "You guys aren't too good at coming up with names around here, are you?"

"*Like I am, he is the only 1 of his kind, so he does not need a further title.*"

"Tanuki the tanuki.. Ok, but he had to be born right?" Jigoro went on. "So he had to have parents, right?"

"*It doesn't register,*" MilkTank announced. "*Tanuki is a very old animal. But enough talking. Allow Tanuki to demonstrate his magic.*"

Nikko stood in silence, Jigoro oddly enough quiet too, and the 2 of them anxiously stood in the rose themed skull house, Nikko excited to see if this tanuki in the bizarre world could really do some magic.. Or a transformation..

"*TANUKI!*" MilkTank's echoed robot voice called out. "*KNOCK IT OFF!*"

And then silence.. The animal's head twitched a little, his left ear twitching more, and at long last he let out a giant yawn, breaking his prayer pose and scratching his ear, then leaning down to stand in a more raccoon-like stance on all 4 paws at once.

".... And that's all?" Jigoro groaned. "Wow, I'd have to say that's pretty unimpressive."

But then something unthinkable happened - The unusual beauty of the small skull house began to peel away, the illusion of the red roses and butterflies falling off like a veil.

"Oh..." Nikko gasped as her Heart filled with a dread. "This.. This is amazing..."

The white walls faded into a more stained white-yellow, the caged cardinals becoming gear and metal robotics, the butterflies and ladybugs transforming into tiny intricate machines. The walls were lined with medicine cabinets and inventor's tools, and the vines were revealed as oversized wires and cables - But worst of all in all of this wonder -

"Fiona..." Nikko whispered as she looked upon the moments-ago fair woman.

Her bed had transformed from the elegant to the depressing. Red sheets turned hospital white, the red curtain canopy was gone, and in it's place was the barrier that Nikko had not been able to push through before. Quarantine-type plastic sheets, zipped closed and completely surrounding... Gears and machinery running medical equipment, fluid tubes and monitors all around...

"*And now,*" MilkTank allowed the 2 to observe, Tanuki sitting at it's robotic feet, "*you are privileged to see Miss Fiona's existence outside of Tanuki's illusion.*"

Nikko looked on, turning Jigoro's skull in her hand to keep his comments at bay. Who moments prior was so impossibly beautiful, now was reimagined in a more age-wise realistic vision. Her face and skin were blotched and worn out, an oxygen mask worn over her once red-lipstick covered lips. Twitching and shivering, she now looked out through the plastic surrounding sheets with heavily glazed eyes. Where her creamy-white powdered wig and rose had been, now was thinning hair and missing patches in most places. Faint attempts at either crying or speaking could be heard from within the clear oxygen mask, and then a choking cough, Nikko having to look away as the transparent mouth-cover was sprinkled on the inside with a spray of her sickly blood.

"This is too much," Nikko said with her face down, Jigoro in silence. "Why is she so sick?"

"*It's nothing out of the ordinary for a human, is it?*" MilkTank offered, now the room around less appealing without the illusion draped over it. "*You grow old, and this is where life takes you.*"

"But she looks so miserable.." Nikko said, her watery eyes looking everywhere but at the bed-ridden women. "Isn't there anything you can do?"

"*I watch over her,*" MilkTank stated. "*I medicate her to ease the suffering.*"

"Ok..." Nikko sounded to herself, now looking to the mechanical insects fluttering about the yellow room. "It doesn't seem fair.."

"*You are in the Medikiss City,*" the robot reminded her. "*Miss Fiona is a lot healthier than the majority of it's inhabitants. You will not see too many out and on the streets. It was surprising, even to a robot, to find you.*"

MilkTank walked back over to the sick woman and continued to talk.

"*Consider how fortunate you humans are,*" it professed, looking down through the see-through plastic and at Fiona. "*You are born and then grow to your personal perfection before the body begins winding down. When robots like myself are created, we are 'born' perfect only to everyday become less so. It's better to build to a peak, and learn about yourself, then to be built at your peak and already know everything that you ever will.*"

"You should be able to upgrade, shouldn't you?" Jigoro interrupted, already returning to his usual insensitivity. "Man - I would think that a machine like you should at least know that."

"*And this is coming from a talking skull,*" MilkTank insulted back, "*who probably doesn't even have a clue how he can hear or see or talk. Shouldn't you know that about yourself?*"

"Hey, yeah!" Nikko agreed, looking down at her friend. "How can you hear? You don't even have ears anymore!"

Nikko and the NLK

"*All that is important,*" MilkTank finished up, "*is that when 1 day the time comes for your body to wind down, you are able to face yourself and all of the uncomfortable things that most likely you will have become. I believe Miss Fiona is finally ready to do so.*"

Nikko walked back over the few steps to the bedside, standing nearly next to MilkTank and now looking a bit more easily at the dying woman.

"*Tanuki has been a great friend to her,*" the robot told the 2, the animal then waddling up to Nikko and sniffing at her boots. "*He was a member of the family even before she was born. Always by her side when she was a little girl, and even up until now. Whenever I returned from my trips to Summerland, I would always see a new fantastic illusion that the 2 of them would come up with. It would almost make a robot smile..*"

Nikko took it in. She had always feared old age, even though it forever seemed like a million years away, she knew in her Heart that it was not. Even this frail woman had been young and invincible at a time, as seen in illusionary evidence only a few short moments ago. She had been beautiful, young, born to parents and a baby - And now here she lay in ruin, helplessly supported.

"How long has she been alone?" Nikko asked. "I mean, other than you and Tanuki? Did she have a husband? Or does she have any kids?"

"*It was always just her,*" the robot remembered, the mechanical butterflies flying past it's face. "*A rare self-sufficient beauty, although I do remember a man in her life - A man as red as a rose like her. 'Mars' was his name, and there was a time when they were very close,*" the robot paused and looked over the woman. "*You probably don't recall him anymore, do you? It's a forgotten memory now.. But they were close once, and eventually he left for war, and the poor lady's letters were never answered. Miss Fiona buried him in her Heart many years ago. He was the last 1 that she had opened up to... A human's life is very long sometimes, but almost always too short to try and find a real love.*"

"Yeah, that's for sure," Nikko agreed. "Was she always so pretty when she was young?"

"*The look that she was in, that was 1 of her all time favorites in the last few years,*" MilkTank told Nikko, sounding now more like it was reminiscing to itself. "*She always admired the Blue Queen, Shiva Angel, all of the way back before Shiva even was Queen -*"

"Hey, wait up..." Jigoro said at the sound of such a name. "Did you just say 'Shiva?' And Queen??"

"*Remarkable, with no ears -*"

"Jigoro, I don't think -"

"No, wait, Nikko," Jigoro went on. "We listened to this lady's entire life story and now I want to hear about this... Who exactly is this Queen that we're talking about?"

Tanuki walked across from Nikko and back over to MilkTank, sitting by the robot's side, yawning yet again.

"*Shiva Angel is the Ruler of the World, the ruler of Daiyomi,*" MilkTank explained to the overly excited Jigoro. "*Miss Fiona has always admired her flawless beauty and grace, her perfection at all that she does, and the perfect look that she effortlessly achieves. The look that you just saw Miss Fiona with was modeled after our ruler Shiva's own.*"

"So she's like, really, really good-looking?" Jigoro asked, his dry jaw almost sounding as if it was salivating.

"*Humans tend to think so,*" MilkTank agreed. "*As for myself, I'm not programmed to be stimulated by the human body.*"

"Well, I may not have a body anymore," Jigoro added on, "but I'm still stimulated by the human body! Nikko, do you understand what this means?? Shiva in *our* world, 'Shiva Angel' in *this* world -"

"Jigoro," Nikko explained while bending to wave her free hand at the tanuki, "it's not the same girl, there's no way."

"But what about that roller-skater girl? She was on the bridge in our world and then we just saw her outside before we crashed!"

"That reminds me," Nikko asked MilkTank, looking up while Tanuki wandered over to her, "did you see a really tan girl when we were outside? A girl with blue hair and roller skates?"

"*No.*"

"He probably did," Jigoro doubted the robot. "That's probably why he got hit by the ambulance in the first place, taking a peak at her bikini.. But whatever - Nikko, listen - What if this Shiva Angel really is my Shiva??"

"*Your* Shiva?"

"Hey, MilkTank - Did this Shiva Angel ever make any, you know... Dirty movies?"

"*The Queen is a very respectable woman!*" MilkTank quickly defended, almost sounding as if it could show real emotion in it's tone. "*She would never!*"

"I'm not talking about being respectable, I'm talking about serious business now!" Jigoro said back and then directed his next words to Nikko. "We have to at least go see her, right? I mean, what else are we going to do in this place? Even if it's not her, the 'Ruler of the World' has to be able to help us, right?"

"I don't know.." Nikko played with the thought in her mind.

"*Maybe you should make a note of the time - Your talking skull friend actually came up with a decent idea.*" MilkTank complimented Jigoro with a mocking insult. "*Having an audience with Queen Shiva is the closest thing to advice that I can give to you. I was actually preparing to suggest that before your friend just did.*"

"You what?!" Jigoro yelled, his bone head bouncing off of Nikko's hand and back down into it. "Don't take the credit for what I come up with!"

"Well, I guess it's our only option then," Nikko took another look at Miss Fiona, her body still slightly shaking within the bed. "We don't even know our way around here, though -"

"*Take a look with me now,*" MilkTank offered, leading the way back toward the tooth-shaped door, directing it's voice back to Fiona - "*I'll be just a moment, Miss Fiona. I'm going to show our friend on her way now.*"

"...Bye!" Nikko called over to her, a wave with her free hand and nothing said from Jigoro - Though as Nikko followed the robot out, she couldn't help but feel her Heart sink when considering the near-death woman. How could anyone understand what it was like to grow so old? Even though here Nikko was herself, seemingly dead or something like it..

A final look at the lady, silent and a shy difference from lifeless..

"Don't forget to say goodbye to that raccoon thing," Jigoro barked a reminder from her hands.

"Tanuki! How could I forget!"

Nikko crouched down once more beside the creature, calling it to her and petting it's brown and black fur, the animal making sounds that sounded as if it approved, and then Nikko hesitantly came back to a stand, following out through the now open doorway - More than happy to leave the room of machinery creatures and medical devices behind.

Outside, and the sky was still a nighttime black, the skull house street of the Medikiss City as empty and quiet as it was before, only now slightly less unsettling.

"*Take a look over the house,*" MilkTank instructed the pair. "*There you will see her castle ahead, the WaterBury.*"

The WaterBury? That was an unusual name for a castle.. Nikko stepped backwards and into the street, far enough so that her eyes could see over the skull shape, and there it was - Dark in the night sky, the barely lit castle of the 'Ruler of the World,' still some ways up ahead. It was difficult to make out, but it looked as if it was a light blue with soft pinks at it's spires - And some form of a black shape sticking out from it's side?

"*Some time ago,*" MilkTank explained, seeming to notice the change of expression on her face, "*an airplane tragically crashed into the western wall of the WaterBury.. I'm not aware of the true circumstances, but it has remained there ever since.*"

"You sound like a tour guide," Jigoro made fun of MilkTank yet again.

"*Oh, the humorous skull.. Though since you mention 'tour guide,' I have a somewhat large favor to ask of you, Nikko.*"

"Me?" Nikko replied in wonder, a little nervous of what the question could possibly be.

"*I'm programmed to be a somewhat above-average judge of character, as shown for my dislike of your friend, and I have come to the conclusion that I can have faith in you for this..*"

Nikko waited for it.

"*Would you consider taking Tanuki along with you?*"

"Are you serious??" Nikko laughed, more than a little excitement in her voice showing. "With us??"

"Um, we're ok, thanks -" Jigoro tried but was cut off.

"*His job of helping Miss Fiona is now coming to it's end, and what remains for him to do? He has always spent his time in this house. Though I haven't been able to enjoy it, I have been fortunate enough to travel to the End of the World, while he has remained here throughout.*"

"Oh, don't be silly," Jigoro argued. "What are you talking about? He can make all of those illusions appear and -"

"Jigoro, be quiet!" Nikko instructed the skull head. "Of course we can take him! We haven't seen this world either, so it can be really exciting for all of us!"

"Hey!" Jigoro bellowed in his increasing confusion. "Where is all of this coming from? I thought we were freaked out about all of this?

And now you're excited because of a raccoon??"

"He's not a raccoon, Jigoro," Nikko corrected him again.

"*Thank you very much, my new friend,*" MilkTank told her as it stepped back into the house again, leaving the 2 bickering alone for a moment outside.

Even the strange world, with it's looming cross skyscrapers behind, it's horrifying hospital, Jigoro's curious skull condition, and the unreal airplane sticking out of their castle destination, even those things could not keep the smile from overtaking Nikko's entire face. A real life tanuki named Tanuki, and now it was going to come with them?? And not just a tanuki like they had in Japan - Those were cool too - But a real, folklore magic illusion-making tanuki??

Nikko realized that she was holding Jigoro with the skull facing up, her friend grimacing as much as he could in dismay over her new excitement, and adjusted to hold him sideways again.

"...Ooooh... Hey, Nikko?" Jigoro tried to interrupt her euphoria.
"Um... I'm thinking... Maybe we should go!"

"Just hold on, give MilkTank a second," Nikko said with an ongoing smile. "I'm sure that they have to say their goodbyes.."

"No, Nikko -Take a look," Jigoro directed her to look, and as she turned to see what he saw, immediately rainbows filled her eyes in the nighttime air.

"That girl!" she said in shock, looking in excitement as the familiar blue haired girl could be seen up ahead, rollerskating in the general direction towards the castle.

"The Dolphin girl!" Jigoro yelled out as he now had the happy face that Nikko had for the tanuki. "Come on! Come on! She's heading the way we want to go anyway! Let's move!"

"Hang on! We have to wait for MilkTank!"

"Nikko!" Jigoro sounded out her name in frustration. "She's our only connection to the real world! We can't just let her get away!"

Nikko thought hard as the unusual tanned girl that Jigoro was now calling the 'Dolphin' skated the street, rainbows being created and then fading in her wake. Long side to side strides with her baggy-sock bare legs, and she was heading off into the distance -

"I thought you were just saying that Shiva would be our connection to back home?" Nikko asked, though feeling anxious at the moment as well.

"Yeah, I know! But..."

And at that second, MilkTank emerged from the skull-shape house, a pet carrier in tow.

"*Ok, Tanuki is ready to see the world now!*"

"In a pet box??" Jigoro laughed and spit air. "Is this guy serious??"

"That's fine!" Nikko said, no cares if it was in a carrier or out walking on it's own. "Does he need to stay in there, or does he get to come out too?"

"*He will come out when he wants to,*" MilkTank explained. "*Inside of the carrier is his Milk flask, should he get thirsty on your travels.*" MilkTank then directed it's pumpkin fire eyes at the skull Jigoro. "*The drink is for him only, none for you.*"

"Yeah, whatever," Jigoro said, his mind still on the girl he called the Dolphin. "Can we just skip the goodbyes and go already?"

"Sorry -" Nikko apologized to the robot, awkwardly trying to take the pet carrier while still holding the skull in her hands as well. "My friend wants to follow that girl down there."

"*A girl?*" MilkTank asked, rotating it's head and body just a bit to try and see.

"Yeah.." Nikko said, having trouble with switching the handle of the carrier to her right hand and the skull over to cradle with her left arm. "Down by all of those rainbows?"

"*I don't see anything...*" MilkTank surveyed the land, it's words mostly unnoticed as Nikko gave up with Jigoro.

"That's it," she said, "I'm putting you -"

"Don't put me in the cage with that raccoon!!" he begged her. "Please! Anything else!"

"I'm putting you on my head again," Nikko told him, "though you keep calling Tanuki a 'raccoon' and I'm going to put you in there for sure!"

Nikko set the carrier on the ground for just a moment, setting Jigoro's skull over her head again and then lifting the carrier back up by it's handle. She looked into the metal grate-door of the pet holder to see, smiling in with her face behind the skull head face, and...

Tanuki?

ZZZZZ........

"That thing's sound asleep!" Jigoro yelled loud enough to wake it, though it only opened it's eyes slightly before going back to bed.

"Not so loud, Jigoro," Nikko quieted him as she often needed to do. "They're supposed to be really lethargic, so just let him rest.. And look how cute he is when he's asleep!"

Nikko and the NLK

"Can we go now?? Please already?"

Nikko looked down the street and saw that the rainbow wake of the girl was so soon nearly gone -

"Ok, I think we're ready to go," she told the robot. "It was really nice to meet you and Miss Fiona.."

"*No need for formal goodbyes, I'm a machine,*" MilkTank reminded her. "*Just please take good care of our friend Tanuki?*"

Nikko reached her right arm around the massive robot in a failed attempt to hug it anyway, her left hand holding onto Tanuki's carrier.

"Alright, I'm going," she said as she let go, starting to awkwardly jog off into the distance of the castle on horizon. "Thank you for being so nice to us!"

MilkTank said nothing and looked on as Nikko ran down the street, Tanuki sound asleep in his pet carrier and the skull head of Jigoro around her head like a mask.

~ Off toward the rainbows in this strange new world, and onward toward the WaterBury castle ~

Nikko and the NLK

~ Biting... ~

~ Choking... ~

~ Hitting... ~

~ Scratching... ~

"Wait!! Ow... I think my front tooth broke...."

"What do you expect? It has to happen!"

"Just maybe don't hit me in the face anymore??"

"I'll hit you wherever I want to. It's what we agreed to."

Nikko and the NLK

CHAPTER 4

We Drink Blood, We Eat Skin

Nikko ran down the street in pursuit of the girl's rainbow wake, the skull over her head and the pet carrier held swaying by it's handle in her right hand, the sleeping Tanuki unphased inside.

Everything was so unclear - From where they had ended up to where they were headed now, Nikko still reeling from the confusion added by her most previous 'blackout,' to the sudden inclusion of a tanuki into their group.. But now, in pursuit of the rollerskating girl 'Dolphin,' and en route to the castle of the 'Ruler of the World' - Nikko had a small sense of purpose, and held to it as she ran through the city streets.

No ambulance sirens, no voices, no signs of any life could be heard in the air - Just the sound of Nikko's combat boots pounding into the ground as she hurried through, MilkTank and Miss Fiona's skull house growing in distance behind now.

"You're too slow!" Jigoro berated her as she breathed heavily against the inside walls of his helmet head. "We won't catch up!"

Nikko said nothing and tried to regulate her breathing, the weight of the pet carrier slowing her mobility.

Not far ahead, and the city was dissipating into open land, a few last small skull houses lined with more space between them, and the amounts of dark open landlots spread increasingly around. It was there that the faint trail of the rainbow lead angled off, still headed in the general direction of WaterBury, but now cutting into a space in between the remaining skull residences up ahead.

"(pause for breath) She turned off -" Nikko told the already aware Jigoro. "Should we still follow her?"

"What do you think?? Just run faster, Nikko!!"

Nikko bit her tongue and didn't exchange words back with him - At some point, she was going to have to fight the urge to smash his skull and leave him behind. After all, now that she had Tanuki to keep her company, what else could she ask for?

Nikko turned, slightly slowing down into the dark spaces, following where the now absent rainbow wake had turned. At the end of a vacant lot, there was a line of taller-than-her-head dark shrouded corn stalks, the rainbow trace lingering for just a moment at their edge.

"In there now??" Nikko wondered hesitantly as she stopped and caught her breath, asking more in disbelief than in a question to Jigoro - Though he decided to weigh in regardless.

"Well, we aren't going to catch up with her just standing and talking, are we??"

Nikko shook her skull-covered head back and forth in disbelief at his behavior. "I'm only going in there because it's kinda the same way that we're supposed to be going," she took a quick deep breath.

"Less talk! More action!" Jigoro ordered, pushing Nikko's nerves from her head. "If I still had a body, I'd be running!!"

This guy...

With a firm grip on the pet carrier, Nikko jogged to the corn stalk end of the lot, seeing the corn now loom high above her head and in tightly planted thin rows. A push in, and she entered the spot where the last rainbows had been seen, entering into the dark and pricking cropland, the night sky and silhouette of WaterBury seen in small visible peeks overhead.

"Oh, this was a bad idea.." Nikko scraped her way through, trying not to bang the carrier into the stalks as she awkwardly moved further in.

"We're never going to find her at this pace -" Jigoro grumbled in disappointment, Nikko uncaring to his concerns at the moment.

"I'm just heading straight through," she explained to him. "If we find her, we find her, but I can barely see where I'm going!"

Ignoring Jigoro's mumbling and with her eyes adjusting to the darkened farm rows quickly, Nikko was able to step a bit more briskly - Only now hearing small sounds that penetrated the thick skull layer.

"Just keep walking..." Jigoro commanded her, Nikko having no problems with his orders this time, already picking up the pace as much as she could without running. Small snapping noises, small buzzes whizzing by, and now tiny brushings up against her arms...

"Whoa!!" Nikko cringed. "Look!! Do you see them?? This place is covered with bugs! All kinds of them!"

"Is that what those noises are??" Jigoro asked, unaware of the insect or 2 now landed and riding on his exterior.

"This is disgusting.." Nikko swatted at her bare legs with her free hand. "Ugh... I can't believe we came in here!"

Forcing her way forward instead of turning back, she struggled on, swiping tiny bugs away from her eyes through Jigoro's gaping eye sockets. A few lit with glowing bodies, the sounds of others rubbing their legs together all around, and after a few minor bites it at last looked like an opening in the cornstalk field just ahead.

As Nikko neared it, she and Jigoro could make out some sort of darkened moving shapes - Without thought of the potential danger or even care, Nikko pushed hard to the final corn row and pushed her way out, the tiny insects scattering and her momentum throwing her to a rocky gravel ground in the clearing.

It was barely a road, a long narrow rock road cutting through the cornfield, equally giant rows of the stalks lined on the other side as well. And before her, the 2 shapes that she had made out now turned out to be standing beside a car, both human, or at least human-like as well..

"Well, howdy there," the man greeted, his voice the same as a midsouth accent from Nikko's world back home, "you'll startle someone coming out of the blue like that!"

"How do, y'all? I nearly jumped out of my skin!" the woman beside him said in a yodeling tone, her voice in surprise with a slightly less convincing version of the accent.

Nikko picked herself and the carrier up from the stone-paved road, small unbleeding cuts above her tall socks from the gravel. These 2 in front of her.. Jigoro said nothing as Nikko looked them over, unsure of them for the moment.

The man was slightly tall, his hair what looked like chin-length green yarn, similar to something Nikko would have seen back at that club they had gone to. His neck was long, skin looking weathered and stretched over his long thin body, tattoo stitchwork seen in parts where his denim patchwork overalls were ripped - No shirt beneath it, no shoes below. His face was slightly protruding, sunken eyes almost looking missing in the night's darkness.

"You not from around here?" the girl beside him asked, her accent and way of saying 'you' instead of 'you're' coming across unnatural and forced immediately.

"Not really..." Nikko unsurely offered.

Now looking at the girl, she was a similar look to her companion. Red yarn hair slightly longer than the man's, her face not quite as protruding but her eyes so dark they looked as if missing as well. Where the man's neck was a bit too long, her stretch of skin came at the nose, extending outward in a small stick length and ending in a nearly needle-sharp point. Her skin had the same uneven stitchwork type tattoo, her clothes a matching patchwork pair of bellbottom jeans, and a dirty, nearly see-through tight white tank-top.

"Unless people have skull heads for faces where you come from," the man said to Nikko as he looked her over from bottom to top, "I imagine you must be 1 of a kind."

"Um..." Nikko tried to breathe normal again, trying to figure them out as quickly as she could - Jigoro still quiet atop her head.

"*Look* at this outfit! And this *style!*" the girl exclaimed as she leaned forward and touched the bottom line of Nikko's skirt, looking more at her exposed legs than Nikko's actual clothing. "You don't see trendy fashion like this around these parts, do you, Bixby?"

"I don't recall ever even *seeing* a woman like this before," the man that had just been called Bixby agreed. "And normal guys like me sure like women! Just look at that pretty face! And the skin tone of these arms!"

Bixby looked more at Nikko's clothing than he did at the mentioned features, his hand reaching forward to try and hold her black tie while he admired -

He failed at the grip, his hand falling lifelessly onto her chest.

"Let's try that again!" he laughed, struggling to make any sort of grip for the other hand either.

Dead hands?

"So, I'm... I'm.." Nikko looked to change the subject as she took a step backward, hoping to avoid any more unsolicited touching. "I'm trying to make my way to a castle.. Called WaterBury?"

Nikko's eyes looked to the open sky of the cornfield-cutting road, the sight of WaterBury actually unseen now with all of the closely looming corn stalks. Her eyes returned to the 2 unusuals before her, seeing that even though it appeared that they had no eyes in this darkness, the woman was obviously staring at the places where Nikko's skin was visible, and the man staring where her clothing covered the skin.

"Well, we would love to help you in any way that we can, Darling," the green-haired man told her, then directing his sunken-eye glance to the rundown car beside them. "But as you can see - We ran into a little dilemma here. I just can't seem to get that dang engine started.."

"Oh, that's ok!" Nikko laughed as she looked for an opportunity to slip away.

"But ~ It ain't *much a problem* if you can help us get this vehicle here down the road," he went on in his forced hillbilly dialect. "We run a garage just down the way - My name's Bixby, by the way -"

"And my name's Natasha," the pointy-nosed woman greeted.

"... I'm Nikko," Nikko hesitantly greeted back, still a little unsure of it all. "Do you guys, like, know how to jump start a car or anything?"

"Oh, he knows how to," Natasha quickly added in before Bixby had a chance to speak, "but wouldn't you know it? Ain't nobody out here to help us out -"

"Well.. I suppose if your place isn't too far up the road," Nikko went on, beginning to wonder why Jigoro had been quiet for so long now, "I can wait here with it while you go get whatever you need.."

"Well, our house may be right around the corner," Bixby told her, Nikko now noticing that he held his forearms out in front of himself, rather than down at his sides, "but even with that being as it may, we'd rather not leave you out here by yourself, young lady -"

Nikko wondered - 2 different things? Was it a garage or a house? Maybe just the same?

"I really can't go with you, I -" Nikko tried but was interrupted by Natasha.

"We can't leave the car out here either, you know," she explained. "Don't want any old buddy just driving off with it!"

Nikko thought to herself - Who would want the old broken down thing? And would someone really drive it off if it couldn't even start?

"Ok, so..." Nikko stood there and looked around, beginning to feel a bit more uncomfortable until just at that moment, Jigoro at last spoke again -

"TAKE YOUR TOP OFF, NATASHA," he announced, saying the horribly inappropriate thing to only make matters worse. "I have been staring nonstop since we came up to you, and I can clearly see through your white tank top - I don't see a point in you even wearing it."

"Jigoro!!" Nikko scolded him, her cheeks red blushed with shock inside of him. "Are you crazy?!"

Bixby and Natasha looked at each other in confusion, seeing the 2 voices from Nikko in an argument. Natasha then looked down at her shirt herself, the red yarn hair falling to the sides, and then looked back up.

"Well, thank you so much for pointing that out to me," she told

Nikko and the NLK

Nikko, seeming to think that Jigoro's voice was Nikko's own. "Is that what normal girls do? Take it off like that in a situation like this? Well then, silly me! I am a 100% normal human girl!"

Nikko then held her breath in disbelief as the woman now removed her shirt, standing before them with an attractive, disfigured body type. Her skin was even more stitchmarked over her torso, discolored bruises at her hipline where her bellbottoms hung.

"Holy crap!!" Jigoro yelled out in a voice that sounded closer to feminine than his usual tone. "I can't believe that actually worked!"

"You got some sort of a multiple personality thing?" Bixby asked, craning his long neck a bit unnaturally to get a better look at the skull.

"I can't believe it..." Jigoro went on talking to himself. "All I had to do was just ask.. I could've did this with that Miavia girl... And the nurses.."

"Oh... Yeah.. Um, that.." Nikko stalled and was racing to think, deciding not to reveal anything at this point to the stitchwork people before her. "Yeah.. Can you believe it? It's like I'm brother and sister, all at the same time.." She paused, hoping Jigoro would catch on to what she was trying to do and stay quiet.

"That is so bold of you," Natasha said, standing closer to also see the skull up close, her topless and leathery-skin body right against Nikko now - No doubt to the enjoyment of the hopefully playing-along quiet Jigoro. "It's like there's a *whole 'nother* person inside of that skull of yours.."

"Heh, yeah," Nikko awkwardly laughed, both characters standing far too close for comfort. "Imagine that? I can drive myself crazy a little.."

"You are a very impressive young thing," Bixby told her, his female counterpart now once again pretending to admire the materiel of Nikko's skirt, while her eyes were to the legs.

"Thank you.."

"And I'll say it again," Natasha repeated, "this is such a fetching style, is that skirt tight? Do you think you could run in it if you had to?"

Nikko, a bit fearing for her safety, made sure to sound strong. "It's not a problem - I'm very fast, even in these boots.."

"And what's that thing down there?" Bixby asked as he looked from her boots to the carrier. "You carrying your pet with you?"

"..Of course! We're inseparable, like a family and everything.."

"And we're looking to give it away!" Jigoro added in, Nikko grating her teeth at this point every time she heard his voice.

"The other personality again!" Natasha observed. "Haha! This is so entertaining!"

"Actually, I'm not really looking to give it away.." Nikko corrected her 'other' voice, miffed that Jigoro would already be attempting to rid them of their new companion. "My other 'self' says some of the most off the wall things sometimes... All of the time.."

"Well, we ain't in need of any more mouths to feed, anyways," Bixby added, finally walking away from Nikko and to the broken down car. "We got us our own little pet, don't we, Natasha?"

"Our little Oliver," she cooed, and as she spoke the name out loud, something like a hog-sized beetle jumped up from the back seat - Costume dog ears fastened to it's head and it's mouth gaping open.

"What is that thing??" Jigoro asked for the both of them, accepting of his role as Nikko's second personality and talking more frequently again.

"It's a.." Bixby tried and then trailed off in thought.

"A dog, Sweetie," Natasha finished the statement, giving him a sharp nudge in the arm for not saying it himself.

Nikko stared at the fat beetle looking out from the passenger side window. Even without the costume dog ears attached, the thing looked so unusual to her - A goliath beetle, too many times larger than a beetle should ever grow, tapping it's head repeatedly against the window in a failed effort to come out.

"Well, are we gonna just *conversate* all night," Bixby asked, ending 1 of the few moments of silence, "or are we gonna get to pushing this fine luxury vehicle on it's way?"

"Actually, I think I should -" Nikko attempted to end her involvement, only to be interrupted immediately.

"Nonsense," Natasha silenced her, pressing her body from behind to force her closer to the car, "we can't let an attractive lady such as yourself walk all of that way by herself!"

"It doesn't look that far, really," Nikko tried, looking up again, trying to remember which way she had seen the silhouette before entering the cornfield.

"Well, we insist," Bixby ordered, coming up to the side of her and going to grab her arm - His hand instead falling limply against her chest again -

Were they broken, just as Miavia's legs had been?

Natasha put her hands at Nikko in place of Bixby, guiding her now to the rear end and closed trunk of the car - Her grip exceedingly tight.

Nikko and the NLK

"You *don't mind* giving a hand to everyday common people in need, do you?" she asked expectantly, not waiting for an answer. "We of course will help you back. You and Bixby just push this down the road a ways, and I'll steer the wheel to make sure we stay on the road, ok? That's not such a big deal, is it? And once we're all set up with that battery jump, we'll get you to the WaterBury in no time, Honey!"

Nikko looked to the cornstalks on both sides of the rundown car, nervously deciding not to just run off, and instead staying to push the car out of fear. She watched as the topless Natasha walked around to the driver's side, pulling her loose hip bellbottoms up a bit, and then getting in to steer - The beetle-dog greeting her upon entry.

"You all ready back there??" she shouted out, Nikko setting the pet carrier atop the trunk as she set her hands against the old car.

"Just a moment, beautiful," Bixby delayed her as he walked a few steps to the side, squatting down to pick up Natasha's discarded tank top. "No need for us to be so wasteful.."

Nikko looked on as the overall clad man tried awkwardly to pick up the white shirt, trying to trap it between his forearms instead of just picking it up with his hands.

"Give me just a second back here.."

"Bixby!" Natasha yelled much louder this time, her accent slipping from southern to cold-foreign for the exchange. "We don't need that old shirt! Let's get this thing moving already!"

"Hey, you listen to me, girl!" Bixby shouted back in a true southern tone. "Clothes don't grow on trees! You remember how hard this here was to get?? If you worried half as much about clothing as you do about feeding your mouth - We wouldn't have any problems between us at all!"

"You always.. have a problem.. with my eating!!" Natasha blasted her words back at him, a little quieter than the last time and with a mix of her 2 accents along with it. "Some of us like to taste different things and not worry about how we're gonna look today -"

Nikko tried to follow their argument as she stood waiting at the rear of the car, Bixby finally with an arm-grip on the shirt and then heading to hand it off to the topless driver. Eating too much? The red-yarn haired girl had looked like dried-skin and bones to Nikko - Did she really eat that much?

"This is *not* the time for the discussion of clothes vs. dinner," Bixby concluded, looking back with his empty eyes at the skull headed Nikko. "Just understand and know how hard I work at these things, and let's move on."

Natasha replied with nothing, and Bixby walked back over to the rear and beside Nikko.

"Sorry about the quarreling," he apologized. "You can't help but fight about food and clothing sometimes."

"I suppose that's true.." Nikko agreed and noticed that the leathery face of Bixby seemed unable to smile, the unusual man then taking his position.

"Ok, now here we go!" he said as he pushed off on the car, using the underside of his upright forearms to push as Nikko used her hands, digging into the gravel road with her boots.

A hard shove, and the beat-up car began to barely roll, squeaking noises and miniature bangs as it crawled along - 4 flat tires wobbling as it rolled.

"Are you sure that this thing was even drivable?" Nikko asked, completely unsure of anything that they had told her.

"Absolutely!" he confirmed, his extra long stitched-up neck and protruding face so close beside her. "This used to be top of the line stuff!"

Nikko pushed off over and over again on the gravel road, using all of her strength to keep the pathetic thing moving. She looked into the trunk-top pet carrier and saw Tanuki still so fast asleep - Even in the tense situation she had found herself in, he was still so cute!

"Turn your head to look at the guy," Jigoro ordered Nikko as she looked on at Tanuki.

"Say what?" Bixby asked, hearing Jigoro talk low.

"Er, nothing," Nikko covered for him, looking over with a courtesy smile beneath and unintentionally granting Jigoro another look.

"I knew it.." the talking skull said, this time loud enough for Bixby to hear him entirely.

"What's that?" he asked, Nikko wondering as she tried to see if Bixby was actually even pushing his side of the vehicle. "What do you know?"

"Ask him if those are really tattoos, or actual stitches," Jigoro said unsuccessfully under his breath, Bixby hearing everything.

"Oh, these?" he asked. "Ha! Of course they're tattoos, don't be silly! You think someone would have this many real-life stitches?"

"Right! How silly of me!" Nikko laughed.

"Although you would have to say," he went on, "if they were to be real stitches, it would be *really* impressive handiwork right? Strictly for the sake of conversation?"

"...Mmm-hmm," Nikko nodded in a 'go-along-with-whatever-he-says' agreement.

"Really?" Bixby stopped 'pushing' and stood up in satisfaction, then coming back to the push - Nikko noticing very little difference in the momentum of the car either way. "That would mean so much to me.. That is, if I could be blessed to be so incredibly talented, so to say."

Nikko pushed on and Bixby at least pretended to as well, the slowly turning gravel road still slowly turning to the left - Still? Natasha sat still in her seat unmoving.

"How we all doing back there?" she called out. "Tired yet?"

Nikko waited for Bixby to answer, then realizing the question was directed at her.

"Getting there.." she called back up to the steering lady. "How far is it from here?"

"We're getting there!" she replied back, and Nikko felt the strain in her arms and lower body.

"So.. What do you think about insects?" Bixby asked her as they went along the road, his voice almost completely accent-less and upperclass for a moment.

"... What do you mean?" Nikko asked. "Like, all of them?"

"Well, how about just a generalization," he elaborated, the voice still close to different. "For example, do you think they are *equal* to humans?"

Nikko made an unsure stretch of her lips. "I suppose so.."

"So you believe that it is completely possible that they are 'good' enough to have insect jobs, insect schools, insect newspapers and whatever it is that humans are so proud of having these days.."

"I never really put too much thought into it.." Nikko confessed, wondering half about what he said and half about why his accent was completely changed now.

"*Of course* you wouldn't think about it," he said to her, sounding insulted and unsurprised. "Someone like *you* does not think about it because humans are too busy to realize the superiority of the insect society compared to theirs.."

Bixby breathed in deeply, the skin at his face moving along with him in an unnatural mask-like movement. "Pardon me - That would be, 'compared to ours' is what I meant to say!" he said, his voice now settling back into the southern style.

"Listen..." Nikko stopped dead in her tracks, the car rolling for not

even half a second before coming to a stop. "I do app_
you are trying to do for me.." she paused and gathered_
"But if you don't mind, I'm just going to continue on by n

As she reached for Tanuki's pet carrier and removed it _ _ top of the trunk, Bixby reached for her, unsuccessfully with the ,ailing grab of his forearms -

"You don't really mean that," he coaxed her, "do you? I mean, it's not more than another few car lengths up..."

"What's going on back there?" Natasha shouted back with a lean and look back from the inside of the still car.

"Is it really only a few more car lengths?" Nikko asked as she stepped slowly backwards and away from the broken down car. "I don't know if I believe you.. I'm looking down the road, and I don't see anything.. The road keeps turning to the left like we're just pushing this thing in a circle.. Like *I'm* pushing it in a circle.."

"Natasha..." Bixby called ahead, his sunken eyes not taking their sight off of Nikko. "You might want to come help me back here.."

Nikko felt a panic in her chest and got ready to run..

"Nikko," Jigoro whispered to her, "let's get out of here.. Like right now..."

"She's gonna make a break for it!" Bixby shouted now without the southern accent, yelling to his partner just as Nikko started backing away faster.

He lunged for her as she turned to run, still wanting to head in the semi-remembered direction of the cornstalk obstructed castle - Grabbing at her stronger this time, Nikko felt Bixby's forearms really clamp around her now, struggling to free herself -

The car door opened and his partner rushed out, the beetle-dog along with her as well.

"Look at you!" Natasha laughed in her cold foreign voice as she came around the side, completely dropping her southern accent as well. "Did you think that you could just leave a nice couple stranded out here??"

"Bite him, Nikko!" Jigoro demanded, Nikko struggling in the grasp. "Headbutt him or something!"

Bixby threw her to the gravel road, kicking her in the ribs with his shoeless feet as she lay there.

"Ow!" Nikko cried and dropped the pet carrier, then quickly grabbing the handle again and clutching her ribs with her free hand. "Let me go!!"

"Just let you go?" Natasha mockingly asked as she kicked her too, her attack just as painful as Bixby's had been. "Who do you think you are? You're not anyone special!"

Another kick, and Natasha reached down and grabbed the free arm of Nikko from her clutching ribs, dragging her off of the gravel road. Bixby walked alongside and the beetle-dog too, Nikko pulled down into the cornstalks.

"You freaks are lucky I don't have my body," Jigoro threatened them, helpless on her head as nothing more than a mask or helmet. "You wouldn't be messing with Nikko like this!!"

"Stop being delusional," Bixby told what he thought was still her other self. "You aren't even making any sense anymore."

"What we're doing is only natural," Natasha explained. "We were going to let you tire out by pushing that car around for us, but you left us no choice! If we have to use force on you, we will! Bixby, cut her open!"

"No!" Nikko screamed with a desperate voice, wrestling free from Natasha's arm drag and pulling herself up to her knees. "Why are you doing this to me??"

And just as she fought to her feet, Bixby broke from his skin, the stitchwork coming apart on the top most part of his body, freeing what had been hiding inside -

"I knew it!" Jigoro yelled at the sight - Bixby in transformation before them -

The stitched-together dead skin dropped off from his body, the awkward human now standing before them in his true form - A man shape of a spider crossed with a mantis, a black skin base with green armor pieces over segments of his body and long mantis neck. He had black antenna and arachnid eyes, the furry fangs of a spider moving independently in and out of his emerald mantis face.

"We can try to make it painless," Natasha offered as Nikko got up and tried to run from the dangerous pair, turning her back and yet again grasped between the outreached arms of the spidermantis, "but if you keep fighting us like this, Bixby can always kill you slowly and in the most inhumane ways possible.."

Nikko tried, refusing to let go of the sleeping Tanuki's pet carrier and now, as she looked back over her shoulder from the hold of the male insect, she could see that Natasha was shedding her skin as well - Still the slim build of a human woman, but now with a complete night-black base, like a bodysuit, and ladybug shell-type clothing over her body with a matching helmet above her eyes. Her long nose now was seen as a mosquito blood-sucking straw, lady bug wings and her eyes glowing electric yellow.

"And just 1 last surprise," the human-shaped ladybug mosquito told Nikko, the beetle-dog coming up and Natasha removing it's costume dog ears. "This... Is not a dog!"

"What?! That 1 was stupid!" Jigoro complained, even during a tense moment like this. "Like we couldn't tell? Couldn't you at least -"

BAM!

Jigoro stopped in mid-sentence as Nikko slammed the back of his skull into the neck of Bixby behind her, pushing off and running as the grip slightly loosened -

"Bixby!" Natasha screamed. "Grab her! Don't let her get away!"

But Nikko fled as fast as she could, nevermind the panic in her Heart or the kicking-pain in her ribs. She moved as fast as she could through the tight cornstalk maze, slamming through little bugs and breaking stalks, the voices and sounds of the insect people never falling far behind.

"This sucks!" Jigoro yelled, managing not to complain about his skull being used as a weapon. "I knew they were trouble from the start!"

"Well, I'm sure you're proud of yourself," Nikko told him in a quiet voice as she stumbled her way through the dark. "All you seem to want to see is a girl take her shirt off -"

"Oh, man! I still can't believe that worked! All these years and I've never thought to just ask!"

"Well, if we get to see her again, you can try it with the real thing this time -" Nikko told him. "You can see a naked ladybug now -"

"Oh, I didn't think of that..." he wondered, paying no mind to the danger as he rode along atop Nikko - His mind free to wander on whatever came to mind. "And it's not like they were going to eat your 'other personality..' I could've just sat there and checked her out.."

"Thanks a lot! Pay no attention to your only friend getting eaten by human-bugs or anything!"

"That does sound... kinda cool..."

87

Nikko and the NLK

"I really hate your imagination today," Nikko scolded him in their whisper-conversation before going quiet again, pushing her way through every stalked row before her.

"Don't think that you can just run away!" Natasha could be heard overhead, her ladybug wings carrying her low over the stalks as Bixby and the beetle pursued from behind.

A push through, and Nikko's hands hit a solid board in place of the breakaway stalks. Not stopping, her eyes and Jigoro's skull followed it up as she angled around it, seeing a skinless body old and nearly meatless - It's remains draped like a scarecrow and covered in small real-size insects.

Nothing was safe anymore, and a bit more urgency as Nikko fled now, the sight of the human remains scaring her at what fate was awaiting in this unsafe world that they had ended up in. Now she not only regretted coming into the cornfield in the first place, but all of the way back to even going out with Jigoro instead of just staying home..

... Back home...

And as her mind drifted between terrified thoughts, Nikko fell out through another and final row, this time tripping and trying to catch her balance in a grassy clearing, in place of the small gravel road from before.

And where was this? Outside of the cornstalk field, and now a slightly hilled area held a 2 story red brick house -

~ So familiar, almost the same as her house back home ~

Within the brief moment that Nikko saw this and gathered herself, Natasha slammed into her from a swooping down attack, grabbing beneath her arms from behind, locking her human-like insect hands behind Nikko's neck and lifting her above the ground.

"Hey!!" Nikko resisted and fought, trying unsuccessfully to do the backwards skull-headbutt that had worked on Bixby. "Let go of me! Stop it!!"

And in her fight, the pet carrier dropped the 2 feet from her struggle to the grass below, falling and hitting the ground with a bounce just as Bixby and the beetle emerged from the cornfield.

"Nice work, Natasha," he said as he walked over toward the dropped carrier, Natasha still struggling to hold Nikko in the airborne full-nelson wrestling hold. "And what do we have down here? Did you want to watch me devour your precious pet?"

"I can't believe I thought you were humans!" Nikko screamed out to them, tears in her under-skull eyes. "You didn't even look like real people!"

Natasha tightened her grip, Nikko's knee-high sock legs kicking helplessly from beneath her skirt.

"You watch your mouth!" the spidermantis ordered her, stalking around the dropped carrier with his mantis forearms held out. "You have no idea how much preparation goes into our productions.."

"Bixby is the best at what he does!" Natasha buzzed, her mosquito long nose uncomfortably close to Nikko's neck while she talked. "If it were up to me, we would just eat - But he works very hard to make these things just right!"

"The clothing, the skin, the voices, the tiny movements," he went on, his black and green insect body crouched down and fumbling at the simple latch of the pet carrier, "everything that goes into the pageantry of what you just saw - *That* is the intelligence that an insect possesses. That is the modern day 'spider web,' wouldn't you agree?"

Nikko felt escape fading away, held helplessly over the grassy hill just beyond the bug-infested cornfield.

"Could you just let us go, and take the animal?" Jigoro pleaded in desperation from Nikko's head. "It's not really even ours -"

"Shut up, Jigoro! He's our friend!"

And in the quarreling moment, Bixby screamed from the bottom of his human-insect lungs, managing the pet carrier open and falling back away from it, the beetle running behind him for protection.

"Natasha! It's hideous!" he yelled to her, a fear in his voice for the first time since meeting him.

"What are you scared of now??" his partner scolded him, flying a foot closer to the ground with Nikko still in the locking hold. "If you're just scared of a little.."

A wild growl came from the awakened Tanuki, stepping out from the opened door of it's carrier.

"A raccoon dog?!?" Natasha screamed to Nikko, letting go of her grip and flying to the side of Bixby at once, Nikko falling the short distance to the ground below. "What kind of a sick creature keeps a monster like that as a pet?!?"

The 3 cowering insects backed away as Tanuki stood his ground, his front quarters low and hind quarters arched up, scratching at the grass below with 1 paw like a motorcycle revving it's engine.

"How dastardly of you!" Bixby argued as the 3 backed closer to the bordering line of the cornfield. "Why would you have this beast along with you?? Don't you know what it does to insects?!"

Nikko picked up the empty animal carrier and backed away herself, backing away from the horrible cornfield and closer to the familiar house. She watched in amazement as the kidnapping couple inched away in absolute terror of the just-now awakened Tanuki, the stout animal still standing it's ground as they backstepped and vanished into the night-darkened cornmaze - Nikko still unsure and feeling unsafe with them only briefly out of sight.

"Tanuki!" she called to the animal, her back now at the wooden stairs of the red house. "Come here, Tanuki! Come on!"

Tanuki turned it's head, and it's cute face went from the defensive snarl of a guard dog to the happy face of a raccoon dog, running over toward her and Jigoro, snapping at small bugs in the air as it did so.

"I forgot that they'll eat insects.." Nikko said to Jigoro as the animal headed up to the stairs as well. "We should have just woken him up!"

"I knew those things weren't people, I swear," Jigoro claimed as Nikko pet her hand over the attention-loving Tanuki. "There's no way that a real girl would take her top off just like that.."

"You want to go back into your carrier?" Nikko asked, disregarding Jigoro's words.

Tanuki stayed out and Nikko closed the carrier door, holding it by the handle now so much lighter than before.

"You know that they'll come back," Jigoro explained as Nikko turned to face the dark house. "When you're so hungry that you start eating people, I don't think you're gonna let them just get away like that."

"Thanks," Nikko said without appreciation. "I *know* they won't give up - That's why we're gonna see if someone lives at this house quick."

"What?? Are you crazy? Everyone we meet here is a psycho -"

"MilkTank wasn't crazy," Nikko told him, Tanuki's ears flicking up at the sound of the robot's name. "And I'm telling you now - If some crazy person lives here, or someone that looks like they're wearing someone else's skin again? You can forget it this time -"

"Well, if it's another girl," Jigoro announced as Nikko rapped her knuckles at the old door, "I'm telling her to take her shirt off right away again. Then we'll see if she's really a girl or not, right?"

"Ha - Nice excuse," Nikko answered, waiting for any answer to her knock. "Hello??" she called out through the door, a look back over her shoulder to make sure they were still alone.

"You've gotta knock harder than that, Nikko!" Jigoro demanded, showing his frustration again at being just a skull. "You have to really bang on it! It's the middle of the night - They're probably not even awake."

"Maybe you're right.." she said, pulling back her hand for another attempt -

And just as she threw her knuckled fist forward, the door softly opened in the slightest, the unlit interior exposed inside and a small 1 foot tall white creature seen at the floor. Before Nikko or Jigoro could even make out what it was, Tanuki made a hissing sound and ran after it inside, dashing into the darkness as the small ghostly white thing turned and fled -

"Tanuki! Stop!" Nikko yelled as it headed in uninvited. "Tanuki!"

"What the heck do you call that??" Jigoro complained as Nikko pushed her way into the quiet house. "He can't just barge in there like that! Who does he think he is??"

Nikko paid the talking skull no mind, instead cautiously walking into the front room of the nearly completely dark house herself, all furniture slightly seen covered in white sheets, an unescapable sense of absolute emptiness surrounding.

"Tanuki!" Nikko shout-whispered at her suddenly wide awake and alert animal friend, seeing it following the small white shape up a set of stairs in the darkness. "Come on!"

She hurried through the difficult-to-see front room, leaving the door open behind and hoping nobody would catch them intruding, if in fact it wasn't abandoned. The house interior was almost the same layout as her own house, though a little reverse, and as she made it to the stairway in the dark, she saw just enough to see the tail of her friend go around the stairs and onto the second floor.

"You better put that thing back in the carrier when you catch it," Jigoro told her as she headed up the staircase, feeling the way up with her free hand at the wall beside her.

"It just woke up," Nikko whispered. "It's probably all excited since it saw those giant bugs outside."

"Well I don't know what that thing it's chasing is, but whatever it is, it must've opened the door for us.."

"It was tiny, Jigoro! You really think it could reach the doorknob??"

And as they whispered and reached the second floor, Nikko saw the only open door, the second floor shrouded in darkness except for a faint light emitting from the space between the ajar door and it's frame.

"Can't we just try to turn some lights on?" Jigoro asked as she crept toward the doorway.

"Be quiet.. We're aren't even supposed to be in here.."

Nikko reached the door and put her free hand at it, pushing it slowly open more -

"AAAHHHH!!!" a highpitched voice screamed in terror as the skull headed Nikko poked her head in, Nikko quickly stepping back and slamming the door shut in fear of her own.

"What was it??" Jigoro asked fast. "What did you see in there??"

"You saw the same thing I saw! I couldn't see anything!"

"Well who was that in there?"

"How am I supposed to know??"

"What do you want??" the high-pitched voice called out from the inside of the room. "You're not here to hurt me too, are you??"

"No - No, we're not here to hurt you.." Nikko promised as she brought her voice back from whispering to a normal level. "My tanuki chased something into your house -"

"Now it's 'your' tanuki?" Jigoro interrupted.

"It came up here, and I just want to get it and then we can go - I'm really sorry! We didn't know if anyone even lived here anymore.."

"Um... Ok," the girl voice continued, "so is this thing a 'tanuki' in here?? It's really scary!!"

"It's another talking bug, I'll bet..." Jigoro warned Nikko as she carefully re-opened the slammed door. "Be ready to run..."

Nikko cautiously stepped through the open door, now seeing a woman standing at the far end of an empty room, her back against the wall, and Tanuki standing in front of her growling -

"Take your shirt off!" Jigoro yelled just as he had with Natasha. "Er... Open that robe up!!"

"You're a horrible monster!" she cried out to Nikko. "You're scaring me to death!"

"Hold on, Jigoro," Nikko asked her friend, waving Tanuki over and seeing the girl in closer detail, "I don't think she's a bug -"

With her white pale skin glowing, she was beautiful and ghostly - Completely different and more lifelike, in a peculiar way, than the 2 creatures that they had met in the field. She was a medium height girl, a black bob haircut with 2 large black cat ears coming from the top sides, her eyes shining honey gold in the dark, almost as bright as her milky skin. She was dressed in what Nikko recognized as a black kimono robe, tied at the waist with a white belt to match the all-white lining at the cuffs and ends.

"Do what you want with me," she cried, "but leave my friends alone! They didn't do anything to upset you, did they? If they did I know that they're sorry! I promise!"

"Wait! We don't want to hurt you," Nikko tried to calm her, feeling unusual to be on the other side of such a fear. "We just wanted to see if anybody lived here, and then our tanuki, Tanuki, chased something in so we had to follow him -"

"Please don't be mean to me??" the pale cat-eared girl begged. "If you're going to eat me, please just do it - Oh, man.. This is so scary.. And look at your face... You're like the grim reaper!!"

Nikko tried not to laugh as she walked the full way into the room, carrier in hand and Tanuki still making small growls. "Please try to calm down?" she comforted the nervous girl. "Really, we're not going to hurt you.."

And just as she said this, 3 skeleton rats poked out from her kimono, their bodies completely skinless - A slightly tall 1 from her right ankle, a slightly heavy 1 from her left ankle, and a third, smaller than both, from the breast of her robe - Tiny animal skeletons, even bone ears in an unnatural un-cartilaged cartoon round shape.

Tanuki growled louder again and began jumping around in hungry excitement.

"Tanuki, settle down!" Nikko commanded him as she set the carrier at the ground, rubbing her hands over his slightly upright hair. "I think 1 of those things is what he chased up here.."

"I sent Chewy down when we heard something knocking," the cat girl said. "He's the bravest of all of us so we thought it was a good idea if he checked it out."

"Chewy?" Jigoro asked.

"Oh no!" the cat freaked out in a small panic to herself. "And now she keeps changing voices... This is so scary.. Um... Chewy is this little guy," she said, looking down at her chest and pointing to the skeleton rat peeking out from her kimono. "And then Chewart should be down by my foot somewhere - He's the big little guy, and then Chewington should be down there by him somewhere too. He's the tallest guy, and the most thoughtful -"

Chewart, the heavier skeletal rat, could be seen looking at the tall

'thoughtful' Chewington with a tiny jealous expression.
"This is really something.." Jigoro said to himself.
"Chewart, Chewy, and Chewington?" Nikko repeated back, making sure that she had it right.
"Mmm-hmm," the kimono wearing girl agreed. "They're my 'Chew Mice,' even though they're really rats... I have a name too, but I don't remember it - It's supposed to be on this charm," she tugged at a metal piece held by the black choker at her neck, "but I have some trouble reading the people words."
"Oh, this is unreal.." Nikko said as her mind began to race. "I know that collar - Do you mind if I see it? I can tell you your name.."
The cat girl looked at Nikko with a little bit of fear, and then slowly nodded her head. "Ok... But please don't bite me or anything? This is so outrageous..."
"It's a choker, not a collar," Jigoro corrected Nikko. "I would think you of all people would know your fashion.."
"I understand that," she addressed him as she walked up to the girl, fear rising in her honey gold eyes as the 'talking-to-herself' Nikko came near her, "but it looks just like the name tag that I made for - Oh, wow - This can't be for real..."
"I think I'm going to get a nosebleed..." Jigoro said as Nikko stood right before the wall-pressed girl, looking down at the collar/choker as Jigoro was able to stare straight down the cat girl's upper curves of the kimono - Chewy looking back up at him in defiant bravery. "What a shapely body..."
"Jigoro, it says her name is *Kimby*!" Nikko read to her skull helmet in bewilderment. "It says Kimby on it!"
"Isn't that your -"
"That was my kitty's name!" Nikko cried as her unthought-of cat popped back into her head, backing up from the cowering girl and taking another look at her.
"Kimby?" the cat girl repeated. "I don't know... I think that sounds familiar. I haven't heard my name said in a really long time.."
Nikko looked her over from a few steps back - The pale skin, like absolute white - The black robe and black hair and black cat ears - Could it somehow really be??
"I'm Nikko.." she introduced herself to the girl, half expecting a sort of reaction. "Does that ring a bell to you? At all?"
"Hmm..." the cat girl scratched at her head in thought. "I don't think so.. But I don't know, I can't remember too many things, I've been in

here for so long.."

"Hold on," Nikko guided Tanuki back into his pet carrier as she decided on trying to figure this out. "Let me show you my face -"

"Nikko, there's no way that this really good looking girl is your cat," Jigoro told her as she pulled his hollow skull from her head again at last. "I mean, come on!"

"Oh......" Kimby whispered as Nikko removed Jigoro, setting it atop the Tanuki closed-in pet carrier. "I don't believe it.."

"You remember me??" Nikko asked in unsure excitement, looking at Kimby and waiting for her to say that she did.

"I don't think I do... But I'm so happy that the skull thing wasn't your real head! That was so scary I couldn't even think straight! Phew! What a relief!"

"Ha!" Jigoro laughed hard from atop the carrier, the 3 skeleton rats leaving Kimby's robe to investigate him. "I told you that she wasn't your cat, Nikko! Give me a break!"

"Well, I'm not so convinced she's not," she told Jigoro, everyone calming down now that the initial awkwardness was out of the way. "She even looks sort of like her - With, like, a human body, or something."

"Hey!" Jigoro yelled, the Chew Mice now over at him, the tall Chewington and heavy Chewart looking all about his skull, and the small Chewy looking into the carrier at the growling Tanuki. "I can't defend myself here!"

"Chewart! Chewy! Chewington!" Kimby called to them by name, their little skull mouse-eared heads looking back at her. "Everyone behave themselves, ok? I know we're all excited, but - Oh wow! Look at these little toys! So cute!!"

Kimby batted at the 3 keychains hanging from Nikko's belt loop, hitting lightly at them just as a little cat would.

Nikko looked toward her skull friend and then back to the girl - The familiar feel of this house, the familiar name of this cat person - This was all a lot to take in, especially after the multitude of events that had already transpired in the evening so far.

"Why does it talk?" Kimby asked Nikko as she came out of her wondering, the girl now standing over by the pet carrier and holding Jigoro in her hands - Chewart standing atop her right shoulder and the skull lined up just right to stare again at her upper body. "Is it like a toy or something?"

As she asked, she played with his bony jaw, moving it up and down and making him talk for herself.

"Jigoro's actually my friend," Nikko explained, "or at least kind of what's left of my friend.. It's a long story - We don't really know how he talks. Or even why, actually."

"It was a little scary at first," Kimby said, playing with the skull in the air like a child, "but now he's kind of funny! Look at him, Chewart!"

"I think she's a ghost or something, Nikko," Jigoro said with the words coming out slurred, his jaw being moved to form different sounds than what he was making. "Her hands are freezing, man!"

"Kimby," Nikko asked, amused by the entire scene at the moment, "how long have you been up here? Do you remember?"

"Oh, it's been a long time.." she sighed, setting Jigoro back down atop the pet carrier. "I couldn't tell the difference, really. I'm always so bored.. I don't have any real toys, or food, or water.. I remember I was going to eat these guys," she said, looking around at the 3 upright-standing skeleton rats, "but then I wouldn't have even had any friends!"

"She's a ghost, Nikko! Seriously! And these dead rats - Did they used to have, um, skin?" Jigoro asked.

"Oh! They still do!" Kimby answered excitedly. "Guys! Go get your hats!"

Chewart slid all of the way down from her shoulder to the ground, his tiny skeleton paws holding to the kimono fabric as he descended. Chewy and Chewington met up with him, the 3 running upright on hind legs to a rounded mouse hole in the wall.

"This is so cute!" Kimby said to both Nikko and Jigoro, her voice with a tiny hint of a purr. "You're both going to love it."

Nikko looked Kimby over as the cat girl stood in anticipation for the rats to return from their hole. The girl wasn't 100% the kitten she had left behind, but the uncanny similarities made her miss her pet even more now - Feeling bad about not making time to play with it, and leaving it alone in that dark and empty room back home.

"And here they are!" the ghost girl announced as the trio returned, hats atop their little skull heads that looked to be their actual former mouse head skin, now just worn as a cute set of hats. "Aren't they adorable? They look like little pioneers!"

"Maybe I could wear my skin like that too!" Jigoro laughed hard as Nikko gave him a frowning 'no-way' face. "Or at least my hair! That would look cool!"

"I could make you some hair!" Kimby agreed, already forgetting her excitement for the mouse hats. "I can make a lot of things!"

"I like this girl, Nikko! I don't know about these rat things, but she's alright!"

Kimby smiled, oblivious to any insult toward her 3 little friends.

"Well, Jigoro and I can't stay here much longer," Nikko told her as she collected her thoughts again. "We're actually trying to make it somewhere.. We got a little sidetracked in the cornfield out there, so we're already falling really far behind.."

Nikko realized they didn't really have a time frame to stick to, but now the similarities of this girl and her cat back home were making her feel a little bit guilty inside, not to mention homesick.

Kimby stood with the saddest face imaginable. "But you just got here," she said in a quiet, depressing voice. "The Chew Mice and I never get to play with anyone.. It gets so boring up here.."

Nikko looked at Jigoro, who probably would have looked at Nikko too if he could have turned his head.

"Maybe... You wanna come with us then?" Nikko asked, Kimby's ghost-like face lighting up as if she herself had seen a ghost. "Jigoro and I are heading to a place called WaterBury -"

"Really??" she cried out in complete excitement. "We never get to leave the house! Ever! And to go to WaterBury?? That would be so exciting!! Look at this! We made a miniature of it a long time ago!!"

Kimby hurried to a dark corner near the window and dragged a small popsicle-stick replica of the castle into the center of the room -

"Impressive!" Jigoro complimented her, Kimby smiling and nodding her head in agreement.

"It's pretty close, you know? We took a lot of time! We can see it right out the window!"

"It is pretty cool, and we would really enjoy your company... But I know you don't like Tanuki," Nikko reminded her.

"We can get along with him!" Kimby promised, the Chew Mice now looking up at her in silence, their skeleton paws held up in the air in disagreement. "Here - I can even carry his little house!"

"You don't have to," Nikko said as she did so anyways, Nikko then taking Jigoro's skull from the top of it and holding it in her arm again. "Are you sure you don't mind?"

"Of course I don't mind!" Kimby smiled. "This will be the neatest thing that we've ever done!"

Nikko looked at the enthusiasm on the cat girl's face as she stood there, pet carrier in her hand, already ready to leave her home so

Nikko and the NLK

quickly - Just as Nikko had been so ready to leave hers.
   Had her kitten back home been this bored and depressed as well? Nikko wondered - Now watching the 3 'skin-hat' wearing skeleton rats climb up into Kimby's kimono robe - Chewart and Chewington again into the low cloth of her ankles, Chewy into the V-shaped opened breast of the top.
   "Hold my head so I can look at her while we walk!" Jigoro explicitly requested from Nikko's arm.

   Nikko had a feeling that this night was only going to get more and more unusual from here on in...

  ~ But at least with some unusual new friends now ~

"I'm glad you wanted to take a break.. Does this look bad?"

"How can I tell?? I can barely even see.."

"Maybe we shouldn't have -"

"It's too late to stop."

"Do we have any medicine?"

"Yeah. As soon as we start again, I was going to force you to eat it."

"Ha - Thanks.. Are you ready yet?"

"Sure.. I don't know how much longer I can do this..."

Nikko and the NLK

CHAPTER 5

Come On, Stacy!

    Nikko and her party traveled outside of the familiar house, Kimby more than happy to leave her prison behind. The skeleton rat 'Chew Mice' hung from her ankles, the third from her chest, all as excited as she was to be experiencing the outside world at long last.
    Nikko wondered - Why didn't they just come outside on their own before?
    But not expecting anything to make sense in this upside down world, she kept her question to herself and traveled on with the additions, the lazy Tanuki now sound asleep again in his Kimby-held carrier, Jigoro still babbling on in Nikko's cradling arm.
    "Is it just me," he asked, "or are all of the women in this world really good looking?"
    "It's just you," Nikko told him without thinking about it.
    "I mean, aside from that dying lady," he went on, "and maybe the heads of those nurses, this place is like some weird version of my fantasies, don't you think?"
    "Only you would know, Jigoro," Nikko answered, her eyes looking forward to the mountain direction of the baby blue and pink spired castle.
    "Even that Natasha, with the dead skin on, what a body.. And then that ladybug mosquito thing underneath? That was actually really good looking too, in a giant lady-shaped bug kind of way.."
    Nikko looked back over her shoulder to the now somewhat distant cornfields, still wary of the evil duo that had tried to kill them not so long before. In the brief glance, her eyes met Kimby, happily skipping along, excited to be a part of the adventure.
    "So where are we going to go play?" she asked them, a kitten like innocence coming from her apparition body. "Are we going to stop somewhere before the castle? Some place else? Something fun?"
    "Um, the castle might be fun," Nikko pointed to their destination in the short expanse ahead. "They might have games there? We're just heading there to talk to the Queen -"
    "Ooh!" Kimby squeaked in excitement, then talking down to the

skeleton rat in the chest of her kimono. "You hear that, Chewy?? You've always wanted to meet her, haven't you? We talk about it all of the time!" she told Nikko and Jigoro as she directed her attention back to them. "We like to watch the castle from our window - It's such a pretty place.."

"Do you know anything about the Queen?" Nikko asked. "Have you seen her? We've heard that she's really something -"

"No..." Kimby thought hard, squinting her eyes tightly as if trying to remember. "I don't think so.. But I know that she's really beautiful and important!"

"That's all that matters!" Jigoro added on.

"Actually, all that matters is that she can maybe help us figure out a way to get home," Nikko reminded him. "Let's not forget that -"

Though as she spoke, Nikko wondered if that was even what they really wanted. Would they be dead back home, or somehow alive again? And go home for what? Nikko at least had her 'real' cat Kimby, not to mention her over-protective family. Jigoro had.. Well, hopefully his car would still be where they had left it, and hopefully he would be able to return with his body intact again..

But at least in all of the excitement and danger, life had felt like life again, here in this place beyond their underwater graves. By this point, Nikko had already given up trying to figure out where in time they had ended up, and what sort of bizarre cross between her brain and Jigoro's brain that they had found themselves caught up in. As long as there wasn't something always trying to catch or eat them, this Daiyomi world might not be such a horrible place after all.

"Do you hear those noises?" Jigoro asked as Nikko came back from her thoughts, walking through the hilly terrain that rested before the castle and grand mountains. "It sounds like a party.."

"I don't think it's a party, Jigoro," Nikko second guessed him as she continued walking forward and listening, hoping that he didn't start up on his 'Monster Party' talk again.

"I can hear it too," Kimby whispered, craning her black furry cat ears. "It sounds like a big deal! Maybe it's something to play with... Can we go? Check it out??"

Nikko looked over the increasingly uneven landscape, searching for where the sounds were coming from. It was definitely ahead, and now that she heard it closer, it sounded like the sounds of wheels turning and wood squeaking, the beat of music and a voice in a megaphone.

Nikko and the NLK

"Come on! Come on!" Kimby yelled as she skipped ahead, faster than Nikko and Jigoro had been traveling. "Come on, let's go see what it is! This is fun!"

"Kimby, wait up!" Nikko jogged a light jog to keep pace with the enthusiastic cat ghost. "We can't just run into danger -"

"Who says it's dangerous?" she asked, still skipping and letting out a laugh, her smile showing a single white little fang, cutely poking out of her lips on the side. "Let's go see what we can play with!"

"Maybe it's another good looking girl!" Jigoro added, Nikko now outnumbered by the enthusiasts. "Let's go! Faster, Nikko! Fast! Fast!"

With a caution in her jog, and Kimby laughing at the way Jigoro talked, Nikko tried to follow along with their excitement, but found herself far too nerve-wracked to do so.

"Oh, I can't believe it.." Kimby exhaled as she stopped skipping and stared down the hill, her eyes expanding unnaturally large at the sight of the commotion. "I think that they call that a parade... Don't they?? I wanna be in a parade.."

"You're supposed to watch a parade, not be in it," Jigoro explained to her, his head positioned to see down at it as well.

"Then, I wanna watch a parade..." she corrected, the skeleton rats looking on in matching enthusiasm.

Nikko looked down, the only 1 of the party unsure of what she saw. A parade off of a road, just cutting through the dark? There were elephant-size black giraffes and black elephants too, black humanoid characters walking alongside a black military tank, and various black oddities trailing the lead float of a giant black swan. The air above was swarming with what Nikko eventually made out to be a sky's worth of flocking bats -

"Does this really look like a good idea to you guys??" she asked. "I mean, come on! This looks like the Devil's parade.."

Kimby looked at Nikko with a giant, unstoppable smile on her face.

"You *really* think so??" Nikko asked again. "This scary looking thing?"

Kimby said nothing, so overcome with excitement that she couldn't even form a word, and with the 3 bony rats hanging on, she started to skip down the hill and towards the black parade without waiting -

"Is she crazy??" Nikko gasped, in total disbelief at what she was seeing.

"Kimby!" Jigoro called out to her. "Wait! I wanna come too! Wait for us!"

Nikko and the NLK

"This is a really bad idea.." Nikko warned as she jogged and let her momentum carry her down the hill with Jigoro, hurrying to catch up with the excited indoor cat's ghost, along with the sleeping Tanuki's carrier that she held. "We can't just make rash decisions like this.."

"Oh, live a little," Jigoro complained.

"Did you seriously just tell me that? From the guy that killed me?"

"You made your own Death Wish," the skull mumbled to himself, Nikko unhearing but not too concerned with what she missed out on.

Up closer, and the dark parade was worse than it had looked from atop the hill behind - Nikko tried to keep her eyes on the mesmerized Kimby while also watching out for any immediate dangers. This close, and she began to have her doubts as to if this even was a parade. The black tank, the closest thing to her at this point, looking as if ready for war instead of a celebration. Black soldiers surrounded it in their marching formations, no uniforms or armor, just complete black existence in the form of human bodies -

Nikko paused in her gaining tracks.. Her Heart hurt. This was the same as him, that black killer in her mind, the thing that kept haunting her and she could barely ever remember. So unclear in her head, but along the same exact lines. That black of their skin, and of the tank, and of everything else that she could see in this Devil's parade now. It was all the same evil-black lack of color that she would see in her mind from time to time..

"Nikko?" Jigoro interrupted her stand-still freak out. "What are we doing? We can't see the parade from back here!"

"No... This really isn't good.. Jigoro, we have to get Kimby and Tanuki out of here..."

"What's the big deal??" the skull asked as Nikko jogged again, this time speeding up to a run to catch up with the now unseen Kimby and pet carrier.

"I can't explain it," she quietly told him as she closed in on the black tank, the shade of the soulless black overcoming her in ways she had only felt in her head before. "I just feel like there's something wrong.."

Beside and around the black colorless war vehicle, Nikko could see the marching soldiers up close and personal now. They only slightly acknowledged her presence, no discernable eyes or mouths on any of them, only blindly stepping forward and throwing candies and rolled up posters into the non-existing crowds.

Nikko and the NLK

"Grab me some candy, Nikko!" Jigoro yelled, unphased by the dangerous feelings she was having about this. "Can't you just grab a piece?? There's nobody here to take any of it!!"

Nikko ignored him and focused on finding Kimby in all of this confusion - Where had she run off to? It wasn't even that big of a parade -

"Kimby!" Nikko called just as she saw the girl dashing in between the black furred lineup of elephant-sized giraffes. "We have to get out of here!"

"Nikko, this is so much fun!" she yelled back over, barely heard in the strikingly opposite cutesy music that played from the midnight procession. "I'm so happy you brought me out of the house! Already we're having such a great time!"

Nikko tried to make her way through to the happy girl, her 3 Chew Mice on the ground and gathering up skull-shaped suckers that were thrown by the featureless marchers. Fire blasts from both the tank and the harnesses of the colorless creatures, and just as she dodged them, Kimby, with rats in tow, had moved further up the parade again.

"That girl!" Nikko complained. "Why won't she listen?? This is serious!"

"I don't think she's ever even been outside of the house before," Jigoro told her. "Imagine how exciting this must be to her!"

And it was exciting, but Nikko felt she had no time to admire it. The giraffes lined up like a caravan, black-bar giant cages held as jail cells atop their backs.

"Kimby!" Nikko yelled again as she raced past the animals, Jigoro biting at the skull-shaped suckers as they flew toward his carrier's body and bounced away.

"Darn it, Nikko!"

More fire blasting, and Nikko struggled to push her way through the featureless marching army. Though they made no effort to hold her back, between trying to follow Kimby through the offroad route and the small mass of animals marching in it as well, it was nearly impossible to navigate through the constantly changing maze. And then, just as her frustration was about to reach the next level -

"STOPPPPPPP!!!!" came a screeching voice over a megaphone, layering atop the cute music, and the entire marching army of the parade came to a mechanically complete stop, even the animals understanding the sudden command.

"What was that all about?" Jigoro asked as Nikko fought her way through the standstill parade now, trying hard not to slip over the rolled up posters and breaking candy beneath her boots.

"I don't know, but I didn't like the sound of that voice," she said, disliking the entire situation for the feelings that it stirred within her. "Why did Kimby have to run through, instead of just standing to the side like you're supposed to?"

"GIRL!" the megaphone voice was heard again, it's distinct yell coming from the head float. "TELL ME WHO THE RULER OF THE WORLD IS!"

Nikko was close to making her way to the front, seeing the giant black swan float modified with the folded back wings of a bat.

"WHAT???" the screechy voice asked in a ear-rattling shocked tone, addressing an answer unheard. "SHIVA ANGEL??? THIS IS EXACTLY THE TYPE OF THING THAT WE NEED TO ABOLISH! SAY 'BLACK QUEEN, BLACK STACY!' SAY IT!"

"Black Queen, Black Stacy?" Jigoro repeated to himself.

"Why does that sound a little familiar?" Nikko asked him, now able to make it to the back and around the side of the swanbat parade float, running around to it's halted front.

"That was on those posters back home!" he told her. "The poster with the girl sticking her tongue out?"

And as they came around the front, they could see Kimby cowering down before the front of it, a featureless black marcher on both sides. Atop the swanbat float, standing in an elevated middle platform, was the girl that had somehow been featured on the 'Black Queen, Black Stacy' posters spread all over the club's alleyway in the real world back home.

"That's her right there! Holy cow, look at that outfit!!" Jigoro said in approval to himself. "Even better than the rainbow bikini..."

The girl looked like yet another fantasy of his, now a cartoon witch - Black furry boots and gloves, a black rubber bikini with a white skull and crossbones design over her fading-trace-of-a-tan skin. Her hair was wavy long, a mix of blonde with an underlaying contrast black. There was even a black and white bikini-matching eyepatch over her right eye, and atop her head was something like a cartoon witch hat, black and bent at the top, a black crown design upright in the circle atop the brim.

Another eyepatch wearing girl?

"AND WHAT ABOUT YOU??" the girl directed her commanding voice toward the skull-carrying Nikko, amplified through a black

Nikko and the NLK

megaphone similar to Jigoro's microphone technique. "WHO IS THE RULER OF THE WORLD??"

Black colorless marchers could be seen surrounding them, holding up unrolled posters from the parade toss - The same exact 'Black Queen, Black Stacy' posters as seen before.

"Say it's her!" Jigoro instructed Nikko, barely heard from her arm with the high volume music. "Tell her what she wants -"

"Be quiet, no.." Nikko answered. "WE'RE ACTUALLY HEADING TO SEE HER NOW -" she shouted in her best yelling voice, keeping an eye on the whimpering Kimby. "HER NAME IS SUPPOSED TO BE SHIVA ANGEL -"

"YOU IDIOT!!" the witch screamed out, jumping up and down like a child. "WHY DOES EVERYONE STILL SAY THAT?? THAT'S WHY WE PUT ON THIS STUPID PARADE! CAN'T ANYBODY LEARN??"

Nikko made eye contact with Kimby, the Chew Mice taking cover within her robe, a few candy suckers protruding from her outfit.

"BLACK STACY IS THE ONLY GIRL YOU NEED TO KNOW!" she told them, 1 leg bent at the knee, it's furry boot standing at the edge of her float platform. "IF YOU CAN'T REMEMBER THAT, WE'LL BEAT IT INTO YOU!"

There was something in Nikko's mind, something about this Black Stacy girl. It wasn't registering at first, but now that she stood here for a moment, it kind of reminded her of something - No, not something, but someone..

A time from her past -

Not Black Stacy...

'Midori Girl...'

And at this important moment, the unreal world fell away, Nikko drifting off into her memories once more, the reminder of someone from her past bringing her into that deadly world of reminiscence again..

No more Jigoro in her arm, no more Kimby, no more pet carrier or parade.. Even the black sky and hills temporarily fell far, far away ~

And then she was standing there, back in her past.

~ Maria ~

That was her friend's real name, though she went by the in-ring name of 'Midori Girl,' and Nikko found herself standing back in the memory of her friend's prowrestling days. It was a small venue, a city athletic center, and a small crowd sat around on folding chairs only 3 rows deep from the ring. She could see all of the faces that she had never met, always sitting in their same spots, never missing a show. And there was Richard Allan, sitting in the second row, drinking a soda even though he was trying not to drink as many at that time back then.
    She saw herself, only a few years younger than now, standing at the vendor tables, talking to Maria, done up in her wrestling gear as Midori Girl. Memory-looking-back Nikko smiled as she remembered this day, Maria making her in-ring debut, trying to sell those Midori Girl t-shirts before anyone had even seen her wrestle yet. Nikko and Richard had been out to support her in full force, and she had 2 shirts ready for them - A small shirt for Nikko, and another for Richard the way he had always worn them, the sleeves cut off in his own style.
    Always so thoughtful - Though even back then, Nikko had often wondered about their connection.
    And then the show began. Nikko was back in her seat beside Richard, matches going, everything moving so fast in this impromptu recollection - Faces blurry, sounds blurry, wrestling moves and the cheering fans..
    It dawned on her what would be happening momentarily again, and her fond remembering turned somber at the thought. The same thing again, the same thing as always. Why did it have to keep happening, even after 'death?'
    The time soon came for Midori Girl to wrestle, making her entrance to the ring in a green version of what Black Stacy had been wearing - Green furry boots and gloves, the green skull and crossbones rubber bikini, and even a matching eyepatch. Though not wearing a witch

Nikko and the NLK

hat, her hair was a similar long wavy as well, though blonde with a matching green instead..

Memory-Nikko was standing to cheer, Richard Allan too, holding a neon green sign for 'Midori Days,' the wrestling hold that Maria had said was going to be her finishing move.

The match went by faster than it had in real time - Nikko couldn't even remember the opponent, so the match was Midori Girl wrestling an indistinct placeholder. And as it continued, the room began to fill with a ground-covering smoke effect that was usually used for the wrestler's entrances.. But it wasn't the same effect, this was a black engulfing smog, filling the ground and lurking up the walls, the crowd of course oblivious to the new component of the old day -

+ It was time, the lights flickered save for 1 above the beat-up ring, Nikko already expecting what would happen next.. +

The dense smoke filled the ground and air like a tarring syrup, and the Black Knight appeared at the wrestler's entrance, fire blasting around him the same way it had been blasted at the parade. The spectators stared at the ring, unknowing to the unseen intrusion that was taking place.

Nikko held in her cry, helpless in these scenes of yesterday as they were taken from her. She looked to herself, so happy and cheering for her friend in the ring, the green-bikini Midori Girl putting on such a great first match - Living out the first day of her dream, right there in front of their watching eyes..

And now the dream would burn to the ground. The distorted black armored creature stalked it's path to the ring, battle axe in it's hands.

This was it - Black smoke engulfed, all lights out but 1, and now the Devil man cut down the 3 ring ropes as he entered, the ropes dropping limp by the turnbuckles.

Midori Girl, unchanged, had locked her opponent in the Midori Days finishing hold, the unremembered wrestler then tapping out, and Nikko's friend Maria jumping to her feet, hand held up in victory by the referee -

Nikko and the NLK

Fire consumed the room, fans cheering as their skin charred from their bodies..

And Midori Girl stood there with her hand raised high, the beginning of her dream and journey, smiling out to the few-years-ago Nikko and Richard Allan in the second row..

The battle axe swung, cutting Maria's top from her bottom half -

Still smiling, fighting back the happy tears in her eyes -

Crashing in pieces to the blood stained canvas of the burning ring -

The memory of Nikko being there with Richard Allan even burned now, their 'Midori Days' sign crumbling in ash, their skin and hair ablaze as well.

And before another yesterday faded to black, the final sight of the memory-killing invader stood tall over Maria's halves, grinding his axe into the cold-cut pieces of blood, skin, and green rubber bikini..

And all went to black ~

Again.

The memory of Maria's first match now destroyed and gone forever from Nikko's Heart and mind..

"...and she's like," a voice came into her unconsciousness, "ok, I'll take my top off - Isn't that what *normal* girls do?"

Nikko opened her eyes from her sudden memory loss -

"Nikko!" Kimby cried to her, the world of Daiyomi coming back to her mind all at once.

"Why do you keep falling asleep at the most inopportune times?" Jigoro asked, his skull now sitting at a fuzzy floor. "I was just telling everyone about Natasha taking her shirt off for me," he said, Nikko looking around and taking in her surroundings.

Nikko and the NLK

Where were they? Shoot! It was 1 of those cages attached to the giraffes, the floor an uncomfortable wide-yet-tight animal's back - And 'him??' Why was he here with them??

"It's a fascinating story," the donkey that had appeared earlier in the elevator agreed, "but I really do believe that what I'm offering you is far beyond just 1 girl taking her top off."

"Hang on," Nikko told the group, sitting up as she was now fully aware. "How did this happen? How did we get up here??"

"Nikko," Kimby sat with her legs folded beneath and the rats atop her lap, the parade's skull shaped suckers in all 4 of their mouths, "you fell asleep on us! You should have told me you were that tired! I would've let you take a nap at the house."

"I wasn't sleeping, Kimby -"

"I tried telling everybody how you just pass out sometimes," Jigoro said to her, seeming to be quite at home in the middle of this still as of yet unexplained dilemma. "Dorchester over here told me that he's heard of something like this before."

"Yes, it's not the first time," the Burrow explained, his miniature body prancing over to her in the small confines of the black bar cage.

"No offense, but I don't really care what you have to say right now," Nikko uneasily stood up and held the cold bars, looking down to the black parade marching again. "Are we hostages or something?"

"Royal prisoners," Jigoro explained to her. "All thanks to Kimby, here."

"Royal prisoners??" Nikko repeated.

"That Black Stacy girl wanted to know who the 'Ruler of the World' was, and we all said Shiva Angel.. Well, Dorchester didn't, he wasn't here yet..."

"Yeah, I remember that - But how did that make us her prisoners? I don't understand."

"She wanted to hear you say that she was the Ruler of the World," the Dorchester Burrow explained. "It's pretty easy to figure out."

"I just said I remembered that part," Nikko said in frustration, feeling like she was in the back of the ambulance all over again. "But wasn't there anything we could've done to avoid this?"

"Royal prisoners? Hello?" Jigoro said with a pause so that Nikko could think. "That means that we might get a fast track straight to the castle! Isn't that where we want to go anyways?"

"I think it's so exciting," Kimby chimed in.

"Well I suppose it's 1 way of getting there," Nikko said, not so sure of this as the best route. "But why do you think she doesn't want to hear that Shiva Angel is the Queen? And who is she supposed to be, even??"

Jigoro sat in silence, not thinking that far ahead.

"And what's with you?" Nikko asked, looking at Dorchester again. "Did you get caught by her too?"

"He just appeared out of the air in here!" Kimby explained for him in her excitement. "Like a little donkey magician or something.."

"I decided to re-extend my offer to you," he proclaimed, sounding when he talked as if reading his lines off of a script, "even if you didn't stick around long enough to really hear it the first time.. And now *especially* that you have a certain *animal*..."

Nikko said nothing back, looking him over and seeing her collected friends stuck here within the traveling giraffe cage.

"I think we should agree to it," offered Jigoro, filling in the silence as usual.

"A wise skull!" the Dorchester Burrow called at him. "My offer, as your friends here have already heard, is to offer you the 1 thing that you truly only want here - An escape from all of this?"

"...Sure, but what exactly do you mean when you say that?" Nikko asked, unsure and still skeptical of the Burrow from his previous appearance.

"Well," he went on, clearing his throat as he made his presentation, "consider what I am. Just a donkey, as you like to say? No.. I am a Dorchester Burrow.. That is, I am a creature that exists in time, that exists for just the moment, burrowing *into* the time that you exist in right now."

"He told us this while you were sleeping.. I didn't understand it," Kimby confessed to the arms-folded Nikko.

"It's nothing complex," he addressed the cat girl. "Everyone, haven't you ever wanted to live in the moment? Things can only get worse, they say, so why not push a pause button, and climb right into where you're at? Your life must hit the end of the road someday, so why not pull over somewhere comfortable?"

Nikko looked away from the enigmatic donkey and to the passing land. It was already the dark forest that had been at the foot of the mountains and WaterBury. She could see that the gate of the cage was padlocked, leaving her only option to listen to the untrustworthy animal.

"I hear what you're saying, but what exactly are you asking us to do?" she asked, looking down to the pet carrier and seeing Tanuki sleeping deeply with his tongue out.

"Burrow into the moment with me..." he repeated. "Step into time, step sideways into my Pocket in time, and let the everyday rush of life pass you by.."

"Nikko, it sounds like a pretty good deal," Jigoro told her. "Don't we want to get out of this world anyways?"

"I thought you were just satisfied that we were being taken to the castle?" she asked, unsure which way he really felt.

"Well, that too.." he said, obviously confusing himself. "Maybe we can take a peek into this Pocket?"

"No peeking!" the Dorchester declared to him instantly. "This is a very definitive matter! Something not to be taken lightly!"

"I don't think that I want to go.." Kimby told everyone. "You guys can go, but why do I want to stay in the moment? I've been doing that my entire life - "

"Excuse me?" the Burrow asked, sounding put off by the ghostly cat girl. "Why would you pass something like this up? It's especially great for young, healthy-body girls! Just do it.. Just come on inside with me?"

"Yeah..." Nikko said and trailed off, now completely convinced that she wanted no part in it. "I'm thinking we're going to take a pass on this."

The Dorchester Burrow looked as if he was going to make another pitch, but then chose to keep his words to himself, his brown-red fur looking redder as he boiled over in contained anger.

"Hey, if it was up to me," Jigoro consoled him, "I'd say we all come in with you. I don't really understand how it works, but I'm always up for hanging out with a talking donkey - Er, Burrow!"

"Sorry," Nikko answered for everyone, "but not this time. We're fine being prisoners, thank you."

And without another word, the infuriated Dorchester Burrow leapt up on his hind legs into the air, entering into an unseen opening, and then with a moving bulge in the space, he vanished without a sound.

Kimby got up from her spot, the Chew Mice standing with her, and waved her hands through the air where he had leapt to.

"He's got some sort of magical powers..." she marveled, turning then to Nikko and smiling her 1 fang animal smile. "He's so cool.."

"Well, if he comes back again," Jigoro asked in a complaining tone, "can we go next time? I really want to see what this 'Pocket' looks like.. It must be like his house or something."

"Let's just worry about WaterBury now," she directed him. "I'm really not sure that this is the best way to meet the Queen. And I still don't understand why we got in trouble for saying who the Queen was."

"The 'Ruler of the World,' you mean," Kimby corrected her.

"Yeah," Nikko said. "Whatever she is."

Past the Burrow's disturbance now, and after deciding not to wake Tanuki to see if his illusions could help, Nikko decided to just sit back and see where the parade would take them. Her mind was still out of sorts from the most recent Black Knight intrusion, again the exact event unremembered, but the lasting image of him burned within her head.

"Same things again?" Jigoro asked, figuring it was the same as always.

"Mm-hmm," she answered, not even bothering to explain how she couldn't remember again, or how it felt like something had died and was missing inside of her in the aftermath.

Just stare off into the passing distance..

The castle drew near, the parade passing through the forest at a decent pace, most definitely heading there as Nikko could see the baby blues and pink spire tops, just over the back of the front-vision blocking swanbat float that preceded them.

Even though captured now and 'royal prisoners,' at least for the time being, this was 1 of the few moments so far where Nikko could stop moving and just soak things in.. The passing woods, masked in the seemingly unending night's darkness - The trees barely blowing in what felt like an autumn wind, not much different then back home - And looking around at her companions now, what an unlikely group they were. The talking skull of the friend that had killed the both of them, the sleeping illusion-casting Tanuki, the pale ghost cat girl of what felt like her pet back home, and the 3 cartoon style bone rats that the cat girl called 'Chew Mice.'

What had Nikko gotten herself into?

At least things were different for a change, versus the everyday staring at the walls and ceiling back home. She couldn't remember how many times she would wish for something exciting to happen, for a ghost or anything, something to mix up her life from the rut that she had made. Even back when Jigoro came to pick her up, it was always just the same things over and over. To the club, a movie, wherever. And in the end, she would always come home to the realization that she just couldn't get away from the thing she hated the most.

But out here, it was feeling like things were different. It was like living in a book, not liking every page, but never knowing what to expect next. And that in itself was almost something worth living for -

~ Even if this was all after death.. ~

As her mind wandered, her hands holding tight the bars of the black giraffe prison, the makeshift parade route led them through the thin remains of the forest and up to the very front of WaterBury. This close it was even more amazing than any of them could have imagined, like a soft color fairytale castle, straight out of a theme park or right off the frosting of a birthday cake. And in contrast, there was the black plane extending outward from the place of it's crash - The same distortion black of the tank and marchers and parade that carried them in now. Nikko tried to look, but could only look away in the familiar discomfort.

"What kind of an idiot crashes an airplane into a castle like that?" Jigoro laughed as it came into his top-of-the-pet-carrier sitting view. "How could you even angle that into here like that?"

"Maybe it bounced off of the mountain," Kimby suggested, looking past the castle and to the vast mountainscape beyond.

Nikko let them wonder as she took it in herself, leaving her brief enjoyment of this world to be on guard again, the parade making it's way into the front black gate of the castle. This was the only lead they had so far, the name of Shiva their only connection other than the rollerskating girl to their world back home. Wouldn't it more than likely just be a coincidence? Going on 1 of Jigoro's many obsessions for her only real lead was probably not the best idea, but it was too late to start second guessing all of that at this point.

Baby blue brick walls as the castle interior was now before them. The parade came to a slowing halt, the castle gate closing behind the tank as it was the last to pull in, and now the Giraffe stood still, silent and resetting the weight around each of it's 4 legs off and on.

"Well, now what.." Jigoro complained more than asked, just sitting there until Nikko picked him up into her arms. "I really think we should have listened to me about listening to that Dorchester."

Nikko and the NLK

"Just hang on a minute," Nikko eased him. "We at least made it here, so let's see if we can explain our story to the Queen. The Shiva Angel Queen, not that 'Black Stacy' girl.."

And there they stood for a bit of time, the voiceless and featureless black marchers from the parade going about the castle before them. The black elephants and other black fur giraffes were led off through stable-sized corridors, eventually even the tank and black swanbat float driving off, leaving only the encaged group of Nikko and her companions atop the remaining giraffe.

"... Have you ever seen an animal like this?" Jigoro asked around, possibly just making conversation as they sat waiting for something to happen. "I've seen, like, some really hefty animals before. But this guy is bigger than a whale, don't you think, Nikko? And who's seen 1 of these things with black fur before? It must be like a hair dye or something -"

"Quiet, Jigoro, I think they're coming now," Nikko said as she saw 2 shadow people come to the reigns of the lone remaining giraffe.

They were nearly the same as the others, though these 2 shadows had the distinct outline of a feminine form - Almost the black design of a maid's dress ruffles.

"Can we see the Queen now?" Nikko yelled to them, no answer as they led the creature and the cage that it carried down a far hallway straight ahead.

"I think they're ignoring us.." Kimby complained as the Chew Mice climbed back into their safety positions with her, the 2 to the ankles and 1 to the chest. "Hello? Can you hear us??"

"Don't even bother," the skull told her. "You just have to know how to talk to the ladies, that's all -"

"Please don't tell them to take their shirts off," Nikko interrupted, interrupting Jigoro's new way of introducing himself to the girls of this world.

"I don't think they're even wearing clothes... Are they?" Kimby wondered.

"Well the shapes of these look like they're maids or something," Nikko said what she had been assuming. "They look like they have skirts on and those little maid hat things.."

"I can't tell..." Kimby studied in disappointment, looking eagerly down toward the pair. "They look like walking shadow people.."

Nikko and the NLK

As they helplessly looked on, the giraffe was led down the blue brick hallway, the colors lit by unseen lighting, and the entire path illuminated until a wide open throne room opened up before them.

"Oh ~ This is *beautiful*," Kimby purred as her sheltered eyes took it all in. "This is like what I dream about!"

It wasn't what Nikko had expected, but then again, maybe it was. The blue brick room, a mix-match of cutes and darks, pinks and blues, and everywhere decorative bats and skulls. There were black army vehicles sitting idle and pink vases with blue flowers. Black furred animals were also there of all designs - From bears to gorillas to ostrich, all in the same black missing blur of a color. Lined against the side walls were pink girl-shaped suits of armor alongside blue boy-shaped suits of armor, and then black 'living' suits of armor - The same featureless shadow people now standing posed as statues, their legs quivering from what was assumed to be a difficult chore.

And there, surrounded by what looked to be all of these things as her subjects, sat Black Stacy, sitting atop the stair walkway to her end-of-the-room throne. Beside her, atop a cushion on a matching royal chair, was what looked like a black goliath beetle sitting as if it were a King.

-Thankfully not as large as Natasha and Bixby's -

"I want to speak with the sleeping girl!" Black Stacy instructed her servants, speaking for the first time without the megaphone, and assumably calling for Nikko.

The black giraffe bent it's legs and came down in a cringe-worthy fashion to a sitting position. What looked like a shadow military man, featureless skin and clothes with just the shape of a machine gun, came to the back and unlocked the padlock, waving for just Nikko to exit with him.

"You sure you want to go alone?" Jigoro asked as he was about to be separated from her for the first time. "You can wear me out on your head if you want."

"No," Nikko turned him down as she followed the shadowed soldier out. "Let me get to the bottom of all of this on my own. I don't even know if we're in the right place. Plus, you'll probably just tell her to take her top off.."

"Give me a little credit!"

The guard escorted Nikko from the cage and down the baby blue carpet, locking the padlock again of the husky giraffe cage.

She walked alertly past the black furred beasts, military vehicles and the awkward statues. The statue shapes, kind of in an uninspired way, reminding her of the thing that lurked within her head -

"State your name, and why you were so tired in front of me!" the girl with the black crown witch hat and skull and crossbone bikini demanded, the blacked-out machine gun guard leading her now straight up the throne stairs.

"I'm Nikko," she introduced herself, "and I wasn't sleeping.. My friends and I were headed here to meet -"

"Don't say it, Nikko!!" Kimby called out from the giraffe cage behind.

"It's ok!" Nikko reassured her as she continued, standing now 1 step down from the throne-sitting girl. "Is this WaterBury? We were on our way here to meet Shiva Angel."

"... So," Black Stacy growled as she stood up and adjusted her bathing suit, Nikko then noticing 2 small fabric strings hanging out from the right side of her mouth, "*you* want to meet Shiva Angel? Just some girl with a shirt and tie off of the street?"

Nikko stood quietly, nodding her head and trying not to look at the side throne of the little beetle. Standing this close to the black crown witch hat wearing girl, she could smell a fragrance of black licorice upon her.

"So you don't have a clue how to move your way up the rankings," Black Stacy said. "You can't just walk up to the Ruler of the World and expect to get a title shot, you know! It takes a lot of hard work and discipline.. Sometimes, someone comes along and gets a shot out of nowhere, and all of the really talented, hard working people are like - 'Huh, what? How did this happen? We worked so hard!' - But things like that aren't going to happen now that I'm in charge around here! Do you even *know* what an arm-drag takedown is?"

"What?" Nikko asked, wondering how professional wrestling was even relevant to this conversation. ".. Yeah, that's a wrestling hold.."

Black Stacy looked flustered. "Listen - Don't show off - Everybody knows what it is, so it doesn't really matter that you know."

"Then why did you even ask me? Look, I just need to see Shiva Angel -"

"You say her name so lightly to me?" Black Stacy complained, seeming to get more and more fired up the longer that they talked. "Do you know what they call me, when they aren't calling me 'Black Queen,' or another really cute pet name? Do you? They," she said, waving her hand to suggest the featureless characters and animals that didn't speak, "call me the 'Bottomless Kiss,' Black Stacy! And as your punishment, you're going to find out why! Guards! Hold her still!"

2 weaponless shadow bodies came upon her and held her in place, Nikko finding it nearly impossible to move in their vice grips. Having them right there and in her face was almost too close to the look of the Black Knight in her lost memories - That void of substance, the illusion of something solid that nearly looked like a hole.

"Someone else!" the 'Bottomless Kiss' Black Stacy called out. "Grab her legs!"

"That really isn't necessary!" Nikko yelled as 3 waiting shadows fell over each other and ran to get at her first, 1 finally diving and holding on to her legs in a most uncomfortable manner. "Hey! watch it! Do you really need to have him do that??"

Jigoro could be heard yelling something back from the waiting cage, but Black Stacy's voice overpowered the sound and blocked it out to Nikko, who was now in a bit of a panic, held against her will.

"The Bottomless Kiss is a secret technique that only 1 beautiful lady can possess," Black Stacy bragged, reaching her furry black glove to the fabric strings hanging from the corner of her lips. "Born out of a tragedy that should have ended her life, during a moment when she was tormented by the little things that haunted her.."

She then pulled and removed an impossibly long black handle sword from her mouth and throat, the 2 strings attached hanging from it's hilt.

"No-no-no..." Nikko said wide-eyed, trying to step backwards as the shadowed person behind held her legs in his uncomfortable groping manner. "We should talk things through instead of this.."

"Nikko!" Kimby could be heard yelling. "What's she doing?? Are you ok?? I'm sending Chewy out there!"

"Relax!" Black Stacy screeched as she stabbed the long sword into the ground beside her throne. "Calm down - I'm not going to use this on you, I just wanted to get it out of my mouth!"

Nikko breathed a sigh of comfort as the black gloved hand let go of the sword, now protruding from the throne's floor.

"Besides," she went on - "I had to clear my throat so that I could do this... BOTTOMLESS KISS!!"

And as Nikko tried to lean back, the skull and crossbone bikini-clad girl lunged at her, her pouty lips puckered up and her non-eyepatched eye closed in await of the attempted kiss -

Nikko and the NLK

   Nikko forced herself harder to pull away, but nothing worked in the grips of the shadow people - Why was Black Stacy coming at her so hard?? It was like she was going to tackle her!

   - And then, in the blue bricked throne room of what was supposed to be Shiva Angel's castle, the sword swallower Black Stacy met Nikko closed-eye to open eyes, her puckered lips to Nikko's sealed closed lips -

   And everything fell away so fast.. Falling inside, but not in the way that she fell into her memories - This was different. This was being pulled into the life of another, a feeling as if being literally swallowed by the blonde haired black crown witch hat wearing girl before her..
The grip loosened from her holders, but already it felt too late. Nikko could see herself sucked into the mouth of the kissing lady, past the full lips and beyond the teeth, over the tongue and the long way down..

   - A view into the neverending drop of the Bottomless Kiss, the dropoff into the black abyss of Black Stacy's throat -

   Physically helpless as if being held still even though she was not, and her body, or at least her spirit, plummeted in the same sick weightless feeling of the drop at the start of a rollercoaster. Falling so fast that her Heart struggled to keep up - Black shapes racing past unseen in the dark as she dropped deeper down the unbelievably massive throat - And what was this? It was difficult to see, but 1 of the skeleton rats along for the ride??
It was Chewy, as Kimby had been yelling she was going to send.. He clung to Nikko as they fell further and deeper into the bottomless pit of Stacy's petite little body, trying to scream as there was no air left in the lungs to do so -

~ Down ~

~ Down ~

~ Down ~

Nikko and the NLK

All of the way down until everything went away - And then the stop? From complete black to something totally different and unexpected, a temporary world appearing in what must have been a place still within the self-proclaimed Black Queen. It was similar to Nikko's revisits of her own memories, only this definitely wasn't hers, and it was more like.. A music video?

From the black bottomless pit of Stacy's soul-swallowing kiss, to the blue-blue skies of something completely different. Music started up, a similar song to the cute song from the black parade, only this melody with horns playing to the upbeat tempo. Everything blurred into focus, but what in the world *was* this place?

- A scene played out before her eyes -

It was a pink-themed baseball stadium, too small to be major league, with all sorts of people watching. Silent cheering girls, sitting still old people, troublesome looking hecklers, and all different sorts that Nikko could see at once, no sounds being heard other than the music playing. There was something being sung in the lyrics about "Come on, Sta-cy, Come on Sta-cy," with the horns keeping it so up-tempo Nikko couldn't help but almost feel happy.

Though in a situation like this?

She found herself cast into this world, or memory, or whatever it was of Stacy's, sitting down in the outfield front bleacher seat of direct centerfield, only the hip-high railing separating her from the field. The odd assortment of spectators were clapping their hands and yelling all sorts of things, their mouths moving and still not a sound coming out in this unexpected scene..

And there was something different here then when she visited her own memories - It was as if she was actually a component of this thing. Sitting on her lap was a foot high basket of nachos, heaping like a small mountain, smothered in sour cream with black olives and lettuce. Chewy was sitting right in the center of it all, feasting away on the nachos as he looked down at the ball field, taking it all in stride -

"I didn't even know a skeleton could eat," Nikko silently said, right away noticing that even she didn't have a voice in this baseball music video.

Even her clothing was different. She saw it just then, looking down to see what she was wearing - A 'Pink Flamingo Lady-Pirates' t-shirt? Cut off shorts and flip flops? Who picked this out??

Nikko and the NLK

    The music really got going now, some more lyrics and "Come on, Sta-cy" again, and Nikko followed everyone else's eyes down to the field to see the action. Even all of the way back in centerfield, she could see everything up close in this modest sized ballpark. The team up to bat had a large logo on their uniforms that read 'RockHopper Witches,' the fielding team the same 'Pink Flamingo Lady-Pirates' as it said on the t-shirt. Nikko looked around and behind and saw an old fashioned 'hand-turn' scoreboard reading 0 - 0, top of the 8th.. And even though it was silent, save for the ska-like horn music, the crowd seemed to really get into the fielding of the obvious hometeam.
    Nikko, so confused on what this was all about, just sat up straight on her bleacher seat, staying alert with her eyes wide open.
    The pitcher wound up for the pitch, kicking unnaturally high and rocketing a fastball straight in for a strike ~ Oh! This wasn't baseball.. This was fast-pitch softball.. Nikko had gone to games with her family when she was younger, but this was a little bit off from all of that. And the girls that she used to see didn't have uniforms like these either..
    The pitcher, #8 'Sweetcheck,' took another high-kicking windup for the pitch. The team uniform, so small on her body, was a primary light pink with banana yellow for it's secondary color. A yellow-button pink button-up jersey, a pink ballcap, pink short-shorts, and then yellow high-below-the-knee socks with pink cleats to color sort it all out. The RockHopper Witches were similar in their style, just a black for every pink, and a halloween orange for every yellow.
    Too bad Jigoro didn't get swallowed by Black Stacy too, Nikko thought to herself - This was yet another wardrobe design straight from his fantasies.
    Another pitch, another strike..
    It looked like all of the RockHopper players were a white-skin pale complexion, while all of the Pink Flamingo girls looked a bronze sun-baked tan. Another look around the stands, and wow - The crowd was really into this Sweetcheck girl.. Someone held up a sign behind homeplate - 'Stacy Sweetcheck #1! The Pink Throwing Star!'
    And as Nikko looked over the rest of the mismatching crowd, she saw what she assumed were the 2 team mascots, wandering through the stands and entertaining, going along opposite sides of the park, both heading from the baselines toward the outfield.
    A look back to the game, and then a returning look to the team's mascots - Speaking of Jigoro, this was becoming even more like something out of his dreams. Who Nikko assumed was the team

Nikko and the NLK

mascot for the Lady-Pirates was walking gingerly through the crowd at best - She was definitely a beautiful girl, just seeming to be a bit uncomfortable with what she was assigned to do. She had the theme of the 'Flamingo Pirate' - A pink belt corset, her upper body nearly exposed, a pink short ruffled dress that triangled open in the front to show matching ruffle shorts, and tan skin to yellow thigh-highs - The leggings flaring out at her boots like pant legs. Excessive gold jewelry, pink lips, blonde spiraled hair locks with pink highlights, a crooked jeweled crown - And seen even from the distance away, what looked like a sparkling pink flamingo sticker on her right cheek beneath her eye. In her hand was a long sword, a toy flamingo at the handle.

Another pitch, the music played on, and a foul ball out of the stands..

The mascot for the RockHopper Witches, contrary to her rival, was someone a little more brash and cocky. She strode through the stands with a black belt corset and orange handless arm-warmers, glittering black fingernail polish and giant gaudy rings. She wore orange ruffled shorts, no triangled open skirt like her counterpart, but similar style black thigh-highs flaring at the bottoms, just over the tops of her black long-heel shoes. She wore black lipstick and heavy black eye makeup, a black and orange witch hat with black and orange rockhopper-like hair spiking out of the sides, and in her hand a staff-like broom with a little rockhopper penguin character atop it.

The same song continued to the point of annoying, and Chewy remained chowing down on the pile of nachos. The crowd was really getting into this, the tight-uniformed girls battling it out, sitting warm under the sunny sky above, and maybe it actually wasn't so bad afterall. Nikko didn't understand what it was all about, or how long this "Come on, Sta-cy" song would go for, but considering that she had just been swallowed into a supposedly bottomless pit, this was turning out to be an alright alternative to an endless falling..

Eyes back to Sweetcheck on the mound - The highleg windup, the pitch, and... Strike 3! The crowd silently went wild, #8 turning around and waving to her fans, showing her appreciation.

That face..

Nikko and the NLK

Though just seen under the low brim of her baseball hat, it was a more than uncanny resemblance to Black Stacy..

Nikko hadn't really seen the Black Queen for long, but she had just moments ago seen her close enough to get kissed face to face.. And now she was in here, playing the role of this Sweetcheck girl? So tan and so... Pink?

Top of the 8th, 1 out!

Another highleg windup, Sweetcheck's long blonde ponytail hanging through the little opening in the back of the cap, and a base hit down the 3rd base line...

Nikko took her eyes off of who she believed to be Black Stacy for just a moment, instinctively following the ball, and then what was the commotion? Down the field line, the Lady-Pirate mascot was having trouble with a rowdy batch of fans - 1 pulling her in by her arm for an unwanted kiss, the lady just escaping him to be tossed down and across another's lap. The scrubby man pulled up the rear of her short dress to slap her hard across her backside! She composed herself and walked away, readjusting the still crooked crown at her head..

That poor lady - Nikko looked away as most fans sat unphased, looking then over to the opposite baseline and the Witch's mascot, who was busy dealing with fans in quite the opposite manner. Though unheard, it looked like she was yelling and winning arguments with every fan that she randomly selected. Slapping food out of hands, stealing sodas for a sip, and then even dumping a can of pop onto the head of what must have been a 10 year old girl!

Such a contrast of personalities, both making their way on opposite sides toward the outfield bleachers..

Back to the game, and Nikko couldn't believe that she was getting into this. That pitcher, Sweetcheck, whether she was really Black Stacy or not, was pretty good.. Nikko had been a fan of the sport way back, but she had never seen a fastball like #8 could throw. The impact it made when it slapped into the catcher's mit was surreal, or at least surreal in a 'real' surreal type way, not to be compared to the absurd surreality of the events that had been taking place recently.

Another wind up from the tan pitcher to the pale batter..

A swing and a miss, the crowd cheering, though this time Stacy looked to be slightly in a daze. Nikko couldn't see her face, but her body language seemed somewhat less enthusiastic as the inning was going on.

Nikko and the NLK

Eyes back to the 1st baseline and then to the 3rd baseline, the mascots making their individual rounds and coming closer to the bleachers.

Foul Ball!

"Come on, Sta-cy!"

Sweetcheck took longer with her pitch this time, just standing there looking toward homeplate. Nikko, along with the watching crowd, waited, and nothing - The catcher stood up, adjusting her shorts after holding the position so long, and headed up to the mound.
Nikko looked to both sides and the team's rival mascots were both coming through the outfield bleachers now, the Lady-Pirate trying to be nice but looking terrified of every lust-hungry man she passed, the RockHopper Witch getting in the face and staring down anyone who happened to be sitting in the wrong seat..
Nikko's attention went back to the suspended action on the field, trying hard to act absorbed in the nothing that was happening down there. It reminded her of the times when she would go to a wrestling show, trying to avoid the bad guy's stare during their ring entrance, hoping not to get singled out.
Music still played, and down on the field nothing was happening.
The 2 were closer, now seen out of the corner of both eyes.
Shoot..
And the RockHopper Witch was even a few strides closer than the Lady-Pirate..
By now, the members of the home team were heading out and onto the field, meeting the catcher at the mound with the still motionless Sweetcheck. Was she going to leave the game? Nikko tried really hard to wonder about this as the Witch stepped next to her.
She tried not to look, taking a few bites of the rat-sitting nachos..
But as the orange ruffled shorts and black thigh-high flared legs stood directly beside her, she had no choice but to look up.
The lady's black lipstick lips sounded out words large and wide that Nikko couldn't make out. Her heavy black make-up eyes were huge and white, grey pupils staring Nikko down into the bottom of her bleacher -
This was almost scary!
A stop of the silent words, and the black fingernailed hand reached

Nikko and the NLK

for the mountain of nachos at Nikko's lap, Nikko grabbing on to them fast, poor Chewy still snacking inside.

Rage lit the woman's eyes for the surprise defiance. She brought her poreless white face down into Nikko's line of sight, face to face, nose touching nose, and Nikko for the first time wished she was wearing Jigoro's skull right about now..

The moment of uncomfortable feelings lingered, Nikko for the most part hoping she wasn't going to be on the receiving end of a girl to girl kiss again, and then the pale witch pulled back - Her attention taken away as the Pink Flamingo Lady-Pirates mascot made it to the centerfield halfway point as well, now trying to make the pass by the Witch in the tiny walkspace that separated the bleachers from the hip-tall fence..

The Witch was appalled, saying things that Nikko could not even imagine, the Lady-Pirate just smiling unconvincingly down to Nikko and then casting a strange look as she noticed the bone rat in the nachos.

The lopsided argument intensified, seeming to do so with increased horns playing in the music heard. Nikko stared forward to the field, not wanting to be any part of this center of centerfield scuffle. The pale Witch to her left, the super-tan Pirate to her right, and all Nikko tried to look at was the confusion going on down at the pitcher's mound..

Stacy looked like she was sleeping standing up, teammates tapping her shoulders and waving hands in front of her face.. Between that and the small shoving match going on right here before Nikko, the music of the song seemed to be reaching a climax, and in moments the 2 mascots were clashing weapons -

Nikko leaned back, pulling Chewy and his nachos back with her, the flamingo-handle long sword vs. the penguin-handle broom-staff. A soundless banging back and forth, the 2 costumed women fencing like 2 people who had no idea of how to fence -

A big swing by the Witch came in almost slow motion, the music a bit dramatic too, and Nikko ducked her head down just in case. The broom-staff struck the long sword so hard that it sailed out of the Lady-Pirate's grip - Slow motion and dramatic music still. And it flew, flying up and out of the centerfield bleachers, high into the blue-blue sky, over the outfield, over the 2nd base, and the players gathered around the standing-still #8 Sweetcheck looked up in terror.

Some ran, some tried to push the 'Pink Throwing Star' pitcher out of the way, and others walked slowly backwards as the long sword's shadow lingered as if hesitating for the music to catch up. And just as the last of her softball teammates scattered from the airborne blade, Sweetcheck came to, looking up in a disoriented confusion at the descending blade from above -

As the tan, pink and blonde girl looked toward the sky, the flamingo-handled long sword stabbed flawlessly through her right eye socket, stabbing cleanly down through her face and continuing down through the inside of her neck. It plunged completely until just the toy flamingo remained, sitting atop her blood-drenched head as she dropped to her knees, still looking alive, but locked in the looking-up position..
Nikko cringed at the grotesque scene of the girl she believed to be Black Stacy, the entire crowd of the ballpark frozen as if only statues now. The music fading off softly, the 2 mascots by her side dissipating as the horrible visuals faded out.

.....

Nothing and black...

.....

"Come on, Nikko! I'm pulling you out of there!"
"Don't forget Chewy! You swallowed him too!"

These voices fading back.. Everything was black again.. And wet??

"Ok! Remember - As soon as she comes out, everybody be ready! We're counting on you, Tanuki!"
"Do you really think she'll fall for it??"
"We'll give it a shot!"

And all of a sudden, like being born out of a mouth, Nikko hit solid ground in a wet 'thud' of the throat saliva from Black Stacy...
What was this? Back in the WaterBury castle, back in her skirt and shirt and tie, and all around her were her friends again - Kimby, Chewart and Chewington, Jigoro on Black Stacy's head(!), and Tanuki

sitting in the meditation pose with his eyes squinting shut..
Though all metallic silver versions of themselves? Like robots?
"We have been waiting for you, oh great legendary Nikko..." Black Stacy said in a completely fake mechanical voice, the sound coming out through Jigoro's skull with her black crown witch hat nowhere to be seen.
"...Huh?" Nikko wondered, not falling for this but wondering what the point was.
"You have been in the Bottomless Kiss..." Jigoro tried to say in an equally poor robot voice, "for... 1 billion... years... Hahahaha!!"
They all laughed as 1, Black Stacy laughing along with them, and even then the meditating Tanuki gave in with a hissy, tongue hanging out laugh. His eyes opened, and the poorly planned 'future' illusions of everyone fell away back into their typical appearances.
"Wasn't that hilarious?" Kimby laughed, the 2 rats jumping around and pointing out that their friend was still missing. "Hey, Stacy? Where's Chewy at? You forgot to get him out too!"
"I'm sorry! Hang on a sec, Kimby," the Jigoro skull-wearing rubber bikini girl told her, Nikko wondering when all of this newfound friendliness had happened.
"Get ready to watch this!" Jigoro told the freshly returned and now standing Nikko, Black Stacy removing 1 of her black fur gloves and sticking her exposed right index finger down her throat, through Jigoro's open jaw.
A few unlady-like choking noises, and then a bent over heave, Chewy then falling out of her mouth in a small wet throw-up puddle..
"Wasn't that awesome??" Jigoro begged Nikko, a thrilled emotion across his face as well as Kimby and the animals.
"Is that... How I came back out?" Nikko asked, slightly grossed out and checking her slow drying saliva-damp clothes.
"Yeah, it was!" he exclaimed, excited to tell her so. "I don't even know how you fit through our jaws, but it was awesome! I threw you up, Nikko! Through her mouth, and then through mine!"
Nikko stood there, half in disgust and half in confusion about the get-along gang before her.
Black Stacy went to taking Jigoro's skull off from her head, her blonde and black hair and eyepatch now exposed again, and she held Jigoro for a moment, face to skully-face.
"Don't kiss me, you sword swallower!" he laughed in jest, Black Stacy wiping a small bit of spit from the corner of her lips and going in

for a fake kiss, instead licking her long tongue over his skull forehead.

"You have to be kidding me," Nikko cringed out loud as the over the top scene of close-friend goofiness was happening, Stacy then tossing the hysterically laughing Jigoro over into Nikko's arms. "Did I... Miss something here?"

"If you had just told me about everything," Black Stacy explained, replacing her furry black glove and Chewy returning to his curiously-sniffing friends, "I wouldn't have swallowed you, silly girl! You're like a big sister to me now!"

"Whoa.. Hang on," Nikko took a step back to take this all in. "A few minutes ago you were sending me into a bottomless pit -"

"Kiss!" Kimby interrupted, obviously a victim of the Black Queen's charms as well. "It's a Bottomless Kiss, Nikko! It's totally different!"

Nikko looked at Kimby in disbelief, Kimby looking back with her innocent ghost-lip smile.

"Well, you were gone for more than just a *few* minutes," Black Stacy turned and walked over to the side of the black tank - A white skull and crossbone image now also seen on the back side of her bikini bottom. "And once your friends told me all about you, I realized that I had made a terrible mistake! So after hanging out for a little while, we brought you back up.."

"You guys hung out before you brought me back up?" Nikko asked, feeling strangely unimportant here. "And where did you even send me to? It was like I was stuck in a music video down there!"

"Seriously??" Jigoro asked from Nikko's hands. "That's so crazy! I want to go next!"

"Oh, I don't know.." Stacy looked up as if looking through her brain. "I usually associate my thoughts with music from those parts of my life. Was it the zoo? Miniature golf?"

"What? No.. No, it was a softball game. It was this team that had -"

"Oh, great, not *that* game..." Black Stacy slapped the palm of her gloved hand onto her forehead. "Was it the August 18th game? Top of the 8th?"

"I don't know.. It was really nice weather, and this pirate mascot lady -"

"Crown Mina," Stacy named her.

"Ok.. And a witch mascot -"

"Polar Mina," Stacy named her as well. "So it must have been the game where.." and she ended her sentence there, sliding her thumb against her throat in the death signal gesture.

"Yeah!" Nikko agreed. "And the girl looked just like -"

"Man.." Black Stacy interrupted. "Of all the bad memories for you to land in, that would be at the top of the 'don't see it' list.. Yeah that was me, the 'Pink Throwing Star,' Stacy Sweetcheck."

"What are we talking about?" Jigoro asked, sounding as if he knew, but not really sure.

"She already told us, Jigoro!" Kimby reminded him. "Remember? The sword through her eye and throat?"

"Oh, yeah! Sorry!"

"You guys already talked so much that you don't even remember everything??" Nikko asked, feeling completely left out from the group now.

"Hey - Chewy's got some type of orange and yellow stuff on him, Stacy.." Kimby noticed, running a finger over the little bone rat as the other 2 looked him over.

"Oh, that's just the nacho cheese," Nikko explained. "He was eating it at the game. I only got to have a bite -"

"But that game was at Tropicaco Stadium, a home game.." Black Stacy recalled out loud. "I don't remember them serving any nachos there... Oh wait! Was it like, a big greasy mess of nachos?"

"Yeah," Nikko described, "like a little mountain of it."

"Oh, geez.. Sorry!" she apologized with an awkward face. "I was eating those during the parade earlier! Some of them probably fell in there instead of into my tummy! Sorry!"

Nikko gagged and looked around with her eyebrows scrunched in disgust, having little clue as to what was going on around here now. Everyone being good friends out of nowhere, a tank just sitting there in the throne room, and all of the parade's other characters now busy making preparations for another trip out or something.

"Getting down to business..." Black Stacy changed her tone as she walked closer to Nikko. "Now would be the time when I ask you about 'him' -"

"I'm sorry?" Nikko asked, assuming she was meaning Jigoro, if anyone.

"Oh, I think you know who!" she expanded. "My man? The No-Life King?"

The group of Nikko and the Black Queen stood in a silence for a moment, Nikko a little confused about what they were talking about.

"I, um, told Kimby and Stacy all about your Black Knight.." Jigoro broke the silence, Nikko's eyes opening wide and her Heart racing.

"Jigoro!" she shouted in a quiet yell. "You aren't supposed to talk about that!"

"Hey, I don't know!" he said back from her hands. "We were about to get swallowed like you did! I evacuated everything that was in my head!"

"He told us his entire life story!" Kimby informed Nikko. "He even told Stacy to take her top off!"

"He's very charming, but what's this about the No-Life King?" Black Stacy asked, a hungry look in her 1 seen eye. "That's why I brought you back up from the Kiss ~ I don't know if you've figured it out yet," she said as she waved her hand around, "but all of this is because of the No-Life King."

"I don't understand what you mean.." Nikko replied, her voice a little shaky, feeling like someone had pulled a rock up and exposed her crawling bugs.

"She's not really the Ruler of the World - Yet?" Jigoro adding on the last word 'yet' as Stacy met him with an evil glare. "But she's the leader of the NLK Cult! That means the No-Life King! That's the guy who's been bugging you!"

"I only came here because of the No-Life King," Stacy went on in explanation. "Do you see all of these weird looking shadow thingys? I don't remember who or what any of them were to me, but I do remember that they used to be things in my memories before he wiped them out."

"What??" Nikko asked, looking at the odd creatures cloaked in their void-like blacks, going about the little odd things that they were doing nearby. "Are you serious?"

"Yeah, she explained everything to us," Kimby said as Tanuki grew bored and wandered back into his carrier. "I didn't even know you had a problem, Nikko! You could've talked to me about these things, you know?"

"Kimby," Nikko said as she tried to keep everything making sense here, "we just met you.. We haven't even had any real time to talk yet!"

"There's only been 1 other person, that I know about, who's ever experienced what we've gone through, Nikko," Black Stacy explained, talking about the now name-revealed Black Knight, the No-Life King. "That was the Ruler of the World, Shiva Angel. Everybody started talking about it - Shiva this, Shiva that - Shiva and the No-Life King, No-Life King and Shiva Angel.. It was really beginning to drive me crazy!"

"Black Stacy," Jigoro added his own commentary, "you are such a romantic, they way you feel so passionate for a guy... Nikko, you could really take some lessons from this girl."

"Aww.." the sword swallower sighed, looking adoringly at the skull. "Thank you, Monster Party!"

They even had time to talk about his nickname??

"While I was out trying to still live my life," Stacy continued, "every day the No-Life King would enter my brain and my memories. And even though I couldn't remember what would happen, I totally knew that something was missing when he left."

"I know, right??" Nikko agreed, now hanging on to Black Stacy's words, this being the first time someone had ever related to her on this. "That's exactly what's going on with me!"

"Then he's moved on again.." Stacy held her head down for a moment. "You know, when he took every happy memory that I think I ever had, I hated him so much, I couldn't stop thinking about him! Then I kept thinking.. And I thought at least I have *something* with him. I keep forgetting everything, but at least I have his really violent visits to look forward to, right?"

"I wish he would have visited me.." Kimby said, sounding as if she was swooning at the romanticized version of this disease by Stacy.

"No you don't, Kimby!" Nikko corrected her, disgusted just a little. "Don't say something like that! He's a horrible thing!"

"But if any of you knew him like I know him," Stacy smiled, "then you know that he at least is a constant in your life. When all of your memories go away, you kinda start to look forward to his cute helmet face.."

Was she sure she was talking about the same nightmare character that had been haunting Nikko? And ruining what might have been the last years of her life?

"And then, once absolutely no more happy memories remain?" the Black Queen posed the question to herself. "No more No-Life King for me. Poof, goodbye. All you're left with are the stupid and bad memories like the 'sword in the eye and down the throat' memory.."

"Well.. At least you can swallow swords and people now, yeah?" Jigoro tried to comfort her during these sad stories. "Having a Bottomless Kiss is pretty attractive to me!"

"Oh, Jigoro.. If it's true I should never see the the No-Life King again," Stacy batted her eye toward him, "you and I will have to get married.."

"Yes! All of my dreams would come true!"

"Yeah, ok," Nikko interrupted the love-fest, "but how come I don't have 'things' like these guys hanging out with me? And what's the deal with you and Shiva Angel?"

"Pumpkin," Jigoro annoyingly addressed her, "allow me to explain. Black Stacy is still very much in touch with her missing memories. There's no need to be jealous! While you seem to just let yours drift away, Stacy holds on to hers for dear life.. She can still see them and even we can see them hanging out with her, caught somehow between a state of existence and suspended existence.."

It was obvious Jigoro was trying to impress Black Stacy, though meanwhile making little sense.

"And as for Shiva Angel," he continued, "how would you feel if you were seeing a guy all of the time, and all of a sudden he just stops showing up? And the next thing you know you hear people say he's visiting some other girl all of the time??"

"You would freaking explode!!" Stacy answered the question in a hot-blooded fury. "So what if it was 'Shiva Angel,' Championship Belt-holder - 'Ruler of the World' - A trampy girl is a trampy girl, and I always hated her anyways! He stops visiting me to start visiting her? So what if I had no more happy memories for him to take away??"

"Well, Jigoro wanted to come meet her because he thought -" Nikko started to explain and was cut off.

"Hey! Nikko! Don't be silly!" he interrupted. "We both wanted to talk to her! We wanted to see if she knew anything about us getting back home.. Even Kimby was wondering too, right, Kimby?"

Kimby shrugged her shoulders in the air, the conversation getting a little too all over the place for her and the Chew Mice to keep up.

"Well, so what happened when you got here?" Nikko aimed to get the conversation over with, the uncomforting shadow creatures still all about. "Did you talk to Shiva?"

"The NLK Cult and I crashed our airplane into WaterBury -"

"That was your airplane??" Nikko asked, thinking of the black jet protruding from of the castle's wall.

"I don't know why," she explained, "but we had it. I figured it was part of my dead memories since it was just sitting around all of the time. So we flew it! All of the way here and crashed it into the place. I came in, totally pumped up with my NLK Cult by my side, ready to wrestle that man-stealing tramp for her belt.. I was going to be the next Ruler of the World! Another happy memory made and I would be watching the No-Life King come roaring back into my life.."

"Ok.. That's a weird plan," Nikko thought out loud as she listened in, "but what happened then?"

"She wasn't here.." Black Stacy sighed in an obvious still-active disappointment. "So, I'm thinking... She'll come back? We wait, we redecorate a little bit, time goes by, and now I'm thinking - Screw it! Vacated title! I declared myself the new Ruler of the World!"

"And no No-Life King.." Kimby added on, standing there seeming to be bored by all of this rapid fire conversation.

"Exactly," Black Stacy concluded with a really fake giant smile. "I'm trying to be happy, but it's not working.."

Fake smile down!

Everyone kind of stood around saying nothing for a few moments, catching their breath and sighing, all in different phases of frustration in the baby-blue brick throne room.

"And now you come along," Stacy stared Nikko down, "finally there is another person that the No-Life King visited, right into my waiting Cult. It's almost like destiny. And it almost makes me happy, but not really.."

"So, are you going to, like, try to wrestle me now or something?" Nikko asked, hoping she knew what the answer would be.

Jigoro's eye sockets lit up -

"Wrestle you?" Stacy laughed a little and covered her mouth. "No way! You don't have any belts! I'm just gonna be hanging out with you guys now!"

"You are?" Nikko's jaw stayed open, unsure of this announcement.

"We already decided on it!" Kimby told her, her enthusiasm picking up out of the boredom. "Before you came back up!"

"Yeah, it's really cool!" Stacy explained, becoming more animated as she grew excited to match. "I figure if I hang out with you, and he visits you, maybe he can visit me again too? Or I can tell you what to say, and you can tell him when you see him?"

"Um..."

"And we're going to go see somebody else too!" Kimby added on, standing up straight and ready to go outside again, the 3 skeleton rats taking their positions in her kimono.

"Yeah!" Jigoro spoke up. "It's some old guy in the forest!"

Nikko just stood there in disbelief, feeling like she was still out of the loop with this group around her. How did they all bond so quickly?

Nikko and the NLK

"In the mountains, there's a guy named 'Oyomi' -" Stacy explained. "Other than Shiva Angel, he's like the most important person in the world here. Well, maybe after myself.. Oyomi knows everything about Daiyomi, and I figure maybe he can help with your problem?"

Nikko put her hands up in defeat. "Well, I guess we're willing to try. Coming here to WaterBury was my only plan."

"Good!" Black Stacy sprinted toward her, running up and giving her a bikini hug, Nikko's arms nonchalantly courtesy hugging back.

"Just don't kiss me again, ok?" she asked and then remembered the scene that had just played out with Jigoro. "Or licking. Don't lick me either.."

"Anything you say, Big Sister! Now - IS THE NLK CULT READY TO MOVE OUT??"

The living embodiments of all Black Stacy's destroyed memories rushed together, lining up in a single file line, starting with a man shape nearest to her, and ending back at the end of the room and a bit around the corner. Characters and animals suddenly all waiting in line -

"Ok, now," Black Stacy quietly said, focusing her good eye over to Kimby and the Chew Mice, "you guys want to see something *really* cool? Watch this!"

She bent over halfway forward, lips puckered for a kiss, and as the shadowed memory in front of her bent to meet her halfway for the lip embrace, the character behind it and each in line all placed their hands and / or paws at the person / creature / animal in front of them -

~ All connected now, like some sort of a black ghost millipede.. ~

The Black Queen kissed the first shadow deeply, his body, followed by each holding-on character in line, sucked in effortlessly fast like an ant spinning up the snout of an anteater. All were pulled into the kiss, the elephants and giraffes and the entire NLK Cult, and at last the final shadow of a bear flew in, disappearing behind her suddenly closed mouth - A smile and lick over her lips with her long tongue, and a quick wipe with the wrist of her glove.

"Ta-Dah!" she proclaimed, raising her arms into the air with 1 leg in front of the other, cheerleader style - "What do you think of that?"

"Nikko, clap for me!" Jigoro demanded. "That was crazy!"

"You put the entire group inside of your stomach??" Nikko asked, feeling a little unsure about this procedure.

"Not just the stomach," she told them, now walking up along the side of the black tank. "I drop them in and they can hang on in my throat, or fall down into the bad memories.. They kind of just wander wherever they want.."

"Do they ever fall out of you when you go to the bathroom?"

"Nikko!" Jigoro scorned her. "That's appalling! Why would you ask something like that??"

"I think you forgot someone over there," Kimby told the tank-side stroking Black Stacy, Chewy pointing back from Kimby's chest to the 2 thrones.

"Choochie!" Black Stacy yelled and ran off towards it, the black beetle jumping from it's throne chair and trying to run off. "You little Devil! You didn't get in line for the kiss!"

Nikko and her group watched as Stacy chased the small black bug all around the throne, finally diving onto it and pulling it up with her gloved hands.

"This little guy is my favorite," she told everyone while holding him up to her lips. "Choochie, give me a kiss!"

A small peck on the lips from the beetle to her, and in a quick blurry warp, he was pulled inside as well.

"What a rascal! Ok! So with that taken care of.." Stacy breathed in deeply and removed her long sword from the throne floor, leaning back and swallowing it until only the strings remained at her lips again. "What do you say we rock and roll!?"

"Yeah, rock and roll!" Jigoro shouted in return, Stacy back to them and taking Jigoro from Nikko's hands, placing the skull back atop her crownless head.

"And we're taking my black tank 'Haifish' with us!" she exclaimed, throwing a black suitcase resting on the floor to the top of it, then climbing up to the front and cannon - "Come on, Nikko! Come on, Kimby! Let's get this show on the road!"

Nikko hesitantly climbed up and aboard to the top of the tank, Kimby handing up the pet carrier of Tanuki before struggling and eventually making it to the top with the Chew Mice as well.

"Do you know how to drive it?" Nikko asked, all of them sitting awkwardly at the top, hanging on to the cannon and various latches and grapple points.

"Me?" Black Stacy laughed, sounding as if she was surprised at the question. "No way, silly! I don't even think you can sit inside of it anymore! I just tell it where to go, and then we hope that it knows what I'm talking about!"

"I'm not too sure about this.." Kimby whimpered.

"Onward, Haifish!!" Stacy shouted, 1 arm in the air like a punch at the sky, the other holding to the cannon as she smiled from behind her Jigoro skull mask. "Through Daiyomi, and to the old man Oyomi! Step on it!"

The black tank Haifish sprang into motion, the black void of some sort of forgotten Black Stacy memory, and now their adventure was about to continue at last..

~ Back into the outside world of the world after life ~

Nikko and the NLK

Nikko and the NLK

~ A pounding in the face ~

~ Plates thrown and forks tossed ~

~ Hand held onto the stove ~

~ Something cut across the eye ~

~ Hiding in the bathroom ~

"Will you just open the door??"

"Go away.. It's not fun anymore.."

"It's what we wanted.. Do I have to break it down?"

Nikko and the NLK

CHAPTER 6

Monster Party

Out of WaterBury, and the black tank Haifish was now on it's way into the mountain region behind the castle. Nikko held onto a latch, Kimby sitting on the opposite side with the pet carrier and the Chew Mice, and Black Stacy rode straddling the cannon, Skull Jigoro atop her head in place of where her left-behind black crown witch hat had been.

Did the night ever end in this world? The forest leading up into the mountains was peppered in darkness. Nikko's eyes adjusted and saw trees and chimney streams, distant Japanese Toori gates, and even Shiminawa ropes wrapped around certain tree trunks and heavy boulders.

"Why are there so many Japanese things in this world?" Nikko asked Black Stacy, looking over the low-vision forest as Haifish bore through it.

"I don't know what 'Japanese things' means," she replied. "But even if I did, I would probably just ask you 'why are there so many Daiyomi things in your Japanese things(?),' right?"

"I suppose so.." Nikko reluctantly agreed, not satisfied at all with the answer.

"Well, in any case, everyone should try to stay extra alert from here on in," the Jigoro skull-wearing girl went on, "this forest is known for all sorts of scary things."

"It's not too scary, is it??" Kimby asked fast, Nikko not knowing if she was speaking for herself, or for the 2 timid of the 3 skeleton rats.

"It can be!" Black Stacy proceeded with a spooky-themed voice. "All sorts of wild pigs and mysterious drownings..."

"Wi.. Wild pigs??" Kimby shivered.

"Well, Jigoro and I should at least have nothing to be afraid of with the drownings," Nikko said in her unresolved anger. "Right, Jigoro?"

"Heh..." he struggled from atop Stacy's head. "Well, I'm sure we can at least try not to die again.."

Nikko looked on and thought about that idea - Could they even die again if they wanted to? She had feared for her life when Bixby and Natasha pulled her off of the road.. But could they have even really killed her? Was she still killable after death? She looked off into the forest, listening for sounds but only hearing the sound of their tank..

And then what about Jigoro? She already had no idea how he could do what he was able to do - Especially without any ears or a tongue, or at least even an eye - But what was she thinking? How could he even exist without the rest of his body there at all? And did he in some way have a brain in that hollowed out skull that so easily fit over anyone's head?

...She had to try and remind herself to stop trying to make sense of it all. Looking at the cast around her, she attempted to suspend her disbelief and just see where the road would take her next. And exactly who this Oyomi person would turn out to be.

"Dolphin!!" Jigoro called out, heard loud even over the roar of the black tank's noise pollution. "Nikko! Dead ahead!"

Nikko looked forward and saw the rainbow trail of the rollerskating girl, ahead and shining in the darkness -

"What are you talking about?" Black Stacy asked, seeing in the same direction as the helmeting skull.

"Straight ahead!" he told her. "Don't you see her??"

"I can't see anything," Black Stacy lifted the skull like a visor for a moment, looking straight through with her eye unhindered by him.

Nikko stood up a bit from her position and tried to see, only seeing the back of the rainbows that would linger in wake of the girl.

"I wanna see too!" Kimby looked forward, her head bobbing up and around like a cat watching a bird. "What are we supposed to see? I can't see any - What?? Nikko! What is this?? Ahhhhh!"

All eyes went to Kimby, and there was a moldy green hand severed at mid-forearm, clamping down on her chest and Chewy pounding at it with his bony fist, it then letting go and falling off to the wayside.

"What was that thing?!" she cried out as she brushed her chest off in a freaked out disgust.

"Wow, that was so cool! It looked like a Frankenstein hand!" Jigoro shouted in amazement toward the startled cat ghost.

"You ok, Kimby?" Nikko asked, unsure herself where the hand had come from, looking over to make sure everything was alright.

"That's the type of stuff we have to watch out for!" Black Stacy went back to looking ahead, the low-visibility darkness of the forest leaving everyone but her on edge now. "Strange things are everywhere on this mountain.."

"And now the Dolphin's gone..." Jigoro complained as Nikko noticed the rainbows had vanished as well, Black Stacy not questioning now what he was talking about, and Kimby too scared to even think.

With the sudden appearance of the groping green hand and it's vanishing act, Nikko's eyes were all over the dark forest. The path Haifish traveled on grew thinner the higher up and deeper in that they ventured, allowing the trees and concealment to grow closer to their road. At this close, it looked at times as if the rocks and trees had grown faces - Shadows draping in a warm breeze that made them dance, forming like hungry mouths and expressions across them coming to life.

"There it is again!!" Kimby screamed as she stood up fast, pointing to the front of her side of the tank.

"The green hand!" Jigoro yelled as Black Stacy had already turned to see. "Look out!"

Nikko craned her neck to catch a glimpse and Black Stacy kicked down at it from the cannon, the severed hand crawling by way of it's fingertips back down the front of the vehicle, descending into the darkness and out of sight once more.

"That thing's crazy!" Jigoro shouted in his own discomfort at such a sight. "How can it run around without a body??"

"Nikko, I'm getting scared.." Kimby cried as she crawled her way over to meet Nikko on the other side, dragging the pet carrier along as she came. "Should we wake Tanuki up? Maybe have him make us look really scary?"

"No, no," Nikko comforted the terrified cat ghost. "We can let him sleep - That's what he likes to do the most. And I don't think that little hand could really harm us too much.."

Black Stacy smiled down at the 2 now on the same side, her smile barely visible through Jigoro's half open jaw. Nikko smiled back and then remained alert, Kimby bunching up beside her with the skeleton rats congregating now atop her pale chest. And with this closeness, Nikko couldn't help but stroke her hand instinctively over the scared girl's black hair.

~ Such a weird familiar feeling, so alike to her Kimby cat back home ~

And as thoughts of her Kimby came to mind, she quickly shut them down, trying in a rush not to remember her happy memories if she could.

Nikko and the NLK

The No-Life King..

At least that was what Black Stacy was calling him...

"Nikko! That tickles!" Black Stacy laughed, Nikko looking at Kimby still and wondering what the sword swallower was saying. "Nikko? Kimby? What are you doing?"
And just as Black Stacy with Jigoro's skull looked over her shoulder, Nikko and Kimby looked toward her - And all at the same time they saw the determined green hand at Black Stacy's upper back, trying to undo her bikini top!
"This is too much!!" Stacy screamed and jumped from her cannon straddling, jumping to the same side as the girls and finally freaking out. "Get it off me! Get it off!!"
Nikko leapt up and reached for it, grossed out by it's rotted flesh and broken fingernails, trying to brush it off but not wanting to actually touch it.
"Nikko!!" Black Stacy jumped around, the green hand fumbling with the bra-like latch. "Hurry up! Eww!!! Get it off!!!"
Nikko finally got a good swipe at it and it fell back to the tank's top, scampering it's way beneath her legs and back to Kimby once more, springing up and grabbing onto her chest yet again -
"No!!" Kimby screamed and began to jump up and down, the skeleton rats all fighting and pulling at it, Chewington showing a bit of uncertainty in his efforts. "Nikko! What do I do?? It's so gross!!"
"It's out of control!" Jigoro laughed as he watched in an obvious enjoyment of the scene. "Maybe we should just let it do what it wants to do!"
"Kimby, stand still for a minute!" Nikko hurriedly asked of her. "And Jigoro, shut up!"
Nikko swung at the hand, this time with more force, and it dropped to the tank's top again, Chewy, Chewart and Chewington all still hanging on and fighting it. It scampered again, this time away from the 3 girls, and then quickly flung itself off of Haifish, back onto the forest path below, all 3 Chew Mice in tow -
"My friends!!" Kimby grabbed at Nikko's shoulders. "No! I can't let anything happen to them!!"
Nikko thought fast and then made an instant decision, jumping off before her next thought would be not to do so, and landed down hard on the dirt road they were traveling.

Nikko and the NLK

"Haifish! Stop driving!" Black Stacy commanded the life-of-it's-own vehicle, the black tank then actually listening and stopping so hard that everyone left almost fell off anyways. "Nikko, that's not a good idea!"

"What do you want me to do??" she shouted back as she ran ahead, the sight of the hand just ahead of her - Bouncing around, running on it's fingers, flipping over and back - Kimby's jealous rats fighting it all of the way.

"Errr..." Stacy growled as she watched her sole connection to the No-Life King now running off into the dark forest alone. "Ok, guys. We have to go too!"

"Huh? What?" Jigoro asked, not wanting any part of going off of the tank into the woods. "Can we wait here for her??"

Without listening, Black Stacy lifted Jigoro's skully helmet and then puckered her lips, planting a wet kiss on the cold black void of the black tank Haifish, the entire vehicle then vacuuming into her mouth and throat - Herself, skull Jigoro, Kimby and the sleeping Tanuki crashing to the ground where the now-swallowed black tank had been.

"Ok, don't freak out, everyone!" Stacy instructed, grabbing her suitcase and quickly coming over to the pet carrier, then opening it's door. "Tanuki! Come on, wake up! We need you to help us go after Nikko! Come on! Get up!"

And inside the pet carrier, the sleepy faced Tanuki let out a gigantic yawn, walking out on all 4 legs and taking a look at his surroundings.

"Come on! Put a leaf on your head and be a horse or something, man!" Jigoro demanded.

The still groggy Tanuki blinked his eyes and looked around still, Kimby standing there terrified with the empty pet carrier now back in her hands.

" Here," Black Stacy said and reached into the carrier, "give me a leaf.. Come on, let's go!"

She set the small leaf atop his head for him, and the sleepy Tanuki transformed without using his meditating technique, growing taller and wider, the leaf unmoving at his forehead, growing in size until he was large enough for both Stacy and Kimby, as well as the carrier and suitcase carry-ons.

The fur broke off!

Nikko and the NLK

The body contorted!

A transformation into a giant frog??

"Oh, now this is good!" Jigoro admired as the 2 ladies hesitantly climbed aboard, sitting with their legs gripped on both sides, the pet carrier stacked on top of the suitcase in front of Stacy. "Wake up and find Nikko, Tanuki!"
And as if understanding, Jigoro absolutely sure that he did, the transformed tanuki-frog hopped in a fast enough speed to gain ground on the small-ways ahead Nikko, still in hot pursuit of the hand-riding bone rats.
"This is really weird!" Kimby cried as she wrapped her arms around Black Stacy. "I hope my friends don't get hurt!"
"I don't think they will!" Jigoro said back. "I think that hand just likes the ladies.."
And the tanuki-frog jumped along the increasingly tight wooded path, eventually looking like the Haifish couldn't have managed through it anymore at this point anyway, the dark world of the forest mountain closing in on all sides.
"Nikko!" Black Stacy yelled as they caught up to her. "Get on Tanuki! He can go faster than us!"
Nikko looked as the transformed raccoon dog was upon her, the green hand already now far ahead of the chase. "Great idea!" she told the 2 girls and Jigoro as she swung her body up to sit behind Kimby, holding on to 2 slimy patches of Tanuki's skin as he sped up again. "This is cool! A frog! What about your tank? Did you kiss it?"
"You bet I did," Black Stacy called back behind her. "Hey, what does Tanuki eat?"
"Bugs..." Nikko said and wracked her brain. "I don't know, and I guess probably like lizards or something?"
"Ok! Tanuki, see that little green thing running around up there? That's a really good looking lizard! You catch it and you can eat it!"
"But not Chewy!" Kimby added in, her voice still high-pitched in fear. "Or Chewart! Or Chewington!"
Tanuki jumped around faster, the moldy green hand still off in the dark distance. The slimy animal, with all 3 girls and their talking skull, seemed extra motivated now from it's sleep, thinking of the hand as a dinner trying to run away. More distance closed, the path nearly swallowed up by the mountain forest, and soon the darkness of the

Nikko and the NLK

closing-in overgrowth was enough to conceal almost everything they saw.

"Tanuki!" Jigoro instructed the speeding animal. "Don't jump into any trees! This place looks creepy!"

"Didn't you say that there were drownings here??" Kimby asked from her closed eyes. "And wild pigs??"

"That's right!" Stacy agreed. "And now dirty green hands too, it looks like!"

The party hung on to the bounding tanuki-frog, the path completely gone now, and the mountain ascended even steeper yet. Nikko could barely make out the fleeing hand and rats, Tanuki winding his way through the woods and jumping over fallen logs, giant rocks and small grey statues. Without the rumbling sound of the Haifish, the surrounding sounds of the darkened forest were overwhelming - Animal sounds and late-night bird noises, the sounds of heavy things moving and small things traveling together.

And now something running up alongside them?

"Something's licking my leg! My leg!!" Kimby screamed, once again the focus of unwanted attention. "What is it??"

Nikko looked down and saw a giant forest hog running alongside the Tanuki, huge but still smaller than their frog-illusioned pet animal, 2 white tusks protruding from it's tongue-wagging mouth.

"It's a pig!!!" Kimby screamed as she saw it too, Nikko wrapping her arms tightly around her friend's waist in case she began to fall. "This is too much!!"

"Move faster, Tanuki!" Nikko instructed her animal friend. "We're racing to see who gets the lizard first!"

"Stacy!" Jigoro asked his wearer in the heat of the chase. "Turn around and let me see this! I gotta see this pig!"

Black Stacy took a quick look and both then saw the forest hog relentlessly trying to lick Kimby's kimono-exposed and kicking leg, Tanuki picking up the pace then to leave it far behind.

"Ewww!" Kimby sobbed. "Why is everything here trying to touch me??"

"Maybe because you're an animal too, kind of.." Jigoro offered a guess. "Or maybe because you're really good looking! But so is Stacy! And Nikko too! I don't know.."

The fleeing hand was a bit closer now, throwing itself forward through the trees, everything even more so looking as if it really had a face now. The sound rose up of more running from behind, Nikko looking back and seeing the forest hog joined by others, choosing not to mention anything to the deeply whimpering Kimby.

A jump over rocks of a mountain stream, the hogs behind following, and then back through the face-shadowed forest. Through more trees, past caves, and up ahead at last appeared a clearing in the landscape, the subtle light of a fire and an opening in the woods.

Another red gate came into view, a giant Toori this time, the same Japanese style as Nikko had seen at the mountain's beginnings. It was centered at the front of the fire-illumination and quickly getting closer, the hand in sight now and the hogs holding back, choosing to remain in the shadows of the forest rather than coming out into the dim light.

"Almost got it, Tanuki!" Black Stacy applauded him, patting her furry glove at his side. "Eat that lizard!"

But just as the green hand reached the red Japanese gate and the entrance to the fire-lit clearing, it stopped it's fingertip running at last, something seen standing at the start of it.

Nikko looked as it came into sight - Was it a man? Wearing a white bathrobe? Bending over to pick up what looked like a newspaper?? The tanuki-frog hopped faster yet, speeding up as the scenery rushed by even faster now, gaining on the standing still rat-covered green hand and the odd bathrobed man.

"Tanuki!" Jigoro tried to control it. "Slow down! We're going too fast!"

And at that moment, only a short distance from the hand and man, the leaf peeled from Tanuki's forehead and he transformed back into his normal size and normal raccoon dog self. Now running in place of leaping, Nikko and her group fell hard to the ground below.

"Ow!" Black Stacy yelled as they all rolled to a stop at the forest's opening. "What did you do that for??"

And all of them could only watch as Tanuki ran towards the wrestled down hand, passing it and leaping into 1 arm of the bathrobed man, licking his bearded face like a dog coming home to it's master.

"Oh!!" the man bellowed out, a deep booming voice that sounded like thunder below the clouds. "Tanuki! How are you, my old friend??"

"They know each other?" Nikko asked herself as she and the others gathered themselves and their belongings, walking cautiously over the remaining ground to the base of the sacred gate.

"I hope my friends are ok..." Kimby whispered as she cowered behind both Nikko and Stacy, walking with the carrier and peeking her head around both sides.

"I see you brought some friends with you!" the man exclaimed in his powerful voice, looking up from the licking Tanuki and setting the excited animal back to the ground. "What an... interesting variety..."

"Hi!" Black Stacy waved as they approached him. "You must be Oyomi?"

"That I am," he said as he stood up straight, rolled up newspaper in hand. "These darn things come later and later, you know what I mean?"

Nikko was in disbelief once more. All of these things that she had been seeing, and now here, in the heights of the forested mountain, she was standing in the presence of a man in the legendary shape of a Hanadaka Tengu. He was a tall and heavy being, faded blue skin and a long 4 inch hotdog-like nose. He had white long hair, bald at the top, and a groomed white beard. His body-builder muscles could be seen in the shapes of his white bathrobe, a 3 skull necklace at his chest, multi-skull bracelets, and single tooth clog shoes seen beneath his robe.

"I take it these are all friends of yours as well?" the Tengu asked, looking down at the green hand's skeleton rats that continued to pound at it.

Tanuki growled slightly at their sight, then returning to his panting excitement to see this man again.

"Chewy!" Kimby stepped in between and ahead of her shielding friends, bending down to her rats. "Chewart and Chewington! I was so worried about you guys! Don't you run off like that again on me, please??"

"Nikko," Jigoro said from Stacy's face and sideways to her, "look at this guy's face... Don't you have pictures of him at home? He looks kind of familiar to me.."

"He's a Tengu, a Hanadaka Tengu," Nikko said in awe of such a man / creature. "You've seen him in my books before.. Why are so many things here a part of Japan?"

She had directed her question to the mythical man, but he didn't answer, instead standing with his breath held and eyes opened wide in a mesmerized stare at the V-cut opening of Kimby's kimono top. A small bead of sweat slid down the side of his enormous forehead.

"Um, Oyomi?" Black Stacy asked, trying to break his impolite daze. "Hello?"

"... Huh?" he asked as his eyes at last blinked, blinking once and then multiple times as he gathered his thoughts about him. "Why is a what?"

"Everything I see is from Japan," Nikko repeated herself to him.

"Well, I wouldn't say *everything,* Nikko," Jigoro interrupted.

"Well, alright," she corrected, "but a lot of things are. Like you, and Tanuki too.."

"Like me??" Oyomi asked. "I'm supposed to be from where? Hmm... I'm not so sure on what we might be talking about at the moment, but shouldn't we allow for formal introductions first?"

He reached to the ground, squeezing the newspaper in between his massive bathrobe-covered bicep and torso, picking up the green hand and reconnecting it to his missing limb opposite -

"Oh, great!!" Black Stacy shouted out as she saw him reattach it. "That was yours? Running around on it's fingers in the woods?"

Oyomi's smile gleamed as he took the newspaper back into his hand, the rotting green hand standing out in contrast to the rest of his faded blue body. "Pretty neat trick, eh?"

"That thing was grabbing me all over my body!" Kimby cried, the 3 rat Chew Mice back inside their kimono hiding spots and looking out.

"No..." Oyomi tried to act surprised. "This thing? It just went out for a walk! I don't think it would do something like that! Are you sure it wasn't a different hand?"

"Oh, we're sure," Black Stacy answered for Kimby. "It was all nasty on my back, and trying to unlatch my top -"

"You're a Tengu, aren't you?" Nikko interrupted the complaints, not able to take her eyes off of the powerful creature. "I never thought that I would get to see a Tengu in real life."

"Well, if that's what you say I am," he said to her, staring down his long nose, "then I'm sure that's what I must be, right? You seem like the leader of this group of Tanuki's friends - What is your name?"

Just to have his attention focused on her was intimidating enough. She knew he was like a Mountain God, capable of anything that he decided on. He would have known the minute that they traveled onto his mountain, and he would have seen them with eyes on every tree and rock that they passed. All of this, but the removable hand? That was something she had never read about before. Could he have possibly been making it do the things it had done?

"I'm Nikko," she introduced to him, then pointing to each of her friends alongside her, "this is Kimby and her Chew Mice - Chewy, Chewart and Chewington - This is Black Stacy, that's my friend Jigoro as a skull on her head, and it looks like you already know Tanuki.. Black Stacy told us to come here and see if you could help us out."

"And I, as you have already figured out, am Oyomi..." he said as he turned and walked away slowly, talking under his breath to himself. "What a bore. All of the time, people looking for some answers..."

"What?" Nikko asked, walking behind as Tanuki walked alongside, Nikko waving for the 2 girls to follow. "But can you help me?"

"Well, in order to help you, I must first know what your dilemma is."

"My friend Jigoro and I -"

"The skull?" Oyomi asked, stopping for a second and turning his head half back before walking slow again.

"Yeah.. Well, he wasn't originally just a skull," Nikko explained as she continued, "he and I were somewhere else, an entirely different world, and then we had something really bad happen to us, and the next thing I know we -"

"Well, it's not unheard of to end up here from another world," Oyomi interrupted, leading them to the side of his boulder and tree lined clearing, then standing near a bonfire that barely blew in the breeze. "Daiyomi is a world between 'body' death and 'soul' death."

"So then everyone here is dead?" Nikko cringed at the question as she asked it, her friends standing around near her in his fire-cast shadow.

"Well, no.. For most of us, this *is* life, not the afterlife. As for me, you've already called me by my Daiyomi name, 'Oyomi,' but did you know that my true name is 'The Vault of Heaven?' I crashed into this mountain 500 years ago, in a wooden-star shaped ark."

"Ha!" Jigoro laughed out loud and then fell quiet. "That wasn't a joke?"

The Tengu looked at Black Stacy's skull-covering head, looking tough enough that Stacy promptly pulled Jigoro off and tossed him over to Nikko.

"Good heavens..." Oyomi thundered through his lips at the sight of the former Pink Throwing Star's face, seeming to lose his thoughts for the moment. "You know I really, *really* wanted to look at you when you first walked up... But that skull was such a turn-off.."

"Oyomi!" Nikko interrupted his swooning over Stacy, now cradling Jigoro's skull again in her arm. "Can you just tell Jigoro and I if we can get back home? You're supposed to know everything about this world."

Tanuki stood rubbing his snout up against the bathrobe covered leg of the Tengu.

"She's just a small bit jealous of all the attention girls like me can get," Black Stacy tried to explain, temporarily forgetting about the wandering green hand reattached to the Mountain God's arm. "And meanwhile here she is, keeping the NLK all to herself."

"... Say that again?" Oyomi asked, hearing the words and breaking his stare at Black Stacy's physical features. "You don't mean the King of Death??"

"She calls him the No-Life King," Jigoro called out, "but we don't know what he really is, right Nikko?"

Oyomi looked Nikko up and down, seeming to not be just checking out the female form this time, Kimby standing by in another of her quickly growing bored silences.

"Well, if you explain him to me, I'm sure that we can clear this all up rather quickly.." Oyomi offered, the seriousness deepening in his voice. "Does he visit you in your brain?"

"I don't really remember too much.." Nikko confessed as she felt put on the spot, wanting more to talk about how to get home than what was wrong with her inside.

"Oh yes he does!" Stacy answered for her, walking up to Oyomi and standing in between them. "And I want to know exactly how I can transfer him from her back into me -"

"Stacy!" Kimby finally spoke, even Chewy looking up from her chest in surprise to hear her voice. "Is that the only reason that you wanted to come up here? You said that you wanted to help Nikko."

"Relax, Kimby," Black Stacy comforted the ghost girl. "I just figure since we're here, we might as well find out everything that we can! And transferring him to me would help her out, actually.."

"Do you remember what this abomination looked like in your head?" the Tengu man stepped aside past Black Stacy to focus on Nikko again. "Was he the darkest absence of light that you have ever seen? Did he find you only in your happiest memories?"

Nikko looked around at all of the faces looking toward her now, all waiting for an answer.

And the world would feel like this sometimes back at home. Nikko remembered the times she had tried to explain these things to other people in her life before. All of her fears from all of their reactions, and now here she stood in another world, along with her dead friend and surrounded by a small group of new friends, along with creatures she had only read about in books..

Was this all really happening?

"I don't remember much," she confessed at last, "but I remember that I can't remember, and I think it's because of what he does.."

"Then that most likely is him," Oyomi decided his mind with the simple statement. "For all of the variable versions of him, that is the description of the single connecting fact... Nikko, come with me. You can have your friends come along too."

The suddenly serious Mountain Tengu walked away from the fire, Nikko and her group following closely, and he led them to a small house-sized hut not too far back in the clearing.

"I want to show you something that I've collected in my journeys across the universe."

"Oh yeah, as if you -" Jigoro started to say, but had his bone jaw clamped shut by Nikko's hands.

"Is it something that could help me?"

"Oh, I think it might help to at least clarify things," Oyomi led the way through a push-aside green sheet that covered the entrance into a nearly primitive hut. "It's a book that I've carried with me since as long as I can remember. All of the stories from the old worlds I've collected here inside of my library."

A library? All that was inside were 2 small bookshelves and a few desks and dressers, white styrofoam mannequin heads with white hair wigs atop them. The walls were crafted out of a bamboo-style tree trunk design, and the floor was matted in some type of nest-like palms.

Scanning his shelves and then selecting a book, Oyomi invited the group to take a seat, cross-legged with him on the floor. Nikko and Stacy did as he wished, Kimby choosing to kneel instead.

"What I am about to show you is something that is very rare in any world," he explained, taking the book and setting it atop his lap. The cover was made of a black leather, an image engraved of a fossilized dragon wrapped into a circle, embracing the also fossilized remains of a human skeleton. "It is an untitled, unauthored story book that explains the eternal struggle of the No-Life King and the Saint Devil."

Nikko focused hard as she heard the names. The No-Life King.. That had to be what he was called if it was even in a book. But the

Nikko and the NLK

'Saint Devil?' Who was that now?

"Is this going to be long?" Jigoro rudely asked, set atop Nikko's crossed legs. "You're not planning on reading that entire book to us, are you?"

But just as Jigoro complained, Oyomi said nothing and opened the cover, allowing the storybook to speak for itself ~

"Wow!!" Kimby cheered as the others' eyes lit up as well. "Look at that!"

And with the front cover set open, the book nearly burst from it's pages, a pop-up book of little things that could move on their own accord. A first page scene literally played out in front of them : A black nightscaped world, a beautiful woman standing on a balcony from the left of the page facing right, overlooking it all below.

Tanuki looked at the book as if ready to attack, Kimby's rats walking up to it and looking it over in curiosity.

She was miniature, but easy to see - Light brown coconut skin, a white flower in her short white hair, and her hair pulled back into the smallest possible ponytail. She wore a black Victorian dress that covered her arms and a collar that went high onto her neck, the woman gazing off of the balcony into a tiny graveyard landscape below.

The subtle unstillness and the scene's slightest motions made the entire page come to life. The woman made puppet-like movements, limbs moving as if different components of the paper, and she lifted off from the balcony a few inches, the book simulating flight as she sprouted black feathered wings from her back and dress, white flower pedals falling all around her.

"This would be the legendary woman known as the 'Saint Devil,' standing in her home world of the SuperCross cemetery," Oyomi explained, reaching to the book and turning the page, the entire scene of the lone woman folding as just the paper that it was. "And next, we will see the Devil of your brain - The No-Life King."

Nikko's body shuddered as the page opened, Black Stacy looking on anxiously too. It was a similar style, a figure standing at another balcony, this structure of bone, and looking out from the right side of the page to the left, standing over a world of empty space and stars.

"Is that supposed to be him??" Black Stacy asked, moving closer to Oyomi's lap to take a better look. "It doesn't really look like it, does it, Nikko?"

Nikko looked him over in his entirety.. The body was the same, covered in the black void-like armor, his scene and body unstill and lifelike just as the previous page, but his face - Nikko could only remember seeing that bat-winged helmet and not a man's face such as this. He had white skin, a handsome face and blue eyes bright enough that they glistened even on this tiny pop-up book scene. His hair was long blonde, slowly blowing in an impossible breeze of the book's space-like scene. He looked to the stars before him, and then the pop-up character slowly faded into thin air.

"Weird... Um, I don't know.." Nikko answered Stacy. "I've never seen his face before.. He always wears the helmet."

"The No-Life King is a creature only in the guise of a man," Oyomi explained, turning the page again to the next, the scene folding in just as the last. "The image that he chooses to be can change if he so decides it, and the man's suit of armor is only a preference. That is just a small taste of what he could be to you. Time and space have very little meaning to him. That place is where he exists when he's not interfering with other's lives, standing in the Living Castle of the universe, 'Drahcir Nalla' ~"

Drahcir Nalla...

The next page appeared and came into it's small animated life.

"They are parasitical creatures, these 2," Oyomi narrated as the group looked upon the next scene, a small boy in a large house, so intricately made, room by room, for a pop-up book. "Watch as they interact in the story now."

"What's he doing?" Kimby asked, the paper boy kneeling at his window, looking outward and upwards, his hands upright in a prayer-like formation.

"It looks like he's praying," Jigoro mumbled.

"But it's not a prayer," Oyomi explained to the explainer. "It's a wish that he's making ~ A DEATH WISH!!"

Nikko's eyes widened, looking down for a moment at Jigoro, who would have no doubt looked back up if he had been able to do so.

A Death Wish? Nikko chose not to say anything and continued to watch and listen. The paper boy of the book walked in an unnatural way to his paper bed, and Oyomi assisted by reaching into the pop-up book and setting him down to sleep. The paper doll of the Saint Devil character then came up from a folded down position on the rooftop, followed by the paper No-Life King, rising up on the opposite side of the roof, also folded down and now standing up.

"The parasites arrive at the same situation, the Saint Devil is first, followed by the No-Life King," Oyomi narrated.

"But I've never made a Death Wish," Black Stacy told him as she looked over the page, the uncharacteristic blond hair of the Black Knight flowing. "At least I'm pretty sure that I didn't, and I still saw him all of the time.."

"And that would make sense," Oyomi explained to her, Tanuki now calming down at the tiny movements of the book. "The No-Life King preys on the suffering of life. If you're suffering deep inside of your Heart, the pain can make him live."

"But then why does he come into our heads?" Nikko asked, wishing she could remember all of his blurry connections to her now. "Can't he just enjoy our suffering from really far away?"

"By coming into your head, he's really only entering your happy memories," Oyomi said to her. "If you're suffering inside, what are you without those? Even worse! And what are you with all of those happy times at a violent end, to kill them before you forget them? That is the absolute limit of miserable.."

"So what about the... Death Wish?" Jigoro asked, Nikko hearing the nervousness in his words.

Oyomi took the book from his lap and set it on the floor between all of them. "The Death Wish is the connection to the female, the Saint Devil. While the No-Life King feeds off of the act of suffering, and the creating of the suffering atop it, she feeds off of the death of suffering. Someone in the world suffers, and I mean *really* suffers, and the No-Life King is there, as the parasite feeding from their pain. Someone in the world suffers so much that they make a wish to die - The Saint Devil hears that wish, and then *that* parasite is there to feed from their death."

Oyomi turned the page again, the fancy paper house folding in and a page of stars and space then opened before them, the 2 characters locked in a fire-engulfed battle through the darkness.

"So they both do different things, until 1 of them tries to eat from the other's food?" Kimby asked, the Chew Mice looking confused by it all.

"Eh.. More or less, I suppose," Oyomi now stood up from the group, the book still sitting there on the floor. "Think of it in this type of way - 2 separate, parasitical creatures in the universe, both feeding from the energy of negativity. 1 from pain, 1 from the death of pain. The 1 from pain can exist easily enough, but when the pain of something reaches it's Heart's limit - The 1 that feeds from ending that pain, in effect killing the hurt, imposes it's survival on the feeding of the first."

Oyomi wandered over to his small book shelves and dresser desks, fidgeting around with the white wigs of the mannequin heads.

"And then they fight like this.." Nikko observed as she stared at the 2 monsters facing off over space in the miniature scene before her.

"It's extremely rare," Oyomi said over his shoulder, "but because of their conflicting natures, it is inevitable that they will eventually meet, over and over. They *are* natural enemies, after all. But there is so much suffering in all of the worlds of time, lifetimes can pass without them ever crossing paths. But when they do, and when something's suffering reaches such a point that it's pain can be felt throughout the different dimensions, these 2 return to their endless struggle. Trying to destroy the other by the pain they can inflict."

"This is so crazy..." Nikko looked up from the book, wondering what Oyomi was doing as he could be seen trying on the white wigs 1 after another. "So if I were to make a Death Wish, I would get killed by this Saint Devil lady?"

"Well, *usually* that's the thing that happens," he turned super fast to face them, the bald top of his head now covered with a white beard-matching pompadour.

"Whoa! Nice hair!" Jigoro exclaimed, seeing his own style emulated. "Right on, man!"

"That's a guy that can appreciate 'cool' right there!" Oyomi broke seriousness and pointed straight at Jigoro. "But, like I was saying, even though that usually would happen.. It hasn't been happening anymore."

"So she's gone?" Black Stacy asked him, leaning backwards on the palm of her hands.

"Well, when they have these battles," he continued, walking back towards them and seeming to be satisfied with the pompadour after Jigoro's reaction, "1 of them always 'dies.' These are some amazing lifeforms, these 2 things. Even after death, they always find a way back. Some tiny hole or crack in the universe to climb through, like a shadow creeping across the room. I have heard of Death Wishes not coming true anymore for some years now, and after hearing of Shiva Angel's experiences with the No-Life King, as well as yours now, I can only conclude that the Saint Devil has been killed off in battle again.."

Oyomi reached down for the pop-up book and closed it, his wig wagging in their faces as he picked it up and stood upright again.

"So what do we do now?" Jigoro asked as they sat around quietly. "Cool pop-up book, but that didn't really help us out or anything.."

"Well, isn't it obvious??" Oyomi asked, a little more character in his thundering voice as he nonchalantly threw the book over his shoulder. "You're worrying about the wrong thing if you're worried about getting back home! You have to find a way to get around the No-Life King.. You gotta find out if you can find that Saint Devil!"

"We do??" Nikko asked, still wondering about the way home. "Didn't you just say she's dead?"

"Maybe dead," Oyomi said. "But even so, death to a creature like that is only a minor obstacle! Didn't you hear what I was saying? They keep killing each other whenever they cross paths. Sometimes 1, sometimes the other, but they always come back. Seasons always change, it's only natural for spring to follow winter.. Somewhere out there, 1 way or the other, the only creature that knows how to kill the demon that plagues you *still* exists! I don't know how, but maybe you could convince her to help!"

"Um..." Black Stacy slowly raised her right hand as if sitting in a classroom. "But.. What if 1 of us really doesn't want to 'kill' the No-Life King, so to say? Maybe they just want to, um, see him again?"

Oyomi looked down his long nose at her as if she were a crazy person. "Well, if that may be the case, and I can't even imagine why it would be, maybe that person should try to just have a good time? Make some new happy memories, suffer a lot, and maybe then he will come see you again?"

Black Stacy sat there and nodded her head slightly, as if making a mental note.

"At any rate, where do you think the likes of you should start if you're searching for the mythical Death Wish granter, the beautiful Saint Devil?" the Tengu asked his audience.

Everyone sat in silence, Oyomi seeming to have changed a bit of his personality since putting on the ridiculous wig.

"In the very place where she drags every suffering soul that she kills!" he answered himself. "Her graveyard world, the SuperCross!"

"Is he joking??" Kimby turned and asked Nikko, a look on her face hoping that he was.

"... And how would we even get to this place, if she was there, and she could help me?" Nikko asked while eyeing Kimby, feeling unsure herself. "The SuperCross?"

Nikko and the NLK

The Mountain Tengu stood still in a silence of his own, grinning an overly-mischievous smile towards all of them. "We're going to open the supernatural gates the only way that I know how," he said, a horrendous look across his face. "BY THROWING A PARTY WITH ALL OF THE FREAKY SUPERNATURAL SPIRITS OF THE FOREST AND MOUNTAINS!!!"

"YES!!!" Jigoro yelled back, nearly vibrating straight off of Nikko's lap.

"A GHOST PARTY," the Tengu yelled, both hands pulling open the bathrobe and throwing it to the ground, standing there in a tacky Hawaiian-shirt print mawashi sumo belt, "A YOKAI PARTY, BABY!!"

"A PARTY!!" Jigoro shouted back, the only 1 of the group as excited as Oyomi. "A REAL LIFE MONSTER PARTY!!!"

"COME ON, SKULL HEAD!!" Oyomi grabbed Jigoro from Nikko's lap and ran off outside of the hut, Tanuki anxiously running along with him, the girls standing up to go and see.

"This I'm going to have to see to believe.." Nikko's Heart thumped as she walked along, exiting the door just behind them.

Outside into the mountain clearing, within the short span of time that had passed, a ghost party and small festival was already under way?? The entire area was filled with paper lanterns, streamers hung and temple zig-zag papers hanging from staffs. All around, from 1 side of the natural barriers to the other, various animals and spirits danced and played games together, spilling drinks and getting into merry arguments.

"I can't believe what I'm looking at..." Nikko marveled at the sights, so many folklore characters now dancing before her eyes.

There were 1-eyed boys and pale faceless men, a snake-neck woman and giant man-sized cats. Mountain grizzly bears were sitting upright, walking skeletons beating on their bear bellies like drums, music in the air accompanying them. Green river kappa were there and a floating fire wheel head, human leg umbrellas, and even a few floating-eye lanterns too..

"Now this is a REAL Monster Party!!" Jigoro was shouting from the arms of the nearly-naked dancing Oyomi. "Nikko! This is the good time that I've been looking for!"

Kimby stood with a dazzled and confused look on her pretty face, looking at Nikko as the girls still stood by the doorway of the hut, not entirely sure what to make of this event.

Nikko and the NLK

"I have to go do this..." Black Stacy gave in as she set her suitcase down. "This looks like it might be too much fun to pass up.."

Nikko smiled and watched as she headed out, the skull on the back of her bikini bottom instantly being admired by the bear-drum playing skeletons.

"You should go too," Nikko told Kimby and her leaning-out curious Chew Mice. "Why don't you go have a good time?"

"... Are you sure?" she asked, somewhat looking as if she wanted Nikko to say no. "We can stay with you if you want.."

"You've been standing around listening to everybody talk so much! Just go and enjoy yourself - It looks like everyone else is having a really fun time."

Kimby let a small smile rise on her pale lips and then headed out towards the mountain party, a ghost among similar spirits.

As the music played, Nikko leaned back against the bamboo of the hut, taking it all in while considering the things she had just learned. Tanuki ran and jumped around, following the Hawaiian sumo-belt wearing Tengu and the singing Jigoro in his hands. Black Stacy was dancing and laughing, showing off her sword swallowing skills to the snake-neck woman and the kappa. And Kimby was off and skipping, Chewy, Chewart and Chewington out of her kimono and running beside her, clapping their bony little paw hands and applauding the drum-belly music.

Was that Choochie? It looked like Black Stacy had even thrown-up her pet beetle, letting him come out and play while leaving the rest of the Cult inside of her Bottomless Kiss.

"Standing here makes it look like you don't know how to dance.." the thunderous voice of Oyomi suddenly came from beside her, the skull of Jigoro now on his head, with the pompadour atop the skull and his blue Tengu nose shooting straight through the bone nosehole.

"How cool do I look, Nikko?" Jigoro begged her from Oyomi's body. "Please tell me! The hair and the nose?? Is this awesome, or what??"

"It's pretty awesome, Jigoro," Nikko laughed as she tried to settle into the Yokai Party.

"Well, why don't you come on then, Nikko?" Oyomi asked of her. "There's nothing else like this in the world!"

"You guys go on," she told them with a smile, "I'm just going to sit back here and watch.."

"How dull!" Oyomi gave up as he headed back to the festivities.

Nikko and the NLK

"Just remember to be ready when I tell you that it's time!"

~ Be ready when he told her it was time? ~

She wasn't sure how this was going to get them to that SuperCross world that he had talked about, but she sat back and tried to wait for it. Oyomi was back into the mix of things, Jigoro off of his head and the skull now balancing on the back of Tanuki, the festive music and drum beating still playing on.

An actual Yokai Party... Right here, and in front of her eyes... All of these crazy ghosts and spirits that *she knew* she knew, but couldn't remember their names. How could this be happening? All of this on top of all of what she had already experienced. All of these dangerous adventures, all of these once in a lifetime things, repeatedly after another. When would it stop?

And as she became almost lost in thought, mesmerized by the sights of the impossible things before her mixing with the impossible problems in her head, the party came to a brief pause.. The music, the drums, the singing and the dancing all holding still as a giant beast burst from the forest, a grizzly bear on it's hind legs and larger than the drum-belly bears, light brown scars all over it's massive face and body.
    Oyomi walked toward the center of the clearing, the Yokai ghosts clearing off to stand on the sides.
    "Is this what we're waiting for?" Nikko called out to him, unsure of what exactly she was supposed to be looking for.
    "What??" Oyomi burst out laughing back at her in the silence. "Are you serious? This guy is just a friend! Hit the music!"
    And the music started up again, the skeletons pounding away on the bellies of the bears, now looking much smaller compared to the new arrival. It walked through the again-dancing spirits, meeting Oyomi at the center of the clearing, about a size and a half larger than the musclebound Mountain Tengu. They stared at each other, and then threw something over their shoulders - Salt? What was this all about?
    "Kimby!" Oyomi yelled to her in the celebration. "I need a referee! Do you want to do it?"
    Kimby ran up, the skeleton rats now busy playing with Black Stacy,

and stood before the the blue-skinned Mountain God. "I don't know how to! What do I do?"

"Easy! No experience necessary! Tanuki! Come over here!"

Tanuki ran across the clearing, Jigoro still somehow balancing on his back.

"Hey, buddy!" Oyomi greeted and leaned down to pet him, setting a leaf atop his forehead. "I need you to transform Kimby's clothing into a sumo referee's! Can you do it?? Use the leaf! No need to strain yourself!"

Tanuki nodded his head, then shaking the complaining Jigoro to the ground beside. A sit into the upright meditative position, and Kimby watched in amazement as her kimono transformed into priest-like traditional referee gear, a match-ruling war fan in her hand.

"No... Hold on, Tanuki..." Oyomi scratched at his groomed white beard. "This is a Monster Party, isn't it?"

"Yeah!!" Jigoro shouted out from the ground in agreement, his voice muffled by the dirt against his jaw.

"That's right!" Oyomi agreed to the like-minded skull. "So why don't we do what real monsters do? Make her referee outfit more revealing! Let's go!"

Tanuki sat there and strained his little face in concentration, Kimby's referee costume changing from the traditional priest style into a small 'fan-service' black and white woman's halloween costume.

"Now you're talking!" Oyomi approved with a giant thumbs up to the illusion-making animal. "That's what I call an outfit!"

Kimby, still holding the war fan, looked over with an unsure glance towards Nikko, Nikko just smiling and shaking her head. Both Oyomi and the bear did their traditional sumo starts, performing their stomps and slapping their opened hands wide, showing no weapons.

"Whoa..." Black Stacy observed as she came walking up from the ongoing festival, Choochie the beetle on her shoulder and looking as if still hoping to get away. "What's going on here? A wrestling match??"

"Not even close," Oyomi bellowed, leaning down with his fisted knuckles to the ground, the giant bear doing the exact same on the opposite side of a Yokai watching circle. "Professional wrestling is a real joke to me! Sumo is the only sport where a God can match his strength..."

"Ha!" Stacy laughed as she helped Jigoro out of the dirt, taking him into her hands. "Is that what you think? I would kill you at wrestling!"

"Another time, woman.. I'm in the zone!"

"Kimby?" Black Stacy looked over her drastic change of clothing. "What the heck are you wearing? Chewy would kill you if he saw that!"

"Start the match, Kimby!" Oyomi commanded. "Wave the war fan!"

Kimby looked from the match to Stacy, and then back to the match again, having no idea what to do and began waving the fan in the most inaccurate way.

Oyomi yelled and the 2 charged, the giant bear and the blue Tengu pushing hard at each other in the center of the circle.

The bear pushed harder at first, using it's colossal paws to grab onto the mawashi tropical-print sumo bottom of the nearly naked Oyomi, pushing him back with all of it's might.

"Come on, Oyomi!" Jigoro cheered. "Don't let me down!! Be a real man! The most muscular!"

"A real man??" Oyomi asked with a few quick breaths in his voice. "Yeah! I'll show you it!"

The struggle now went the other way, Oyomi pushing the brown scarred bear all of the way back into his end of the Yokai watching circle, the festival's music playing even more rampant now.

"Come on, sumo bear!" Black Stacy cheered the opposition. "Hey, Oyomi! Look at me for a second - Check it out!"

Black Stacy stepped to the edge of the circle and turned around, Oyomi's eyes on her from the grapple.

"Rubber... bikini... bottom..." he stuttered as he lost a bit of his focus. "... with a cute.. little picture... of a skull..... on the back..."

"Ha!!" Stacy laughed and turned back around, sticking her tongue out as the bear pushed and sumo slapped the distracted Tengu back into his edge of the ring. "Serves you right, you dirty old man!"

"Hey, is that cheating?" Kimby questioned as she stood waving her fan, no answer as Oyomi quickly regained control of the impromptu match.

"This has gone on for nearly a minute," he shouted, "and almost exactly a minute too long!!"

The Tengu pushed back with a large show of strength, the grizzly bear sliding back on it's hind legs without the Tengu's hands even touching it past the halfway point.

"Heavenly Wind!!" Oyomi called out and stood with both legs apart in a squatting position, taking a deep breath of air, his blue cheeks expanding beyond the normal size, and then the exhalation -

Nikko and the NLK

A hard wind blew from his impossibly strong lungs, blasting the opponent bear up and into the air, blown hard over the treetops of the forest with several watching Yokai being blown along as well.

"YEAH!!" Jigoro hollered as Oyomi stood tall in victory, the Tengu quickly scooping up Kimby and setting her atop his broad shoulder. "The Champion of the Mountain! King of the Hill!"

Tanuki broke his meditation and Kimby's revealing referee outfit instantly transformed back into her black and white-lined kimono, the ring outline in the ground instantly disappearing as well.

"Well.. I still think wrestling is better," Black Stacy walked away, taking the cheering Jigoro in her hands and Choochie still at her shoulder. "Shiva Angel would've won in a second against a guy like you.."

"Bring her on!" Oyomi bragged, strutting around with the laughing Kimby, Nikko standing back and watching all of it in amusement. "I enjoy wrestling women more than bears any day! Oh, yeah!"

Nikko laughed to herself as the party raved on, the skeletons and floating eye lanterns coming and going past her, and Nikko's friends all looking to be having the most fun since she had met any of them, Jigoro included. Almost the same as when she was at the club in the real world, she found herself sitting outside of all of the celebration. Unable to let herself go, but at the same time, enjoying this so much more compared to the other. Maybe, if she tried, she could actually be a part of this single moment. Try to make 1 more happy memory, and why not? The No-Life King was ruining everything that she held important, so why should she aid him by creating nothing new? Even if he was killing her memories, she was killing her future by forcing life to pass her by - Or whatever this existence was.

~ So maybe just this 1 time, 1 more time again ~

"Nikko!" the voice of Oyomi cut into her thoughts. "It's going to be time! Are you ready??"

~ Or maybe wait until next time ~

The celebration was at it's peak - the forest clearing of mountain ghosts, Yokai of folklore and the miscellaneous animal spirits - and Nikko now saw Oyomi, along with her friends, quickly running toward her.

Nikko and the NLK

"We opened the gate to the supernatural world!" Oyomi proudly claimed as they all ran up at once, Kimby with her Chew Mice and Tanuki back in the carrier, Black Stacy holding her suitcase and Choochie at her shoulder. "Our Yokai Party was so loud that we broke down the door into the spirit's world! That always does the trick!"

He handed Jigoro to Nikko, and in her confusion she nearly dropped him.

"You better hang on tight to this guy if you're going in!" the Tengu warned. "You're on your own once you get in there!"

"Put me on your head, Nikko!" Jigoro begged in a hurry, a sense of urgency about all of them.

"And swallow that bug, Stacy!" Oyomi demanded, Black Stacy then promptly taking the the leg-flailing Choochie and kissing him into her Bottomless Kiss.

When did Oyomi even have time to learn about her secret?

"Ok, everybody ready then?" he drilled them, Nikko not really sure what they were all about to do.

"Hang on, Oyomi!" she tried to slow him down, the expression on his face showing that he didn't want to listen. "What are we even doing?"

"Just find the Saint Devil!" he explained as Nikko set Jigoro's skull atop her head again, the Tengu then grabbing her by the hand and running in the direction of the clearing past his bamboo hut. "If she's even in there, you need to find her and explain your connection to the No-Life King!"

Nikko looked backwards as she was pulled and forced to run along, seeing her friends willingly chasing after.

"What if she doesn't listen to us?" Nikko asked, her Heart racing as she wasn't ready to make this trip so unprepared. "And what do we do if she really *isn't* there anymore??"

Oyomi stopped running, the end of the clearing opening up into a beautiful night-shrouded cliff face -

Wow... Had they really traveled so high up in that brief tank and Tanuki ride? The forest mountains stretched out all before them, the sounds and lights of the Yokai Party the only interruption from behind.

"If she isn't there anymore," Oyomi answered, "then you have no choice but to face your own reality!"

"I can't do it it by myself," Nikko said to herself, all of her friends around her hearing. "I've already tried that.."

"Well, he didn't say by yourself!" Jigoro told her. "We're all here with you!"

"That's right!" Kimby added and then looked confused. "... But what am I going to do?"

"We can be all together, like 1," Black Stacy reassured the group. "We were all alone, and now we're all in this together!"

"Exactly..." Oyomi told them, standing there with his arms folded in his flamboyant sumo belt and wig. "And now, the door of opportunity is briefly open for you," he added, directing his eyes at the edge of the cliff and straight up into the sky. "The graveyard world of the Saint Devil's victims, the SuperCross..."

High over their heads and above them, they all looked and saw a large cross shaped cut-out of the night sky - It was as large as a house and it's edges a glowing white, the inside of it a hard-to-see landscape of rolling hills and trees, the light of a sun that they had not yet seen in this forever nighttime world.

"Oh, my..." Kimby spoke first, her fears keeping her from making another word.

"We're supposed to go into that thing?" Black Stacy asked, looking up to the door of the Death Wish world. "And how do we do that??"

"I'm so glad you asked!" Oyomi told her, a small animosity still between them. "Would you like to be the first to go?"

Stacy looked around at the others and made her decision quickly. "Yeah, sure... As long as everybody meets me in there.."

"Will we be able to find each other?" Nikko worried, the glowing sky cross looking a bit smaller already.

"Of course!" his voice thundered. "You are all 'walking through' the same doorway! It's not anything to get worried about! But, time is of the essence! We need to get you in before the opportunity closes itself from us.. Black Stacy, are you ready??"

She nodded, Oyomi then motioning for her to stand closer to him. The others all watched as she stood, suitcase in hand, and Oyomi reached for her and bench-pressed her body up over his head -

"You like wrestling better than sumo, do you?" he asked, sneaking in a free rear-end grope with his decaying green hand -

"Hey!!!"

"Sumo will always be superior!" he yelled and threw her effortlessly, up into the air with his supernatural strength and toward the shrinking SuperCross window-like opening.

Nikko and the NLK

Her body flew through the sky, toward the cross and then vanished into the inside.

"Ok, who's up next??" Oyomi offered, looking over the remaining friends beside him.

"Kimby, do you want me to hold Tanuki's carrier for you?" Nikko asked, looking and seeing Tanuki temporarily still awake inside. "I don't want you to drop him.."

"Not a problem!" Oyomi answered for her, taking the pet carrier and holding the bar entrance up to his face, looking Tanuki eye to eye. "You take care of these good people, Tanuki! I always knew you and I would meet up again sometime.. And don't forget, your tanuki-magic isn't going to work inside of that SuperCross! Just try to sleep through it!"

Tanuki licked his tongue through the space in between the carrier's bars, licking Oyomi across his long nose in agreement.

"Haha, yeah!" he laughed and threw the carrier like a hammer-throw up into the sky, Kimby gasping as she watched it fly into the cross as well. "We go way back.. Ok, the cat girl next!"

Nikko wished there was time to hear about Tanuki's connection to Oyomi, but the SuperCross was nearly half it's size by now.

Oyomi walked up to Kimby, the Chew Mice looking on defensively, but then quickly ducking into their kimono sections for safety. "Um, can we maybe wait a little??" Kimby begged, the scared face coming over her as usual. "Like maybe next time I can go.."

"Hmm.." Oyomi stopped and contemplated, his brain turning like old clock gears. "Actually, yeah.. Do you want to just stay here with me for a while instead?"

"No!" Nikko answered for her, not even considering leaving the poor ghost girl behind with such a guy. "Kimby, we're all going to get through this together, and we're going to need your help too! And your friends!"

Chewy popped his head out of her chest for just a moment before ducking back inside.

"Ok..." she hesitantly agreed, trying hard against her fear. "I guess I'm ready then..."

Oyomi reached for her in the same way that he had pressed Black Stacy over his head -

"But please don't touch me in any weird places?"

"Ooops, sorry!" he apologized as he launched her with a quick and inappropriate feel of her body as well. "Hand slipped!"

Nikko and the NLK

Nikko and Jigoro watched as Kimby flew through the shrunken entrance of SuperCross, screaming the entire way in, fading away and then gone.

"And that leaves just the 2 of you," Oyomi said as he stood before them in the mountain night scene.

"How are we supposed to get out of that place once we get in?" Jigoro asked, Nikko preparing for the throw.

"Hmm.." Oyomi stopped and thought, a slow scratch at his white beard. "You know, I don't think I've ever thought about that... That's a surprisingly good question.."

"Oh great!!" Jigoro yelled in a panic. "We're never gonna get back out!!"

"I'm sure we can find a way," Nikko made a quick effort to calm him, realizing that it was too late to turn back now anyways. "Come on, we're ready.."

"Excellent, Nikko," Oyomi said as he stood towering before her small frame. "I have an unusual feeling about both of you, different than the friends that you travel with. I'm not sure what it is, but you stick together, no matter what happens to either of you. Understand?"

"Of course, man!" Jigoro agreed. "Nikko's my buddy! We'll always stick together!"

"You're a good man, Jigoro.. Well then, now is the time," he warned while lifting the skull-wearing Nikko. "You know, as good looking as your friends were, I've been waiting to do this all night -"

"Huh??" Nikko panicked and swung her arms, but it was too late - Oyomi and his decayed green hand then sneaking a bunch of quick touches in on her upper body and legs before rocketing her off into the sky -

"You freaking jerk!" She yelled as she sailed off in the air toward the SuperCross.

Oyomi laughed his thunderous laugh and folded his arms, watching the girl and skull fly into the closing entrance before then returning to join the winding down Yokai Party.

"I can't help but love those ladies..." he said to himself, the gateway now completely gone in the sky high above the mountains. "Pretty girls are *everywhere* ~"

Nikko and the NLK

~ Anything I can find, smash it over your head ~

~ The hollow thud of a fist on your chest ~

~ Furniture tipped over ~

~ A small fire burns in the kitchen ~

~ Absolute cries of pain ~

~ After today, 1 of us isn't around anymore ~

Nikko and the NLK

CHAPTER 7

Diemania Level 1: SuperCross

    For the first time since the day of her 'death,' Nikko stood with a sun brightly shining in the sky above her, now once again standing alongside her reassembled party. It was the sub-world of the SuperCross, surrounded by green hills, empty of all life but the dark clusters of trees and the breeze-blowing grass.
    "It sure is quiet in this place," Black Stacy broke their silence, taking a few beginning steps down the treeless face of the hill before them, her suitcase still held tightly in hand. "No wonder it's a place where all of the Death Wish people go.. It really is just a graveyard.."
    "I think I like this place better!" Kimby playfully told them as she began skipping down the hill ahead, Chewart and Chewington coming out of her kimono to run along with her, Chewy meanwhile staying put in the top. "No more creepy guys or monsters!"
    "Don't forget about Jigoro," Nikko reminded her, now cradling the skull again in her arm. "He can be both if he wants!"
    "Well, whatever Nikko.." Jigoro said in pretend indifference. "Hey, Stacy - Why don't you just Bottomless Kiss your suitcase instead of always lugging it around with us?"
    "Hey, yeah!" Kimby overheard and slowed down. "Maybe you could kiss Tanuki's carrier too? Or Jigoro!"
    "Tanuki's staying outside of Black Stacy," Nikko addressed her friends, "thank you very much."
    "I don't just kiss everything, guys," Black Stacy defended herself, the group wandering now at the bottom of the hill and then up the small incline beyond it. "I'm perfectly fine carrying it."
    "What do you have in there, anyway?" Kimby asked, coming up then beside her and looking really closely into her face. "Did you bring some clothes to wear?"
    "Let's not get all excited about what I brought with me, ok?" she asked with a little embarrassment showing on her face. "Besides - Shouldn't we be more worried about how we're even going to find this Saint Devil lady anyway??"
    "She's right," Nikko agreed, ending the small conversations. "We don't have the slightest clue where to begin in this place. And we

don't even know how big this SuperCross thing is!"

"It looks like a whole other world to me.." Jigoro stated what Nikko had inside been fearing. "We'll be lucky to find anything if we just wander around."

And yet what other option would there be? The group walked on, over the sunlit hills and past the tree groves bunched together on the landscape. Near and in the distance, every direction held tombstones and graves, crosses and mausoleums. They were peaceful looking enough in this daylight, but the large number of them was unworldly. Was this how many people had made the Death Wish to the Saint Devil? And if it was, did she bury all of them in here herself?

Nikko and Stacy took turns trying to read the headstones as they wandered onward, all of them weather damaged and unintelligible as far as they had gone so far. The eerie quiet was striking - Only the sound of the warm wind through the trees could be heard, a peaceful and empty echo over the hills of nothing and final resting places.

"At least the sun is out here," Nikko comforted everyone as they kept moving, making sure not to trip over any of the grave markers scattered around. "It's almost a beautiful place..."

"I don't see anything like that picture in the pop-up book..." Black Stacy walked beside Nikko now. "It looked like a castle balcony, or a fancy house or something."

"That lady was so beautiful, the Saint Devil?" Kimby asked as she said.

"A little too much clothing for me," Jigoro added, "but she looked pretty good otherwise.. Stacy, maybe you can give her a little more fashion sense once we meet up with her?"

And as Black Stacy set to talk back, Nikko stopped walking for a moment, and then picked up her walk again with a light jog - Holding Jigoro's skull in the direction she was looking -

"Again?? Unbelievable! Jigoro! Look! It's her!"

"The Dolphin!" he exclaimed, the same excitement in his voice as Nikko's.

"The what?" Black Stacy asked as she quickly followed, Kimby along as well. "Like who you thought you saw in the mountains?"

"Another dolphin??" Kimby asked. "I couldn't see it last time! Where is it??"

And Nikko ran, the others as well, careful not to trip and fall over the tombs of the hillsides. The rollerskating girl was far ahead of them, impossibly skating up and down the dirt and grass hills, skating

Nikko and the NLK

as if on straight solid ground, the small fading rainbows still appearing right behind her.

"You can't see??" Nikko asked back to her group. "She's right there up ahead!"

"Is she in the trees or something?" Black Stacy asked. "I don't see anyone.."

"She's right there!" Jigoro repeated Nikko's words. "With all of the rainbows?? She looks like Nikko - Only a really tan rainbow bikini version! Rollerskating!"

And it was the same as earlier, none of the others able to see the rainbow girl ahead, effortlessly skating with the bulky headphones, never looking back. It seemed that she would always show up now and then, always too fast, but somehow forever just ahead. Nikko tried to keep her in sight this time -

"Ow!" Kimby cried as she tripped and quickly regained her balance, almost falling over a half-unearthed headstone.

"Stacy," Jigoro called from Nikko's grasp, "can't you cough up that tank? And we can ride it through here?"

"We're not driving over all of these graves," Nikko answered for her. "Let's just try to catch up with this girl! That's what you wanted us to do before, remember?"

"I know! I'm just saying we should drive or something!"

Nikko ignored Jigoro and tried to continue catching up on foot, never able to gain on the rollerskating girl in any of her appearances so far. This arrival of her now in the SuperCross made her all of the more important - She had been seen, sort of, in the real world, the Daiyomi world, and now inside of this graveyard world. Not only was she able to travel between the 'worlds,' it was evident that she was invisible to everyone but Nikko and Jigoro, not to mention that she always was appearing everywhere that they went. Just as they had sought Shiva Angel, Oyomi, and now the Saint Devil, this girl, with her blue hair and rainbow-themed attire, was now atop Nikko's list of someone they needed to speak with -

"Look at that body!" Jigoro whistled as Nikko unsuccessfully tried to keep up. "Nikko, maybe you should start rollerskating as much as she does. She looks great!"

"Please shut up, Jigoro -"

"I wish I could see who we are talking about here," Black Stacy complained as she ran unwittingly along. "I think you're both getting delusional on me.. Do you need to eat something? Or lay down?"

Nikko and the NLK

And then moments after, just as always, Dolphin vanished into the distance, the trail of rainbows fading off until they too were soon gone. Nikko ended her jogged pursuit by trailing off into a defeated walk, a lot of distance passed behind them now.

The landscape changed a bit this far in - The hills had combined into less and wider hills, and the patches of trees mixed into thickets of forest around the distance. Even the sun was already lower, not yet setting but closer to the horizon than above.

"Is it safe to guess that she isn't around anymore?" Black Stacy wondered, sounding unbelieving of the things she couldn't see.

"Yeah," Jigoro sighed as Nikko was slightly winded, "Nikko's not fast enough to catch up with her."

"I didn't even see anybody," Kimby added in.

"It was nothing," Nikko felt defeat again in trying to catch up with the mysterious stranger. "Jigoro and I just keep thinking that we see this girl, that's all."

"Well, there's nothing out here," Black Stacy looked around. "Not anything living at least. Maybe we should just stop and try to think this through? Maybe come up with a plan of attack or something."

"Yeah," Nikko agreed, still upset that the Dolphin girl had gotten away. "We're just walking blindly here.. Let's just try to sort this all out."

"Come on," Stacy motioned with her furry gloved hand, beckoning the group to follow her further up the hill they were ascending. "Let's get a better look of where we're even headed. Maybe we can see where that big house-castle thing from the book is before it gets too dark."

The group continued up to the cemetery top of the hill, and at it's heights, the land opened up before them. Dead-leaf forests were seen, fields of broken graves and tombstones in disarray. A full moon rose, the sun descending quickly now, but still no castle or giant house in sight.

"You would think it would be close," Black Stacy complained in her guesswork, sounding disappointed to see nothing but the world. "I mean, how big is this place supposed to be?"

"Maybe there are a lot of people that made a Death Wish," Kimby mumbled as she decided to sit on the ground, the Chew Mice sticking close by. "This world would have to be *really* big if it goes all of the way back to 'forever.' That Saint Devil lady is probably really old now."

"Ugh.." Jigoro moaned as he tasted a bitter thought in his mouth, the image of the book version turning into the 'Fiona Rose' version. "Let's all hope that she's at least aged well..."

"Well, look at these graves, guys," Black Stacy wondered as she walked around the hilltop cemetery. "Can you tell how old they are?"

"Do you even keep track of the years in Daiyomi?" Jigoro asked from Nikko's hands.

"I don't keep track of them," Kimby answered for herself. "Everyday is the same to me..."

"Me neither!" Black Stacy agreed, Nikko's question of what year it was in Daiyomi going unasked. "But let's see what they say.."

And as they continued talking, Black Stacy wandering in search of a tombstone with a year, and Kimby sitting in the grass with her rats and the carrier-sleeping Tanuki, Nikko was deep in thought..

Too deep to turn back - Already in her mind she was remembering a time from not so long ago, all of the graves triggering a happy, yet not so pleasant memory.

The voices of her friends began to fade away, and she fought to cling to them, knowing that she was about to slip into another piece of herself to be destroyed.

The hilltop graves disappeared to her, the darkening landscape fell out of her mind, and from complete black, she opened her eyes again inside of herself and her memories ~

~ A sad reality happening 1 more time ~

The sight before her was a moment she thought of often..

A white hospital room, the smell of vased flowers and perfumes..

It was a horrible time, though something held close to her Heart, nonetheless. She could see her other self alongside her Parents, her Cousin, her Aunt and her Uncle - They were gathering around the hospital bed of her Grandmother, now at the nearing end of life.

It was a depressing memory, but a somewhat happy time at the same moment. So much suffering and pain - All finally going away for her. The people she loved, gathered around her and representing a lifetime of experience and memories, now still together even at the very end. It brought the revisiting Nikko to soft tears, even more than she had shed at the time, being able to appreciate what it meant ever so much more these short few years later.

It almost allowed everything to make sense - All of the struggles to be with people, the fights within the family, the falling in love and arguing through the most difficult little things - All to leave the world 1 day, surrounded by the faces that you loved and of course that loved you back..

She now could see how much pain was in her Mother's eyes, the generations changing so fast, losing the past and trying to hold in the sorrow.

~ To be strong for their own child, Nikko ~

It was this versus the selfish life, and of dying alone in an empty room. Maybe this was the only thing to be considered a meaningful death? Not in a war or an imagined cause, but in a tucked away room with only the emotion of Heart. It was all so hurtful to see again, but so importantly held in Nikko's mind..

+ And then time ran out +

The moments before the pain went away, and before the dying woman could close her eyes 1 final day in peace, the walls caved in - The hospital white room turned death-black, the lights flashing and the vases falling to the floor.

Nikko could only stand there and witness the nonstop mis-placer of the only things that mattered anymore. Already her eyes were red from the looking-back tears, and she cried more now with her hands over her mouth, her family standing there unaware of the changes as the No-Life King made his way into the thought.

Again there, black axe in hand, black-void armor pulsating like a charcoal Heart. Nikko knew of course he would come, and looked at the scene in helplessness as it came apart before her -

+ Her Mother and Father, cut down to the floor with blood sprays and a thud +

Nikko and the NLK

+ Her Cousin, the axe entering halfway through the middle of his body and then removed, the wedge of separation pouring out the intestines +

+ Her Aunt, lifted by his axeless free hand at her neck, snapped in the undead grip like a straw, her spine crushed and head dropping by such force +

+ Her Uncle, the lone remainer standing beside the young version of herself, cut off at the legs and left bleeding to death on the floor +

All that remained for Nikko to see was that memory of herself standing beside the bed. This was the part where her Grandmother would take her hand, and hold it with a final smile, but it was not to be in this change. The No-Life King was already on top of the bed, standing over the elderly woman, skin-covered axe in his grip held directly at her body.
The revisiting Nikko cried loudly now into her hands. Why did she have to see these things? She couldn't turn away, stuck in the only room of the memory, subject to helplessness.

+ The sound of a heavy swing +

+ The artery spray of the Heart poured out +

The monster swung continuously into the woman, so many times, from her head to her legs..

Why did he have to do this??

The room now as black as his Devil-like armor, all traces of the hospital white now the dark and red of the blood, and he then turned his attention to the bedside memory of Nikko - The last of the family still living in the room.
"Why..." the real Nikko cried voiceless and unheard. "Why do you do these horrible things to me???"
The No-Life King stepped off from the bed and held his axe to use again - The memory-Nikko oblivious.

"God, I hate you...." Nikko pulled her hands from her mouth. "I hate you... No-Life King..."

And then, for the first time, the Black Knight stopped in his tracks, looking away from the scene and dead at the vantage point where the remembering-Nikko was looking back from - Acknowledging her presence for the first time ever -
He heard her?
The monster stepped toward her now, towards the actual *her* and not the memory..

A slow delay in his steps -

Nikko's tears held up as her Heart froze - What would happen now? Was this the end, as in the real end?? Oyomi had said that the evil creature strictly fed off of the suffering of people, so he wouldn't really kill her, would he??

- "Nikko!! Come on, already!!" -

A voice from the outside of her thoughts, calling in to her..

- "I swear, you better not be spending time with him again!! We're getting scared out here! Wake up!!" -

And as he drew near, the lone memory of Nikko standing bedside in the background, the scene fell away, blurring into just a thought and the 'reality' of her whereabouts coming back to her at 1 million miles per hour -

"Nikko!" Kimby yelled as the world of the SuperCross was back in view, the sun now down and a complete shroud of darkness. "Please, wake up!!"
"I'm up - I'm up," Nikko gasped as she came out of her standing-sleep, now seeing the most unusual things all around. "What are..."
"We gotta keep moving!!" Jigoro told her with an extra volume in his

voice. "This place is seriously haunted, look around!"

And as Black Stacy tried to ask her questions, Nikko saw the nighttime version of the hilltop they were still at, blurry red images floating around, fading in and out of sight.

"Nikko!" Black Stacy shouted, tugging at her necktie. "I'm trying to ask you a question here!! Were you just hanging out with the NLK again??"

"Yeah..." Nikko confessed, confused by actually being able to remember what had just happened this time. "And I can finally remember what I saw..."

"What??" Jigoro asked, still settled in her hands. "Wow - You can never remember what happened! Tell us what it was!!"

"Can we just go now, pleeease???" Kimby begged, the shivering Chew Mice peering out of their kimono spots. "This place is so scary I can't take it!!"

"Not until I hear about what just happened!" Black Stacy demanded, completely unphased by the wandering spirits. "What did he do? Did you ask him about me??"

"Are you serious?" Nikko came back to her senses, her brain still lingering with the NLK-killed memory. "Kimby, you carry Tanuki and let's go."

"Hang on -" Stacy tried but was denied.

"Stacy, I promise I will tell you all about it just as soon as we get away from whatever these things are.."

"Where are we supposed to go??" Jigoro asked. "Do you realize that this entire world is a graveyard? We should have never come here!"

"Well it's too late to say that!" Nikko started walking, heading down the front of the hill and Stacy looking her over in fierce jealousy. "And if that's all that the ghosts do is fly around in little red balls, I'm sure we'll all be fine!"

"I can't believe you won't tell me now," Stacy whined. "It's not fair to me!"

With her attention kept away from the complaining Jigoro and the questioning Black Stacy, Nikko kept the nerve-wracked Kimby near and walked cautiously through the nighttime cemetery. The red illuminaries were less numerous after the hill, and with the lasting images of the No-Life King still playing within her head, she tried to guide her group now through the dark, still no idea of where to go. A black sky forced everything even darker than the WaterBury forest, black enough to hide some of the uprooted headstones underfoot, and they all carefully traveled on. Towards anywhere, trying not to stay still in the overwhelming place.

"It's pretty freaky when you think of all the dead bodies under the ground," Jigoro thought out loud to a cry from Kimby. "I mean, just think about it - We're totally the minority here.."

"Don't say those things," Nikko asked as just then there was a sound from up ahead in the darkness.

"What was that???" Kimby stopped walking in another panic.

Nikko froze, and then Black Stacy too, all faces forward and seeing nothing.

"I don't think that was your rainbow girl," Black Stacy warned as she leaned her neck back, pulling the 2 strings from the corner of her lips to slowly unsheathe the swallowed sword.

"Can that thing kill ghosts?" Jigoro asked her in doubt, held at just the right angle to see. "I don't think that's gonna be able to protect us in this place.."

Another sound filled the quiet air, not far ahead and like a heavy pounding on the ground.

"Ok," Nikko pulled the carrier-carrying Kimby by her kimono sleeve, leading her - and the others to follow - sideways toward a patch of trees. "We're not going that way anymore."

"You think this is better?" Jigoro asked from her other arm. "Into the woods, somewhere even darker??"

"Do you have any better ideas??" she shot back to of course no answer, Black Stacy walking ahead of everyone again, now leading the way into the trees with her swallowed sword out.

"That noise didn't sound like a ghost," Kimby whispered as they walked into the wooded area. "I thought there wasn't anyone else in here? You really don't think it was that girl you saw before??"

"Shhh..." Nikko quieted her as they crept forward, the trees mostly leaf-covered and concealing in their space. "Let's try to be quiet and not make so much noise.."

And Kimby listened as the party slowly walked past the graves and above ground roots, squinting to see in the dark, no noises from around yet. The vast peacefulness of the SuperCross was gone in this nightscape, now the all-encompassing graveyard getting into their minds and fears, even Black Stacy noticeably offset. It felt as if their presence was unwanted in this place, getting deeper in now, their surroundings close to total black a few feet forward of every step.

Nikko and the NLK

Something unseen fell in front of them, and then a heavy drop behind, instantaneous and halting them yet again in their tracks.

Nikko motioned for silence before anyone could even speak, then leading on in an angle through the vision swallowing darkness ahead. Hearts were racing now, walking faster and trying not to fall over any of the black-engulfed tombs. Whatever it was around them, it seemed to be watching, like the green hand had been in the mountains. But even that seemed like nothing compared to this fear - Almost a silly thing in difference to this real sense of danger.

"I don't want to be here anymore.." Kimby whispered as quietly as she could, the group heading diagonally through the tree grove and close to back out again.

"This really sucks..." Jigoro whispered back, acknowledging his own fears that were being felt.

"Hang on, guys," Nikko stopped them, just then remembering what had happened when she ventured into the cornfields earlier. "We're getting back out of these trees.. It was a bad idea.."

And as she led the way, Black Stacy now in back, another sound came from behind them as the tree grove ended. The group quickly stepped out into a different patch of the SuperCross world - A moon behind the clouds, and land stretching far with grass here overgrown to just below her knees.

"Well, this is bad!" Black Stacy looked all around, the ground here in much worse shape than before. "How are we even going to see where we're walking now??"

"Guys, you're coming up with Chewy!" Kimby told Chewart and Chewington, lifting them from her ankles and setting them atop her chest, the 2 of them squeezing in behind the fabrics along with their partner. "This place is giving me the creeps!!"

"Just everyone please be careful," Nikko warned as they ventured out into the untamed grass, a long stretch of flat land with a few tall gravestones and dead trees. "We're going to stick together and we'll be just fine.."

The others came along behind her, Nikko's thoughts still juggling between what she was now experiencing and what had happened in her brain.. The No-Life King noticing her looking on, hearing his name, and not getting to kill her memory of herself before she was brought back to reality ~ What would that all mean now? Would he be back sooner next time? Maybe he would see her right away then, now that she had made her physical presence known to him..

A step forward and a trip over an unseen gravemarker -

"Careful, Nikko!" Jigoro yelled from her arm. "Don't drop me here!"
"Walk really slowly, guys," Nikko gathered herself, paying more attention to the tall grass underfoot now than her NLK dilemma. "There are graves all under the grass here.."
"Ouch!" Kimby cried as she tripped too, walking fast as she fought not to fall and then regained her step. "I can't see where they are!"
"If we walk slow, at least it won't hurt so bad.." Nikko commented as she tried to move with her feet feeling out each step before it was taken.
They made it a small bit out into the tall grass, away from the trees with frequent look-backs to make sure that nothing was following them in the now moonless night.
Black Stacy tripped, moving too fast along. The graves beneath felt overturned and unearthed, Nikko stepping on them at times when she couldn't step around them. It was beginning to feel as if she stepped on more wobbling graves than on the actual ground itself - And even when she did, the ground felt soft and unstable, as if there were roots or even body parts hidden in the unkempt weeds and grass.
"Something just touched me!!" Kimby shouted loudly, standing in place and then jumping up and down in fear.
"Calm down, Kimby!" Black Stacy tried to settle her, Kimby then screaming again -
"And it's doing it now!!" she cried. "Right now!!"
"Kimby," Nikko stopped and faced the cat girl, a grave unsteady under foot, "don't freak yourself out.. I know it's really scary here -"
"Hey!" Black Stacy interrupted, swinging her sword at the grass around her. "Something just got me too..."
"Owww!!!" Kimby cried in an outburst more of pain than of fear this time, trying to run away but tripping over the many unseen graves and falling to the ground, the pet carrier along with her. "Stop it!!"
Black Stacy then let out a shriek as well, only a split moment later, an uncharacteristic scream coming from her lungs, and Nikko's eyes shot between the 2 - Black Stacy standing upright still but struggling with something at her leg.
"It's biting me!" she screamed, a deep pain in her voice, Nikko then tumbling over the graves to the nearer Stacy.

Nikko and the NLK

"Kimby, hang on!" Nikko yelled back as she rushed first to Stacy, only making it halfway in steps before something took a solid bite out of her right leg and thigh, forcing her to scream out in a horrible pain as well -

"Oh, my God..." she cried as her body fell into the tall grass, Jigoro going down with her and her other hand holding at the spot of the bite, her eyes though seeing no mark or blood in the place of her pain.

"No!!!" Nikko could hear Kimby crying and looked over from her spot on the ground, the tall grass low enough for them to still see each other somewhat.

A red apparition of a dog, or something shaped like a dog and then changing, was at Kimby. It's see-through red jaw started biting down and gnawing at her body, the 3 skeleton rats, even the brave Chewy, all hiding away in terror.

"Kimby!" Black Stacy yelled. "Get away from it!! Run away!!"

"I can't..." Kimby screamed, wrestling with the spirit that violently bit but left no bleeding marks. "It hurts so bad - Stop it!! Leave me alone!!!"

And in another moment, Black Stacy began screaming in a pain just as loud, unseen things from Nikko's vantage point fighting her within the tall cemetery grass -

"Nikko..." Jigoro said with a shaky voice from her grip. "Can you try to get back up? Please stand up and get out of here?"

Nikko looked down at him, and in that same moment, another bite into her leg happened, this 1 coming down lightly, but strong enough to feel as if it were trying to tear the skin clean off of her body.

Another cry in pain, different cries now coming from all 3 of the girls. Nikko looked and saw red clamping jaws, the same color as the ghostly dog thing, all around her at the ground, some taking tries at her flesh and others combing through her pulled hair. Bites and misses, small prickly teeth bit down and then disappeared into her knee-high socks and skirt, creating holeless punctures and bloodless cuts.

"Leave Nikko alone!!" Jigoro desperately tried to help, his words offering no assistance in this overturned graveyard of the SuperCross world. "Go on! Get out of here!!"

"Jigoro...." Nikko cried, tears rolling down her face rapidly into each other. "This is too much..."

Her voice was interrupted by what sounded like a scream of death

coming from Black Stacy, and even in her suffering, Nikko couldn't help but look to her newest friend - Seeing a full-sized red body about her, human-like, a foggy and transparent vapor shape.
"I'll kill you!" Stacy threatened as she swung wildly, her sword only meeting the air.
It grabbed her with both terrible hands, biting down onto every bit of her body that it could, falling atop her as she continued to scream and cry from the unseen pain of the attack.
And then small yiping was heard, Nikko's tear-blurry eyes quickly over to Kimby, now seeing Tanuki out of his carrier and wildly jumping around, trying to scare the red dog creature to no avail.
Nikko's attention was forced back to her own attacks, 1 of the jaws digging into the bones of her free hand. The pain was so real that she made no sound, only an open mouth gasp as she unwantingly fell completely on her back, all at the mercy of these restless spirits, her face for a moment sideways against an unearthed gravestone.
"Nikko, you have to get up!" Jigoro ordered her, the hungry ghosts so far uninterested in his presence. "You can't stay on the ground with them!!"
Nikko, feeling the pain through her legs and hand, said nothing and went to make a move, but then felt the jaws at her body again. Now they formed attached to small distorted faces, and deeper bites came, overriding the small pains with larger pains. The screams filled the air as Nikko tried to block each clamping mouth with her arms and boots, but with each try, they bit whatever was placed in front of them. No blood, but the undeniable suffering pain of countless violent bites, matched together with the natural fear of the supernatural, was far too much to bare..
"How long will the suffering continue?" a familiar voice asked, sounding near, but Nikko's ears unsure. "I can never understand what would possess anyone to come to this wretched world, of all of the wonderful places that they could travel to.."
"Dorchester?!?" Jigoro burst out in happiness at the sound of anyone's voice in this horrible moment. "Dorchester Burrow?? Is that you?? Tell me that's you!! We need your help over here!!"
"It would appear that you all need a little help, at the moment," he went on, Nikko able to lift herself up in the pain and take a look towards his voice, seeing him peer out of his hole in the air, placed roughly in the center of them all. "What a dire predicament you've managed to find yourselves in," he observed as his head rotated 360

degrees around, Kimby crying hard in the background. "But at least I can say that I might have your attention, at least for another chance to hear me out again?"

"We're listening!" Jigoro answered for the girls, all in their own states of bloodless pain.

"Although I can understand the beauty of a cemetery stroll," he kept calm in the hurting moment, "what sick mind would decide to come to the SuperCross - The world of the Death Wishers - And then decide to feed themselves to the horrible things that live here??"

Black Stacy seemed unnoticing of the Burrow's appearance, still wrestling and crying with the man ghost atop her, biting and tearing at her relentlessly.

"We were trying to find the Saint Devil lady!" Jigoro yelled from beside Nikko's shaking body. "We thought maybe she could help us!"

"Ha!" the Dorchester burst out laughing, hardly bothered by all of the torture taking place around. "You came *here* looking for the Saint Devil??"

"...That's what Oyomi told us..." Nikko tried to yell, the pain she was suffering from her still-happening bites evident in her voice. "I need to find her.."

"Well, that's fine and all," the Burrow claimed, his hovering head now floating over to Nikko's face in his slightly-distorted air pocket, "this is her home, after all.. But you of course know that she isn't here anymore, don't you?"

"How can you know??" Nikko begged him in her struggle, his head from the air pocket now nearly face to face.

"How?" he asked back. "Because I have time on my hands, and doesn't everyone know?? The Saint Devil has been gone for a very long time now. And no offense, but I doubt that you would be the first to find her, especially right here in her abandoned home of all places!"

The Burrow's head and unseen body floated away, sailing around the 3 girls and the barking Tanuki, surveying the situation and then returning to the cringing body of Nikko.

"Looks as if you 2 keep adding to your following..." he told Nikko and Jigoro, pleasantly smiling despite what was taking place. "Extra girls are always welcome.. And my offer still stands, even if I can't promise that I have a lot of room for everyone in here.."

"We'll take -" Jigoro tried to agree, but Nikko, despite her pain, stopped him at once.

"Just tell us if you know how to get out of here," she demanded, giving up trying to fight off the attacking faces, now just letting them clamp down and chew into her writhing body. "Otherwise, just leave.."

"Nikko!" Jigoro defied her amid another of Black Stacy's screams. "Why can't we go??"

"No, my skull friend," the Burrow stopped him, his donkey head still levitating, "it's nothing to complain about. She's in an unimaginable amount of pain here, so it's understandable for her to be so unkind to me.. However, I must regret to inform you, there is technically no way out of the SuperCross."

"What??" Nikko cried, new tears ready to form atop her pain tears, another deep bite into the white of her shirt, forcing her to go quiet and pound the graves where she lay.

"I'm sorry, but that's true," the Dorchester Burrow confided. "The Saint Devil could come and go, but otherwise this is a place where you are typically 'brought' to, not a place to just visit and leave."

"So now you're stuck here too?" Jigoro asked, the sound of defeat in his voice.

"I only said 'technically' there was no way out, I myself am not bound by the laws of the world, of course."

The cries and pain-filled screams of the girls continued, a sickening sound as their fear of the red spirits was wearing off, and now the physical anguish was the only ruling factor.

"If you come into the Pocket with me," the animal began it's pitch again, "I can at least take you away from these relentless things. Do you think that they will let up? They'll never stop, you know. And even though you can't see the cuts, or the blood, I can tell that the pain you're in is very real. And don't think that the suffering alone wouldn't be enough to finish all of you off.."

"... Fine!" Nikko gave in with all of her frustration and helplessness. "But what happens to us if we go??"

Nikko rolled to her side in the hurting, feeling as though she was left without a choice anymore.

"We step outside of the bad times!" he sang to her in the same well-rehearsed tone he had used the first time he offered. "Step sideways, and leave all of your problems, especially things of this nature, behind you.. Step into the moment, and live for it! How can you beat that?"

"Nikko, we can't beat it!" Jigoro told her, his original enthusiasm of just wanting to go now replaced with actual concern for her and the others.

Nikko and the NLK

Nikko fought with her pain, knowing in her mind that she had no other option anymore but to take a chance with this questionable creature. And if what he said about the Saint Devil and there not being a way out of the SuperCross was true.. What was there to even consider?

With tears covering her face, dirt from the grave and soil ground, she nodded as best as she could, agreeing with no alternative left.

"GREAT!!!" the Burrow shouted, overjoyed, his eyes looking 2 times larger for a moment. "And not just you, all of the others?? Those 2 girls as well?? And that tanuki?? Especially the tanuki?"

Nikko continued to cry as she nodded, a complete opposite from the overly-enthusiastic animal.

"Everyone will come!" Jigoro said for her. "But can we just do it right now?? I don't think they can take it much longer!"

"But of course they can come right now!" the Burrow laughed and lowered his pocket of air to their level. "Consider it done, and now you will truly be living in the moment, my friends!!"

His head popped back inside of the unseen pocket, and then, with a larger distortion of the air space, it rushed at Nikko and the skull Jigoro - Passing over and engulfing them, swallowing their forms and the red ghosts dissipating as it passed through -

A travel of the air pocket over to Black Stacy and her wrestled spirit, and it swallowed her the same - Engulfing her and her carried sword, the red ghost man fading into a mist and then unseen -

And finally, the pocket rushed over to the unhappy raccoon dog and Kimby, along with the inside-the-kimono Chew Mice - Another pass through, and all were absorbed in as well, the red dog spirit breaking up and fading off into the air as only tiny red specks -

~ All went instantly quiet, the screams silent and the enraged spirits back into their resting night. The unwanted visitors now left and gone, unwantingly traveling from the SuperCross graveyard world into the hidden realm of the Dorchester Burrow's secret 'Pocket' ~

Nikko and the NLK

Nikko and the NLK

~ My breathing is so fast while his is fading away ~

~ It didn't last as long as I thought it would? ~

~ Maybe I should call a hospital ~

~ It's too late to fix that now ~

~ I always assumed he would kill me first ~

~ Unless he let me win ~

~ The final breath on earth - He looks so happy ~

Nikko and the NLK

CHAPTER 8

Diemania Level 2: Burrow's Pocket

Nikko and her companions arrived on the other side of the moment, the Pocket in time that the Dorchester had been so adamant about them joining him in, and as initially expected, it was immediately revealed to be a trap. Nikko was the first in, shortly followed by the others, all falling from the mid-air entrance in SuperCross and landing down on the warm floor of a zoo style cage.

~ Flashing colored lights ~ Furry walls ~ A humid smell that reeked of animal waste and stale perfumes ~

Jigoro fell and bounced across the floor upon arrival, picked up by the mouth of the Dorchester and carried away through the open bar door of the prison cell.
"Nikko!" Jigoro called back, carried in the oversized donkey mouth, and now taken by the hand of a black-dress wearing woman at the door. "Give me back to Nikko!"
Still feeling the effects of their individual and non-visible graveyard attacks, the girls slumped together in shared agony, Tanuki running toward the door just as it closed. The woman shut it with a locking key, then turning to walk away with a swoosh of her long jet black hair.
"Nikko.... It hurts..." Kimby cried, laying between her and Stacy and clutching at her body, the skeleton rats cautiously looking from her clothing.
"I know it does," Nikko sat up, letting Kimby rest her head at her folded legs. "We got pretty beat up back there - And it's looking like this wasn't such a great idea after all.."
Tanuki walked back from the closed gate, Nikko's eyes following the black-dressed woman and the Dorchester as they walked away, Jigoro stuck in their possession.
"What kind of a stupid place is this?" Black Stacy asked, standing up a little unsteady, her sword still in hand. "It smells like crap! COME BACK AND LET US OUT OF HERE, YOU STUPID ANIMAL!!"
"Hang on -" Nikko said to quiet Stacy down, her biggest concern

Jigoro's predicament. "I knew it was trouble right when I first met that thing, and we walked right into his trap... But what other choice did we have?"

"NIKKO!!!" Jigoro yelled out yet again, this time louder and from further away, prompting Black Stacy to walk to the front of the cage and try to see her surroundings better.

"Oh no.. Are you kidding me?? You have to see this..."

Nikko got to her feet, helping Kimby do the same, and they walked up alongside Stacy to look into the dark fur-covered room - Any small doubts Nikko may have had about the Dorchester Burrow's intentions quickly disappeared, the complete vision of the dome-shaped room coming into her eyes all at once -

"This is horrible..."

She could see the black-dressed lady walking a route along an elevated walkway, suspended above masses of wall to wall donkeys below, each making noise and pushing each other around in violence. Trampled in their mess, there were hundreds of female bodies, naked and some in undergarments, laying dead and smeared with animal waste - Some lay propped across the support beams as if they had fallen below, their corpses appearing fresh and not yet decomposing.

At their level, above the slaughterhouse-like pit, the girls could see the circular pathway from their cage connected to other elevated cages in the room. A girl with a black hooded sweater sat quietly in the cage nearest to them, and then another hard to see girl in a cage further down. At the center of the room, there was a giant platform suspended just as the cages were, designed like a stage, with the walkways connecting like spokes of a bicycle tire.

But the worst vision came last - Eyes back to the walking away woman, and Nikko could see where she was taking Jigoro's skull at that very moment -

"Jigoro!!" Nikko shouted, yelling in the way that he would yell to her. "Bite her!! Do something!!"

But the lady carrier just looked and smiled back, her black lips seen curling up beneath a donkey masquerade mask, saying nothing in return.

"What is that thing??" Kimby asked as she too saw the end of the lady's route. "This is *really* bad, Nikko.. I don't want to stay here...."

Black Stacy offered nothing as they all looked on, seeing a broken clock throne against the furry wall of the walkway's end. It was seated directly facing the stage, naked and un-decomposing bodies laying all to the side of it. And sitting in the clockwork chair was a sleeping giant with a man's body type, impossibly muscular and with an obese stomach. It's body was covered in a short black and red fur, with a mammoth donkey shaped head and a short snout, it's eyes closed and it's mouth gaped open in a deep sleep, massive teeth showing with each heavy breath.

"I don't think this is just that little donkey's home, guys.." Black Stacy said as she watched the Dorchester Burrow wander off into the mix. "It looks like that big guy is the King here or something..."

Before Kimby or Nikko could respond, the black-dressed woman could be seen pushing at the beast, his gigantic head moving back and forth before finally waking up, closing his mouth and opening his large, completely black eyes.

"I think that's her friend, maybe," Kimby said as they watched from their cage, all of them uneased and still in their pains. "She doesn't look like she's afraid of him too much.."

"I just hope they don't try to hurt Jigoro..." Nikko worried as a new fear rose inside of her now, adding to all of the things she still hadn't been able to sort out yet. "He's helpless out there.."

Black Stacy reached her furry glove hand across the front of Nikko, bracing her for something - "Nikko, stop looking.."

And the moment after, Nikko and the others watched in horror as the creature took the skull and set it within his gaping jaw, a thick muscle tongue seen as his mouth slowly shut, a complete swallow of Jigoro without any struggle -

KImby gasped and Nikko backed away from the bars in silence, too shocked at the sudden event to react, completely voiceless and drowning in a deeper fear now -

- Jigoro, her partner in all of this, gone just like that -

- This was the end of the road, it had to be now -

Nikko walked backward all of the way until the back of her head touched against the rear bars again, letting her body sink to the floor in defeat - No words left to say.

1 bad choice after another, and something like this was bound to happen eventually.. Her friend, completely gone. And now what would

be left for her, not to mention the others??

Tanuki ran up and licked at her hand, but she could only stare blindly at the nothingness before her.

"Nikko, I'm so sorry," Black Stacy came and sat down, Kimby doing the same at the other side. "There's nothing we could've done to help him, you know? Or we would have.."

"I'm sorry too!" Kimby bawled her eyes out onto Nikko's shoulder. "I didn't want to see stuff like this... I only wanted to play with you guys... I didn't want anything bad to happen..."

Chewy and Chewart came out of Kimby's Kimono and then sat at Nikko's lap, Chewington looking on mournfully from atop Kimby's chest.

"If there is a way out of here..." Black Stacy told her, staring straight into her welled up eyes and ending without finishing.

"Maybe Tanuki can help?" Kimby asked with a gleam of hope in her voice.

"I don't know.." Nikko looked at the small animal's innocent face before her. "Guys, I can't think right now.."

The place had turned out to be a nightmare. The smell of the waste and bodies, the fuzzy walls and containment of the cage, the colored flashing of the lights and the animal sounds from below - It all made Nikko feel as if she wanted to throw up.

Looking for the Saint Devil?

Why did it matter..

The revelations of the No-Life King?

Now she couldn't care..

All of those things plaguing her brain were now unimportantly cast aside. The hope inside, the desire to fight back from the moment that she woke up in the Medikiss Hospital, suddenly it was all falling away, pushed back up against these bars.

"So that skull was really important, I guess?" a voice called out from the near cage.

Nikko looked, her eyes in a heavy wetness, and it was the hooded girl. She was standing at her bars, hands in her pockets, and looking curiously over the short distance between them. The hood hid her face only a little, short orange-fruit colored hair seen and combed over her left eye, black make-up seen in the shadows. Her skin was a pale fair, the hoodie serving as a full outfit as it dropped to her upper thighs, leaving her bare legs exposed to black buckled boots.

"It was my friend's best friend," Kimby told her from the huddled 3, Tanuki standing with his short snout through the space between the bars.

"And I see you have an animal with you too, nice..." she said, an unphased demeanor about her voice. "Good looking bodies, a tanuki.. At least 1 of you should go far here!"

"What do you mean by that??" Black Stacy stood up in a bit of anger, facing the girl across the way.

"Take it easy?" the stranger asked of the unsettled Cult leader. "I'm just a prisoner here, like you guys. And a word of advice? Maybe you should try hiding that sword," she whispered, "if you plan on getting to use it, duh?"

Stacy eyed the girl somewhat suspiciously before deciding to follow her advice, then leaning her head back to perform the sword swallow, her eye carefully staying focused on the orange haired girl.

"Wow..." she admired as Stacy throat-sheathed the sword. "I see the most unusual things, stuck in here.."

Black Stacy brought her head back down, the sword's 2 ribbons back at the corner of her lips, and Choochie poked his little beetle head out from her mouth, Black Stacy forcing him back in again.

"Um," the girl in the hoodie continued, perplexed by the beetle's short appearance, "like I was explaining, the reason I said 1 of you should go far - Isn't it obvious? 3 hot girls, no guys, a tanuki already with you - What's the little guy's name?"

"His name *is* Tanuki" Nikko finally spoke from her silence. "He got named that because he's the only 1 of his kind around here."

"Oh, is that right?" the girl laughed a little, looking back into her cage as if calling something over. "I'm sorry, but check this guy out... Q-Sopp! Come here, boy!"

From the dark end of her prison cage a tanuki came waddling over, an all black fur variation of their own animal -

"Look!" Kimby exclaimed to the unpleased Chew Mice. "Another cute little guy.. Awww!! What did you call him?"

"His name is Q-Sopp," the girl answered to the bewildered looks of Nikko. "And as if 2 isn't enough," she said and pointed to the hard-to-see-into cage of the girl's cage beyond her, "Venrra's got her own down there as well... It's like a tanuki party in here!"

"... Why does everyone here have the same animal..." Nikko said more than she was asking, her eyes looking floorbound and not really caring, her Heart lost on Jigoro.

"Wow, you really don't know?" she laughed, looking for an answer from either Nikko or her friends. "Well, not *everyone* that comes here has 1. But come on - Really pretty girls? Magic casting animals? Together? In 1 area? New girls come here all of the time, but when someone arrives with a tanuki.. Hmm.. I guess some things are better left to see than explain! You're gonna get to watch in a few minutes anyway, now that the Burrow's Devil is up again.. Whoa! Hey, are those little bone rats for real??"

Kimby proudly lifted the 3 of them with her hands, Chewart then scampering off and back toward her Kimono.

"Radical!" the girl admired, squatting down to see better. "Does your tanuki make them, or are they able to run around like that on their own?? So cute!!"

"They run around on their own," Kimby proudly explained. "They're called the Chew Mice!"

"Too cute for words!" the girl admired, Black Stacy then deciding to interrupt -

"You said that monster is called the Burrow's Devil?" she asked, motioning back towards the throne sitting beast, Nikko unable to look in it's direction.

"Yeah, it's his place," she told them. "That woman with him is the Burress, she's kinda like his Wife, although it's probably not quite what your definition of 'Wife' would be.. I'm Miyakki, by the way."

"You can call me the Black Queen, Black Stacy," Stacy introduced herself. "That's Kimby, her little bone rat friends Chewy, Chewart and Chewington - Tanuki, and our friend Nikko."

Nikko sat unacknowledging of all of this, hearing it but not caring. If the SuperCross had felt like a dead end, then this was feeling like a purgatory now. Alone without Jigoro, just waiting here to see if the worst was yet to come.

"Man," Miyakki stood back up from her rat-looking squat, the tanuki Q-Sopp at her side, "she doesn't look so good.."

Nikko looked at her with no words but a face that said enough, her green amber eyes squinting and her mouth hanging open at the edge of mean words.

"Well," Kimby tried to ease the moment, "we don't really want to be here... All of these dead girls and donkeys around.. And the furry walls, I don't think Nikko likes it here either..."

The music volume raised and all of the talking went silent for a moment. The flashing color lights turned brighter and more vivid, a burst of smoke from a machine, and the woman that Miyakki had referred to as the Burress began walking her way back down the walkway.

"Ok," the hood-covered Miyakki called over to them, a bit muted by the music but still able to be heard, "now you're gonna see why they brought you here. Whatever you do, please don't say anything to the Burress when she passes."

"Why not?" Nikko asked back, standing up and the girls seeing the venting rage across her trembling lips.

"Because she'll kill you!" Miyakki shot back, her un-hair-covered eye opening wide to emphasize her seriousness. "I'm not joking around!"

Black Stacy and Kimby held onto the shaking Nikko to restrain her as the Burress passed their cage, looking in through her masquerade mask, her floor-clicking high heels heard even over the sound of the generic club-style music.

Miyakki and Q-Sopp smiled pretend-style, looking as sincere as they possibly could, the Burress passing the 2 of them as well.

And to the next cage of what may have been many more hidden in the flashing lights and shadows, the simple black-dressed woman stopped and opened the door of the cell, standing guard at the opened lock as the female inside made her way out and onto the connecting walkway. The sounds of the donkeys below seemed to amplify as she made her way across the elevated path, the Burress remaining at the opened door, and the girl wandered halfway towards the girls' cage before turning to head toward the center of the room stage and platform.

Accompanied by a grey and white tanuki, the girl was dressed in a plain-white ruffled short-sleeve shirt, with brown slacks and a simple long, straight blonde haircut. She made her way out to the center of the stage and just stood there in wait, her grey tanuki the only thing still moving.

"Are they going to hurt her??" Kimby whispered to Black Stacy, terrified for the poor girl and animal.

"I don't think so..." she replied, watching back and forth between the platform stage, the door-waiting Burress, and the throne-sitting

Nikko and the NLK

Burrow's Devil. "But this is a very odd place..."

The tanuki took a leafless meditative position, and then from below, 2 female corpses magically floated up to the platform, hovering on adjacent ends of the stage. The tanuki deep in concentration, the music pounding, and a scene of illusion came to life on the platform right before them.

"Venrra's the best at this," Miyakki told them from her cage over, almost sounding envious of the girl on stage. "That's why she's lived here as long as she has.."

In illusion, and now understood as the evil creature's entertainment, an entire diorama came into being. The 2 dead women were jolted up on make-believe wooden crosses, looking like the human scarecrows that Nikko had seen in the fields a while back. A pretend cornfield emerged from the entire diameter of the stage, and most unusual of all, in the place were the girl stood, she now became a human-sized and female-shaped windmill.

Nikko couldn't help but watch, shaking her head with teared eyes looking on in absurd disbelief.

"The Burrow's Devil has unusual tastes," Miyakki said as she also watched, spellbound by the start of the performance. "Venrra always comes up with something so crazy like this, it's impossible to beat her... Look at this stuff!"

"I don't understand," Kimby said as she and the Chew Mice stared, Tanuki eyeing Q-Sopp more than the illusion it was casting.

The music began throbbing, the smoke machine spewing just enough smoke to mix below into the rancid scent of the animals and decay, and the flashing lights went on and off to a faster rhythm - An illusion of fire overtook the stage-covering scene.

"It's part of her act this time," Miyakki explained as Kimby became spellbound, gasping at the false sense of danger. "He's going to love it.."

And Nikko looked over to the throne sitting monster, glaring at him in hatred as he sat there, naked as the animal that he was, watching in judgement at the show put on for him.

The fire took over the made-up corn field, slowly engulfing the scarecrow crosses and the broken barely-turning fan of the windmill - And now the truth of the illusion was coming out. The body of the girl shaped into the windmill was moving and slowly dancing, her real shape slightly seen in the burning fire of the performance. First 1 arm came free of the structure, moving in a subtle yet suggestive way, and then the other, the shape of the human-sized windmill in a provocative pose.

Everything was becoming obvious now.

"We're stuck in a freaking strip club..." Nikko said as she looked on from the cage, almost a laugh at her lips. "I really, truly, cannot believe this..."

Kimby and Black Stacy looked to her and then back at the scene, understanding it now too -

~ Music pumping ~

~ Lights flashing ~

The illusion fire crackled over the bodies of the 2 dead women high atop their scarecrow perches, and then outlining the shape of the woman bursting from the windmill. What was the point of all of this scenery? Her body now was seen nearly in full as the pretend-frail wood burned clear off of her skin, the windmill fan in flames, slowly turning behind her, almost looking now as if worn like a propeller-type backpack.

"Look at the way she moves her body," Miyakki told them. "That's where her real trick is. She moves so hypnotic.. You mix that with her creativity, and nobody can outdo her.."

Completely covered in the blaze, Venrra danced a slow style unlike anything imaginable. Such slow movements and then subtle fast bursts, using her body in a way that shook tiny pieces of dust off in a slow-to-fast rush, the fragments bursting into flames all around. The gyration of her curves, now seen in sparkling grey undergarments, moved in motion with the flaming turn of the back-attached fan of the windmill..

The Burrow's Devil looked pleased, and then all at once the music stopped to silence, the illusion dropping, and the Burress could be heard shouting.

"THAT'S ENOUGH!"

The stage suddenly fell back into it's original empty style - The grey tanuki stood back on it's 4 legs, and the girl Venrra was once more dressed in her simple ruffled top and brown slack pants.

"WELL DONE, VENRRA," the Burress applauded from the waiting door of the cage. "YOUR PERFORMANCE IS PLEASING TO YOUR MASTER. PLEASE RETURN TO YOUR CELL NOW."

And the watching girls stood in silence as the dancing girl took the long route away from the stage, allowing her to walk past Nikko and her companions before returning to her cage.

"Oh, great..." Miyakki could barely be heard saying. "Here she comes.."

"I thought you liked her?" Kimby asked to no response as Venrra and her tanuki passed, stopping for a short moment in front of their locked door.

"Don't even *think* about taking my spot," she told them, a cold voice coming from her beautiful high cheekbone face. "You can have the donkey girl's spot if you want," she directed her eyes over at Miyakki, "but I'm at the top around here, got it?"

"VENRRA!" the Burress called to her again. "A REMARKABLE SHOW DOES NOT ALLOW YOU TO STAY OUTSIDE OF YOUR CAGE! GET IN HERE THIS MINUTE!"

And with a final glance, focusing in on Nikko more than anyone, Venrra continued down the walkway, passing Miyakki's cage and then back to her own. The Burress stood aside and allowed her in, then locking the door behind her and the illusion-casting animal.

"Why did she call you donkey girl?" Kimby asked, walking over to the side bars that faced Miyakki's cage, being interrupted before she had her answer.

"THERE WILL BE A SHORT RECESS," the Burress announced, walking by the 2 cages from Venrra's cell en route to the Devil's throne, "AND THEN MIYAKKI WILL PERFORM FOR HER MASTER."

She cast a disgusted look into the cages as she passed by, then heading off to rejoin the Burrow's Devil. Once near, she removed her 1-piece dress with a single swift pull of it over her head, revealing an intricate back tattoo of a black skeletal system, then throwing the dress aside and climbing atop her demon lover.

"This is really nasty," Nikko vented her frustration. "We're stuck in this sadistic strip club now... And right when I felt like we were getting close to something.."

Miyakki stood there with a 'what-should-I-say' expression on her face, not offering any words to the agitated Nikko.

"But what were we supposed to do?" Kimby innocently asked. "We couldn't stay in that SuperCross place. What about all of those scary ghosts??"

"It doesn't even hurt so much anymore..." Nikko said of her wounds, the other 2 noticing it along with her. "It felt like the worst pain ever, didn't it? And now it almost feels like it didn't even happen. Why is it that nothing ever makes sense here?"

Black Stacy stood at the bars and offered nothing, her mind still waiting for the right time to ask Nikko about what she had learned about the NLK back at SuperCross...

"And what happens next?" Nikko directed her look to Miyakki. "You have to dance now?"

Miyakki nodded her head, keeping quiet towards the upset Nikko.

"And then what? 1 of us after that?"

"No!!" Kimby said quickly at the suggestion. "I don't want to take my clothes off!!"

"After I go," Miyakki explained to them with exactly what Nikko expected to hear, "the Burress will probably pick 1 of you to go next.."

"And that's it?" Black Stacy asked. "Just 1 of us? I'll go then.."

Nikko looked unsure towards Stacy as Miyakki continued.

"Well, she'll probably pick 1 by 1 until everyone goes... I don't think she'll let all of you use the tanuki though.."

"So we're screwed then," Nikko concluded. "We have to make up a stupid dance routine to please that monster, and then if we don't..." she looked at Miyakki and waited for her to fill in the blank.

"...You probably won't get to come back to the cage..."

"Exactly..." Nikko sulked, looking down to the scattered bodies below. "And if we all can't have Tanuki help us, how are we supposed to come up with something as ridiculous as what we just saw?"

"There has to be a way out of here," Black Stacy offered toward Miyakki. "I mean, that Dorchester thing came and went, he brought us into here -"

"The burrows can go anywhere they want," Miyakki explained, "but I've never see anybody else do it."

"What happened to the Dorchester guy?" Kimby asked, Miyakki answering immediately.

"They're *all* Dorchesters, every single 1 of them. They're just an extension of the Burrow's Devil."

"And he's behind all of this..." Nikko said as she could see him being friendly, his disgusting face tongue to tongue with the no-dress Burress. "Where did he even come from..."

"From what I've heard," Miyakki leaned against her bars in telling secrets, "he used to be a pretty cool guy - And he found a way to burrow into time and live forever. He wanted to escape time, to read and learn things, and change the world."

"What the heck happened??" Black Stacy laughed, looking at the furry-walled strip club around them.

"I don't know..." Miyakki looked around too. "I guess it doesn't look like that, does it? The first girl I met here told me she used to see bookshelves beneath the cages. Some of us even saw the animals throwing books out when they visited us - And then they brought us back instead.. I guess that's what happens when a guy is left to his own devices.."

"Nonstop girls," Nikko looked and considered the creature's obvious weight, "eating, and lethargy.. It really is just living for the moment, like that Dorchester told us. I always thought that Jigoro was the most selfish guy I had ever met.. But this monster's a million times worse.."

The music came back on, and all eyes looked back towards the Devil's throne, seeing now that the unwatchable grossout-makeout session had at last ended, and the show was getting ready to start again.

"Boys will be boys, right?" Miyakki laughed it off as she gathered herself and Q-Sopp. "Sometimes you just have to accept the hand you're dealt, and at least try to stay alive."

"MIYAKKI, DO NOT CONVERSE WITH THE OTHER DANCERS," the Burress commanded as she walked the walkway, adjusting her worn-again dress as she made way to the cages. "YOU ARE MUCH SMARTER THAN THAT. LET THE NEW TALENT DISCOVER WHAT THEY MUST DO ON THEIR OWN, UNDERSTOOD?"

Miyakki stood enthusiastically at her jail-cell door, nodding that she understood as she waited for the Burress to open the lock.

"WE WOULDN'T WANT SOMEONE TAKING YOUR SPOT," she said as she passed the girls' cage and arrived at Miyakki's. "WE WOULD MISS YOUR PRESENCE IMMEASURABLY HERE."

The Burress unlocked the keyhole and stood by the door in wait, Miyakki and her tanuki Q-Sopp walking the path that connected to the center platform, taking time to wave to the 3 girls.

"I think I like her," Kimby told Nikko as the music now played loud enough that the nearby Burress wouldn't be able to hear. "Do you think if we get out we can bring her too? I don't think she really wants to be here.."

Nikko looked over at the Burress and saw her splitting her time between watching them and the stage-bound Miyakki, then deciding to give Kimby a simple smile in place of an answer.

The lights flashed and the smoke machine kicked out a sputtering of smoke, Miyakki ready at the stage. Q-Sopp took his place and spell-casting position, and Miyakki for a moment looked a bit unsure, pulling her hood off before she began - What were those things? Devil horns?

"That's why that girl called her donkey girl!" Kimby answered her unanswered question, looking at the hood-down Miyakki and seeing 2 devil horn-like black donkey ears, going backward in an uneasy manner. "She's like me! Only not a cat!"

Black Stacy and Nikko watched, Kimby with her rats and Tanuki awake and looking on too - And Q-Sopp was already hard at work bringing an intricate scene to life.

A desert sun, make-believe and beating down above the stage in the Burrow's Pocket, and a desert scene appeared from the room-centered platform. Sand, cactus, and even a donkey-style cattle skull were created - Train tracks appeared next then, going from a black tunnel opening and to another black tunnel opening, crossing through the middle and where Miyakki stood alone.

"This might be even better than the last 1..." Kimby admired as she and the Chew Mice looked on, sounding as if she had momentarily forgotten their dangerous situation. "What do you think she's going to do?"

"... No idea.." Black Stacy automatically replied, her mind lost in thoughts.

The illusion continued, Q-Sopp making it so Miyakki was tied to a 5 foot stake in the center of the stage and tracks, posed like the damsel in distress of an old western movie. She stood in place, waiting until the illusion of her binding looked complete, and then - with increased music and lighting - she began to try and free herself, moving and pulsating with the beat. She danced with her body tightly rope-bound against the stake, her back up against it, the binding just slightly free enough for her to shift her body sensually around.

A moment or 2 into this, and a train horn blared from the stage, a small light growing larger from the far end flat-black tunnel-hole.

"SHE'S GOING TO GET HIT BY A TRAIN!!" Kimby screamed out, noticeably catching the attention of the cage-door waiting Burress.

"It's just an act, Kimby," Nikko reminded her as she looked on as well, waiting for the inevitable illusion train's arrival.

Another blare of the horn, Miyakki dancing her body looser from the train-track centered stake, and with the Burrow's Devil intently looking on, a runaway train raced at full speed from the tunnel - Barreling across the small set of tracks until it reached the stake of Miyakki.

- And then the moment of impact -

The train froze in place, the sound of it's horn full-blast mixing with the music, and it was as if still racing full speed down the track, only held steadily in place as it did.

Miyakki moved her body with the new rhythm, freeing herself from the binds as the locomotive sat no less than 1 foot from where she stood. The girl then stepped from her stake to the barred-grill of the powerful train, holding to the front bars of it's engine and dancing in a fast-beat, at the same time simulating a slow-motion impact of her body to the machine. Her no-pants thigh-length hoodie tore open slowly, grinding her hips as her arms held strongly to the in-place racing train. Her clothing ripped across and down, and now she stood in her clothes beneath the covering top, making Black Stacy stand up and notice in an instant -

"Hey! What the?!" she said loudly to her herself in shock. "That's not fair! This is supposed to be 1 of a kind!"

Beneath the now train-torn away black hoodie was a black rubber bikini, matched to the style of Black Stacy, the only difference being an orange skull and crossbones in place of Stacy's white.

"I thought I was the only girl that had something like this!!" Black Stacy complained, looking the dancing girl over in disdain now.

"Maybe she just copied it for the illusion," Nikko told her. "Or her tanuki did."

"And you've got the eyepatch," Kimby told her. "At least that's something different -"

Miyakki swooshed her short orange hair's long bangs through the air, quickly lifting her head up, showing a black and orange crossbone eyepatch before being covered by the bangs again -

"You can't be serious!" Black Stacy cried in an outrage, feeling her individuality being stripped.

"She doesn't have furry boots or gloves..." Kimby tried to make nice, Black Stacy just watching the dance with her head shaking back and forth.

Miyakki continued the simulated train-death striptease, her body moving all around in the dance while now small squirts of blood sprayed out from her limbs and arms - Seemingly no harm to Miyakki, just provocative dance and make-believe disaster. A few more moves,

Nikko and the NLK

and the cloudy smoke of the train's active smoke stack dropped down to add to the performance, engulfing the blood and dance with a low visibility that eventually overtook it.

"MIYAKKI," the Burress called out to the stage, "THAT WILL BE ENOUGH."

She hesitated on saying more for the moment, the illusion of the tanuki Q-Sopp dissipating, and Miyakki emerged from the now-gone smoke and scene, dressed back in her black zip-up hoodie.

"I liked her alot..." Kimby rated the second of the 2 so far to her friends, "I didn't like that blood part at the end, but I liked the rest of it."

"That Burrow's Devil has some messed up taste if they have to come up with stuff like that..." Black Stacy whispered out through the side of her mouth, hoping to avoid being heard by the nearby Burress.

"YOUR MASTER IS NOT PLEASED BY THE SAME SHOW OVER AND OVER," the Burress announced in the now music-less room. "YOU SHOWED HIM NOTHING NEW THIS TIME THAT HE HASN'T ALREADY -"

"I can do a different dance!" Miyakki quickly defended, Q-Sopp coming to her side. "I have something different that I was originally going to use -"

"DO NOT INTERRUPT ME WHEN I AM SPEAKING TO YOU!!" the Burress coldly scolded her. "YOUR MASTER'S DECISION IS FINAL!"

Miyakki trembled in fear as both she and the Burress directed their eyes to the throne of the Burrow's Devil - The monstrous creature who said nothing but sat there in his own filth, not even a showing look of displeasure across his warped animal face.

He pounded his hoofy-fist at the armrest of his throne, and either by enchantment or machine, the platform stage of the room's center began to rotate upside down, flipping it's side so that the top where Miyakki and Q-Sopp stood would end up the bottom.

"Wait!" Kimby cried out - "What are they doing? They can't do that to her, can they??"

Nikko put her arms around Kimby from behind, neither her or Black Stacy saying anything as they hopelessly watched from behind their locked cage door.

The orange hair Miyakki and her grey tanuki fought to stay on, hanging, and then sliding down the turning stage -

Nikko and the NLK

- The girl screamed as her body fell, then vanishing beneath the sounds of the hungry creatures in their horrible mass below -

"I SUGGEST YOU COME UP WITH A PERFORMANCE A BIT MORE INNOVATIVE THAN THAT," the Burress told the cage of Nikko's friends as she passed, leaving the vacant Miyakki's cage with it's door half open. "SOMEONE WILL BE UP AFTER THIS NEXT RECESS - AND WE ASSUME BY NOW THAT YOU UNDERSTAND HOW THINGS WORK IN HERE."

Kimby stood still with a shaken Heart, the group now seeing the Burress head again to the Burrow's Devil, her high heels clicking with each step, and then again - the same as the time before - fastly pulling her black dress off in a quick slip over her head, bounding atop the throne-sitting animal.

The sight sickened the girls as they looked away and back to each other.

"... You really don't have to go first," Nikko told Stacy, answering the suggestion she had made not long ago. "I got us into this stupid mess, I should have to go before anyone."

"And what?" Black Stacy asked, a hastily tone in her voice, not wanting to waste any time that would be allowed in this recess. "Go out there to dance and die? Even if he likes what you come up with, then you're going to be stuck in this place - What's worse, that or death?"

"I don't want to dance out there," Kimby added in, Chewington standing atop her chest and holding the kimono together with his miniature bone paw-hands. "I don't want to take my clothes off.."

"You're not going to," Black Stacy calmed her, looking back toward the scene of the clothing-less Burress and the monster Burrow's Devil. "Let me go first, Nikko. You 2 wait with the rats and Tanuki in here.. I'm gonna try to break us out of this place."

Nikko's woeful eyes perked up a bit at her friend's defiant stance. "But without Tanuki? How are you going to even try?? You saw what happened to that Miyakki girl.."

"Just leave it to me," she replied. "And all that I'm going to say is that if it works, you still owe me all that stuff about NLK, got it?"

"If you get us out of this place," Nikko told her, a small measure of doubt subsiding within her, "I promise I'll tell you anything you want!"

"But Stacy! What are you going to do without Tanuki?" Kimby pulled at her arm. "If you don't do an illusion they're gonna drop you down there right away!"

Almost as if listening, the sounds of the animals below increased, the noises sounding like a fight or a battle was breaking out.

"I've still got the NLK Cult inside of me.." Black Stacy showed a pre-victory smile across her lips. "I can make my own scene just by bringing them out.."

"And then shoot them with that tank!" Kimby excitedly suggested.

"Yeah, that would be awesome! But the tank doesn't shoot..." Black Stacy admitted after looking to the ground in a small disappointment.

"What about kissing us," Kimby suggested, "and taking us out there with you? And then Tanuki makes pretend versions of us to stand around in here??"

Nikko looked to Black Stacy, a bit of surprise at Kimby's quickly thought of idea -

"Well, yeah," Black Stacy said and thought, not sounding nearly as convinced as Nikko's face looked, "but I think they're going to notice anything we try to do in here like that..."

A quick look over, and the suspicious Burress watched from her generous make out session.

"Even an illusion to cover up *making* the illusion may be too risky right now..." Nikko suggested as much as she hated to. "I'm surprised they didn't see your sword before you swallowed it.. Are you sure you really wanna try going first? It's do or die now.."

But it was too late to try and figure things out any further, the evil Burress back up and her eyes deadlocked onto the 3 of them, pulling her slip-on dress back over her head 1 more time again.

"LADIES..." she shouted as she began to walk away in a female slither from the throne-sitting beast. "DID WE MENTION THAT IT ISN'T SOCIAL HOUR? YOU SHOULD BE PLANNING ON WHAT YOU WILL BE PERFORMING, NOT GOSSIPING WITH YOUR FELLOW CELLMATES."

The music began again from the room of the Burrow's Pocket, the time already at hand for the next dance of the show.

"I wish you would take Tanuki," Nikko insisted to her friend, worried about her fate the moment that she would walk through the door.

"I'm leaving him with you guys," she whispered through her lips, saying a repeat of her intent, "and if something goes wrong with what I'm going to try and do, you and Kimby are going to need him if you want to stay alive in here.."

Nikko didn't respond, the Burress making the short walk up and to their cage, emotionless mouth just below her masquerade donkey mask.

"WHO WILL IT BE?" the lady asked, slime-like beads of saliva still hanging at her neck. "HOW ABOUT THE CAT GIRL?"

"I want to go before these amateurs," Black Stacy boldly stated, stepping confidently to the front of the cage, Kimby cowering back to Nikko. "I don't want to waste any time with the baby stuff."

The Burress looked back at the 2 girls and their tanuki and rat companions, Nikko quickly faking an expression of disgust for the pretend-boastful words of her scheming friend.

"VERY WELL..." the Burress said with a trace of doubt in her voice. "BRING YOUR TANUKI CENTER STAGE WITH YOU."

"I'm going to do it without him."

"OH?? YOU THINK YOU WILL?" the lady laughed at Black Stacy's intended stupidity. "WELL THEN, THIS SHOULD BE BLAND! YOU ARE ALREADY MORE THAN HALFWAY NAKED, GIRL!"

Black Stacy said nothing, standing there at the door waiting, the music and lights at full speed now. The Burress held up the key from a giant keyring and then turned the lock open, Black Stacy stepping through and the door being immediately closed behind her, closing Nikko and her remaining group within.

"THE STAGE IS YOURS," she invited Black Stacy to walk the rest of the way to the platform, standing in wait by the door behind. "WE LOOK FORWARD TO WHAT IT IS YOU THINK THAT YOU CAN DO! GIRLS WITHOUT MAGIC ANIMALS ARE ALWAYS SUCH A LAUGH.."

Black Stacy walked to the stage, glancing down at the bodies and animals below, possibly trying to see something for an escape. The smoke machine kicked on again for a small burst, and soon the sword swallower was at the center of the platform stage, the lights bounding off of her blonde hair and rubber 2-piece bathing suit.

"THIS IS YOUR FIRST CHANCE TO IMPRESS YOUR MASTER," the Burress called out to her through the loud club music. "GIVE HIM EVERYTHING YOU'VE GOT - STRIP OR DIE!!!"

Black Stacy stood still for the moment, the empty stage quite a contrast to the earlier 2 beginnings. The Burress watched patiently, Nikko hoping her friend would do something before the Burrow's Devil lost interest already.

And then with an illness-type hunch of her back tipping forward, Stacy put a furry-glove finger into her mouth and throat, the sound of her gagging somewhat audible within the music beats.

A small bit of water and spit fell to the floor, and then the contents of the NLK Cult began to spill out, some sliced and nicked from her still throat-sheathed sword. First the black featureless soldiers fell, small from her lips and then growing to their right size. Then the black fur giraffes and other shadow animals fell out, followed by the black ammo-less tank, Haifish. And with a last gag and a little cough, the beetle Choochie tried to come out, Black Stacy quickly pushing him back inside again -

The NLK Cult stood in full force, and the Burress looked on in half amazement, her judgmental body-language unchanging. Nikko and Kimby felt a rush of adrenaline, the sheer amount of force in Black Stacy's Cult inspiring them, even still behind the bars. Was this the method to take back their freedom, after all of the unfortunate events that had transpired?

"You want to wage war with the Black Queen, Black Stacy??" the former Pink Throwing Star climbed atop her tank and demanded of the Burrow's Devil. "You treat girls like garbage, and you expect them to dance??"

The Burrow's Devil pounded his fist at the throne, just as he had against Miyakki - Black Stacy braced herself as the platform vibrated hard, struggling and then slowly turning upwards, trying to invert with all of the added weight now atop it.

"Stacy!!" Nikko yelled, receiving a fast look from the Burress, the lady now alert to what they were attempting.

"Don't worry, Nikko!" Black Stacy yelled back to assure her. "You didn't come this far just to take your clothes off!"

The no-firepower cannon of the tank tilted backwards, raising all of the way up until it was standing nearly vertical on the trying-to-flip platform stage. Black Stacy climbed it, her arms and legs around until she could stand atop the tank's weapon, balancing her furry boots on the cannon hole.

The Burress stood with more of a reaction, her knees slightly bent as if she couldn't decide to run back to her Master or stay standing at the cage door.

The stage platform let out a gear-grinding sound as it finally was able to overcome the extra unnatural weight, the NLK Cult of shadow memories sliding backwards as it turned halfway over, Black Stacy leaping at the very last moment. She threw her body with all of her momentum and dormant athleticism, hurdling herself over the tipping stage and across the elevated walkway. The Burress immediately took off in a high-heeled sprint towards her creature Master -

"She's really going to do it!" Nikko's spirit came to life, inspired by the ferocity of Black Stacy's Heart.

"DON'T APPROACH HIM!!" the Burress screamed as she reached halfway, Black Stacy coming down just before his throne, standing up fast from a landing kneel.

Behind her the Platform finished it's half revolution, dropping the entirety of the thrown-up NLK Cult to the animals and body pit below - The entire Pocket quaking as if it's lower half was about to fall off -

"You're not going to do what you've done to girls anymore..." Stacy told the sitting animal before her, tugging the strings at her lips, then pulling her long sword up through her neck and tilted head.

The room was smoking now - Not the foggy mist from the club-type smoke machine, but true machinery smoke - The 'in the moment' space of the Burrow's Pocket was vibrating with an overload from the crashed weight of the massive NLK Cult inclusion.

"MASTER ! DON'T LET THAT GIRL GET ANY CLOSER TO YOU!" the Burress shouted loud enough to be heard across, just a few long strides from his side now.

Black Stacy swung her long sword at his stomach, a squealing cry of deep pain, and steaming yellow blood fell in a thick gravy to the throne and floor around him -

The beast screamed out in a primal howl, bone segments, skulls and other undigestable pieces rolling out of his obesity at the gaping slice -

"WHAT HAVE YOU DONE????" the Burress cried as she ran to him, pushing his assailant Stacy aside and hopelessly coming to the horrible creature's aid.

"Stacy!!" Nikko called over in a Heart-rush of excitement. "Get us out of here! Hurry up!"

Black Stacy, a surprised look of what-did-I-just-do across her face, turned to run to the girls, just then Nikko stopping her fast -

"Wait! Do you see Jigoro?? Was he in there??"
"And get the key!!" Kimby added.

"Oh, this is so humiliating..." Black Stacy could hear a muffled voice say, already turning back and now beside the grieving Burress and her dying monster.

"Jigoro??" she called down at the soupy blood, the Pocket still shaking and filling with eye-limiting smoke. "I can hear you! Where are you??"

"Just get me out of this nasty slime..." he moaned, the macho voice without a doubt his own. "What is this junk??"

"You are a fowl, evil creature..." the Burress quietly said to the searching Stacy, rubbing the oversized head of the whimpering-to-die animal. "You have no idea what you have done to all of us..."

"Jigoro!" Black Stacy cried, finding and reclaiming his jaw-agape skull from the stomach poured bones and skeletons. "Talk to me! Are you ok??"

"I think... I heard some music..." he said to her in a daze, trails of the gravy blood rolling off of him and to the ground. "I wanted... To go dance..."

"NIKKO!!" Black Stacy yelled as she stood up from the stomach pile. "I GOT HIM! HE'S OK, TOO!"

"I can't believe it!!" Nikko could be heard through the thickening smoke of the place. "Thank you, Stacy!! Come help us!!!"

"Girl..." the Burress stopped her and eyed her face to face, talking in a quiet voice and tossing the ring of keys over without a care or concern. "Go ahead, go let everyone out - Do anything you want. Do you think it's even going to matter?"

Stacy caught the ring with her free hand, Jigoro cradled in her arm and the sword still held in the other.

"Hey -" Jigoro said as the situation was just now coming to him. "What did you guys do out here?"

Not caring about the woman's reasons, Black Stacy grabbed the opportunity to run back through the smoke, carefully stepping so as to not lose her footing on the scaffold walkway.

"NONE OF YOU ARE GOING TO MAKE IT OUT ALIVE!!" the Burress screamed, returning to her domineering loud voice. "THIS POCKET CAN'T HOLD ALL OF THAT WEIGHT!! THIS POCKET CAN'T EVEN EXIST WITHOUT THE BURROW'S DEVIL!!"

Black Stacy ignored her, coming up to the locked bars of the cage, fumbling the keys and successfully opening the door. The Pocket quickly dropped a foot in the air, a light-stomach elevator feeling for a moment.

"Jigoro..." Nikko cried as she quickly took him from Black Stacy's arm, looking him in the face to speak directly to him. "I almost thought you were gone this time!!"

"Hey, Jigoro!" Kimby greeted, leaning her head into his line of view for just a moment.

"All I could see was black and bones," he said, still sounding just a bit disoriented. "I thought I could hear dance music, like strip club music, so I thought I was maybe on my way to heaven. But I just sat there in the dark.."

"You killed *everyone* in here," the Burress calmly said in her quiet voice again, coming through the smoke in a high-heeled clicking at the walkway. "Does that make you proud? You try to save friends just to die free?"

The Pocket dropped another steep foot in the air, Kimby letting out a squeak and holding at the jail bars beside her.

"I thought this was just 'in the moment,' right?" Nikko asked, a strength returning now that the tables had turned and Jigoro was back. "How can things fall apart so easily?"

The Burress laughed, folding her arms and leaning back against the outside of the bars, all signs of giving up now. "It was *his* moment - Everyone else's moments still go on, time doesn't stand still for us, you stupid girls. But now without him, and that ton of crap that your friend created out there, we're all crashing down.. Back down to Daiyomi, back down to that horrible place that he never wanted to see again!"

The smoke was almost choking now. Another fast foot drop of the room, stomachs all feeling it, and then a foot and a half more -

"Nikko, is she lying??" Kimby asked in a nervousness at the doomsaying words, the Chew Mice gathered up around her top.

A drop again, at least 3 feet this time, and the flashing club lights flickered off and on, then staying mostly off.

"Aww -" Jigoro moaned as the Pocket grew silent, only the sounds of the upset and confused burrow animals below. "Well this sucks.. Why did you guys even save me?? Now we have to die??"

"Die again," the Burress muttered as she walked back off in the direction of the presumably dead Burrow's Devil, pulling her dress off 1 final time as her body disappeared into the covering smoke. "It seems nothing lasts forever, after all. At least now you have a quick reunion to cry about death.."

Black Stacy quickly ran back to the rear of the cell, grabbing at her suitcase and after a small thought, at last putting it to her lips and kissing it, the medium luggage shifting and funneling into her mouth.

This was going to be something bad, and everyone now tried to brace themselves for the unknown disaster -

~ Jigoro said a few words, Kimby grabbed Tanuki, and the sounds of the room muted everything, the short drops of moments earlier now 1 long descent down ~

~ Stomachs to the ceiling, and like a plane dropping out of the sky, the Burrow's Pocket was falling straight out of the frozen time it had been burrowed deep inside of ~

~ Human screams and animals crying, the screech of metal and the smell of rotting waste in a weightless plummet ~

All crashing into the unknown...

Nikko and the NLK

Nikko and the NLK

~ When I met him, we were both broken ~

~ We fixed our problems by poison ~

~ What was he really like? ~

~ Did he ever understand me? ~

~ Our time went by so fast ~

~ Our fight to the death ~

~ And now I'm here alone.. I was the 1 who wished for death ~

Nikko and the NLK

CHAPTER 9

Diemania Level 3 : World's Teeth

High above Daiyomi, a circular distortion crashed through the air, flames bursting from the top and sides of it, creating the illusion of a flaming ring. It burned it's way out of the sky, flaming amid a black night of fire clouds - The only motion in a stark empty landscape.

Toward a jagged ground, fire at all sides, and then an impact into the land of Daiyomi beneath -

CRASH!!

Like a small world colliding, the outside-unseen Burrow's Pocket smashed hard into the ground, collapsing in onto itself and creating an instant crater. A howling metallic sound filled the air, imploding as a series of rips tore at the base, vermillion blood and a mixed stench seeping out as the surviving burrows escaped, hee-hawing into the dark world.

And then the familiar shapes of the final survivors -

Nikko with Jigoro, Kimby with her arm around Nikko's neck and shoulder, Black Stacy holding her sides and Tanuki walking gingerly. All emerged even worse than they had entered the trap of the Pocket, their SuperCross-faded wounds nothing compared to their crash and burn from the sky,
"... Are we... all ok?" Nikko took inventory as they hobbled from the invisible wreck. "I can't tell if I'm in 1 piece.."
They all took a moment to gather their senses, adjusting to their pains and shock within the new cut-rock stretch of land before them. Their skin was stained in patches with blood, Nikko's white button shirt half dyed by it now, Kimby's kimono wet, and the crimson juice just rolling off of Black Stacy's rubber bikini.
"I think I broke my leg..." Kimby whimpered, walking softly with Nikko's aid, the Chew Mice visibly shaken from their kimono spots as well.

"Once we get away from here, we can take a look at it," Nikko offered, feeling a strong desire to put distance between herself and the crash site. "We'll make sure you're ok, Kimby - really - I promise."

"Do you think that lady with the mask survived?" Jigoro asked of the Burress, asking just to ask.

"Or what about that Venrra girl?" Nikko wondered out loud as well. "I can see some of the animals made it out."

"I left my sword in there..." Black Stacy remembered, mad at herself and looking back before Nikko interrupted her thoughts.

"We're leaving it there, Stacy," she told her, not wanting her friend to even consider returning to the evil place. "It's probably lost in the crash anyways - We have to get away from it!"

"And my NLK Cult..."

Nikko said nothing, not knowing how to answer for Black Stacy's loss of already lost memories -

"I knew they wouldn't make it..." Stacy answered herself, a forced smile shown to the ground. "They always fade away anyways.."

Nikko had trouble making sense of her friend's plight - Such things held inside of her, then brought out and so heavy, only to fade away as if they never existed at all..

"Let's just keep moving," Nikko repeated her idea. "We'll stop and figure this all out once we've put some distance between us and that place."

The group walked into the uneven and treeless land around them. It wasn't clear exactly how they could crash out of the burrowed moment and into a place like this, but Nikko didn't understand how 1 could burrow into time in the first place, so she didn't waste her thoughts on it. They moved at a very slow pace, breathing unnaturally heavy and uneven, their bodies under stress from the twice in a row torturous events, and now Nikko hoped that the worst would be behind them.

"Don't forget our deal..." Stacy mentioned to Nikko as they traveled beneath the broad sky.

"... I know," she told her, having trouble understanding why Black Stacy was still so obsessed with the No-Life King, especially after all of this. But after a thought, she remembered that this was the only reason Stacy had even decided to travel along with them at all. And after what they had been through together, and after what Black Stacy had just done for all of them, Nikko almost felt wrong that she didn't have much to tell her now.

"There's still not much to say," she confessed, everyone listening in as they walked through the silent night, "but I'll tell you what I know."

~ They passed in the shadows of the rocks towering all around them, the floating fire shaped clouds unmoving overhead ~

"Before we went to SuperCross," she began, "I wasn't able to figure out what was happening when I blacked out. I knew about him, not by his name yet, but that was the only thing I could remember. And then when we were in the SuperCross, all of those graves made me start to get depressed, and I started to think about my family - I thought about my Grandma, and then I just drifted off."

"So you saw him again," Black Stacy prodded her along, anxious even in their collective pain for any new detail.

"All of a sudden," Nikko described to them, envisioning it again so vividly in her brain, "I'm remembering seeing her at the hospital - It was like a memory, but like living in the memory. I wasn't myself, I was watching everything from behind, like a tv show, or a dream.."

"That's weird.." Jigoro added. "You never told me anything like that before."

"I know! And then it got worse. *Really* worse.. I had no control, I couldn't talk to them, I couldn't interact with anything - And then he showed up, the No-Life King."

Black Stacy filled with hope, Nikko not surprised, and she refused to let it upset her.

"He came into my head, like he was already a part of my memory. Only they couldn't see him, but I could.. Not the memory-me, the now-me, looking back. It was so bad.. He was killing everyone - Swinging an axe, and they didn't even know they were dying.. They had the same exact looks on their faces after he hurt them, and all I could do was watch.. He killed my family, he killed my Grandmother before she died.. And just when he went to my memory of myself.. He heard me.."

"What did you say to him?" Kimby asked, absorbed with every word of the story.

"I said his name to myself, and he stopped what he was doing to look at me - Not the memory me, but the *real* me - I was never so scared before, it was like the Devil was facing me right inside of myself..."

Nikko stopped talking, and the air was silent again.

Nikko and the NLK

"AND WHAT HAPPENED??" Black Stacy demanded, sounding more excited than the group knew she could have mustered.

"You guys woke me back up.." Nikko responded. "You brought me out of the memory -"

"Aww, man...." Black Stacy frowned in disappointment, wishing there had been more before the end. "That's all? I thought maybe we figured something new out about him.."

"What do you mean??" Nikko asked. "Don't you think that's really something?? He invades your memories! The things you keep inside of yourself - The only thing no 1 is supposed to be able to take from you! And this time I can remember the memory.. Kind of, a little.."

"Yeah, but I already knew that.." Black Stacy reminded her. "That's just how he is -"

"Ok, but hang on," Jigoro split his voice between the 2. "He actually looked at you? Like he was coming at you and going to kill you? All because he heard you say his name? Whoa.. What do you think would have happened??"

"I have no idea..." Nikko wondered, Tanuki letting out a concerned yipe.

"Give me a break! I'll tell you what would've happened!" Jigoro went on. "You would have really died! 'Probably' really! Like, as in the 'real' you, not just the memory!"

"Jigoro.." Kimby tried calming him, not wanting him to be so mean to Nikko. "You don't know.."

"Do you really think so?" Nikko asked, thinking about it herself now that he mentioned it.

"Yes, I do! So what if he feeds off of suffering? He'll probably kill you anyways!"

"Yeah," Black Stacy coldly agreed. "Now the next time you see him in your memories, he's probably going to come straight after you.."

"Stacy!!" Kimby looked at her now, bothered the same as she was with Jigoro. "Don't say that!"

"Wow - Thanks, guys..." Nikko's Heart pumped even faster. "So now I have to try not remembering anything. What if he can come into any memories? Like even bad memories?? Or the 1 we're making now??"

"Don't panic, Nikko," Kimby told her, Tanuki eyeing the rocks around them. "We'll just try waking you up every time that you look like you're blacking out!"

"That's too difficult..." Jigoro said. "She always looks like she's going to black out to me.."

"Hey!" Nikko cried to her original friend. "This is serious, Jigoro! I'm freaked out right now!"

"Well then we just have to figure out a way to stop him on our own," Black Stacy explained. "Or at least transfer him back to me, now that we know the Saint Devil is out of the question -"

- And at that moment of the conversation, something long and solid swung through the group of them, like a baseball bat or pipe, clipping Black Stacy just enough in her head to knock her to the ground -

"Hey!!" Jigoro yelled as Kimby screamed and Nikko leapt back - "Stacy!"

"What is it??" Nikko confronted the darkness, seeing something reaching for Black Stacy from a rocky hole in the ground - Another swing of the long object came at Nikko as she looked to her friend, moving back just in time - "What the heck?? Who's there??"

There was an alien shape of a man before them - Tanuki leaping and barking about it. It was a curving-forward thin body, no details seen, with spiny upright appendages protruding from it's back.

"Nikko, help Stacy!!" Jigoro ordered, the knocked to the ground sword swallower being pulled into the hole by an unseen other shape.

As Nikko looked to her, another swing of the heavy object came, this time clubbing Nikko enough in her already sore body to level her to the ground, the weak-legged Kimby dropping down along with her in tears.

From 1 hell into the next, and now into another - Kimby cried as the solid weapon struck down again at Nikko, hitting her not hard enough to finish her off, but at least hard enough to knock her out, the dark and firecloud sky falling into a blacker black -

A third strike, and another nightmare from nowhere was happening. The sounds faded away, a pull and tug at Nikko's tired and worn out body, and almost like the end of life, she was dragged defenselessly into the ground below.

How many more times could these nonstop horrible things happen?

Nikko and the NLK

~ Maybe only 1 more time, for 1 last time ~

Nikko was knocked out into her mind with no dreams or memories, only a deep hurting sleep from the blows and consistent dealings of pain - And it faded away - Why was everything like a trap, growing worse the further along they went? From the graveyard to the Pocket, and then this brutal attack. With all of the things that were happening both now and before - It had to be for something, right?
Nikko's unconscious mind and soul clung to that hope, drifting away inside of her pain-stricken body.

~ An unknown but brief amount of time passed, followed by the sounds of a television, and eventually a kitchen sink... ~

Home at last? Something completely different appeared before her dizzy eyes - The walls here were wallpapered in a retro decor, an old fashioned television illuminated the room with a black and white show she had never seen before, and there were neatly placed picture frames and a tabletop vase as well.
All coming at her in 1 waking moment, it was the most comforting thing she had seen in such a long time - Even a coffee table with a newspaper, a sofa and 2 reclinable chairs - It had to be a place back home.. Somewhere, somehow, perhaps a doorway that she had stumbled through, leading her back from the dangers of Daiyomi.. And as it all came back to her - Her pain, the memories, her friends and the No-Life King - Her senses took in everything, and something was terribly amiss.
This wasn't back home, this still had to be Daiyomi.. With her eyes able to refocus, she could see the vase now as a sealing-coated organ, the picture frames not of family photos, but of tattooed pieces of flesh -
Nikko's anxiety kicked in and she pulled herself up from the floor.
A little kid before her? A monster?
"Dad!!!" it yelled in terror just as soon as Nikko moved. "It's awake!! Hurry up!!"
It was a human boy, or at least it must have been - He was the size of a 9-10 year old, his body 100 % covered in a black latex suit. He

had long extending fingers, a gas-mask snout of a mouth and nose, and suit-attached reflective eyes, overly large and goggle-lensed.

"What are you??" Nikko asked from her pain, seeing him just sitting there at the couch, possibly in charge of watching over her.

But before she could soak in another moment, a loud thundering of steps came fastly down a set of stairs from behind.

"Devi Jr., you get away from it!" a metallic man's voice could be heard in step with the arrival of the stair-rushing body. "We don't know if it's good with children yet! You leave it to Daddy!"

And just as Nikko tried to turn her aching neck to see, another black latex shape jumped atop her, straddling her at the living room floor and holding her down in place. It was a similar suit style as the small boy, only this the same size as what she had seen outside.

He held her in place, swinging his material covered hand in a slapping strike, but then instead folding his long fingers and hitting her with a closed fist -

"You woke up really fast," he marveled through the gasmask snout. "You must be a feisty thing! Well, we'll have none of that in this house. You will conduct yourself like a well behaved female - We expect nothing less from you."

"Oh, my!" came a similar metal-snout female voice, coming from the sound of the running kitchen sink from behind. "Look at the both you... This is too much..."

"*What?*" the male asked back to her, standing up and bringing Nikko to her feet with him as well. "Do you think this is funny?"

"A little bit, I do..." she laughed, Nikko now able to see her standing in the doorway of the kitchen, the same suit only in obvious female proportions. "You look ridiculous, struggling with a frail little thing like that! Devi, look at your Father..."

The little latex-suited boy looked up at them, peering through his large goggle lenses, and then laughed a small bit as well.

What was so funny? Nikko felt an unmanageable pain coursing throughout her entire being.

"Heh.." the man laughed a bit himself, directing it back to the both of them. "Well it looks to me like you 2 must have been bit by the silly bug!"

He lifted Nikko up effortlessly with his hand and then held her with 2, almost like a wrestling body slam position before pressing her up and down over his head 3 times.

"Not a struggle!" he bragged with his metal voice, then bringing her back down to her unsteady feet. "Let me put this little girl upstairs with the rest of them."

The rest of them? Nikko felt relieved to know her friends would be here and hopefully still alive.

"Oh, Honey, wait wait wait -" the woman stopped him, turning back to the kitchen for a moment. Nikko could now see she had a high, long and straight black ponytail extending from the head of her suit, no black protrusions from her back as did the male. "Here, give their toy back to them - It looks... 'cleaner' now."

The man walked near the stairs, leading Nikko with a strong grip on her wrist, and they met the female at the staircase bottom. She handed something to him in an ivory white contrast to her black - Jigoro?? It was the skull of Jigoro, cleaned off in the kitchen sink by the unreal creature-type woman. Now held by the man and saying nothing, Nikko elected to say nothing in return, keeping quiet so as to not cause anymore pain to herself or her friend.

"And I really want to do something about these things.." the woman said as the man turned to face the steps. "Look at how filthy this creature is.. It must have never even had a home! Do you know how many diseases she must be carrying??"

"I'm sure they had an owner at some point - They certainly didn't dress themselves! Let them get settled in first, SweetHeart..." he paused in his step to reassure her. "We don't want to traumatize them with too much at once.."

"You're right, of course," she lovingly said to him. "But I do think we really need to disinfect them.. At least a good scrubbing.."

"We'll get to it, Darling.. Let them settle in."

And as the woman returned to the kitchen, the male led Nikko up the stairway, Nikko finding it all but impossible to fight back, the man's grip twice the strength of what it should have been. Everything was happening so fast and Nikko didn't even take a chance to talk, trying to cope with the return-pain causing even newer suffering. This family in their latex suits talked as if she were an animal, as if she couldn't understand a single word they were saying..

She focused on her pain for now, Jigoro silently held as they were brought up the stairway, the wall lined with more morbidly framed skin artwork. To the top of the stairs, and he opened a door in the hallway to a girl's themed room, where inside Black Stacy, Kimby, the Chew Mice and Tanuki were scattered about and just sitting around in boredom. A look of joy lit their eyes when they looked and saw Nikko along with the skull Jigoro too.

"And at last, here's your other little friend, and your toy," the latex man said to them, pushing Nikko in and then throwing Jigoro to the bed where Kimby lay.

"Try not to talk, Nikko," Black Stacy immediately instructed, sitting on a dresser and holding a gloved hand over her cheek. "He'll hit you if you do."

The man looked to her and she quickly quieted. "Don't make so much noise.." he warned, then looking over the gathering of Nikko and her party, all in dire form about the room. "What a shaggy looking group you are..."

Nikko headed to stand among the others, nearest to Kimby who now held the bed-tossed Jigoro, and the body-suited man closed the door behind him, leaving the group of friends all alone in the room together.

"... Ok," Nikko said just as soon as a moment passed, "what the heck is going on here??"

"We have to be really quiet," Kimby told both of them, adding to what Black Stacy had said about not talking too much, everyone now gathering at the mattress of the bed. "If you make too much noise, they get really mean.."

"I was trying to talk," Jigoro said, his tone only a small bit quieter, "yelling at them and stuff, and they thought I was like a squeaky toy or something! I've been getting washed in the sink since we got here!"

"And for some reason, unless they're just acting," Black Stacy whispered to the group, focusing her words on Jigoro and Nikko, "I don't think they can understand anything that we say - even though they use the same language as we do. It doesn't make sense.."

"Ok," Nikko said, now understanding only a little bit of why they were treating her like an animal, "but what *happened*? How did we end up here? Was that them hitting us outside?"

"They really hurt you, Nikko," Kimby told her, the Chew Mice now cautiously walking about the bed, Tanuki laying down to rest with his overtired eyes half closed.

"Yeah, they really laid into you for some reason," Jigoro added. "I saw them hit Black Stacy and Kimby too, but not like how you got it.."

"They dragged all of us into the ground, it's like some sort of an underground house down here," Stacy explained, making extra sure to stay quiet. "It looked like the tunnel connected to another room down the hallway, but it went by so fast I don't even know - They took you away from us and downstairs, you were really knocked out cold. I think they thought you were dead! And then they took Jigoro too, he wouldn't stop yelling at them -"

"Well, man! I'm getting tired of seeing you guys get beat up!" he defended himself, Kimby shushing him as he struggled to speak quietly. "But at least I got all of that donkey juice off of me down there in the sink.. You know, I can't remember the last time I was given such a thorough bath by a lady.."

"Well, don't get too attached," Black Stacy leaned in for a deeper conversation. "We're not planning on sticking around here, are we, Nikko?"

"Well, um.." she said and thought, nursing her wounds and worried about the others as well. "I don't want to, but that guy was really strong right now.. I don't know what we could even try to do against someone like him.."

"Why doesn't Stacy just kiss them??" Jigoro asked. "3 quick little smooches, and we're out of here - No problem!"

The others looked to Black Stacy in wait for her response -

"Are you nuts?" she asked, sounding surprised that they all seemed to go along with his thinking. "I don't want those weirdos inside my body! They'd probably try to climb right back out!!"

"I don't understand why you have this amazing super power and all you do is keep a bug in there," Jigoro complained, disheartened by her turn down. "You kept that entire group of shadow animals and dead people inside of you, but you don't want to help us?"

"That was different!" Black Stacy quickly explained. "Those things were maybe important to me, I just couldn't remember them. And Choochie's my little pet - Totally different!"

"You kissed me," Nikko added in, then getting a look from Stacy that made her wish she hadn't mentioned it.

"That was different too," she argued. "I was defending my kingdom.. And you were a lot prettier than these creepy things."

"I still think that's our only option," Jigoro added, staying firm with his decision. "Or have Tanuki make up some illusion."

"I'm not doing it," Black Stacy whisper-shouted, Tanuki walking beneath the bed to hide at the mention of his involvement. "We're really tough - Look at all of the junk we just went through, and we're ok!"

"I still think my leg is broken," Kimby added in, Nikko feeling sorry for her still.

"Things keep getting worse," Black Stacy went on, "so right now, before we even break out, let's make an actual plan this time - And not just to have me kiss things I don't want to kiss. Something to help you, Nikko."

"Me? Ok, but we're all pretty much in trouble together now, I don't want to be selfish.."

"Be selfish!" Black Stacy told her, the group of them still all sitting at the bed. "All of this, even my involvement from when I met you until now, It's all been because of the No-Life King, right? So let's just face him already!"

"Ok, yeah, but how would we even do something like that?" Nikko asked. "He's in my head, and no offense, Stacy, but he doesn't affect any of your memories anymore.. And we all know he hasn't been to anyone else's memories here.."

"That's why we're going to come up with a way to beat him right now together," Stacy said to her. "All or nothing!"

"But why do you want to beat him," Kimby asked and reminded her, "I thought you said that you loved him?"

"Yeah, well... I'm still kind of hoping that when he sees me, he'll leave Nikko," Black Stacy admitted, returning to her true colors, "but for now we have to plan our most drastic measure yet!"

"Well, if we could figure out a way to have all of you face him with me," Nikko thought out loud, "then at least we would have something to try. And just making a happy memory with each of you wouldn't be enough - When I saw him this last time, I could tell that I was the only 1 in the memory that could see what was happening. It would just be the same thing, except with all of you dying.."

"I don't want to die in your memories!" Kimby cried to her, the Chew Mice agreeing with their body language.

"I don't know what all of the commotion is up here..." the metal voice of the latex man came through the reopening door. "But you are making quite a disturbance! Which 1 of you is it?"

Nikko and the others went into silence, the rats fleeing to join the hiding Tanuki beneath the bed as the overpowering man stepped into the room.

"Who wants to accept the responsibility? Who was it?"

All remained silent, aware of his violent temper.

"Well, luckily for you," he went on, relaxing his stance with his back still angled on a forward slouching lean, "Mrs. Lexington has decided to let you all come down and play in the living room for a little while.. I know you probably can't understand what I'm saying, but I want you to follow me down there now. Mrs. Lexington and Devi Jr. are both patiently waiting to see everyone."

He turned and headed out of the room into the hallway, leaving the door open and Nikko getting up to lead them out.

"I don't think we have a choice.." she whispered to her group with her eyes held in fear.

"Leave me here!" Jigoro whispered as he was set back on the bed, Tanuki and the rats still quietly underneath.

"And everyone keep thinking about what our plan should be while we're down there," Black Stacy whispered to all of them, careful to not be too loud.

"Come on, girls, come on," he beckoned them, patting his leg with long rubber fingers, waving the group out into the hallway.

Nikko followed the stairs down, and was able to see the framed skin on the stairway in definite detail now, seeing body art of insects and meticulous writing, a bat-winged strawberry and an octopus too.

Downstairs, Mrs. Lexington and the small Devi Jr. sat anxiously at the couch, waiting for their 'guests.' The television was showing an old black and white tv show, and as they all reached the first floor, the male of the family spoke up and made their formal introduction.

"My beautiful Wife, and my handsome Son," he announced, both of their heads turning to see, "it is with great honor that I introduce to you the newest additions to the Lexington family! Go on, girls, march!"

He pushed at Black Stacy in the back, forcing the line of them to walk into the center of the retro-styled room, Stacy using everything in her power to keep from pushing back.

"They're so adorable!" Mrs. Lexington admired as her Son moved closer, looking like he was just a bit afraid of their appearance. "... But you're not going to let them on the couch, are you, Dear? They still look a spot or 2 'dirtier' than I would like to have in the house..."

"I know.. But they are something to behold, are they not?" the man proudly beamed. "The finest collection that we've had through these parts in some time!"

"What do they do, Dad?" Devi Jr. asked of his Father, looking on from behind his expressionless mask.

"What do they do? Well they probably can do many things! Here, let's find out... You, bikini girl - SIT!"

Black Stacy stood in denial.

A short wait, and he commanded her again. "SIT!"

"I'm not a dog!" she said to him, not caring if he could understand or not. "Don't even think about telling me what to do again."

"She's a noisy little thing," Mrs. Lexington said, Stacy's words not making any sense to the unusual family. "It looks like she doesn't respect her new owners."

"Ha.." Mr. Lexington laughed to himself, taking a step to the coffee table and pushing it off to the side. "She just needs to be broken in, that's all. She's probably been out in the wild so long that she's forgotten what it's like to have people who care about her. Come here, girl.."

Nikko and Kimby looked on from beside Stacy, Nikko cautiously so, aware of the power of Mr. Lexington.

"I said COME HERE, GIRL," he repeated, firmer in his order now.

"She doesn't listen, Dad!" his Son complained. "I like the pale girl better!"

Kimby smiled a pretend smile with all of her teeth, hoping to not draw any more attention to herself as Mr. Lexington made another unsuccessful attempt.

"COME.. HERE.. GIRL..."

"I'm not doing anything for you," Black Stacy pointlessly declared. "I don't take orders from weird freaks like you."

"Stacy..." Nikko carefully whispered, keeping her voice as low as she could to appease the dangerous family. "Please??"

"She's going to need a lot of work," Mrs. Lexington shook her head back and forth. "Maybe we should put her to sleep."

"Nonsense," the Father pulled Black Stacy to the spot where he had pushed aside the coffee table. "She's just a healthy girl. She'll learn the ropes around here -"

"Hey! What are you doing??" Black Stacy tried to fight back as Mr. Lexington put her in a headlock, slipping his arms around her neck from behind in something close to a wrestling sleeper hold.

"Guys!" she called to the panic-stricken Nikko and Kimby. "Get this creep off of me!"

Nikko, defying the pacification that she was trying to maintain, came up to his strong thin arms and tried to pry them from her friend's neck, her strength feeble against his unmatchable might.

"Oh, my!" Mrs. Lexington laughed at the scene, Devi Jr. seeming to join in with the enjoyment as well. "Look at the skirt girl! Haha! Look at her go!"

Mr. Lexington laughed too, amused with Nikko's attempt. "You like that?" he asked, then slipping 1 arm free to push Nikko off to the ground, returning to his wrestling hold.

"Nikko, do something!" Kimby begged, standing back from the scene in nervousness.

Nikko got back up and tugged again hopelessly at his arms, the family laughing even louder this time as if the Father was playing with new puppies on the floor.

"Stacy, can't you get out of it?" Nikko asked as she failed to loosen the hold. "You said you were a wrestler!"

"I never wrestled someone like this!" she yelled as he let go of the hold on his own, her lightheaded body dropping to the floor. "He's a lot stronger than he looks.."

With Nikko pulling at his cold latex skin, Mr. Lexington squatted above the face leaning-down body of Black Stacy, pushing her chest down onto the ground and pulling her legs up into his arms.

"Boston Crab!" Black Stacy shouted as she cried a little bit in pain, the move applied tighter than it would be in a wrestling ring. "This guy's trying to paralyze me!!"

Kimby carefully walked up to stand beside Nikko, adding a helpless effort in trying to pull him off of their friend, the family members on the couch just laughing all of the more.

"I think.. I can beat him, guys..." Stacy stuttered from a short-breath sideways cheek to the ground. "I wanted to fight Shiva Angel -"

"But he's probably a lot stronger than she was!" Nikko argued as she remained fruitlessly yanking on the thin man's arms and body.

"They're making so much noise..." Devi Jr. said as he put his hands where his ears would be. "Mom, they're too loud!"

"Shiva Angel was the best!" Stacy defended, even in this dangerous match up. "If I wanted to beat her, I'd have to be better than anyone!"

Nikko tried to swing an energyless punch at the Husband and Father-figure, her fist just striking him and causing no recoil in his frame.

"Honey!" Mrs. Lexington called to him at the sight of it, no sense of urgency in her voice outside of her enjoyment. "The skirt girl is as wild as the bikini girl!"

"That's alright!" he said as he loosened an arm from the wrestling

Nikko and the NLK

hold, grabbing at Nikko's arm and dropping her beside them with an overly applied armbar hold. "Devitri Lexington can discipline 2 pups at once! Not a problem!"

Kimby tried in small attempts to kick at his body, standing on her good leg and trying to kick with her bad, causing even less of an effect than the attacks of Nikko. Black Stacy remained face down in a 1-legged Boston Crab, Nikko to her side in an escape-less armbar.

"Oh, Dear..." Mrs. Lexington worried as the scene went on. "The carpet.. That skirt girl is getting it all dirty with those filthy clothes of hers!"

"Would you relax?" Mr. Lexington asked his Wife, Kimby still making attempts at helping her friends. "It's not that bad - It'll come right out!"

Mrs. Lexington got up from the couch, her Son clinging to her side, and walked around the wrestling holds as she leaned in to inspect the dirt marks.

Nikko's squinting eyes unintentionally caught a quick glance of the television again - A girl in black and white - Was it the rollerskating girl again?? Seen now, and on tv??

Here eyes shut in pain and then reopened, the girl now gone and the channel back to a show -

"Honey! Really!!" Mrs. Lexington begged her Husband as she wiped a long black finger at a spot that Nikko rolled from. "Look at this filth! I can't get this out! Do you have any idea how much bacteria this must be?"

"Oh, such a neat freak!" he joked, letting go of his single leg hold on Black Stacy, her body still held in place by his weight sitting atop her. "We need to have a little fun once in a while! Right, Devi Jr.?"

The Son nodded just a little, seeming still scared of the helpless girls before him. Mr. Lexington swiftly grabbed at Kimby, pulling her in with a 1 armed headlock to have all 3 girls under his control at once.

"Hey!" he said, jokingly proud of his own feat. "Look at this! No sweat!!"

"SweetHeart!!" Mrs. Lexington screeched, her voice shrill through the metal snout of her mask. "That other girl's as dirty as the skirt girl!! Don't get her on the carpet too -"

"Oh, you worry too much..." he said as now all 3 struggled, Black Stacy growing frustrated just being sat on.

Devi Jr. leaned down and looked at the Black Queen's face, Stacy gritting her teeth and then trying to bite at him, Devi quickly running behind his carpet-checking Mother.

"Darling...." she pleaded again to her husband, this time in a gentle asking manner. "Can you please get those 2 off of it?? That bikini girl isn't so bad, but these 2 are covered in yuck..."

"Oh, have it your way, Dear," he gave in and at last stood up, finally releasing his holds on all 3 of the girls. "I don't think they're really that bad.."

"Well, you wouldn't," she told him as Nikko and friends nursed their aching limbs. "But the woman who's in charge of scrubbing all of this mess believes so..."

Mr. Lexington rolled the sore Black Stacy over to face up, wrapping his rubbery latex legs with hers and then sat down facing her, their legs locked in an extra tight Figure 4 Leglock.

Black Stacy bit hard at her lip, the pain evident across her whiter than usual face.

"Why don't you go on ahead and clean those 2 up then?" Mr. Lexington suggested, Nikko holding her arm and Kimby rubbing her neck, still favoring her previously hurt leg. "I'll finish up with this girl down here, and then we'll put them back in their room."

"Oh! Do you want to get a really nice warm bath??" Mrs. Lexington delighted at the idea and leaned down toward Kimby, asking as if she really was an animal. "And what about you, you dirty girl?" she asked Nikko, Nikko saying nothing back in fear of a stricter punishment.

"Devi Jr.," his Father ordered, the boy cowering behind the thin legs of his Mother, "help your Mom get those girls upstairs, would you?"

He nodded, Black Stacy looking on in a sorrowful look from the leg hold.

"This will be so much fun!" Mrs. Lexington led Nikko by her hurting arm toward the stairs, Devi Jr. following behind Kimby.

"Come up.. with something.." Black Stacy tried to remind them as they were brought back upstairs, still hurting in her floor-discipline wrestling hold. "All I can think of... is.. a wedding.."

A wedding??

"Don't be too long with that girl," Mrs. Lexington called down as Nikko slipped a confused yet acknowledging look to Stacy below. "I don't want her getting even wilder!"

Mr. Lexington showed a thin latex bicep, flexing an arm from his leglock floor hold to his Son and Wife, both now up the stairs.

What did Stacy mean by a wedding? Nikko almost gathered the strength to yell down to her, knowing that none of the family could understand them, but feared the repercussions she would face for making such a loud noise.

    To the top, and Mrs. Lexington led the 2 hurting girls past the closed door of their holding room - Jigoro, Tanuki and the Chew Mice still closed within. Down through the hallway, and Nikko wondered which door led to where they had been pulled from the surface. Before she could even try to see, she and Kimby were brought into a simple small bathroom. It was tiled in white with a white high sink, no cabinets or mirrors, and a white old-fashioned 4-leg bathtub, no toilet seen in sight.

    "Devi, start the water for me, would you?" the lady asked as she made sure that Kimby came all of the way in too, neither girl trying to fight back as they feared the black-covered woman. "That's a good boy," she told her Son as she prodded for the girls to walk the short steps to the tub, bringing them to the lip of it. "Now both of you get in, and don't force me to discipline you - I'm not as kind-Hearted as my Husband."

    Nikko, unknowing how to react to this, stepped into the high white tub with her clothes still on, her boots leaving dirty prints from the slight water in it's base.

    "And you as well," the woman gently moved along Kimby, forcing her to stand just in front of Nikko, facing forward towards the faucet. "There's plenty of room for both of you in here, don't be shy."

    She pushed at Nikko's shoulders to sit down, and the force was just as strong as her Husband's had been, a sheer brute strength through her long thin body. Nikko came to a sitting position, facing forward and Kimby forced to sit in front of her as well, Nikko's legs on both sides of her and both now sitting like 2 young girls being bathed by their Mother.

    "I'm glad that you both seem to be more docile than that bikini girl," Mrs. Lexington said in a quiet metallic voice, on her knees beside the tub and letting the water run without a stopper into the drain. "I hope you're not too attached to her.. I'm not sure how long a temperament like that will last in this household."

    "Nikko, I don't want to be here -" Kimby cried to her friend. "These people are scaring me..."

    Mrs. Lexington looked at her and made no immediate motion, Nikko fearing that she was about to strike the terrified girl.

    "Oh, you poor thing..." she said as she stroked Kimby's short black hair with her latex fingers. "Devi, I think your new favorite is cold -

Could you make the water warmer for your Mother?"

Nikko looked over Kimby's shoulder, setting her chin against it as she shivered, not from the cold but from the pain and the fear, and watched as Devi Jr. turned the hot water control to it's limit. The water came out only a little faster, though the temperature quickly grew much higher.

"There," she said, splashing a hot dose of it onto Kimby's kimono, "that'll be better for you, don't you think?"

"Nikko, it's hot," Kimby whimpered, Nikko wishing Kimby would just stay quiet and try to make it through this.

Mrs. Lexington slapped a water-heated hand against Kimby's face, the wet latex making a sound that rang louder than just a woman's hand against the skin. Kimby cried and Nikko squeezed her, hoping to keep her voice down and just suffer through the worst.

"WE DON'T MAKE SO MUCH NOISE," the lady scolded Kimby with a voice reminiscent of the horrible Burress. "Is it that difficult to understand me??"

The water was heating up past the level of tolerability. Without the drain plugged, a small level of it collected as a pool and constantly emptied out into the drain. Nikko could feel it on her bare legs and underneath her skirt, her skin already turning red where the water touched. A splash of it, 1 after another onto mostly Kimby, and she could feel the heat rising even higher.

"All of this grime," Mrs. Lexington stood up and looked them over, then reaching for a black scrubbing brush hanging beside the shower head, "and to think Mr. Lexington was letting you roll all over my living room!"

Devi Jr. stood back and looked on as his Mother pulled a release above the faucet, stopping the water flow and sending it up into the wall-mounted shower head. It made a chugging sound, the water pressure lifting the hot stream up through the pipes, and just as Mrs. Lexington removed it from the wall, the hot water sprayed from it - Kimby jumping up as the scolding hot spray hit her skin first -

"Sit back down!" Mrs. Lexington pushed at her with the scrubbing brush, forcing her back down into the space between Nikko's legs. "Don't make this so difficult for me!!"

Kimby screamed and now Nikko felt the pain too, the water spray from the hand-held shower head many levels above burning. Rapid-fire drops scorched onto their flesh and Nikko pushed off to stand up from instinct alone, Mrs. Lexington screaming at her and pushing her

Nikko and the NLK

back down, both girls helpless against her might.

"I know that you're scared of the water," she said as she held the shower head and scrubbed at Kimby's legs and kimono, "but you are both *far* too dirty to live in a nice house like this. That's what happens when you wander around the World's Teeth like you were doing.."

~ The World's Teeth? Nikko remembered the name of the strange sounding place, a place MilkTank said it had traveled through just before it reached Summerland ~

"No!!!" Kimby cried with all of her Heart, in the front and stuck with the worst of the fire hot water. "Nikko!!!"

Nikko had to stop thinking, instantly crying from the burn of the water splashing back at her and under her legs, trying to ease her pain by shifting her weight from 1 leg and to the other.

Mrs. Lexington stood with a spike-heel shoe on the tub lip, standing on an angle to spray the water more effectively. "And don't think I'm not going to get you," she laughed as she sprayed back at Nikko - The full on blast blistering every exposed inch of her -

"Please... stop!!!" she cried out, the words a raspy scream in her suffering.

The evil woman took her leg back off of the tub and worked her way to the back half, focusing more on Nikko as Kimby wept and shook against her. The scrubbing brush was placed on her shirt and beneath her tie, scrubbing her clothes so rigidly and pressing hard against her skin beneath. Nikko gasped for air, the stove-hot water never ending, and her body felt as if it was going to go into shock.

"Devi, be a doll and get your Mother some clean towels?" she asked her watching Son, thinking nothing of the torture she was dealing out.

After all of the scolding abuse and suffering, their screams no doubt easily heard throughout the entire house, at long last Mrs. Lexington set the brush aside, turning the water shower head off and placing it back in the wall-mounted holder.

"Thank you, young Sir," she said to her Son, taking the white towels from his hands and motioning for the poor girls to rise to their feet. "Just a little rinse and scrub for today. Come on, now. Up and out."

Nikko pushed to help the shaking Kimby stand up again, and as she slowly stepped from the tub, Nikko rose to her feet as well. She felt unsteady and off balance, her skin stinging and steam rising from her drenched clothing.

"Use the towels to dry off," Mrs. Lexington said as the girls held them around their bodies, shaking from the burns. "That wasn't so bad, was it?"

Nikko held her mouth open, her lower lip trembling at all of these assaults on her body. Even if she wanted to risk the abuse, there was nothing she could have said to describe the physical pain she felt.

"Silly me, as if you could talk!" the lady waved for them to follow her back out the through the door, Devi Jr. by her side and the 2 girls slowly stumbling behind her. "It's easy to forget you're so different then we are sometimes, but we'll learn to love you regardless. We always do."

She led them back to the door of their room, opening it and forcing them in. Stacy was back inside, sitting on the floor and rubbing her limbs from the impromptu wrestling match downstairs.

"Clean as a whistle!" Mr. Lexington observed as he looked over the returning girls, walking up behind them from the hall.

"And I see you listened to me and stopped horsing around with that bikini girl," Mrs. Lexington joined him, Devi Jr. peaking in around the corner.

"As I always listen to you, Dear.." he wrapped his arms around her from behind, both looking in as Nikko and Kimby softly stepped to their worn out companion. "Now, we would like all of you to get a good first night's rest here."

"That's right," Mrs. Lexington added. "You're all very lucky to be taken in by a kind family such as ours."

Mr. Lexington squeezed her with his arms, affectionately holding her. "Tomorrow, we're going to spend some more time with each of you, and we'll try to get you more accustomed to your new home. That means a little more playing, and a little more discipline!"

"Say goodnight to them, Devi," Mrs. Lexington told her Son and looked down to him, her loving look hidden by the goggle eyes and gasmask.

Devi Jr. shook his head, shyly looking away from the new additions to his family.

"Oh, you'll come around, Buddy!" his Father laughed, letting go of his Wife and reaching in to turn off the light, closing the door then to leave the room in total darkness.

At last they were alone again...

"...What happened to you guys?" Jigoro whispering in the complete black. "It sounded like you were being murdered over there.."

"I tried to open the door after he brought me back up here," Black Stacy said in a lighter-than-Jigoro whisper, her voice floating through the no-light room as she was walking across it, "but it doesn't open from the inside.. I think the knob only works from the hallway.."

The light came on and Black Stacy was standing near the switch, looking a little better off than she had in the light just a moment ago.

"Seriously," she said, "are you both ok??"

Kimby shook her head back and forth, a frown as the Chew Mice came out from under the bed and investigated her.

"...We'll be ok..." Nikko whispered, the blistering burns coursing across her entire body. "But we have to get out of here - Are *you* ok, Stacy??"

She held her shoulder and swung her arm around, winding it up. "I'll heal.. That guy's not so bad at wrestling, but I had to make it look worse than it was so he wouldn't do it harder."

Nikko believed her, but wasn't sure if Black Stacy would really tell her how bad it was or not.

"Man, everything keeps getting worse in this world.." Jigoro said, Nikko coming to sit down beside his skull on the mattress of the bed. Her legs stung when she sat, the cooling wet of the towel helping ease it only just a little.

"Did you hear me when I said wedding?" Black Stacy asked Nikko, looking at her as if this was of the utmost importance. "You were going up the stairs, so I didn't know.."

"I heard you," Nikko tried blocking out her pain as she saw poor Kimby sulking with her rats. "What were you talking about?"

"Oh, brother," Jigoro spoke loudly until Stacy brought her finger to her lips to remind him. "This girl thinks we can beat the No-Life King with a wedding."

"What do you mean?" Nikko asked, Kimby looking up from the floor as they talked.

"Yeah, she told me all about it right before you just got here," Jigoro went on, sounding unimpressed by Black Stacy's solution. "Tell me we're not doing it?"

"Let me explain it, Jigoro!" Stacy sat next to Nikko and waved for Kimby to move closer.

"Ugh, please spare me," he complained as Kimby and the Chew Mice slowly came to the bed. "Once was enough.."

"Well, let them hear me out, please" she added a serious tone to her whisper. "I've been trying to think of an indirect route to the No-Life King. I know we can't just go in your brain and see him, right? So why can't we bring him out into this world, where he can face us right here outside of a memory?"

"But he only shows up *in* my memories," Nikko reminded her, not following what Black Stacy was getting at.

"I know," she agreed. "And that's the only way that I ever saw him too. But we forget that he doesn't live in the past, like our memories. He exists in the present, the same as all of us."

"I don't understand what you want us to do.." Nikko apologized, wondering how this plan could even be attempted.

"That's exactly what I said," Jigoro added in. "And I told her, why don't you just lay a giant kiss on this entire family the next time they walk through that door, and -"

"Well, listen!" Black Stacy stopped him, a sense of accomplishment behind her voice. "Things have gotten so bad now - None of us have even been happy since we were at the Yokai Party with Oyomi.. We may not be able to help you in your memories, Nikko, but we can make something even better than them. Take that happiness that we had at the ghost party and do something like that again, only like a *million* times better.."

"And what exactly are you thinking?" Nikko asked, hoping Stacy was on to something.

"I'm thinking of all of us getting away from this suffering we've been going through. Then we try as hard as we possibly can, with all of our Hearts, to create the single greatest moment in each of our lives - all at the same time. Something that would be so perfectly wonderful, so memorable, that it would be the best day ever.."

Nikko felt a little light turn on in her Heart - It wasn't what she was expecting them to come up with, but it was the only idea they had right now.

"I like it..." Kimby said, almost a small smile on her sad lips.

"Truthfully, I can't remember much of anything from my life," Black Stacy told them, "but you know that feeling when something really great is happening, and you catch yourself thinking - 'This is going to be something that I look back at 1 day?' If we could take that, and explode it to be so many times bigger - And don't hold back? What if we made a real-life happening memory so great that the No-Life King stood up and noticed, and came into our world?"

Nikko and the NLK

"How could we do it?" Nikko asked, liking the idea though not really convinced it could actually work.

"We get married!" Black Stacy declared - Jigoro laughing almost too loud, and Kimby gasping even in her pain at the thought.

"That's the wedding you were talking about?" Nikko questioned her, now the idea sounding too ridiculous. "You and I? Are you joking??"

"Well, what else could it be??" she asked. "That's like the ultimate, isn't it? I think that I used to want to get married.. Didn't you?"

Nikko bit her lip. She hadn't thought about it in a very long time, but getting married used to be 1 of her taken for granted dreams. Something that she always assumed would have happened, but now, after 'death...'

"Yeah..." she admitted, though thinking not to someone like the sword swallower, let alone a girl.

"Great!" Black Stacy beamed with enthusiasm. "And obviously it's important that you be the Bride or Groom, just to maximize the chance that it reaches NLK.. And for me, I don't think Kimby would want to be standing next to you if the No-Life King showed up.. And Jigoro -"

"I'm not doing it," he answered for her.

"So it would have to be you and I!" she concluded. "But we couldn't just get married here.. We would have to go somewhere that would be really wonderful for a wedding."

"Yeah," Jigoro laughed, "like there's going to be somewhere in this world that won't have something trying to kill us the entire time.. What an outstanding place to get married.."

"The World's Teeth.." Nikko thought out loud, thinking back to what Mrs. Lexington had said during the horrible bathtime.

"The world's what?" Jigoro asked.

"The World's Teeth," Nikko repeated. "That's where Mrs. Lexington said we were right now. That's the same place I remember MilkTank mentioning."

"That stupid robot?" Jigoro let out an angry sigh. "I don't remember what it was saying."

"Of course you don't," Nikko told her skull friend, "you were too busy talking - But I listened to it - MilkTank said that when it traveled to the End of the World, Summerland, it passed through all sorts of places, and the last place was the World's Teeth."

Tanuki came out from under the bed at all of this mentioning of MilkTank and Summerland, yawning from a nap and now sitting down to listen.

"So if we were to have this wedding, we would have to do it in Summerland..." Nikko said with a firm belief in her Heart about it now. "It would be our only chance."

"I'm not buying it," Jigoro still complained. "It's so far-fetched, how could it even work?"

"We just have to believe it will," Nikko told him. "Jigoro, if he comes into my mind again, even you said that you think he's going to kill me.. Don't we have to try something?"

"But how do we even get out of here?" Kimby still wondered, Black Stacy offering nothing and all eyes at Nikko, except for Jigoro who was set facing forward.

"Well..." she began and thought hard, getting used to Stacy coming up with the ideas as of late. "Um..."

Nikko thought about what had been happening deep down inside. Somewhere on this road, she had lost her leadership role and Black Stacy had become the person to help them, to save them in the Burrow's Pocket and now to come up with the only thought-out idea. Nikko realized that it was time to make an effort again - All of this, after all, was revolving around her it seemed.

"The only reason that we even made it this far," she stated, "was because all of us clung to whatever was left of our lives - Against all odds. We *are* going to leave here, and go to Summerland. And we're going to have the happiest day of our lives, together. Tanuki," she said and looked down to him, "I appreciate everything you've been through with us, but now we need you to use your power and really come through."

Nikko leaned over and looked at Kimby, her eyes then going down to the skeleton Chew Mice and focusing her attention at them.

"Chewy, Chewart, Chewington," she said to them, "I know that the 3 of you love Kimby more than anything, and she needs to get out of this horrible place just like the rest of us. I need all of you to be brave and help her now."

Everyone felt a sense of duty, the pain of these past experiences weighing down their Hearts for too long.

"Jigoro," Nikko looked to the friend she was closest with of all, "I need you to do this 1 thing for me.. Please?"

"...Yeah," he hesitated before finally answering. "Ok, I'll do whatever it takes.."

The room was silent, everyone waiting for Nikko to give her orders. They had survived so much, showing weakness and fears, but now they were ready to maybe stand strong, asking no questions and banding together.

"Tanuki," Nikko called to the yawning animal, sitting there and patiently waiting her commands, "I need you to take the skull of Jigoro and the bones of the Chew Mice, and I need you to use your magic... Do you know what the 'Odokuro' is?"

The Tanuki yawned again, and then after a moment nodded his sleepy head in acknowledgement.

"Yes!!" Nikko almost celebrated too loudly, Black Stacy and Kimby unsure of what they were talking about.

"We are going to create the Odokuro, right now," Nikko explained to her friends. "It's a Japanese giant-skeleton legend, made up of infinite bones and skulls.. And that's what's going to get us out of here and carry us to Summerland.."

The group looked around at each other, unsure of the sudden idea Nikko had come up with.

"Hmmm..." Jigoro hummed to himself, not wasting anymore time. "Ok. Let's do it right now!"

Nikko and the NLK

Nikko and the NLK

~ Someone must have called the police ~

~ I can hear the sirens driving closer ~

~ Will anyone remember the 'me' before this? ~

~ Even if they remember, I suppose everything changes now ~

~ It's time to get going. Nothing lasts forever ~

~ No need to clean up or put anything away ~

~ I won't be coming back this time ~

Nikko and the NLK

CHAPTER 10

Summerland Wedding

With Tanuki's eyes closed in a no-leaf trance, the group anxiously waited in the locked room of the Lexington's household. Kimby's Chew Mice stood before him at the bed, Jigoro set there in wait as well, and in a small moment, already the transformation was about to begin.

"Do you know what this is going to be like?" Black Stacy asked, hoping that this was definitely the best way to put her own idea into action.

"Well, of course I've never really seen it before," Nikko stated as she watched the magic unfold. "But I've seen them in drawings, and video games..."

"Whoa... This feels weird.." Jigoro said, glowing as he began to slide across the sheet of the bed. "Nikko, I hope you're right about this!"

Chewy stood strong, Chewart and Chewington trying to back away as the gravity pulled their tiny bodies into the skull, an overpowering light from the encasing glow.

"I think this is it!" Nikko quietly exclaimed, her face smiling and pain to the side in anticipation of the creature. "Jigoro, don't forget to pick us up! And don't step on us!!"

"..Huh??" he asked, his voice from the illumination and then silent, a fast flash and then a full-bone skeleton lay there at the bed, normal size and growing.

"Oh, gross!!" Kimby said in shock as she stood up, letting the towel drop from her wet kimono to the ground. "Is *that* the Chew Mice??"

And the skeleton grew - Growing from it's human size to a larger mass, the bone-set of the body taking the tiny shapes of many bones to make up each larger single bone. The little skeletons of the Chew Mice continuously multiplied, making up more and more bones as they stretched even longer.

"Jigoro!" Nikko called to his growing skull atop the magic body. "Do you feel ok?? It doesn't hurt, does it?"

But the black eyeless holes looked down in silence, the body still growing and no words to say.

Nikko and the NLK

Tanuki strained as he leaflessly concentrated.

Still growing..

"This is amazing," Black Stacy admired the sight before her, looking up as the skeleton began filling the entire room. "I can't believe what I'm looking at.."

It's legs were bent in hundreds of smaller bones for each side, it's upper body and skull bending down to even fit inside of the bedroom now, the growing bones pressing against the ceiling.

And as it began to outgrow the room's capacity, it held a multiple bone constructed skeletal hand open at the floor. Nikko hurried Stacy and Kimby onto it's ivory palm, carefully picking up the trance-state Tanuki and setting him inside beside them.

The walls began to crack, long single cracks appearing 1 after another, and pieces of dirt fell from the pushed-against ceiling. The group sat down within the bone hand, the tight quarters of it's palm growing larger still, all girls staying huddled together as they were unsure of what to expect next.

"WHAT IN THE WORLD IS GOING ON IN -" came the voice of Mr. Lexington as he opened the bedroom door, nearly the entire room filled with the bent-knee giant Odokuro now, silencing the evil man the moment he lay eyes on the impossibly growing creature.

"Honey, what did they do -" Mrs. Lexington asked as she and Devi Jr. walked into view. "WHAT IN THE WORLD IS THAT THING??"

The Odokuro grew, it's tiny-bone large bones breaking the side walls in a structure-crushing press, the Lexington family fleeing in terror. It pressed against the dirt-falling ceiling, it's right leg then breaking through the floor, Nikko and her group holding on tightly as they could see the first floor through the splintered floorboards and dust. The skeleton's left leg pressed next, pushing off of the destroyed ruins of the room.

"Hold on tight, you guys..." Nikko warned as she gathered her friends around her, Tanuki controlling the overpowering illusion from the center in between them.

"Why didn't we do this before??" Black Stacy laughed amid the destruction. "We're so stupid! This is awesome!"

And the Odokuro pushed it's spine and free hand against the ceiling of the home, the tiles falling and a waterfall of soil spilling in. It closed it's bone hand in a protective fist around the girls and continued to press upwards, stretching to the world above as it clawed with it's free hand at the ground covering the home.

"It's working!" Kimby yelled as she joined in on the excitement, feeling the power in their control at last. "Nikko, you were right!"

The Odokuro broke out from the underground house, it's bones continuing to multiply as it emerged into the outside world of Daiyomi, clawing from the ground of the World's Teeth like an actual skeleton rising from it's grave.

The outside air poured into the now-ceilingless house as the giant Odokuro took it's first full step out of the hole, standing tall in the deserted landscape. It towered 8 stories high and began a slow and steady stride, each step covering land that would have taken minutes to travel, the horrible home of the Lexingtons demolished behind in ruin..

"I can't believe this worked!" Nikko laughed, hugging Black Stacy and Kimby too as they relaxed held in the cupped bone hand. "This is amazing..."

"Seriously..." Black Stacy agreed, carefully standing up on the palm of bones, the skeleton staying steady now at the gargantuan size it was. "Why the heck didn't we just do this from the start?? I didn't know the Tanuki could do stuff on this scale!"

"And my little guys, too!" Kimby added, staying seated with Nikko and seeming a bit unsure of standing up. "They're all of these little bones right now?? How cool!"

"And don't forget Jigoro.." Nikko said admirably, looking up at his eyeless and now giant skull, untalking and staring straight into the distance. "This is everybody working together! I really had no idea Tanuki could actually do something like this. That giant frog thing was pretty outstanding, but this is better yet! And I didn't know he could do that kind of damage with just illusions!"

The girls took a moment to soak it all in, letting the supernatural skeleton carry them across the land. The jagged rocks of the World's Teeth passed by beneath the giant steps of the Odokuro, and the fire clouds in the sky seemed so close to his skull this far up. Of all of the things they had been through, Nikko held a new admiration for Jigoro at this moment of their adventure. Looking back, she found herself amazed by his strength to live on without a body, and now with the aid of illusion, being able to carry them to safety from the worlds of horror behind.

"He's taking us to that Summerland that you talked about, right?" Black Stacy asked, standing at the cupped fingers of the hand and looking out into the distance.

"I would think so," Nikko hoped. "He seems to know where he's going.. I don't know if Tanuki's making it walk, or if it's walking on it's own, but I think we'll be ok.."

"Well, no matter what, we got away from that place.." Kimby added, happy to just be outside again. "My clothes are still all wet though.."

"Maybe Tanuki can make them feel dry?" Stacy asked, looking over at the waterlogged Nikko as well.

"We'll be fine. Let's let Tanuki just concentrate on the Odokuro for now.. He's doing all of this without a leaf on his head, remember? We don't want to wear him out!"

They continued further through Daiyomi, the methodical steps of the skeleton like clockwork, it's bones-shaped-into-bones moving like the gears of a machine, long stepping over large patches of black earth and broken rocks. Jigoro still made not a sound, his skull so high up above them, never-stopping his looking forward into the march.

"*So....* How are we going to go about this wedding?" Nikko asked the girls, serious now that the first phase had been put into action.

"Um..." Kimby looked around and thought. "You still want to get married to Stacy?"

"Sure," Nikko told her, "why not? And I'll be the groom."

"Ha! Seriously?" Stacy smiled. "Are you sure?"

"Yeah, it'll be fun," Nikko said with a little laugh. "I'll even get a marker and draw a goofy moustache on my face."

Kimby laughed and then Stacy too, Nikko smiling as at last they could enjoy a moment together.

"Well, we'll have to pick a really beautiful spot once we get there," Black Stacy said, leaning a bit forward and spreading her hands across the bones of the palm, as if demonstrating a scene. "I know we could just have Tanuki make the grounds, but we should think about having him do something else."

"Yeah," Nikko agreed, "but not like attacking the No-Life King.. I think we should see if he can create people to attend the wedding."

"Oh! That would be really neat!" Kimby bursted out.

Black Stacy leaned back now, resting on her hands. "But it can't just be anybody. We should have people that mean a lot to us.. Only I don't know if I can remember anyone, really.."

"And I don't even know anybody!" Kimby pouted in disappointment, a worried look across her face.

"Well, that's ok," Nikko assured them. "And I'm not going to use any of the people from my life before. I can talk to Tanuki about all of the different people and things that we've met.. He can have them come, and even the mean ones would act nice, since they aren't really real!"

"Yeah," Kimby agreed, sounding a little unexcited, "but don't bring that family we just saw."

"Well, of course not."

"Or that Burrow guy..."

"We won't bring anyone like that," Nikko told her, "we'll just bring who we're all ok with, ok? It's supposed to be the best day, and we won't let anything ruin that."

"And what will you guys wear?" Black Stacy asked them both. "I already have something planned ahead."

"Really?" Nikko asked her in surprise. "Tell us! What's it like?"

Stacy hesitated. "I really don't want to say yet - Besides, isn't the groom supposed to wait to see?"

"Ha... Yeah, I suppose you're right.." Nikko laughed. "I think I might have Tanuki put me in a black tuxedo, something super traditional looking.. I really want to get into the spirit of this.."

The dark world was passing so rapidly. The winding turns around rock formations were cleared with a fraction of a single step for the Odokuro, a break coming in the seemingly forever night sky ahead.

"Look, guys..." Black Stacy instructed from her lookout at the skeleton's upward bent fingers. "Do you see it??"

All 3 looked to the light at the end of the sky - It wasn't a sunrise, but something closer to a natural end of the black. Like a painting, the blues, reds and oranges of sunlight smeared into the colorless, 2 opposites pressing together, ending and beginning where they were brilliantly intermixed.

"That has to be it," Nikko smiled, her Heart unexpectedly jumping as their idea became even closer to realization. "I can't believe it - This is all actually coming together.."

"It's looks so beautiful," Stacy marveled, "doesn't it?"

Nikko grinned and just looked on, looking ahead to the closer change in the world. So much black was at last falling away to light, nevermind the brief and deathly sunlight of the SuperCross. This was real and like a Heaven after death, each step of the giant skeleton bringing them closer to the sunlit colors than the midnight blacks behind.

The ground cut up, the broken World's Teeth rocks stabbing and ending beneath the new sky, new land just ahead and the deep world of the Summerland opened up before them -

"This is the place, guys," Nikko told her friends as they passed into it, all of the black landscape put behind. "This is what someone I met told me was the 'End of the World' - Summerland.."

The Odokuro took a long and final step over the dangerous rocks, it's towering body continuing on into the warm new world of paradise. The colors of the sky now locked into a bold and bright blue, perfect green grass over small hills and fairways - Up ahead, the arched shape of a familiar rainbow, only now an actual rainbow in the sky.

"This is so great.." Kimby let out her final shiver, the warmth of the Summerland sun heating and beginning to dry her wet clothing.

"I've never seen anything like this, I don't think," Black Stacy admired, looking down with the others at the scenery they rode above.

There were actually a few people down below now too, their hair powdered white wigs and dressed in Rococo period clothing. The ladies were in elegant fall and summer color dresses, the men in petticoats and fancy fashions. They were far and wide separated, and as Nikko and her party passed within the hands of the giant skeleton, they nonchalantly looked up from their picnics and parasol strolls, some even offering a friendly wave to the travelers.

"They aren't even scared of us.. Or the Odokuro!" Nikko said in amazement, everything happening so well at last. "I wonder if any of the people here would come to the wedding??"

"Er, they would probably end up getting killed.." Black Stacy grimly suggested, waving back along with the other girls. "We might not want to bring strangers.."

"You're right," Nikko almost forgot in her excitement what they were planning. "This really is such a nice place. No wonder MilkTank made the journey here every year."

The other girls, unsure exactly of who or what MilkTank was, continued to watch the scenery, captivated by the elegant beauty of the painting-like land they rode through. There were fountains below and gazebos, weeping willow trees and romantic couples out drifting by in rowboats, glancing up to the creature that passed, not in the least phased by it's presence.

Nikko looked to the rainbow and now saw that it was nearing like a landmark, not just a creation of light and rain in the air. Could it mean something? All of those attempts to catch up with that rainbow girl, and now here was an actual rainbow, static and unchanging..

"Do you think we should keep heading in?" Nikko asked, hoping for a little guidance from her friends. "We're already here now.."

"Oh... I'll let my groom decide on this," Black Stacy replied, Kimby laughing at the words. "Would my 'Husband-to-be' like to be married in the flower garden down *here*," she pointed down, a beautiful flower-wall garden just below them now. "Or would 'he' prefer to be married.. In the statued yard over *there*?"

Nikko looked briefly at the spots Black Stacy jokingly pointed to - It was all very nice, and probably any location here at all would suffice for what they planned, but she couldn't keep her eyes from looking ahead to the fast-approaching rainbow. She had never seen a such a thing so close-up in her life, it's colors unfading, almost solid colored and nearly without transparency.

"I think I want to be by the rainbow," she told her friends, hoping either Tanuki or the Odokuro could hear her and understand. "Don't you think? It looks so beautiful.."

"I think so too," Kimby agreed, a happiness returning to her face that Nikko hadn't seen in some time.

"Then near the rainbow it shall be, my future-Husband!" Black Stacy joked to her, a smiling smirk across her lips. "Although, I must tell you.. I don't think we can get a whole lot closer than this.."

Nikko looked again towards the color arch in the sky - Only moments later, and they were nearly beneath it! "This is.. Incredible.." she said in disbelief. "I didn't think it was even possible to do this.."

"It's right here!" Kimby craned her head to look skyward. "Jigoro's almost touching it!"

"I don't think they're normally this close to the ground.." Nikko explained. "But this is it then, right? We should go down here??"

"Whatever you think we should do," Black Stacy answered, Kimby nodding in agreement. "We're right behind you, Nikko!"

"Ok! I don't know exactly how to do this," she said as she spoke towards the others. "Tanuki? Jigoro? You can let us down now."

With a finished, careful-stepping last stride, the Odokuro skeleton came to a stand, kneeling then to 1 massive bone knee.

"They heard you!" Kimby exclaimed, happy to not just fall from the sky, and the giant skeleton lowered it's carrying hand to the grassy ground below.
The girls stepped off, Nikko helping Kimby with her still-hurt leg, and they stood at the ground of Summerland, so much more beautiful down here in all of it's details.
"Wow.." Kimby gazed wide-eyed, white butterflies dancing past her face. "This is like Heaven here.."
"It's everything I imagined," Nikko thought out loud, thinking back to how long ago MilkTank had told her about it. "It's the End of the World, and paradise.."
Black Stacy picked the concentrating Tanuki up from the palm, and as he opened his sleepy eyes, the entire Odokuro illusion came to an abrupt end -

The uncountable bones zoomed down into a small size, and the massive skull shrunk just atop them - In the blink of an eye, Jigoro, Chewy, Chewart and Chewington were all back before them, none looking worse for the wear.

"My brave little guys!" Kimby cried to the Chew Mice, the 3 restored skeleton rats running to their best friend. "I'm so proud of you!!"
"And hey - Good job, Jigoro!" Nikko congratulated him as she picked his regular sized skull off of the grassy ground. "And you too, Tanuki.. You guys did everything better than we could have ever hoped for.. Thank you so much!!"
"I kept on trying to talk," Jigoro said, right back to his ways, "but nothing would come out! I was talking about everything! Did you see those women with the powdered wigs?? I've waited to see stuff like that my entire life!!"
"And then an *extra* thank-you, Tanuki," Nikko added on, "for the non-talking version of the Odokuro!"
"Hey!" Jigoro countered, Tanuki already off and following Stacy.
"Guys, look at this place over here," she called to them, walking just ahead. "What do you think about it?"
Nikko walked along, Jigoro back in her arms, and Kimby slightly limping with her rats beside her. Black Stacy waited atop a small hill

directly in front of them, looking down over a scene just out of their sight. As they walked up, Nikko couldn't help but breathe in the breeze, so warm and clean, fighting to hold back any summertime memories it could possibly stir.

"This.." Nikko stopped and stood atop the hill. "This is it.."

"Really?" Stacy looked at her and then back at the scene.

"Yeah... This is where we'll have our wedding."

It was another simple paradise of the Summerland, nothing greater than the rest, but special in it's own sort of way. It was green grass and perfect flowers, a tiny circular pond of water, white swans and floating lilys, and a short white wood-railed walkway that led to a pond-centered gazebo - All directly beneath the impossible rainbow.

Kimby walked carefully, Chewington and Chewart running ahead of her, Chewy back riding atop her chest.

"We should look for that Milk the stupid robot was bragging about," Jigoro suggested as the others gazed at the beauty of the scene, Tanuki growling at his unsavory words.

"If we survive the No-Life King," Nikko said, her words a reminder of the danger they would soon possibly face, "I promise we'll go find that Milk he talked about.. Stacy?" Nikko asked to her friend, Kimby and her rats down and in the gazebo already playing. "Does a place like this bring back any memories to you?"

"Not so much, I mean, I remember summer afternoons like this, but nothing happy.. Why, do you?"

"Yeah," she replied. "I'm trying really hard not to, but I think I'm remembering a lot of happy things - I don't know how long I can do this."

"Ok -" Black Stacy said, an urgency quickly coming over her voice. "We can't rush the celebration, but we need to get started right away. Let's get married right now!"

"Holy cow, I still can't believe this.." Jigoro sighed.

"Well you need to believe it," Black Stacy ordered him. "We all have to believe in this 100%, or nothing... KIMBY!" she called down to the ghostly girl, heading a few steps towards her. "You have to help us tell Tanuki what to do now!"

Tanuki widened his sleepy eyes in surprise at his name, Nikko noticing and immediately feeling bad about his involvement.

"I know you must be exhausted after what you've done for us," Nikko said, holding Jigoro and petting Tanuki with her free hand, "but we need you to just do a little bit more, and then afterwards you can sleep all day! I promise!"

"That's 2 promises!" Jigoro said as Tanuki rubbed up against the petting hand. "Don't forget about the Milk already!"

"What's going on?" Kimby asked as she and the Chew Mice returned, traces of her hot-water burns seen in the sunlight.

"We're going to have you guys tell Tanuki what you want," Stacy explained. "And while you get ready, I'm going to go get dressed for the big moment!"

"Aren't you just going to have him dream up a dress for you?" Nikko asked, looking down at Tanuki and then back to her.

"No..." Black Stacy said, unable to look up from the ground as if holding a secret. "Here, just a second.."

She hunched over like she had back in the Burrow's Pocket, her furry gloved middle finger pressed into the back of her mouth and throat.

"I love when you do this.." Jigoro swooned as she made her small gag and throw-up noises, Kimby looking on grossed out.

And out from between her lips, from the Bottomless Kiss to the grassy Summerland, out came the black medium suitcase she had been carrying, her pet beetle Choochie standing atop it and sopping wet.

"When I agreed to come with you, I only wanted to bring 1 thing, other than my Cult," she told Nikko, picking up the handle and Choochie scampering to stand atop it. "I've dreamt of marrying the No-Life King if I ever saw him again, so I've always carried a dress with me just in case."

Nikko said nothing, hoping Jigoro would do the same.

"Now," she went on, "it looks like I'm not going to get that chance, but at least I'll get to wear it, and maybe even see him again 1 last time!"

"Sounds good!" Nikko ignored the absurdity of it all and just let Stacy be herself.

"Wha??" Jigoro asked and ended, Nikko quickly shutting his jaw.

"I can't wait to see it," Kimby told her, Stacy turning to walk away from the group with a smile. "I bet it's really pretty!"

"I'm gonna go get some privacy and change," she called back, walking just over the hill to an unseen side. "Do you think you guys can have the wedding ready? I know you don't want to wait, Nikko.."

"Leave it to us!" Nikko shouted out, ready to face her fears at last. "We'll be ready and waiting for you!"

"Ok! And everyone - Don't forget! We have to try really hard to believe in this! Who knows if it will work? But even if it doesn't, let's make today the best memory ever!"

"What are we going to do if he actually shows up?" Nikko asked before Black Stacy disappeared out of sight, nervous now getting so close to the moment. "We haven't even planned that far yet -"

"Don't worry, Nikko!" Black Stacy relieved her. "It's a wedding, I'll have my dress, and when he shows up, I'll kiss him - Then everything will go away.."

"Do you really think it will be that easy?" Jigoro yelled. "Come on, get serious!"

"It will work if we believe it will," she told the talking skull. "And besides, what do we have to lose?"

Nikko agreed, smiling as Black Stacy vanished over the hill, then turning to Kimby and the others.

"Ok, so here are the details that I think we should use," she said to Tanuki, the final preparations at last under way.

She and Jigoro re-lived their adventures to the animal, and all of the characters, both good and bad, that they had met. She explained things before he had joined them, as well as the things he may have been sleeping through.

And with the exception of those who had deeply hurt them, Nikko shared who she thought should be there to witness and celebrate this, if only in a dream.

After a brief time of planning, the thrown together illusion of the wedding was under way, the pond gazebo scene's beauty amplified by the once again meditating Tanuki. There were white tablecloth tables covered in a wealth of fruit baskets and cupcakes, strawberry shortcakes and cookies with a non-Summerland variety of Milk. There were tiny cordless lights along the gazebo and bridge, checkerboard grass square patches, and everlasting ice sculptures of human-size skeletons, in honor of the happy memory of the Odokuro.

~ And an illusion of guests, so real ~

Keeping out their own families and people from their 'real' lives, Jigoro and Nikko had shared everything about the characters and creatures they had traveled past, Tanuki conjuring up near identical replicas to populate their mock wedding scene. MilkTank was there and the young illusion of Miss Fiona too, double illusion now both in her age and existence. The horrible Head Nurse was back again, Miavia, though now friendly and in a torn-Heart replacing wheelchair, attended to by 1 of her own skull head nurses. Oyomi and his sumo wrestling bear were present, the presumed-to-be-deceased Miyakki and her grey tanuki Q-Sopp, and a great number of Black Stacy's NLK Cult - Including the black tank Haifish, the giraffe and elephants, and an army of the featureless human forms. A peaceful Polar Mina and Crown Mina made an appearance, Stacy Sweetcheck's softball team of the Pink Flamingo Lady-Pirates as well, dressed exactly as they had been seen.

Nikko and her group were in the spirit, the Chew Mice - never once straying far from Kimby - wearing small black bowties, the same as the meditating Tanuki. Jigoro was still the skull, only now held upon the shoulders of a minister's body, happy to be in control of his full range of body movements now 2 times in a row. Kimby had elected to remain in her Kimono, stating her uncomfortableness with sudden change, and at last Nikko was ready and waiting at the altar, her skirt and tie outfit transformed into a black suit and tie tuxedo, a curly tip black marker moustache comically drawn just above her lips.

"This is outrageous," Jigoro said with pride, standing at the gazebo before the now-groom Nikko. "I never thought I'd see the day you would actually get married. Especially not as a man.. Or with me as your pastor! Hilarious!"

"It's all really crazy!" Nikko bit her lip with a smile, trying not to feel silly as the whole thing was unfolding before them.

And it was a bit ridiculous - Seeing all of these characters pretend-mingling with each other, sampling the make-believe cakes and cookies, chatting with each other and just wandering around. And to see a once-sinister character like Miavia mix in with the others, a smile on her mean little face, that was something in itself.

Nikko stood and soaked it all in, no memories to mess things up and no thinking about how it was just an illusion, like she already caught herself doing.. Just try to make it work, all or nothing.

She looked above at the rainbow, so huge and near in the sky, and let herself go..

~ This was it ~

Nikko and the NLK

~ It was today ~

"She's coming, everyone!" Kimby called from the hill, a basket of flower petals in her hands. "The Bride is coming!"
Nikko's Heart leapt into her throat, never expecting to be waiting to see *her* bride walk down to the altar. The crowd stood to the sides of a checkerboard path and patiently awaited the appearance of Black Stacy, any second to appear over the top of the small hill.
Kimby started walking down the aisle, the tuxedo-tied skeleton rats standing in her flower basket, tossing flower petals to each side as she carefully walked in limp-less strides. Off to the far sides and behind the gathered crowd, Tanuki created pieces of the Yokai party, the skeletons beating on the obese stomachs of the bears again, only now in a wedding march theme.
"Hey, nice touch!" Jigoro complimented, Nikko not quite used to him being back in full body form yet, let alone in the clothing of a holy man. "Even Tanuki's adding his own happy stuff!"
"Mm-hmm!" Nikko sounded with her lips closed, nervousness matched with trying really hard not to acknowledge it was all just pretend.
And as Kimby neared the altar, smiling up at Nikko with Chewart and Chewington fighting over who threw the last pile of petals, the silhouette of Black Stacy appeared over the hilltop - Though now in a new shape of a different style of clothing.
"Oh, wow.." Nikko looked on at her friend, finally in something more than just the bikini. "It's beautiful.."
Black Stacy walked down the hill, an evident smile as she had her first glance at the illusion crowd, noticeably happy to see her NLK Cult back to 'life,' or something close to it.
Her gown was unlike anything Nikko was expecting, something closer to the girl she may have been before than the girl she had been up until now. It was an unexpected pink dress with a flamingo theme, ruffled out low and wide like an umbrella, a pink glittery top and matching fingerless gloves. The ruffles of the bottom continued up her back, riding high as an unmeeting collar, the front points of it extending forward below her chin, black colors at the tip as if the beak of a flamingo. Her blonde hair blew slightly in the breeze, the skull and crossbone eyepatch still held across her missing eye.

The wedding march played, continued by the skeletons beating on the bear stomachs.

As Stacy approached the pathway through the illusionary crowd, the illusions of Polar Mina and Crown Mina appeared and walked to her, meeting her on opposite sides and escorting her to the altar, pink on 1 side and black on the other.

Nikko smiled as her Bride neared the small railed bridge to the gazebo, Stacy still looking around in marvel at the cast of characters from her life gathered here.

~ The NLK Cult ~

~ The Pink Flamingo Lady-Pirates ~

A few more paces forward, and both softball team mascots let her continue the walk alone, stepping back into the crowd as spectators. Black Stacy now continued across the bridge and to her friends, Kimby standing aside and Nikko waiting before Jigoro.

"*Nice* dress!" he broke character and completely checked her out, Nikko holding her hand to her forehead at his inability to go along with a plan.

"Oh, yeah? Nice *body*, skull head!" Black Stacy shot back, Kimby laughing and Nikko realizing to just relax, and only worry about trying to enjoy herself. "What do you think, Nikko? Is this everything you ever hoped your Bride would look like??"

"I can't say I really gave it much thought.." she admitted, both of them now standing before the waiting crowd of pretend characters. "And even though I have no idea how you squeezed that entire dress into your little suitcase, it does look very beautiful.."

Black Stacy smiled and then looked back to the skull minister, trying not to laugh at the absurdity of his appearance.

"Shall we?" Jigoro asked, not looking like he had the slightest clue what he would even say next.

"Oh! Just a second.." Stacy said as Nikko nodded she was ready, Stacy then reaching into her mouth and removing Choochie, promptly placing him atop her shoulder. "Ok! Now I'm ready!"

Jigoro stood there for a moment in disbelief - Either real disbelief or roleplaying, or somewhere in between.

"Alright, then..." he began and tried his best to carry on. "Dearly beloved.. We are gathered here, in Summerland, to witness the unbelievable union of Nikko Heinlad, and her, er, *his* Bride to be, Black Stacy -"

"Um, Stacy Sweetcheck," Stacy interrupted, changing her name with a nervous uncertainty on her face.

"Huh?" Jigoro asked, both Kimby and Nikko taken aback as well. "You sure?"

"...Yep."

"Ok," Jigoro went on, "the unbelievable union of Nikko Heinlad, and Stacy Sweetcheck."

Upon hearing her real name said aloud by him, Stacy let out a satisfied smile, quickly replacing her nervous uncertainty in a flash.

"Stacy, do you take this, um, *man,* to have and to hold, for better or for worse?" Jigoro asked, trying his best to remember what he was supposed to say in this role.

"I do," Stacy firmly agreed, a silly eyebrow-raising look at Nikko.

"And Nikko," he continued, "do you, um.. Do you do the same thing? To have and to hold?"

Nikko waited a moment and cracked a smile of her own - This was as close to a wedding as she was ever going to have.

"Oh wait a second!" Stacy interrupted, quickly taking Choochie from her shoulder and handing the small beetle to Nikko. "Put him on my finger!"

Nikko snorted a tiny laugh, taking the always-terrified pet beetle of her Bride and then returning it, setting it's gripping legs onto her ring finger.

"I only have 1 beetle ring.." Stacy told Jigoro, Tanuki then creating another instantaneously from across the way. "Whoa! Nevermind! Check it out - 2 Choochies!! Awesome!"

She took the duplicate of her pet and set it at Nikko's ring finger in the same fashion, the original Choochie as well as Nikko eyeing it with hesitance.

"... To have and to hold??" Jigoro asked again, Nikko still looking at the finger-gripping beetle curiously.

"Oh, right! Of course I do," she replied, facing Stacy with a serious look and flashing a silly eyebrow of her own.

"Then, by the power invested in me, I now proclaim you *Husband and Wife!* Nikko, kiss the Bride! On the cheek!"

Nikko and the former 'Black Stacy' pretend kissed on alternating cheeks, and then turned to face the illusionary gathered crowd, Stacy holding Nikko's hand up high like they had just won the tag team belts. Right on time, Tanuki's created crowd cheered and applauded them, Jigoro quickly stepping in front of the new couple at once.

"And now.." he called out, heading over the bridge - "Who wants to party?? MONSTER PARTY, BABY!!"

The Yokai music picked up and the celebration began, Jigoro out and already taking full advantage of his temporary body, harassing the illusionary women as Kimby and the Chew Mice wandered out as well. Nikko remained in the Gazebo, side by side with her new 'Bride,' Stacy.

"So we're *Newlyweds* now," Stacy mused. "Who would of guessed? And cool moustache, by the way.."

"Sophisticated, don't you think?" Nikko joked. "We didn't really plan this out so well, did we?"

"What are you talking about? Shhh! This is perfect! You just need to loosen up! We're Newlyweds and Honeymooners now! Let's live it up!"

Black Stacy, back to Stacy Sweetcheck now, ran off and into the pretend gathering of people. Nikko watched from outside of the great time - Almost again like standing aside at the Yokai party, and all of the way back at the nightclub too.

But now this time, why not? All or nothing was the plan, so she forced herself to cross the bridge into the illusion of the celebration, letting herself go and enjoy the moment for everything it was worth ~

Jigoro was dancing with the Pocket girl Miyakki, back in the hood over her orange hair and donkey-ears. He held her hands, jumping around as the girl's grey tanuki Q-Sopp sat beside the illusion-casting Tanuki, a miniature smile seen at the base of it's snout.

Kimby was off with the Chew Mice, excitedly talking to the pretend MilkTank and Miss Fiona, the new Bride Stacy Sweetcheck telling stories to her former softball team and their mascot Crown Mina, along with Polar Mina peacefully standing near.

Beneath the summer sky and rainbow, with everyone getting along and so happy, the day was turning out to be everything that they had hoped and more -

"Do you remember me?" the old familiar voice of the Head Nurse said to Nikko, calling up from her wheelchair and a pushing skull head nurse. "It's me, Miavia!"

Nikko and the NLK

Nikko looked to her and felt a bit at odds - 1 of the characters that had tried to cause her so much pain, now sitting just before her. Why did Tanuki have to recreate her?

"Um, of course.. Hi!" Nikko greeted, trying to remember that this was only a happy illusion of her adventure, not the syringe-stabbing medical team that she had met.

"Yay!" Miavia uncharacteristically cheered, her nurse of course voiceless behind her. "I just wanted to say congratulations, and I'm really sorry about whatever mean things I did to you!"

"Ok, thank you..." Nikko said in humor, getting a kick out of how Tanuki's creations were a little off from their true selves. "No big deal, of course!"

"Ok, well please enjoy yourself!" Miavia said as she was pushed off by her nurse, almost like a bizarre puppet of her real identity.

"Super cute moustache, by the way!" the skull head nurse said as she pushed the wheelchair past, Nikko laughing and realizing she forgot to tell Tanuki that the nurses didn't talk.

This was even better than the real thing. Everyone nice stayed nice, and everyone mean turned polite. Nikko took a sigh of relief - Nothing was dangerous here. Everyone was in celebration, a fun and happy time, and the longer that it went on, the greater her enjoyment became.

"Nikko!" Jigoro called, running up with Miyakki hand in hand, a skull-tooth baring smile across his face. "Check it out!"

And before Nikko could greet him back, the minister-bodied Jigoro grabbed Miyakki around the waist, giving her a deep passionate kiss, skull face to pretend face, then grabbing her rear end with a little too much enthusiasm.

"See?? This is even better than that 'take off your shirt' thing I was using when we first got here!! Remember??"

Nikko just smiled at Jigoro 'unleashed,' and he turned to run off, Miyakki still hand in hand.

"I like your moustache!" the orange-haired hoodie girl called back, pulled away into the crowd.

"*I really like your moustache!*" Stacy mocked as she walked up again. "*You're so cool! Oh, my God!*"

"Shut up!" Nikko joked back. "Hey - Do you think everyone's having a good time?"

"Are you?" Stacy asked, making sure Nikko was giving it a try.

"Actually, I am," she admitted. "This is a little weird and all, but it's the best thing that's happened to us. Everyone is getting along, laughing and smiling.. Kimby looks like she's already forgotten about all of that bad stuff that -"

"That we aren't going to talk about today!" Stacy finished for her.

"Ok, ok.." Nikko caught herself as well. "You're right."

"Of course I'm right! And listen.. I just wanted to thank you, Nikko.."

"Yeah? For what?"

"Well, for helping me out... I don't know if you noticed, but I've changed a little since I met you guys -"

"A little?? Try a lot! You were gonna kill me when I met you!"

"Details, details.." Stacy looked at the ground in a half joking embarrassment. "Look, I just wanted to say thank you. When I met everyone, I was really obsessed with myself, you know? I kind of gave up being happy too. I just stuck around with all of my old bad memories and ideas. Man, I was really freaked out when you came back from the Bottomless Kiss and said you saw me all pink and girly!!"

"Kinda like you are now?" Nikko asked, looking over her flamingo wedding dress.

"... Yeah, you could say that. I guess the real me is somewhere in between. I felt pretty cool in that bikini, until 'what's her name' over there took off her hoodie.."

"Miyakki," Nikko reminded her, holding down a smile.

"Whatever! When I saw her in it, I kinda felt like I wasn't so unique after all."

"Oh, trust me," Nikko told her, the celebration still at full speed around them, "pink, black, or anything else you can cover yourself in - You are definitely unique, Stacy.."

"Well, I just want to thank you. I've been lost for a really long time, and because of you guys sticking around with me, I was able to let go of what I was holding on to, and get back to who I really am.. So thanks, ok?"

"... You're welcome," Nikko told her with a smile and hug, a few of the nearby NLK Cult members clapping at their embrace. "Oh, knock it off!" Nikko laughed and told them.

"Anyway," Stacy said as she walked away into the illusion, "now I have to go find my pet 'ring,' Choochie. He's off and running all over the place!"

Nikko waved her own beetle-ring hand as her Bride headed off, the gratitude really reaching her Heart. The words of Stacy were touching, but the emotion of happiness in her face said so much more, and Nikko truly felt great in return.

"Every time we were gonna come up and say hi," Kimby said as she now approached, out of breath and walking up from behind, "someone else beat us to you! So popular!"

"No..." Nikko greeted her ghost cat friend with a hug. "And are you guys having fun too??"

Chewy, Chewart and Chewington all nodded their little heads in agreement, walking confidently and not lingering near the kimono for a change.

"That's awesome!" Nikko gave them a thumbs up, cracking up at their crooked tuxedo ties.

"Yeah," Kimby looked down proudly at them, "we wanted to thank you for taking us along with you. It's been really exciting for us.."

"I'm sorry about all of that bad stuff that happened," Nikko told her, trying to avoid it, but feeling so guilty when it came to Kimby. "Are you feeling ok??"

"I feel better. I think my leg is alright, and the burns aren't as bad as I thought they were."

"Good!"

"All of us just really wanted to tell you that we appreciate you," Kimby continued, the 'thank-you's beginning to pile up. "It gets really lonely when you're closed in a room all of the time. I know we got to look through the window, but that's just the same thing everyday.. Now look at all the fun we're having! Nikko, if you and Jigoro and Tanuki never came along, we would still be up there in that room and all depressed. We're happy that we get to be friends with you now!"

"Oh, Kimby," Nikko said and hugged her again, so much a reminder of her own cat Kimby back home. "And thanks for being so strong through those bad times with me.. You really are wonderful, and your brave little skeleton rats are too!"

Chewy waved, Kimby then waving too as all 4 of them headed back into the crowd and it's party celebration. The illusion created a basis for this happiness, but the words and gratitude of her new friends were the pieces of joy that could not be make believe. This was something truly valuable, and appreciated even more so after such hardships together.

A missing piece of life, now found at last in this End of the World 'afterlife' of Daiyomi.

Nikko and the NLK

Nikko mixed herself into the party, now taking the time to greet and talk to each of the illusion characters at least 1 more time. She admired the decorations and the skeleton ice sculptures, laughing at the scenes of Jigoro and his latest obsession, Miyakki.

A feeling swept over Nikko - Such happiness and joy surrounding her, both real and convincing illusion, and maybe this could be the happiest day after all. A world far away from her life back home, the possible conclusion of a great nightmare, and surrounded by this celebration created strictly to aid in her struggles. She remembered being little, and always thinking life would some day become a great adventure, only to grow up and realize that nothing really exciting ever happened.

And now here it was, 'real life' adventure, in spite of real life..

+ A crash +

Lightning struck the ground just beyond the gazebo, a thunder loud enough to bring Nikko's hands to her ears.

+ Another immediate crash +

The joy fell away, Nikko's Heart soaring back into the feelings of horror in her soul - Was it time? So soon??

Clouds loomed above the overhead rainbow, raindrops beginning to fall and the illusionary people barely noticing, only going about their celebration with a small disturbance by the weather.

"Do you think.." Stacy asked as she ran close to Nikko, stopping in her tracks. "Is this it??"

"It has to be!" Nikko's stomach knotted in fear.

The wind grew stronger and carried flower petals up and away, a nearby weeping willow tree struck by the next bolt.

Through the crowd, someone was moving fast and pushing the gatherers aside -

"What's happening??" Kimby cried as she ran up, the Chew Mice back into their kimono positions.

"Kimby, go and wake Tanuki up from his trance!" Nikko ordered. "I think we're going to need his help protecting us!"

The wind swooped through in a tablecloth-whipping speed, Kimby holding her hands to shield herself from the sudden rainfall as she fled.

"What if it's just a storm?" Stacy asked, standing guard over Nikko as the sky blackened into an oblivion.
"It's not a storm, Stacy! Trust me! I can feel him - He's coming! Where's Jigoro at??"
Their eyes searched the surrounding grounds and eventually Stacy picked him out of the crowd, seeing him pushing his way through the softball team.
"JIGORO!!" Nikko yelled. "GO HELP KIMBY! IT'S TIME!!"
He nodded and went to her, heading out into the direction Nikko pointed to.

+ And just then, the Black Knight himself came walking from the storm, the No-Life King stepping through the tempest out of nowhere and approaching the celebration +

Steady, methodical steps, black void-like armor reflecting the now void-like sky, the colorless axe gripped..
Stacy pressed her arm against Nikko, knowing the shared feeling and hoping to calm her fear.
"Stacy..." Nikko struggled to speak as the being approached the outside of the party, the girls slowly backing into the cover of the gazebo. "I don't think we're ready for this - I didn't think the wedding would work.."
"Don't say that!" Stacy locked eyes on the man-shaped creature she had waited so long to see again. "We both knew it would work, the same as we both know the Bottomless Kiss is going to work.."
"But what if it doesn't??"
"It will! And if for some weird reason it doesn't, we'll find a way anyways! Tanuki can make something if we need him to!"
"..*Why are these pretend people still around*?" Nikko asked herself, hardly able to divert her own attention from the No-Life King's impending walk. "Isn't Kimby supposed to be waking him up??"
They both looked and couldn't see, the bodies of the illusion guests blocking their view.
Another lightning strike, followed by an ear-cracking thunder, and the horrible barbarian was at the crowd, walking unphased past the pretend revelers, his path set straight to Nikko.
"Stacy..." Nikko felt her body weakening, something like the feeling of not being able to run inside of a dream. "He's coming right at us..."
"I know... It's the minute I've been waiting forever for.. And it's about

to all be over. It's a wedding, I've got my dress on, and he's walking directly down to the altar... This is how I always imagined it!"

In that moment and the words that she had said, Nikko once again saw the dark side of Stacy Sweetcheck. She truly wanted to help Nikko, but still couldn't escape her own obsessions. It was no matter now, the time for both of them had at last arrived, and the No-Life King was straight ahead, midway through the party.

"NIKKO!!" Jigoro yelled across from the far side. "WE CAN'T WAKE TANUKI UP!! I THINK HE'S SOUND ASLEEP!!"

"How can that be.." Nikko whispered, unable to even concentrate as the Devil advanced.

"Tanuki illusions are like dreams, aren't they?" Stacy asked, taking a small step forward ahead of her friend. "It's no surprise he can fall asleep once he starts them.. Hey, Nikko.. Do I look ok?"

Stacy glanced just a bit sideways and back, using her eye and barely turning her head. How could she wonder about that at a time like this?? Nikko nodded, remembering that this moment alone was what she was living for - Seeing the ruiner of her life, and finally, her wait was over.

"Wish me luck," she forced a smile, the obvious fear overpowering her own Heart. "He wrecked every important memory I ever had.. But I still wonder if he'll even remember me.."

Nikko held her breath as Stacy followed through with her plan, taking hesitating steps out of the gazebo and onto the rain-pelted bridge. Watching her flamingo-dressed friend stand in the downpour, blocking the connecting path of the No-Life King and herself, Nikko wished they hadn't gone though with this. Even if it would have meant the end of herself, at least she wouldn't have yet again put her friends into the path of danger.

But no more time for regretful thoughts, this was the moment of truth.

With the pitch black clouds pouring rain from overhead, and the gusting winds with booming lightning all around, Stacy Sweetcheck - the Black Queen, Black Stacy - stepped into the advancing path of the killer, standing with her back to Nikko.

The monster stepped toward her, and she leaned forward for the deep Bottomless Kiss she had been saving, waiting all of those dark and empty days to use -

Nikko and the NLK

He cut through her, effortlessly swinging his black weapon into her body, the axe tearing through Stacy's flesh and bone, ripping her apart sideways and dropping her in a blood-drowning scream -

All went silent, the moment frozen to Nikko.. The tormentor of her nightmares walked over Stacy Sweetcheck's fallen body, now lifeless and torn apart...

Just a moment ago, everything had felt so right.. And now the dark reality took over, her friend Stacy at the floor, dead and severed in half -

- No time for thoughts -

- A bottomless emptiness filled her Heart in shock -

What was the back-up plan??

Her stomach sank, leaving her no option but to look into the face of her fear, his black armored body bearing down on her so close..

Tanuki?

Kimby?

Jigoro??

There was no time to wait for anyone, the armored Devil was upon her, and Nikko mustered all of the might in her trembling body to stand tall, to 'stand out loud' and face her memory-devouring monster right now.

In a desperate attack, she threw herself at the No-Life King with more fear than she had ever felt before, anticipating the cold solid swing of his axe..
But in surprise to even herself, she managed to catch him off guard and her thin frame body plowed against his armored chest - Pounding

until he easily brushed her off, knocking her to the gazebo floor in her illusion-created tuxedo.

Why couldn't they wake Tanuki up yet?? With Stacy gone, he was their only chance.. But there was no time to wonder -

Before he could swing at her, Nikko took advantage of his slow movements and threw herself at him yet again, this time grabbing onto his body and struggling for a grasp at his neck and helmet.

"NIKKO!!" the voice of Jigoro called to her in between deafening claps of thunder. "I'M COMING, NIKKO!!"

And as the No-Life King shoved Nikko off again, the illusion-bodied Jigoro ran across the short bridge to the scene of the struggle.

"Stacy!" he cried in shock as he stepped to her split and collapsed body, the blood running off into the tiny pond beneath. "What did you do to her?!"

And as he ran the short steps across the bridge, the Black Knight turned and swung his axe at the aiding Jigoro, cutting the illusion into the ground and dropping the body beside Stacy's, Jigoro's hollow skull bounding off of the floor and into the shallow water below.

"Stop it!! Stop hurting my friends!!" Nikko screamed from the depths of her soul, bounding 1 final time at the constant ruiner of her life, this time just missing a late axe swing. "What do you want from me?? I don't understand!!!"

And he fought with her, 1 fist holding the axe and the other pushing her off, Nikko hanging on stronger than before. She gripped beneath the bottom of his helmet, holding as he pushed until her fingertips felt like they were going to rip out from her hands.

- Rain and lightning, the storm blowing close to a tornado now -

"NO!!!" Nikko could hear the voice of Kimby crying, not able to look away from her fighting pull. "NIKKO!! DON'T LET HIM HURT YOU!! I CAN'T WAKE TANUKI UP!!"

Nikko had no strength to call back to her remaining friend, having to focus all of her energy into her hopeless pull at his helmet. Even if Tanuki had woken up from the trance, it was too late now.

Everything had fallen apart.

All of these adventures beyond death, seemingly for nothing.

Nikko and the NLK

The No-Life King dropped his axe to the ground and went to push at Nikko with both arms now, the end coming into sight. He shoved her off again, both hands now and in full strength - But in doing so, matched with Nikko's never-let-go hold, the black bat-winged helmet came loose, breaking off and crashing down to the gazebo floor with the toppled Nikko.

His body stood there, it's ancient face finally revealed - No beautiful blonde hair, no pale fair skin or blue eyes as Oyomi's storybook had depicted him. All that remained beneath was an emptiness and dying face seen straight across, soulless eyes with a white beard and bald head.

His face began fading the moment it was exposed, small blue-white tentacles extending from his beard, feeling their way into the air until no form of a head or skull remained. Nikko held the empty helmet in shock, watching the headless armor and it's feeling appendages exploring outward through the neckline.

And before she could return to her feet or spot Kimby, or even realize what she had just done, another tornado cyclone appeared out of the gaping neck and tentacles of his armor.

Nikko pushed herself backwards seated on the floor, watching the gazebo roof pulled off and swallowed into his raging body.

"This isn't happening..." she told herself, all alone before him. "This can't be happening..."

Pieces of the nearby scenery lifted in the tempest storm, from the ice sculptures of skeletons to the tables and decorations. Nikko could see the bodies of the illusionary guests, still so lifelike and colliding into each other, pulled into the tornado vacuum and devoured, being swallowed up in a stinging reminder of the Bottomless Kiss.

Nikko held to the railings as her legs lifted off of the ground, even the destroyed body of Stacy lifting up and drawn into the opening of the sucking neck - Her remains fed in by the octopus-like tentacles, the other 'still-living' bodies cramming tightly up against hers to be squeezed through the tight spot.

"No! Kimby!" Nikko screamed, now seeing Kimby and her rats immediately after, all of them helplessly swept away in the air current, crying and reaching in vain for anything to help save them -

- But nothing -

Nikko and the NLK

The blue and white tentacles snatched them once they were near, the group then quickly vanishing into his body.

Nikko cried, her already weak fingers fighting to hang on, a No-Life King tentacle just barely reaching and pulling at her leg -

She wished this entire wonderful day had never happened, now not even the happy parts before this nightmare-come-true. In her Heart, she could still see their smiling faces, an instant haunting memory as her life held on by a thread.

And then more depression -

The illusion of MilkTank, Miss Fiona and the real-life Tanuki - still in sleeping meditation? - passed by and into the No-Life King, Nikko seeing the group together again of sorts, Tanuki peacefully unaware of the tragic results all around.
Into the funnel storm from the neck, and gone just like the others.

Nikko's grip loosened to nothing..

The skull of Jigoro, in silence, rose from the tornado-lifted water and rattled against the standing armor, clinking as it was pulled in and swallowed inside as well.

Everything gone..

And with all hope lost, not a single friend or happy thought left, Nikko gave in. A few illusions still remained, but with all of her friends now gone and drained into the body of the headless No-Life King, she let her desire die away inside and gave in to her fears -

Let go..

Every tentacle pulled at her...

Her body banged around into the outside of the black armor, rising up then into the air. Blown by the evil winds and then swallowed whole inside, the tentacles and internal tendrils fed her to the body.

Nikko and the NLK

All along, the No-Life King's empty helmet remained on the floor, unmoved by the impossible storm -

~ This was what it was to truly die again ~

Nikko and the NLK

Nikko and the NLK

~ Sirens in the rear view mirror ~

~ Doesn't matter.. I'm racing away toward my Death Wish ~

~ Is there a happy ending on the other side? ~

~ I left it all behind ~

~ A cold splash into the river ~

~ Which way is up? ~

~ This is where I picked to die ~

~ My brand new world awaits ~

Nikko and the NLK

CHAPTER 11

Death Wish

    Nikko tossed and twirled like a mouse swallowed whole into the body of a snake, violent winds blowing at her body in an absolute black. She remained conscious, though in a striking similarity to the feeling she had felt when drowning back in her 'real world' - Flailing, out of control, and suspended with little awareness of what was up or down.
    Seeing Stacy die, and then seeing her friends thrown around in the storm like ragdolls.. Why did it have to come to this? Nikko felt as if the simple plan of the Bottomless Kiss was her fault, and that she should have come up with a different idea then her sacrificing friend, or just avoided the confrontation altogether. And what was fate now? Haunted by the No-Life King was 1 thing, but to be engulfed by his living body was beyond comprehension.. Was this a new world again, or was this finally true-death?
    From the living world to Daiyomi, the Bottomless Kiss of Stacy to the graveyard world of the SuperCross, and from the Burrow's Pocket in time to the End of the World in Summerland - When would it stop? And if this could be death, how much longer until her mind turned off now?

    Through the dark, and the only sound heard was the vacuum wind howling in her ears, her body descending helplessly..

    Then the stop, a crash and land in the black, the feeling of landing in a garbage dump with so many unfitting shapes beneath her. And as she sat up from her fall, the weight of more falling debris landed atop and around her, forcing her down, heavier and heavier while she fought hard to push against it.

    Nikko climbed her way up and out of the pressing weight, almost the same as the Odokuro clawing itself out from the World's Teeth underground -

    ~ It was the devoured aftermath of the illusionary wedding ~

Nikko and the NLK

Nikko's eyes could see now, tiny lighting from the pretend lights Tanuki had created, now swallowed in and haphazardly scattered around the pile of bodies and destruction.

Nikko choked, her heavy Heart not ready to see even the pretend bodies piled up of the faces from her adventure.. The softball team, the mascot girls.. The split-separated body of Stacy Sweetcheck - Blood drenched and as motionless as the dead pretend characters surrounding her.

"Stacy... I'm so sorry.." Nikko cried and leaned down onto her, pulling up a dead half of the body into her arms for an end of life embrace. "I didn't know it was going to turn out like this!!! If I did, I would have never..."

She stopped, words pointless and unable to express the regret running so deep, and she let go, allowing her friend to rest lifelessly on the crash of the wedding beneath them.

Nikko forced herself to move on, her Heart either stopped or racing as 1 solid beat. A cold, unleaving shiver shook her body as she walked over the soft and hard shapes of the pretend characters, standing at a bottom limit in the illumination of the tiny lights.

"Kimby?" Nikko coughed with a shaking jaw, falling and trying to run towards the laying body of her cat ghost girl. "Kimby! Kimby!!"

But as she approached, it seemed that even the body of a ghost could die - Her doll-like face lay expressionless and her great eyes stared off into nothing, her rats most likely lost in the wreck as well..

"Kimby..." Nikko moaned, her hope that the girl had survived the swallow now crashing into depression.

She was for the first time utterly alone, seeing no survivors even in the illusional remains. Nikko rushed and pulled at the bodies, tripping over them as she pulled and pushed her way through - If the illusions were here, Tanuki had to be alive, didn't he? She searched in the dim illumination, her small strength not helping in the slightest, and there, beside the shut-down MilkTank, was the still eyes-closed Tanuki.. A smile at his snout as he slept through his meditation, unknowing of the fate that had befallen them.

"Tanuki!" Nikko called out as she climbed over, stepping off of the pretend Polar Mina with tears cascading over her cheeks. "Tanuki, wake up! It's over.. You can stop..."

Nikko picked up and held the animal for a quiet moment, no sounds

Nikko and the NLK

of his small breath or Heartbeat...

    Kimby and Jigoro hadn't been able to awaken him, because he had finally stopped living..

    Nikko sobbed over his still-warm fur.. He had done so much for them, using all of the power in his old animal body to create the Odokuro, and then to create the illusion of the wedding with all of it's make-believe guests.. All without an aiding leaf.. Had it been too much for his elderly Heart? Nikko wondered in her sorrow and felt guilty of asking so much. He hadn't fallen asleep, he had just died somewhere in the moment, his illusions locked as his final thought and now remaining in a lifeless heap..
    At the very least, Nikko thought, at least he had died with an animal smile, surrounded by the illusion of the robot and woman he had spent his life around.

    With everything in wreckage, the bodies of yesterday slumped with the broken ice sculptures and tables, all that remained was the search for Nikko's missing friend, Jigoro.. Maybe he had survived the black hole into this evil pit? He had already survived death enough to live just as a skull so far -
    Nikko looked for him, holding her pain of Stacy, Kimby and Tanuki at bay well as she could, feeling all along her overwhelming despair build up. This was so much to handle - She pulled at the limp arms and legs of Stacy's illusion NLK Cult, tears dripping over her lips and to her neck.
    "Jigoro??" she called for him, hoping to hear his obnoxious voice once again. "Jigoro, please.. Say something.. Where are you??"
    No words were returned, just the quiet call of the bodies as the poor girl rummaged through the lopped pile of remains..

    ~ And then the polished-white bone of his skull, seen through the surrounding black of the laying NLK Cult ~

    "No..." she whispered as she pulled his head from the wreckage, holding it's cold brittle jaw and feeling the reality in her hands. "Not you too.. Please say something? Please say that you're joking?? This is just a really bad, horrible joke??"
    She held his skull to her face like she had done so many times so

far, and he answered nothing back. He was only a skull, and this time it was real. No friends were left, not even the only connection to her real world back home.. This was everything gone and Nikko alone - More alone than she ever could have imagined, all of the way back to when she used to stare out from the window at her Parent's home so long ago.

Holding tight to Jigoro's skull, she placed it 1 final time over her head and black hair, wearing it as she often had in this world, only now worn just as a lifeless helmet.

Why did it feel like everyone had to be sacrificed just for her? Nikko wondered how she couldn't have anticipated such an outcome.. Even through the skull, her sobbing tears could be seen running off, though there was no 1 left to see her. No 1 to talk to, no 1 to laugh with anymore at the unbelievable things - Just emptiness and the pile of death beneath her. The storm had ended, and nothing but her life in a final disarray existed now.

~ From nowhere, just as it would have come in the clearing sky after a storm, just as it had been held overhead at the make-believe wedding, and just how it had always been ahead and out of reach, a rainbow materialized - illuminating the area in it's spectrum of lights everywhere near that it touched ~

Nikko lifted her head, 'what' and 'why' mixing in her mind at once. How could it even be? After the suffrage and death of anything that was important to her now and here, this girl appeared again. The rainbow knit bikini with baggy socks and rollerskates, the tan skin and the long blue hair, the wake-behind rainbows and her sound-blocking headphones..

There was no way it could be, but once again here she was and skating happily in her own little world, long-stretch leg strides and all of her colors displayed behind.

Nikko followed along without thought or any reason why. Maybe, if anything, only to get away from the horror of her piled up losses and mountain of depression. She walked and then jogged, her legs hardly listening to her brain anymore. It wasn't much, but this was the only thing in her world right now, to follow this rainbow and Dolphin to see where she would go..

Always moving, never stopping and never listening with her bulky headphones always on. Nikko picked up her jog as best as she could, leaving the pile of bodies behind.

Was this the type of girl she should have been? Never slowing down, happy and always moving forward, never listening to anyone? It didn't matter anymore. Follow the colors of the rainbow ~ Red, Blue, Green and Yellow ~ Just follow the beautiful girl that cast them, each full rollerskate stride creating a fading color path behind.

Nikko still felt afraid.. Nothing left to lose, but the pain was so unending. As she ran behind and kept up enough not to fall behind, the surrounding black lashed out to her. She could feel the presence of the No-Life King, knowing that this was either within him, or just within a world of his.

~ The hard-to-see walls pumped like black blood-filled organs ~

~ The rainbow-lit ceiling dripped with the pus of infected tissue ~

And underfoot, every hard-fought step met a mix of soft and swollen membranes, the uneven footing not affecting the graceful glides of Dolphin still ahead.

The thought continued to cross her mind of why did she even try. From the living world bridge, all of the way to right here and now.. If Jigoro hadn't seen Dolphin himself all of those times, Nikko would have thought the girl was just a figment of her imagination. And if she was real, how could she survive so much where others could not - Now most notably making it down into this No-Life King living hole, not a speck of dirt or sign of bruising against her flawless body.
Nikko drifted, her mind upset and trying to keep her pace, leaving her friends behind and out of sight. The worn skull of Jigoro and Tanuki's illusion-created tuxedo were all that she was left with now, still wearing her pretend-beetle wedding ring.
So far past the point of return, following the rainbow deeper into the body. She felt her breath shorten, breathing heavier with every other step. Still in stride, Dolphin was no closer or further away from her yet, just a short distance for Nikko to touch the leading rainbow ahead. And she tried, but it was nothing, her hand feeling right through the fading rear of it all.

Nikko and the NLK

Deeper and angled up, a forward path through the body corridor, and then something new -

The walls opened up and the pathway immediately continued like a bridge inside of a castle, Dolphin skating on. There was a fire-filled pool beneath, far below but dancing and licking the highest air, rising up in bursts alongside the traveled path.

Nikko kept on in pursuit, not letting anything hold her back from the last connection to her world, the fire light and rainbow mixing into an explosion of colors.

~ Nikko, with nothing left, followed ~

The bridge continued into a tunnel, a black organ-formed similar tunnel to the path before, and now it spiraled up. Dolphin kept her pace even with the winding incline, forcing Nikko to do the same. Around and around, upwards in the intestinal tower, and the rainbow girl never once looked back. Nikko felt the rubbing sweat build up beneath the skull-head helmet, irritations and the deep itch of no concern - Forward forever until her body came undone, and nothing else mattered.

Dolphin was all that she looked to now.

And in the moment that she thought this, her eyes picked up something besides the nonstop girl, something lining the walls and things she wasn't ready to see -

Were these her memories??

All along the upward-bound spiral path, the walls were lit with filmed images, just turning on now like a remote control television. They lined up on the angle, like projection screens side by side and within.

Every great memory, from start to finish, lost and stolen by the No-Life King now played as if on tape, all coming back to Nikko. Every missing piece of her life was finally here inside of him, where she now saw and was reunited with the nightmare turn they had taken.

Nikko fought her looking eyes as the ruined happy memories came flooding back, killing her over and over again inside. Her birthdays, the times with her family, the times with her friends.. All of the things that the No-Life King had invaded and destroyed, now held here inside of what made him live - If he even was living..

She averted her attention, wanting to regain her lost pieces but not in the forever ruined state they had become. These weren't her real memories, these were the rotted remains of her happiest days, now no longer hers. Nikko couldn't bare to look, leaving yesterday behind and running upwards around the constant turn, chasing the rainbows while her destroyed life broadcast on both sides of the narrow path.

Make it go away.. She wished anyone was here to be with her..

The spiraled path straightened, still angled but forward on a slant like a stairless staircase. Dolphin skated up, her rainbows Nikko's only focus as the entire path, both walls and even the ceiling now, displayed movie-like scenes of her happy life's demise. She fought herself not to see, but even in hiding eyes she unintentionally picked up a little, noticing that the memories now were forgotten times with Jigoro.

And all along, she had always thought she didn't enjoy her time with him. Now, even in trying not to see, she could see the happy times were already just forgotten.

If only he could watch this with her now, her eyes looking through his empty skull in shame.

At last, and out of breath, the internal pathway through the No-Life King came to an end with a black door at the top of the path, closed, and Dolphin quickly reached it - Her body passing through as if it wasn't even there, followed by her trailing rainbow path as well.

An illusion, or a just a ghost?

Nikko finished the remaining distance of her ascent, eyes locked onto the withering door just to avoid her memories, both in her Heart and all around. Only a few more steps, and she would finally be able to see what was behind all of this, the last doorway at the limit of her journey..

~ This end, and the end of her trials ~

Nikko and the NLK

She turned the rot-covered doorknob and blindly walked into a blue-light bathed room, the door then automatically closing behind her.

Within was simply a woman, the blue lights encompassing the empty room draped over her exposed body. Without any sight of the girl Jigoro had called Dolphin, Nikko took it all in -

The woman before her was restrained to some sort of an alien contraption. It was a crucifix in design, needle-like appendages and bars extending outward, cords and thick tubing dropping to the ground with entrances into the walls. She was held to it by thick black straps, straps across head and over her eyes, bound by her arms, legs, ankles and torso.

Her skin was so white, locked away in here and her long hair as well, both looking blue beneath the ceiling's shining lights. Her body was the exaggerated type that Jigoro would have loved, bound up completely naked, save for the unusual exception of a wrestling championship belt worn around her waist.

"Are.. Are you alive?" Nikko asked, her hands at her tuxedo pant-leg knees, bent over trying desperately to catch her breath.

The woman's thick white lips slowly raised from the expressionless, transforming into a welcoming smile -

"It's you..." she said with a satisfaction, the words coming through her lips in emphasized-syllables. "It's finally you.."

Nikko looked up from her slumping stance. "Do you know me?" she asked, knowing that there was no way the eye-bound lady could have seen her.

A silence in the air as Nikko stood upright, more air in the lungs of her worn out body.

"I don't know you," the woman answered, "but I do know what's inside of you ~ What is your name?"

"...Nikko," Nikko hesitated and then replied.

"Glad to meet you, I'm Shiva Angel," the cross-bound prisoner introduced herself -

Nikko's mind jumped - This was the person she had sought out after descriptions from the robot MilkTank - The generally-proclaimed 'Ruler of the World,' and the 1 person, other than the No-Life King, that Stacy Sweetcheck had been seeking out all of that time before.

"... Are you really her? The Ruler of the World?" Nikko asked, not expecting to find such an important person in this place.

"It's still me, and is there still a World Title at my waist?" she asked in reference to the wrestling belt and her only piece of something close to clothing.

"Yeah..."

"Then it looks like I must *still* be the Ruler of the World," she said with a smile, "even if it doesn't really look like it at all.. Let me ask you a question, Nikko," she asked, speaking comfortably as if she were not bound up in such a position at all. "How did you end up here, right in front of me?"

"I... It's a really long story..." Nikko told her. "I came here from a really far, far away place.. Like, not even in your world.."

The woman's lips went from a smile to a slightly sideways mouth scrunch, looking unsatisfied with Nikko's answer.

"But what *specifically* brought you to this exact moment here?" her mouth carefully sounded out each sound, her lips the only moving and expressive part of her body. "It couldn't be by accident that you would end up in such a place."

"No, I, uh, I lost my friends and got pulled into this body," Nikko explained, unable to easily describe things without going into a greater detail. "The No-Life King.."

"The No-Life King," she repeated, the evil name almost sounding more tolerable coming off of her carefully word-forming lips. "There's a name I haven't heard in a very long time."

"So you know about him too??" Nikko asked, a small spark inside the closest thing to life she could now feel. "That was why we were looking for you in the first place.. A robot I met told me to go to your castle to meet you."

"Oh, WaterBury.." Shiva Angel sighed. "You know, I miss that castle now, I probably had so many great memories inside of it. All of my people - My manager, my cooks, my plastic surgeon, my pets - Tell me, did you get a chance to see what became of it? I have always wondered.."

Nikko thought and decided to keep the truth to herself, of Stacy and her castle-ruining No-Life King Cult.

"No.." she lied to the World's Ruler. "We didn't go, everyone said that you were gone.."

"Did anyone in the world say that they missed me?" she asked, then answering herself before Nikko could have a chance - "I guess it wouldn't matter if they even did or not.. So, you say you know the No-Life King. Have you been able to figure out what he does yet? It took me at least a little while."

"With what he does to your memories and stuff? Yeah... It took me a while too."

"But he's done more than just that to you, too, you know," she went on. "Do you even know his real name? It's 'Drahcir Nalla.' You and I are inside of the body, the Living Castle, of Drahcir Nalla."

Drahcir Nalla.. Nikko thought of the name and it felt quite unusual bouncing around inside of her head, as if something important to her she could somehow not recall.

"What do you mean when you say he's done more to me? Is it something else that I forgot?"

"It's more complicated than we might have time to explain, Nikko. What matters is that at last all of the pieces are in place.. Tell me, are you alone in this room with me?"

Nikko pulled the mask-skull of Jigoro from her head, holding it in her arms once more.

"I brought the skull of my friend, Jigoro -"

"And that is exactly something that should have happened, you and another important piece being drawn together, the same as how the both of you were most likely drawn to me," she replied to the answer, none of this making sense to Nikko. "And tell me another thing, was there ever a 'guiding light' that brought you here to me? Something like a star, or a sign, that led you to this *exact* place?"

"There was a girl... Jigoro called her the 'Dolphin,' and she was always 1 step ahead of us - From where I started, far away from here, and all of the way until your door."

"A girl?" Shiva Angel asked, sounding slightly more amused than just surprised. "And the form 'she' took, was it beautiful? Did she look like I do at all?"

"She was really beautiful," Nikko agreed, feeling strange explaining Dolphin under such circumstances, "but I wouldn't say like you - She was different.. She was really tan, and rollerskating. And Blue hair."

"Hmm.." the lady interrupted, her lips smiling high in enjoyment. "Blue hair.. How wonderful.."

"Yeah, and she had headphones on - I could," she looked down to the remains of Jigoro, "*we* could never get her attention or catch up, and everywhere that we saw her, there were always rainbows just behind her."

"And only you and your friend could see her?" Shiva Angel asked, her lips remaining parted, anxious to say so much more.

"Yeah, it seemed like that.. What do you know about her?"

"Nikko..." she said and took a deep breath, so much it seemed on her mind.

"Can I at least help you get out of that thing while we talk?" Nikko started to feel guilty standing free before the prisoner.

"Something like my life doesn't really matter anymore," she warned, sounding out every word carefully. "I have so much to ask you and so much I've been waiting to say to you, but we can only share a little in this time.. The pain inside of my body overrides every feeling in my bones, and I can only even speak to you with every single focus of my mind.. This takes so much out of me.."

Nikko held her questions in, now realizing the sounded out words were to hold in the agony of the suffrage, and now she carefully listened.

"When I first began encountering Drahcir Nalla," she said, calling the No-Life King with his true name, "I was the same as anyone else. I didn't know what was happening - All I knew was that little by little, I was losing pieces of myself. He preys on the suffering from creatures in every world of the universe, a God-like species. He is concentrated suffering - I had a Death Wish and I thought that by killing myself I could end it. But I ended up in Daiyomi.. I talked to everyone there, I wrestled my way into being the Ruler of the World, and when I finally met others who had discovered a likewise fate - I then realized that I was different than anyone he had preyed upon."

Nikko fought to hold in her thoughts and just listen.

"I can't explain it," the woman continued, "but the way people talked, the way black things surrounded them, some even becoming so obsessed with the creature - That wasn't what I wanted. I only tried to be free of him, and that was when I met a man named Oyomi, someone from the stars who had landed in the world."

Nikko stayed quiet at the mention of the Mountain Tengu's name, waiting to see where the story went.

"He explained what he knew about who he was still calling the No-Life King, and when he got to the part about the Saint Devil woman, the personification of suicide, something spoke to the inside part of me."

Nikko's Heart was still racing from everything that had happened prior, but the words of Shiva Angel had just explained the exact same feelings Nikko had felt herself.

"And from that moment," she explained, "I knew that Drahcir Nalla had defeated the Saint Devil, 1 time again, because I knew a piece of her resided within me -"

Nikko opened her mouth and nothing came out, unsure of what to say at such a bold statement.

"It was true," she laughed. "I don't say these things lightly. I saw him again, in a dream or a memory, and I didn't hold back - I called out to him, I called his attention to me before I could forget, and he stopped killing my memory and instead came to me -"

"I'm sorry, but I really don't understand you," Nikko interrupted the recollection. "I did the same thing - I called to him, but that doesn't mean that I'm the Saint Devil.."

"People can't recognize him while they are in their memories, Nikko, but do you see? I did - When I called to him, he took me away, he hid me from the outside of all the worlds, and kept me inside of himself. I've been here for so long now, bound like a prisoner, the only thing I can do is let my mind wander. I felt I was still myself, Shiva Angel, but I knew that there was something else breathing inside of my body. And while at first I thought I was the Saint Devil, I eventually figured out that wasn't entirely true.."

Nikko waited for her next words, wondering how all of this could connect to her and Jigoro.

"Time is short and I don't know how much longer until something is going to happen, but please hear what I have left to say. I came to the conclusion, from the feeling and other voice inside of me, that I was the Saint Devil only in part.. The battle that happens eternally, the conflict war between the Saint Devil and the No-Life King, had happened again in recent history and Drahcir Nalla had won.. The Saint Devil crashed down to Earth, and the remains of her broke up and manifested into living things.."

"And you expect me to believe everything?" Nikko asked, starting to lose faith in the story she was being told. "Everything has become so difficult to understand.."

"Nikko, please hear me?" Shiva Angel still went on, unphased by the words. "I was just a piece of the puzzle, the spirit of the body, but somewhere out there, in *our* real world, the body of the Saint Devil herself still existed.. When Drahcir Nalla realized that I could call to him in my memories - Something that his prey could never do - He knew that he had come across 1 of her pieces, and that his arch enemy would reform and be reborn, the same as always. The gravity of the soul and body would find a way to reunite, and come together against the odds, like it always had throughout time."

"So hold on," Nikko said, figuring out what the unclothed woman was now getting at, "are you trying to tell me that I'm the body of that thing? The Saint Devil??"

"No.. Not exactly 'you.' By putting me locked up here inside of him, hidden from all of the universe, Drahcir Nalla made a new plan. He figured the Saint Devil could never come together again if he hid a piece of her within the last place she could ever be. And as the voice grew stronger inside of me, I could only confirm that my entire human life was just a vessel to hold her soul. Forgotten inside of him, unable to move, I wandered my mind across the infinite worlds. I imagined everything that existed, even beyond the realms of understanding ~ I spent my time here dreaming as far as I could reach and set aim for *our* world ~ A nonstop daydream, an infinity-reaching projection of my mental freedom and of the Saint Devil's mental freedom. And when it at last returned, I prayed that it would lead that remaining piece of the Saint Devil back with it - The gravity that always brought the losing entity back to life in their struggle across dimension and time. So no, I don't believe that you are the body of the Saint Devil, but I believe that it resides inside of you, Nikko -"

"Ok. Now listen to me.. This has been a really bad *long* adventure for me.." Nikko held Jigoro's skull close to her body. "I've seen so many things that I want to forget, and I've seen really impossible things happen right in front of my eyes. But how can you tell me something like this is true? This has to be impossible - It can't be real.."

"It has to be real. There's no other way you would have been led into here, and to me."

"You've been locked in here so long," Nikko told her, now walking backwards towards the door, no other exit in the empty room, "you have no idea what you're even saying anymore.. You've lost your mind in this place.."

A feel for the door, and she turned as she failed to find it, looking to the doorless wall that she had entered through -

"And now the door just disappears??" Nikko laughed in frustration, looking around the blue lit room, seeing nothing except the binding contraption that held the naked Shiva Angel in place.

"It's his Living Castle. It changes like a body changes, nothing stays the same for too long inside of him."

"So then what happens to us now?" Nikko asked, feeling at the end of her limit, Jigoro in her hands and nowhere left to flee. "Is this the end of everything?"

"Only for you and I," Shiva Angel said, a peace in her slow voice that could say such things so easily. "But what's inside of us will live on, don't you think? It's the life that we've been dealt - What do you think the odds were?"

A sharp pain clawed at Nikko's body inside - What was this now? It was like a knife turning in her stomach, cutting unseen from the inside walls of her skin.

"Are you hurting? I can't see you -" Shiva Angel asked, only hearing the sounds of discomfort. "Nikko, while you are still able, and even if you don't believe me about all of this, can you please do something for me? It's been so long, could you please uncover my eyes? Let me see again -"

Nikko, holding her side from the sudden discomfort, did what was asked of her if only to be kind. In pain, she headed to the strapped in woman, then pulling the cold leathery bind from her eyes up over her forehead - Uncovering crystal grey-white eyes.

Shiva Angel smiled, the look as if she were blind, and Nikko stood back, standing a few feet between the woman and the wall.

"Tell me what you wanted to be, while we still have time," Shiva asked of her. "What did you always want to do?"

Nikko wondered why she would ask such a thing, getting to know someone in a condition such as this? It made no sense to her, but there was nowhere left to go -

"I only wanted to be important to someone," Shiva Angel answered herself as Nikko considered the question, "not even to get married. I just really wanted someone to be attached to me, and never leave. I wanted to be a professional wrestler, but I ended up making adult movies.. I wanted to be famous, or a star in the world.. But even when I found something close to that, I was stuck with my depression and boredom. I put my body together with money and surgery until I never looked like myself again.. And even then, I still hated myself.."

"I guess I don't know what I really wanted.." Nikko admitted, unsure of why she would even share her own desires. "I think I used to know, but it's gone now. Everything's so complicated.. I think I wanted love too, maybe.. To trust people, have friends again. I think I wanted to be a teacher a long time ago, I can't remember anymore. Everything feels so detached from me now.. I just want to go back to how things were.."

"Things can never be how they were, Nikko. Everything changes, and even now, I think our gravity can't keep us apart much longer -"

Nikko felt the pain churning inside of her, almost on schedule with the words of the woman. How had it come to this, and were these things that she had said true, or only just delusion?

"I'm sorry that we both got drawn into this event," Shiva Angel told her. "I think we both could have been wonderful people, if our lives weren't so destined to suffer. Maybe we could have been friends, don't you think? Maybe here, since there's nothing left anymore, we can say that we're friends now?"

Nikko didn't know what to say, trapped in the doorless room within the Living Castle, and in the middle of a terrible pain.

"We can be friends.." she said after a pause, looking into the woman's cold grey eyes. "We can be friends now."

"Thank you, Nikko! I wish you knew how much those words mean to me - Things are hurting so bad now, it's the only thing that sounds good anymore. I know it sounds childish - But I wish I were dead."

With a hurting look in her eyes, Shiva Angel breathed a breath that could be seen, a rainbow colored Breath of Life out from her body and into the air before her. It sailed like a snake, winding it's path to Nikko - And in less than a moment, it entered into her gasping mouth, solid as if a frozen shape. Nikko struggled to talk as it made it's way down her throat and into her lungs - "God... What was that??!"

~ Shiva Angel said nothing, her eyes lifeless and her lips parted forever open, the leaving breath of the Saint Devil's soul ending it's vessel's own carrying life ~

"Oh, my God, oh God..." Nikko began to panic and placed her hands all over her body, dropping Jigoro's skull in the process. "This isn't really happening.. This can't be real.. There's no way..."

All over her skin an odd feeling was taking place, as if her skeleton was trying to move on it's own, her brain saying one thing and her body doing another.

Nikko and the NLK

"No, no, no...." Nikko cried and tried to regain control, ripping pains surging through her insides. "Stop... Oh, God, stop - What's wrong with me??"

She fell to the ground, on her knees and out of control with her movements, tears erupting from her swollen eyes - A consuming nervous breakdown and all remaining memories rushing before her mind -

Mom...

Dad...

Her pet Kimby...

Everyone and everything, sunsets and simple problems - She cried and wanted it all back, at the end and everything ripping apart inside of her now - Carefree days, busy days, taking naps and being bored.. The stupid little things all gone. She wanted anything to have them back and have her problems back, anything back to get away from this..

The bones inside shifted, the movement like a child birth of a head to toe replica of herself. Every tiny nerve stretched, the fossilized Saint Devil stirring within, unknowingly carried inside of her all of this time.

"*No...*" Nikko cried more, at the ground and covered in her deepest tears. "I don't want to die... I wish I was dead.."

And those were her final words, words she had never said before followed by words she had said far too often, and the only sound to follow was her voice in heaving sobs. Everything shut down as her role in the new rebirth was now complete. Traveled from 1 world to another, following the mental projection Dolphin girl to lead her all of the way in here, beyond the End of the World. All for nothing, just a role in a bigger play - The following of Dolphin, the choices of her own, the results of her actions and curiosities.. The gravity of the Saint Devil's remains were too strong to not come together again..

Nikko and the NLK

And now, no breath left and the Breath of Life entered into her body from the deceased Shiva Angel, Nikko watched her vision cloud up and felt her racing Heart wind down.

~ Another end, again.. ~

And like a butterfly pulling it's way out of a discarded cocoon, the female body of the Saint Devil broke from it's cage, emerging from the torn-open back of Nikko's body husk -

~ The beautiful Nikko reduced to a lifeless dressing ~

It climbed out wet and reborn, a completely different entity than it's carriers of either soul or body, Nikko's flesh hanging to hers as she stiffly pulled completely loose. An impossible appearance of an entire woman coming out of another - She had rich caramel skin and full dark-lash green eyes, short long-banged white hair and white devil horn nubs. Her body was clothed in a white ghost-skin suit split from mid torso and up, exposing a 'V' of her coconut skinned upper body, the ghost material covering her arms and legs with heel-shape spikes at the soles of her ghost-covered feet.

She stepped out and was free, alive again, just as she had been many times throughout eternity - The Saint Devil this time resurrected inside the Living Castle of the No-Life King, Drahcir Nalla..

Nikko's remains left at the floor, and the Saint Devil reached to the lifeless skull of Jigoro - Now it too took it's true shape and form, held within the Saint Devil's supernatural grasp -

The Death Wish weapon, 'Space White' - Jigoro's skull transformed into an oversized halo-shape, hand-held and with a pure white tone. The skull facial expressions of Jigoro, in actuality Space White's expressions, appeared flat and changing across it. An un-living weapon, it was the Death Wish granter of the Saint Devil, and now with the transformation complete, Drahcir Nalla could instantly sense his mortal enemy's presence within himself, and everything began to change -

Nikko and the NLK

Nikko had battled the No-Life King with all that a human could, even going as far as to dismantle a piece of his evil-containing armor. But now the time had come for the eternal struggle to begin again, the prey of the suffering versus the prey of the suicide.

~ And with a blue-light explosion, the room of Nikko's body and the contraption with the remains of Shiva Angel lit with evil fires ~

~ Drahcir Nalla aware of it's enemy's rebirth, and the Saint Devil ready to fly ~

Through the doorless wall with an unstoppable crash, and once again the eternal struggle was already under way -

Nikko and the NLK

~ So this is where we go when we die ~

~ I always wondered where it would be ~

~ Can anyone hear me from the other side? ~

~ I'm still empty ~

~ Even in death, I can't find escape ~

Nikko and the NLK

CHAPTER 12

All Night Galaxy

    The manifestation of suicide flew through the inside of Drahcir Nalla with the aid of no wings, her beautiful body soaring by the will of her ghost-skin bodysuit alone.

    Downward through the stairless staircase and the memories of Nikko were now absent from the corridor, lost in a montage of stolen life memories from across the dimensions - The Saint Devil aware of the suffering, but paying no mind. A Devil's look rode across her face, the Space White weapon held in her grasp the same way Nikko had held onto Jigoro, and she sailed down as the furious explosion of Drahcir Nalla bit at her white spiked heel feet. Through the Living Castle's spiral that Nikko had traveled up, and the memories were replaced here as well, Nikko but an afterthought in death.

    The explosion followed behind, kicking up pieces of the organs and infected tissue around. From the spiraled ground, the uneven walkway beneath her wingless flight now birthing black void-like beings, the same as the NLK Cult, pathetically lunging at her flying body as it roared by. Their countless arms, heads and torsos blew up and spewed forward in the momentum of the following explosion.

    Down to the bottom of the spiral with Nikko's path-in retraced backwards, and the Saint Devil's body rushed across the fire bridge and opening. Each far wall and the ceiling of the wide room came into it's own life, the void creatures pouring out of every clogged pore space. Groups from overhead dropped down from the ceiling, masses falling to the flames and in a wreck some smashing onto the bridge.
    The Saint Devil flew above the footing and cut through the hive of dead memories, unleashing Space White, throwing it out and around the dropping crowd like a boomerang. With a razor's edge it sawed and danced it's way through their shadow bodies, the skull face cast upon it's flat shape reveling in the carnage.
    A spinning return to the forward racing Saint Devil, and she grabbed it in mid air, holding onto it again with it's large hoop shape slung over

Nikko and the NLK

her shoulder.
Out of the fire bridge room, and into the tighter black living tunnel Nikko had first entered - All 4 sides, from the floor to the walls and ceiling, were transformed from the black organs into the shadow creatures here as well. In this tighter spot they grabbed at her body, latching on as she swung the Death Wish weapon violently around her, cutting the black nightmares into ribbons, never slowing down.
As she cut, the more the expressive eyes and mouth of her weapon seemed to bask in it, doused but unstained in the black juices raining from their severings.

Out of the tunnel, and now through the room that held the remains of Nikko's friends and Tanuki's illusions, the ruins of the wedding and the lifeless bodies of the similar black shadow creatures.
The mound of death meant nothing to the Saint Devil, and she soared without a care up and over them, upwards into the long tunnel that Nikko and the others had been swallowed down into.
The explosion followed, countless black bodies blown by it's might before it, and now as it lifted upwards through the once swallowing passage, the entire mound of the deceased wedding party rocketed in it's momentum as well - The Saint Devil refusing to look, following her instinct straight up and Heaven-bound, flying faster and holding her body in a graceful pose.
And just as the rest of the Living Castle, the vertical tunnel came to life, all of it's nightmare creations fighting her - Missing and falling to the relentless blue fire, heaping atop the dead and rising body masses collected.

- Higher, higher and to the limit -

The Saint Devil never slowed down, flying faster than ever, Space White in her hand smiling a reckless smile as she burned a path ahead of the burning explosion. Reaching the point where Nikko and her friends had been pulled in, she continued higher yet and faster, the black walls reaching for her, though never fast enough.

~ And then, to the end ~

Nikko and the NLK

~ The body limit of the No-Life King, the Living Castle of Drahcir Nalla, and the Saint Devil flew through a black and white explosion ~

~ Her end of the life 'ghost-white,' and his suffering of the life 'night-black' ~

The Saint Devil at last burst from the cage of the Living Castle body, not exiting outside of him where Nikko and the others had come in from, but instead out into the deep and vast emptiness of space.

The true home of their struggle and the Saint Devil spent no time in thought, already being here in infinity so many times before. It was a different path this time, but the same result as always.

~ The neverending fight, and the unending battle of suffrage versus suicide ~

As she flew forward through the black space and distant starlight specks, the explosion that had pursued her emptied out into the nothingness of the universe, the collection of bodies thrown out of the Living Castle and scattered into the weightlessness of the outer space.

- The Saint Devil turned and stopped her racing speed, holding still for the moment and surveying the scene she had just escaped -

The bat-winged helmet of the No-Life King hovered bodiless and fortress-size in the unending dimension. Drahcir Nalla... It was his Living Castle at the deep reach of the worlds, the home of the vile black-armor contained suffrage. And now, back to life, the Saint Devil looked towards it unflinching, just as she had throughout time and ready to go through the motions again.

The explosions ceased and the silence returned, the momentum-propelled bodies no longer pouring out, their mangled debris of lifelessness littering the soon-to-be battlefield.

Nikko and the NLK

The Saint Devil waited, the Space White halo weapon anxiously waiting for violence in her hand. She stared down at the Living Castle and knew that soon he would be on his way. What would his form be this fight? A creature that was bound by no physical laws, other than it's necessity to feed.

Lightning flashed in space - It was almost time.

The SuperCross appeared behind the Saint Devil, the portal to her home world and the same cross shape that Nikko and the others had been thrown in through by Oyomi, now floating silently in the black.

The Saint Devil levitated patiently, black void-skin bodies drifting by and bursts of thunder-less lightning beginning all around. As the battle time drew near, each flash revealed a giant silhouette of surrounding universe-encompassing Gods and Devils from the reaches of outer space. Featureless world-sized shapes of human-like and monster forms, unknown entities entertained by the time after time wars the minor Gods would wage.

The Saint Devil sat atop the floating horizontal Space White, a leg crossed over the other before the time at last would come.

~ There was movement from ahead, and then at last the ageless war was continued yet again ~

From the black helmet shaped Living Castle, the entity of the No-Life King appeared, now no longer the human-like barbarian shape the girl Nikko had encountered so many times. Instead, it took a shapeshifted cast into a segmented worm-like dragon, black-plate scales and bat-shaped dragon wings. It hovered before it's helmeted fortress and stared across at it's resurrected rival, now ready to battle for the conflicting things that they fed upon once more.

~ From behind the Saint Devil, the red spirits and hungry ghosts emerged from her cross-shaped door to the SuperCross graveyard world ~

~ From behind the dragon of Drahcir Nalla, winged void-skin creatures amassed, emerging from the holes of the Living Castle ~

And with the deities of the universe watching, everpresent with the constant revealing of them through the unnatural galaxy lightning flashes, the Saint Devil charged her war path forward. The dragon form of Drahcir Nalla then wound it's segmented body forward as well, the lightning strikes growing in a fever -

The red army of ghosts plunged forward beside their halo-holding leader, it's legion of winged shadow creatures beside their bat-winged dragon.

And the warring beings of suffrage and suicide clashed in the shadow-body filled battlefield of the stars, meeting together in the center of the doors to their domains, acting out the unending conflict.

+ +

Far below and away on the mountain realms of Daiyomi, the Mountain Tengu Oyomi stood at the cliffs of his home, arms folded and watching the sky above. Small flashes of light could be seen hidden amongst the stars, and he looked on with his great nose tilted upwards, his eyes gazing at the night scene. A look of satisfaction came across his face, the natural struggle so infinitely far away, but as he sensed, well underway just the same as the seasons always came again..

+ +

The opposing sides clashed, red spirits of all designs clawing and tearing, the black winged monsters ripping into the essences of the red souls. Countless followers were destroyed and at odds, lightning blistering throughout the emptiness.
The No-Life King dragon pursued the nimble Saint Devil, her ghost-skin body suit keeping her forever just out of his reach, dashing about the space all around them. The scattered bodies brushed aside and severed into unrecognizable black pieces, all blending into the starry space and floating off into infinity.
Drahcir Nalla lunged, his black gaping jaw clamping down onto

nothing, the Saint Devil propelling out of his range and swinging her Death Wish weapon in a short returning throw, just clipping his armored body and sawing a portion of his black plates clean off. The returning Space White halo smiled at the God's familiar blood flavor.

+ +

All of the way across the universe, Maria - the 'Midori Girl' - exited the nightclub Nikko and Jigoro had visited, hand in hand with Richard Allan. They laughed, happy after another wonderful night, and left down the alleyway back to their car at the street -
"Whoaa.." Maria hesitated in the narrow alley, her eyes straight to the starless city sky. "Did you see that?"
"Huh? See what?"
"I don't know.. It looked like a shooting star.."
"... A shooting star?" Richard asked with a mocking laugh. "Come on already, you can't see anything in this city!"
Their voices trailed off as they continued down to the street, the light-years away battle seen only with small hints in the sky of Nikko's home world.

+ +

The Saint Devil bit down, her own gentle mouth as strong as a monster's, tearing into the giant snake neck of the No-Life King and tearing at his armored body with her Devil's teeth. The background flashed, the onlooking Gods amused by the 2 forces and their unholy armies obliterating each other all around.
The dragon coiled, biting hard itself now onto the Saint Devil's upper body, her frame vapor-like and unaffected, fading out and then fading back in unharmed.

+ +

Nikko and the NLK

Far away, further than Nikko's World and everywhere at once, the sounds and bright flashes of the warring predators reached across time. The cries of a God creature's pain, and the clashing sounds of the Space White weapon striking against the armor plates of the No-Life King. Worlds at the end of time saw and heard these things only as a tiny whisper on the wind, a speck of light lost in the far off distant sky.

+ +

The battle raged, the female body and the creature body battling for some time, their supporting armies falling and then unendingly replenished. Lightning, illuminated Gods and Devils, and the No-Life King Drahcir Nalla was at the absent mercy of the reborn Saint Devil. Relentlessly at his neck, she bore the Space White halo ruthlessly into the dragon's skull, the spray of black juice unstaining her. Her eyes lit with bloodlust, matching the Death Wish weapon's own.

From her head and beneath her white bangs, the devil horn nubs grew rapidly outward - Long thin white horns extending from her skull, multiplying her power as she drove the weapon deeper, her Devil's power unmatchable and her rage uncontained.

With Space White completely submerged into the dragon's head, the Saint Devil spun it, grinding and then letting go, letting it spin with it's own lifeforce. It dug like a machine into the cosmic bone and brain matter of the suffrage-feeding entity, the Saint Devil reveling in it, animal-screams of death pouring out from the invincible nightmare.

With Space White unrelenting, the Saint Devil then attacked the serpentine body, clawing at it's armored scales with her ghost suit covered hands.

Piece by piece she hurled it through space, black soft-skin eggs floating out from beneath each scale with every rip -

Drahcir Nalla wailed, it's cry echoing throughout the cosmos -

The Saint Devil raged across it's body, her beautiful caramel skin and white skin-tight suit untouched by the blood pouring out among the eggs and torn black scales. She reached deep inside of him, grabbing fistfuls of whatever she could hold, ripping his insides out and throwing them aside, tearing him apart in a lustful killing, the Space White still grinding in place within the skull..

Nikko and the NLK

And then, the galaxy-illuminating flash of war - The ghost-skin of her suit possessed, continuing to clothe her and at the same time extending off in multiple biting jaws. Stretching from her body, they attacked and chewed entire pieces from the dragon No-Life King.

~ The Death Wish weapon Space White cut through the head of the suffering ~

~ The Saint Devil ripped the body to pieces by her hands ~

~ The possessed ghost-skin mauled the remains until they broke into a frail pathetic thing ~

~ And it fell, as pieces, into space ~

~ Lifeless ~

The deceased Nikko's dream came true at last..

The shadow-wing army disintegrated, disappearing into the black as the Living Castle sat quietly now in death, then fading away as if it had never existed at all.

A few scattered lightning strikes finished off, a flash revealing the still surrounding Gods, and then a following flash revealing the vast emptiness - The Deities back into their omnipresent existences, bored and uninterested by the aftermath of the tiny war.

The Saint Devil levitated victoriously - Countless times won and countless times lost - No feeling of satisfaction, just the temporary survival that would someday lead to Drahcir Nalla's own eventual resurrection.

But for now, for a brief time, all of the suffering created by the memory-stalking No-Life King came to an abrupt end. All of the happening and forgotten nightmares that had been plaguing girls like Nikko Heinlad and Stacy Sweetcheck went away again. Drahcir Nalla's own created-suffering stopped for now around the galaxy, allowing the Saint Devil to return to her world and her ways - Granting the Death Wish on those who would give up on their lives.

~ Suicide over Suffering, for now ~

The resurrected Saint Devil hovered through the floating wedding remains of the lifeless bodies in outer space, briefly searching for something as Space White returned to her side and floated on it's own accord.

There they were...

Now it was finally time to go home.

+ +

A warm wind blew over the land, the sky dark and cloudless. Time stood still after death, and a calming peace once again ruled over the graveyard world of SuperCross. The Saint Devil stood at the balcony of her castle within, overlooking her world of rest and the undisturbed graves of those she neverendingly would bring there. The red spirits rose in the night, wandering happily without the worries of their lives, and now just able to sleep or exist in the peace that they deserved.

~ No intrusions, no invasions ~

Only the Saint Devil, their savior for the suffrage in their lives.

The unholy lady gazed over her land in satisfaction, Space White grinning at her side. Her hair was pulled into a tiny white ponytail, her body covered in the black victorian dress just as she had been in the pop-up story book.

The Saint Devil waited longingly until the next life in a world called to her, wishing to die - And now at last back, she would once again be able to save them, and to grant their dreams come true.

A beautiful silence in the world of endless graves, the newest stones of Shiva Angel and Nikko Heinlad placed respectfully beside each other, their brought-back Death Wish bodies resting peacefully at last.

It had all been so long and painful, now at last they could sleep forever away, unforced to ever hurt again.

Nikko and the NLK

Fin

Nikko and the NLK

OUTLETTER

Here we go again - Time's really flying by now! Who knows how much longer we can keep meeting up like this?

It's been another long journey from 1 book to the next, and finally, after giving it everything I had with 'CoolToDie World,' I squeeze a little more blood out of my Heart. Nikko and the No-Life King is at long last in your hands.. What a relief! It's a strange feeling at the release of each book, I feel like I'm at the start and end of something, and opening another door into my personal world. Some of you know just how secretive I can be - Since I started publishing under the 'T.B.O.A. Sad' name in 1997, I know I've never been easy to reach, but take it from the King Antisocial Creature himself - Your undying enthusiasm and support still means something to me.

Overdue gratitude deservedly goes out to Go Nagai for his classic and masterpiece manga 'DevilMan,' as well as Eichiro Oda for his dedication on the epic 'One Piece.' Elements and emotions of these 2 favorites are perfect examples of what I strive for. I think of the new 'Saint Devil' character as my book universe's DevilMan, and I hope to include her in future stories some day. And speaking of that, I hope you caught the return of Venrra - Appearing as the main character in my second book, a few readers have asked me where she flew off to at that story's end. As we found out in Nikko and the No-Life King, her ultimate destination was not exactly a happy ending! And we also saw the return of the 'Burrow' race, an unmistakable connection to my long-ago character of the 'Burrow Reincarnate.' Catch any of the other continuations?

But no need to confuse new readers even more, the story stands well enough on it's own without these tributes to yesterday. Nikko and the No-Life King was founded on the idea of memories being secret and individualized. No matter who it is, all humans *usually* have some small form of memories existing in their head. Isn't that strange? Some share them with you, some keep them quietly to themselves, but these are always the individual treasures that a human constantly looks back on. These can mean everything, and even sometimes feel like the only thing we might have left as time goes by.

And I really love yesterday. Old movies, 1980's video games, toys, cartoons and Ben Cooper plastic monster masks. I'll never forget those Christmas mornings, the family vacations, the childhood friends and pets I can never see again. I'll always remember those old trips

Nikko and the NLK

to the movies and arcades, those long days watching the clock way back in school, and how fast summer break would always fly by. Without even closing my eyes, I can see yesterday so perfectly.

If our memories are mostly the 1 thing that no individual can take away, what if there was a God monster that could? To violently destroy these memories is to destroy the makeup of who we are as individuals today. This is what I considered - I wanted to make it, just to see, and then step on such important things.

Anyway! A 'thank you' is in order, of course, to my Mother and Father, and entire family - Without them, what's the point of all this junk?

A super special thank you to Megan V - Thank you for your advice, patience and encouragement to see this project through.

Thank you to Cool S., Carmen and Lydia, Zoey and Haze, Jen, Julie Skidd, Criss, Shawn, Jeanette S., Kelli, Ryan, Scott, Tst Chris, Willie Vargas (R.I.P.), Dragon, Jessie, Ann, Stitches, Cheryl, Basil, Meena, Stef, Faith and Fayth, Erica, Deborah, Sheri, Miki, Dawn, all former members of the NF, former members of the 818 SDC, and to all subscribers of my T.B.O.A. Sad 'Bullet' Newsletter.

Finally, a long distance thank you to my forgotten 'growing up' friends of Gene, Tommy, Wayne and Mark - R.I.P. Pegasus, and God Bless DevilMan.

The T.B.O.A. Sad mailbox is open at tboasad@aol.com, or mail your letters direct to :

> T.B.O.A. Sad
> P.O. Box 2262
> Northlake, IL
> 60164

Did you think this is all we do?? Please take some time to enjoy the entire world of T.B.O.A. Sad at the official website:
TBOASAD.COM
Check out stuffed animal monsters, clothing and more -

Nikko and the NLK

~ Project Made in Heaven vs. Made in Hell 20XX ~

~ T.B.O.A. Sad steps on your memories and now he's finished, Nikko and the No-Life King completed + out, and so back into reality we go. It wasn't too long of a wait, was it? Nothing lasts forever, but maybe someday we can meet again ~

Nikko and the NLK

: Official T.B.O.A. Sad Seasons and Holidays :

Seasons : August 19 - May 14 K.O.D.
     May 16 - August 17 N.H.A.B.

January : **11** The Space Ball, **18** WhiteSoft Day, **23** Devil's Cradle

February : **13** St. Adam's Day, **27** GameDay Blue

March : **8** NeoShe, **22** DieMania, **26** WrestleFest

April : **10** Trainer Day

May : **15** T.B.O.A., **26** F.S. Memorial

June : **16** SummerLand

July : **14** Motorama, **21** CastleEggman, **30** N.F. Peace Summit

August : **10** SouthTown Memorial, **18** SuperCross

September : **3** 8-Arms Day, **6** NagaiSlam, **13** BluthWorld

October : **1** Monster Party, **(2nd Saturday)** S.M.C. Day, **16** Wild Paw Cup, **27** Southern Cross

November : **7** Darkade, **24** GameDay Red

December : **(1st full weekend)** Disney FGC Fest